THE TRAIN TO ORVIETO

THE TRAIN TO ORVIETO

Rebecca J. Novelli

Black Heron Press
Post Office Box 13396
Mill Creek, Washington 98082
www.blackheronpress.com

The Train to Orvieto is a work of fiction. All characters that appear in this book are products of the author's imagination. Any resemblance to persons, living or dead, is entirely coincidental.

ISBN (print): 978-1-936364-23-7
ISBN (ebook): 978-1-936364-22-0

Black Heron Press
Post Office Box 13396
Mill Creek, Washington 98082
www.blackheronpress.com

For Billy

All the more pleasurable, then, to mock the witlessness of those who believe that with present power it is possible to extinguish the future's memory...

—Tacitus, *Annals*, 4.35.5

THE TRAIN TO ORVIETO

ORVIETO

At the top of a volcanic outcropping nearly a thousand feet high and hidden behind walls of yellowed stone, the town of Orvieto arises from its distant past. Tourists move through its narrow streets and quaint shops, imagining the shouts of long ago artisans and traders. Like pilgrims at a shrine, they believe that ancient verities can be found within our ruins and that by drawing close to our past, they will know *truth*. Their preposterous quest is doomed.

Inside the Duomo, with the famous golden façade, Signorelli's 15th Century fresco depicts the damned in hell. See in the lower right corner where the face of Signorelli's beautiful lover is contorted in suffering? This was his vengeance for her infidelity. Six centuries later her betrayal is remembered, but no one asks whether Signorelli was faithful to her, whether he deserved her loyalty. That the answer is uncertain isn't easily accepted and may cause unwelcome controversy. For us it is enough to say, "She dishonored him," and continue on our way. This is how we keep faith with truth.

In the museum near the Duomo, tourists marvel at an exhibit of amphorae exhumed from the ancient caves formed in the crumbling *tufa* on which our town rests. Some of these vessels are thought to contain wine. The more adventurous want to taste it, while the timid fear that it's poisonous. It's likely turned to vinegar by now, but the amphorae remain sealed and the exact nature of their contents uncertain.

In the afternoons tourists can be seen following a guide along a steep path leading to the base of our outcropping. There they will visit the Etruscan necropolises, tombs frescoed in silent accounts of sumptuous banquets and passionate assignations. Whether the beautiful people pictured there lived as they were depicted or whether their memory was confined in a palace of wishes remains unknown.

Memory is easily confused with truth. Memory is that half-drowned survivor heaved up on the uncertain shore of awareness. It offers an account of what happened when the ship foundered on treacherous shoals or ran aground in the gale. Was there a mutiny? Murderous pirates? Or was the captain drunk and the cargo and crew lost to negligence? Because no one remains to contradict the captain's story, what he remembers becomes *truth*. Given the choice, tourists almost always prefer pirates and mutinies, so the castaway need not fear contradiction.

We Orvietani have a word for tourists. We call them *stranieri*. It means foreigner, outsider, alien. More importantly, it means someone who doesn't—and never will—share our memory of what we know to be true. Indeed, on certain feast days we offer one another our own good luck toast: "To fine memories and the best wine: may you never have to share them with *stranieri*." This is how we have lived with one another for centuries, our memories entangled like a vine that engulfs a house, choking off the original structure in favor of its own.

What I tell you about Willa, my mother, and our family, and about those we knew and loved is only the account of this half-drowned survivor. Is it the truth? The truth never mattered.

I. GABRIELE

1

ERHART, OHIO, JUNE 1934

Darkness fell just past nine, and the humid evening curled still and breathless around The Pavilion, enveloped by sounds of crickets, frogs, and a nearby brook. Fireflies competed with lanterns and stars until the rising moon, round as a lemon slice, lifted above the trees and bathed in silver-gold the hardwood dance floor and the two twirling figures in the center. My mother, Willa Carver, and her father, Howard Carver, had just begun the first waltz. The party celebrated my mother's twentieth birthday and her graduation from Miss Waltham's, where young women were prepared for "thoughtful and gracious living" and where for two years she had studied drawing and painting, art history, home management, and the Italian language. Formal debuts were unheard of in small, midwestern towns like Erhart, Ohio, but her party nevertheless affirmed her emergence into a somewhat awkward status that conferred adult privileges and freedoms without actually permitting them.

The two dancers dipped and turned in front of the musicians, ten local men, friends of Mr. Carver, who were seated in the band shell at one end of the dance floor. According to family stories, Mr. Carver had hired the conductor from nearby Oberlin Conservatory for the evening.

"With a little professional direction you won't be able to tell them from the Cleveland Symphony," he had promised Willa and Ruth, his wife.

"Spending money on a conductor in times like these! What will people think of us?" Ruth had said, mindful of how many of their friends had been affected by what historians and economists would later call The Great Depression.

"I don't care what they think," Mr. Carver told her. "We're going to do this right or not at all!"

The Pavilion and its transformations typically marked the seasons in Erhart. Thus, on December first, the volunteer fire department removed the hardwood platform to expose the basin below and then flooded it to create a frozen rink for ice-skating and the Holiday Ball. The reigning "Winter Princesses"—Willa had been one the previous year—arrived in a sleigh pulled by three horses and driven by the mayor dressed as Santa. The sleigh glided to the center of the ice rink and stopped next to a Christmas tree, which was felled for the occasion and remained there throughout the holiday season while several reindeer wintered in a nearby field. In its promotional literature, the Erhart Chamber of Commerce labeled the entire Winter Festival "a popular regional attraction." More importantly and more often, The Pavilion was the site of the most significant passages in the lives of the citizens of Erhart. For many, including Willa, it was there that they first noticed the direction of the compass that would guide them toward their dreams.

As they passed in front of the refreshment table, Mr. Carver twirled Willa out under his hand. Over his shoulder Willa saw "Aunt" Leonie, her mother's spinster cousin and an English teacher at Erhart High School, sitting on a folding chair and knitting a tiny sailor suit. Against Aunt Leonie's stasis, Willa felt her own liquidity, as if she had joints and muscles unbounded by gravity, as if she were made of moving water. She knew that her pale gown of violet silk chiffon, the skirt layered like butterfly wings beneath a ruched bodice, contributed to the watery impression and emphasized her rosy skin, already freckled from the sun, though summer would not officially begin for two weeks. Her thick, auburn curls fell over her shoulders and flashed in the moonlight. Earlier that afternoon, she had gathered pink roses and dianthus from her mother's garden and had woven them into a crown held in place with grandmother Carver's mother-of-pearl combs.

Willa and her father swept past Willa's cousin Lawrence, who had just turned twelve and whose too-small suit revealed several inches of his ankles and wrists. Prodded by his mother's elbow, he raised a cup of punch in their direction. Willa giggled.

"Daddy, look! Lawrence has one white sock and one black one." Mr. Carver glanced at his nephew and then at his nephew's mother.

"My sister looks like she's missing more than socks," Mr. Carver said.

"She expected nothing and gave up early," Willa said dryly.

"Nonsense. She married a rich man. He's a terrible bore, but she has everything she could want."

"But she wanted to be a singer." Willa twirled again.

"She had no voice," Mr. Carver said. "It's better this way." They swirled past Aunt Leonie once more. Mr. Carver drew back and winked at his daughter.

"I suppose you'd say Aunt Leonie has lost something, too."

Willa looked at her father. "Her sailor, the one grandpa wouldn't let her marry."

"That story isn't true, at least not entirely. She had other chances," Mr. Carver said.

"She gave them all up to knit for other people's babies."

Mr. Carver smiled at his daughter over his bow tie. "Perhaps Aunt Leonie likes what she's doing. Have you ever thought of that?" Willa shook her head. "I take it, then, that you don't intend to give up anything."

Willa held her father's gaze, smiling. "No. Nothing." Mr. Carver chuckled and turned his daughter around and around until some of the guests began to clap.

"I guess your dad isn't such a bad dancer after all."

Willa laughed. "Daddy, you're a wonderful dancer."

"It's you, honey. You make me remember how I used to dance with your mother. Right here. We were just twenty—like you," he continued with a sweep of his hand. "One evening we stopped over there by that wall to look at Orion. That's when I proposed to Ruth. Didn't think about it. Just said, 'Ruth, I'll die if you don't marry me.' Imagine!" The music stopped and the guests clapped again. "There's Maestro Ottaviani. I believe he's been waiting since the music started for a turn with you."

Willa glanced at her drawing teacher, a slender man, nearly thirty, elegant despite his inexpensive suit. A recent émigré, Maestro Ottaviani had taught both drawing and Italian at Miss Waltham's, and Mrs. Carver had insisted that Willa continue her lessons with him, though it had been Mr. Carver who questioned that expense. Willa had already noticed Maestro Ottaviani and took a certain pleasure in his uninterrupted gaze. He was holding a gift.

"Punch?" Mr. Carver said. They entered a covered structure where Mrs. Carver had set a dozen tables for ten covered with pastel linens, silverware, and china, all of which had to be rented in Cleveland. The roses in the centerpieces were from Mrs. Carver's garden. The menu consisted of Willa's favorites: roast chicken, potato salad, peas, and, for dessert, chocolate cake with frosting roses and raspberry sherbet all prepared by Mrs. Carver and Belle, the housekeeper. Willa paused at the buffet table and stuck her finger into the frosting at the back of the cake, pulled her finger out and licked it. She walked around the table nearby, this one piled with gifts, some from as far away as Memphis, Chicago, New York, even California.

Another cousin approached them with cups of punch, balancing carefully in her white dress and first high heels.

"Oh, champagne, please," Willa said waving the cups away.

"Willa! You have to wait until you're twenty one."

"Tonight I can do what I want." Willa wanted—no, assumed—the possibility of living in a state of artistic enchantment in the same way most people in Erhart believed in God and rising early. Her desire to exist in an unhampered, creative state was the scale on which she weighed the desirability of any choice or decision about her present and her future.

Maestro Ottaviani appeared in front of her. *"Tanti auguri."* He held out a white package tied with pink grosgrain ribbon.

She smiled. "What a lovely surprise. *Grazie mille,* Signor Ottaviani."

He looked into her eyes, his expression buoyant but uncertain. "First open. Then the *grazie,*" he told her. Willa sat down on a nearby chair.

Maestro Ottaviani sat next to her, adjusting his chair so that it touched hers. Willa pulled at the ribbon and let it drop into her lap, then tore away the thin tissue. The book was bound in leather the color of lapis lazuli. Willa ran her fingers over the gold sun embossed on the cover, touched the raised silver moon on the back, let the blank pages play between her fingers. "For your *disegni, Maestro,*" Ottaviani said.

Willa understood the Italian word for drawings. Indeed, under Maestro Ottaviani's tutelage, she had become quite fluent in Italian. "What a beautiful sketchbook. Thank you." As an artist Willa intended to make her ideas and feelings manifest in her work and to live a life dedicated to art, beauty and love. Such things were difficult to explain to most people, particularly in Erhart, but Maestro Ottaviani had understood from the very first day of her classes with him and had helped her to express her intentions on paper and canvas.

"The artist's art is the artist himself," Maestro Ottaviani had often said. He understood her aspirations better than anyone else, Willa felt, because he was Italian, and Italians were a very empathetic and artistic people. Maestro Ottaviani put one hand over hers and touched his chest with the other. "Art is the *emozioni,* the things of the heart and the soul. "

Willa squeezed his hand and smiled, pleased that he thought that the ideas and images in her heart and soul should be recorded, that what was within her mattered. She hugged the album. "*Bellissimo.* "

Maestro Ottaviani leaned so near that she felt the warmth of his breath next to her ear when he spoke. She kissed him quickly on the cheek, then set the sketchbook on an empty chair and stood up.

"I make dance with you now," Maestro Ottaviani said, "and we make talk together about art...and...our friendship." He led her outside to the dance floor.

By the standards of Erhart, Willa already enjoyed artistic success. She had sold some of her paintings—figurative oils of children and small watercolor landscapes–to her parents' friends and acquaintances and at church bazaars. She had also received a few small commissions to document the homes and gardens of Erhart's more prosperous citizens. With

Maestro Ottaviani's encouragement, however, she imagined something more for herself as an artist, something more significant that she could not name yet, but that she would surely find in Italy, in places like Roma or Firenze, where Maestro Ottaviani had studied art himself.

"You and I...we paint together in Firenze," Maestro Ottaviani said to her. "Later in Roma. I have friends. We will be together. I teach you."

"I want to study in Italy," Willa said, "but my father doesn't think it's important."

"I talk to him...how you say?...man with man."

When the music ended, Willa and Maestro Ottaviani paused at the edge of the dance floor. Immediately, Eddie Ingersoll, who would soon take over his father's business as the Security Insurance, Ltd. broker in Erhart, asked Willa for the next dance.

"I've got something important to tell you," Eddie said breathlessly, his hair and tie askew. He led her to the edge of the dance floor, and they looked outward toward the darkened land. Moonlight etched the fringe of clouds floating just above the horizon and silhouetted the shapes of the trees. "Willa, I've always been in love with you...and besides we've known each other since we were in elementary school...."

"I already know what you're going to say." Willa pushed her hair back. "You have a job."

Eddie nodded. "...and our families are friends...and my father gave me his old Packard, too, and I just asked to speak to your father." He rushed on. "Now that I can support us, I want us to get married. Your father will approve, Willa. I know he will. I know we're meant to be together." He paused for breath. "We can settle right here in Erhart just as soon as you can plan our wedding. In fact, I saw a house for sale on Greenleaf Avenue. Want to take a look after the party?"

Though they had gone to the high school prom together, Willa was surprised by Eddie's proposal. She had never considered their marrying a possibility. "Oh, Eddie, it's a beautiful evening. I don't want to spoil it."

"Spoil it? How?"

"I'm going to be leaving Erhart." At that very moment she had become certain. "I'm going to be an artist."

"But how can we get married if you're not here?"

Chip Larson, another classmate, approached them, his left hand still bandaged from an injury in a recent motorcycle accident. People shook their heads and said that Chip preferred fast engines to good sense and one day if he didn't stop...well, one day, things would end badly. The orchestra struck up a jitterbug."Hey Ingersoll! Willa's *my* girl!" Chip sped off toward the center of the dance floor with Willa in his arms.

"That Ingersoll can't even find a beat," Chip said. "Watch this!" He whirled in front of her. The guests whistled, urging him on. When the orchestra stopped, he did a cartwheel and landed in the splits. He wiped his hands on his pants. "So, whadja think of that?"

Willa considered—and not for the last time—her effect on men. She had become aware of her own power and so had others. Earlier the saleslady in downtown Cleveland had commented that the gown Willa had chosen for her party "makes you look like Helen of Troy."

Willa's dress did set her apart from other girls, those whose customary clouds of white suggested not so much epics as christenings, first communions, weddings, and, of course, virginity. Perhaps it was obvious to some of those present that Willa didn't share their acceptable aspirations. Perhaps Willa's rejection of what was expected of her called up their long-suppressed memories of possibilities foreclosed or lives not lived. Perhaps her rejection raised a more troubling question: What if one had had the courage to bear the risks of one's true desires and had been willing to endure the terrors of opportunity? In this way, Willa left some feeling uncomfortable, off balance, as if their idea of themselves and their secure place in the world had tilted without warning, spilled them out onto the empty shores of forsaken dreams and the companionship of regret. And among a very few, Willa's rejection of what was customary, symbolized by that party dress, represented an even more threatening possibility: Could one, in defiance of custom, inertia, and expectation—still, even now—change and become that larger being one had once believed oneself to be? And so it was that these guests clucked and whispered among themselves about Willa's "risqué costume" and the unhappy fate it foretold.

"Is it my turn?" Lawrence asked Willa, his eyes fixed on his own feet. The pockets of his boy's jacket strained to contain his hands.

"Would you like to dance?" Willa said. Lawrence worked his jaw like an old man trying to remember something he has forgotten. Finally, he nodded. She put her hand on his shoulder and held his sweaty left hand in hers. "Put your other hand against my back," she told him. The music began. "Are you enjoying my party?"

"That's a pretty dress."

"Thank you. Did your mother tell you to say that?"

Lawrence nodded. "She says your dress looks 'risky.'"

"Really? What do you think?"

"My mom says you're not beautiful and that you've got that long Carver nose and that space between your front teeth like aunt Ruth's, but you still fascinate men." Willa knew the women talked about her, but this was the first time she had known what they said. *If I fascinate men, surely I must be beautiful enough*, she thought.

"Is that so?"

Lawrence nodded again vigorously while he counted aloud to the music.

"And do I fascinate you?" She was curious about what he would say.

"No." He looked around as if to find an escape. Seeing none, he took a deep breath. "My mom says you can bewitch men with your voice because they want to hear you talk." He stepped on her foot. "Sorry."

It pleased Willa to be thought bewitching. "Do you want to hear me talk?"

"Not if *bewitch* is something bad. My mom says I only have to dance with you for one dance because it's your party."

Willa laughed. "Only one?" She glanced at Lawrence's mother. "Let's make it worth your while then."

2

Willa waited before her tall, wooden easel while Maestro Ottaviani arranged a still life on the table in front of her. The scarred wooden floor of the cramped studio creaked under his footsteps. Stacked in the corners and on any available surface, Maestro Ottaviani's drawings and paintings seemed disordered, but Willa knew he could find any work immediately when he wanted to demonstrate to her the meaning of *grisaille, sfumato,* or *chiaroscuro,* words he pronounced like poems or incantations, words shimmering with possibilities. In the uneven and peeling white of the walls that were crowded higgledy-piggledy with Maestro Ottaviani's drawings, in the programs and advertisements from the shows he had held in Italy scattered about the tiny studio, Willa saw a world that fit her idea of the artist she wanted to become. She picked up one of the programs. On the back it said that Maestro Ottaviani had "received the very highest honors at the internationally famous and most distinguished art school in all of Italy."

"What school in Italy did you attend?" she said.

He glanced at her. "*Aspetta.* Work now," he said. "Not talk." He returned to the still life he had arranged—a cracked marble ball, dead flowers in a thin vase, a skull with a hole in the back of the cranium, a walking stick, a small mirror, an open book—and then went to his easel.

"Now, draw together," he said.

"I'd rather paint," Willa said.

"First, draw. After, paint. Must discover life inside—even in object. Object dead. Artist must give life. No life. No art."

When he drew, Maestro Ottaviani's eyes seemed filled with light. With a few, quick strokes he reproduced not only the forms on the table, but also something more, something Willa was learning to notice. While he imparted to her the nature of line, value, and hue, Maestro Ottaviani confided to Willa other secrets as well.

"*Cara*, you have the *amore* for *l'arte Italiana*," he told her. "It means we share *una fortuna,*" a destiny, a fate. "I will show you my drawings." Signor Ottaviani removed the charcoal stick from Willa's hands and gazed at her. "They are…how you say in English…*molto personale*." Very personal. The moment hung between them, until, with a slight shrug suggestive perhaps of the futility of love and beauty, Maestro Ottaviani opened a black portfolio and took out his drawings of a famous soprano, who was popularly known in Italy as *La Voce*. "In my *desegni*," he said, "I show my experience of *l'amore* and *la sofferenza,*" love and suffering. He wiped a tear away. "She spurned me for a tenor." He looked at Willa and smiled. "Now that you know everything, *cara*, you may call me Ottavio."

3

Nearly two weeks after Willa's party, Mr. Carver summoned his wife and daughter to the living room after the Sunday evening dinner. He closed the sliding doors into the front hallway, a sign that he intended to discuss an important matter, and sat down in his maroon-leather wing chair. With deliberate slowness, he took his pipe from the rack on the mahogany side table next to him. Mrs. Carver made herself comfortable on the chintz-covered couch and took up her needlepoint, a familiar gesture that signaled she was listening. Willa sat in the caned rocking chair, her feet planted firmly on the Aubusson rug. She and her mother waited while Mr. Carver covered the bowl of his pipe with his hand, blew through the stem, and then took several fingers-full of his favorite Mapleton tobacco and tamped it into the bowl. At last, he struck a long wooden match, lit the tobacco, and puffed several times. Satisfied, he turned to Willa.

"I believe you received a proposal of marriage. Is that correct?"

"Two." Willa examined her fingernails closely, picking at a bit of skin near the middle fingernail of her left hand.

"Two! Gracious me." Mrs. Carver threaded a length of red yarn through the eye of a large, blunt needle. "Who was the second?"

"At my party, Eddie and Chip both proposed to me," Willa said. Mr. Carver puffed on his pipe.

"You might have told us," Mrs. Carver said, inserting her needle into the canvas picture of a large Christmas package with a red bow. "Lovely boys. Fine families. Good prospects, too. Both of them." Willa recognized her mother's tone as identical to the one she used when discussing pork chops with the butcher. "Which did you accept?"

"Mmm." Willa picked at the hangnail and bit the piece of skin off.

"What was your response?" Mr. Carver said.

"No." Willa pulled her feet up and hugged her knees. "I said 'no.'"

"Because?"

"My own prospects interest me more."

Mr. Carver exhaled slowly and lowered his pipe. "And these are?"

"I'm going to be an artist...in Italy." Willa unwound herself and settled in the rocker.

Mr. Carver held his pipe in one hand and observed his daughter carefully. Mrs. Carver held her needle in the air like an exclamation point. "Italy? What about your reputation?"

"The art schools in *Firenze* and *Roma* have fine reputations," Willa said, emphasizing the Italian pronunciation of the names of the two cities.

Mr. Carver sucked on his pipe. "I thought you said you planned to become a teacher, not a vagabond."

"I meant only if I were starving." Willa shifted in the rocker again without finding a comfortable position,

"*If?*" Mr. Carver gave Willa a severe look. "A young woman in a foreign country with no family, no husband, no connections, and no means of support is certain to starve. Likely worse."

"I'll be fine, daddy." Willa crossed her legs tailor-fashion. "Italy is a very good country for artists. Much better than here."

"I don't want to hear any more of this, do you understand?" Mr. Carver said.

"Daddy's cousin's daughter taught first grade and lived at home until she got married, and she's perfectly happy," Mrs. Carver said. "She paints in her spare time." She smiled at Willa. "And what's more, she's going to have a baby."

Willa made a face. "Not that silly Janet?"

"Please don't take that attitude, dear. It's unbecoming." Mrs. Carver held her canvas up to the lamp. "How do you like it?"

"Ruth!"

Mrs. Carver paused with her needlework and looked at her husband. "I *am* listening, Howard."

"If this is some idea you've gotten from that Ottaviani fellow…" Mr. Carver put his pipe down on the metal tray with a clang. "Ruth, did you check his references?"

"You won't find a better husband than either Chip or Eddie in all of Italy," Mrs. Carver said, adjusting the stitches in the canvas with her needle. Willa studied her bare toes.

"Maestro Ottaviani says I'm a true artist and that I must follow my gift."

"You tell Maestro Ottaviani that these are hard times for us as well as other people and that you're going to get a job," Mr. Carver said. "I'm not paying him real money to give you silly ideas."

Willa looked up, wounded.

"Perhaps later, if you still want to go abroad and the economy gets better, we could think about another trip," Mrs. Carver said. She brushed some pieces of yarn from her work. "Or you could go to Italy on your honeymoon. The museums are excellent." Mr. Carver grunted and emptied his pipe, filling the room with a sweet-smelling odor of just-burned tobacco that would turn acrid by morning if Mrs. Carver forgot to wash his ashtray.

Willa felt as if her dreams were being stolen from her. "You mean you won't pay for my lessons, then?" She began to cry.

"I won't pay for someone to fill your head with this nonsense," Mr. Carver said.

"But daddy, I have a real future as an artist. Don't you believe in me?" Before he could answer, she rushed from the room, leaving the door open behind her.

Willa found work first as a babysitter, then as a receptionist in a dentist's office, and finally as a salesclerk at Reynard's Department Store. At each, she was found sketching when she should have prevented a child from wandering into a pond, when she should have kept track of patients' appointments, when she should have been attentive to the correct change for twenty dollars. Asked why she had been fired from these legitimate jobs, Willa explained that she had been thinking about a drawing or a painting she was working on. Meanwhile, she continued her lessons with Maestro Ottaviani under a new and secret arrangement in which they bartered his teaching her drawing, painting and Italian in exchange for her teaching him English. Alone in her room, she memorized Italian verses by Leopardi from a book Maestro Ottaviani had given her just as Italian students learned them in school. Maestro Ottaviani had also given her a copy of Manzoni's *I Promessi Sposi*, *The Betrothed*, inscribed with a declaration of his love.

A week later, when Mr. Carver came home from work, he heard Willa reciting Leopardi aloud. "What's that you're saying?"

"Poetry, daddy." She sighed. "Did you know that Leopardi is the greatest Italian poet since Dante?"

"No, but I think I know where you can get a job as a secretary."

Willa thought of the series of paintings she was working on, how very much she wanted to finish them. Stopping her work seemed to her akin to giving up on life, but she knew it was better not to mention her work just then, especially not in a way that sounded like what her father called "melodramatic."

That same evening as they were preparing dinner, Mrs. Carver said to Willa, "When I was your age, we didn't do just as we pleased. We were grateful for whatever our parents could do and we did for ourselves." Willa knew the rest.

"But I do help you and daddy," she said, her voice edged with irritation as she jerked a drawer open and took out a peeler. There was a brief silence before she began peeling the pile of carrots that lay on the counter. "Wasn't there ever anything you ever really wanted to do?"

"I wanted to marry your father," Mrs. Carver replied as she shelled peas.

"I didn't mean that."

Mrs. Carver wiped her hands on her apron. She seemed to glow at the memory. "When I was your age...no, younger...I wanted to be on the stage. A great actress. You probably can't imagine *me* doing such a thing."

Willa stopped peeling and looked at her mother. "No, I can't."

"In my day, respectable girls didn't go off alone and join the theater," Mrs. Carver continued.

Willa ran the peeler the length of a carrot letting the skin drop onto the counter. "Why didn't you go anyway?"

"I preferred the local productions—musicals and such." A distant look crossed Mrs. Carver's face. "This one evening–we had just done *A Midsummer Night's Dream* at the Pavilion—after we took our bows, a handsome young man stood up and handed me an armful of red roses. I had noticed him before because he sat in the front row at every performance. He followed me all the way backstage. 'My name is Herbert,' he said, 'and I'm going to marry you.' Just like that. I still remember that moment every time I smell roses. He said that first he had to go away on an important business matter...I remember this clearly...and that he would write to me. He made me promise to wait for him. All that summer we exchanged letters, and then in the last letter he said he had completed his business and that he would be coming back for me just as he'd promised."

"But he didn't." Willa said. She laid the peeled carrots in a line like fallen soldiers.

"Many years later after my parents died, I learned that he had continued to write to me. I found several of his letters in my father's desk drawer. The letters were addressed to me and they had been opened. He wrote that he was now certain that he could make his fortune and asked me to go away with him. 'Now I can give you everything you could want.' That's what the last letter said."

"Don't you wonder...about going with him, I mean?"

"Life is what really happens to us, dear. It's just a memory. Besides, I'm very happy, probably happier than I would have been with him. Think of it this way: if Herbert had come back, you and your brother would never have been born."

That summer Mr. and Mrs. Carver continued to nibble at Willa's artistic ambitions like moths in a wool coat, and Willa continued to refuse the invitations from young men Ruth Carver considered "perfectly suitable," unconcerned that she might fulfill her mother's prediction of permanent spinsterhood. Mrs. Carver often reminded Willa that art "is a pleasure that leads to poverty." At Willa's insistence, the Carvers attended a traveling art exhibition of "modern" paintings in Cleveland. Mr. Carver gazed at a Toulouse Lautrec for several minutes and then said to Willa, "Clearly, an artist's life is squalid and erratic. Artists are almost never recognized before they die, so they can't make a living. And it says right here that Lautrec was independently wealthy. And a hunchback."

"They're always men, too," Mrs. Carver added. "You'd have no one to talk to."

Willa saw something different in Lautrec, namely, an escape from the constraints of Erhart, and she decided that escape must be her subject, her art, her life's work. Under Maestro Ottaviani's tutelage, she produced increasingly abstract works in which the viewer could identify disconnected body parts—principally breasts and penises—in a maelstrom of sweeping colors. She began to paint at night in the studio she had arranged in the unfinished attic, feverish images of monkey spirits dressed in orange shirts and rising out of peacefully sleeping bodies, of cars toppling off bridges into roiling waters, and of coffins both empty and full.

"Do you paint like that because you're crazy," Roy, her brother, asked one evening at dinner, "or because you can't paint very well?"

"I paint what I feel," Willa replied without looking at him.

"She's using her imagination, honey," Ruth Carver added.

"In that case, she should imagine a real job," Mr. Carver said, "because she must have one by two weeks from today."

"Perhaps it's time for a checkup, too," Mrs. Carver said. She had consulted among her friends, mothers of more predictable daughters, and these conversations, Willa knew, produced in her mother an intense, unremitting anxiety. The next morning, Willa went straight to Maestro Ottaviani's studio.

"They want me to stop painting," Willa sobbed into Maestro Ottaviani's sympathetic embrace. That very day, Maestro Ottaviani requested a meeting with Mr. Carver. When the two men met, he asked for Willa's hand in marriage, suggested that his request was a mere formality, and then inquired about the status of Willa's dowry. Mr. Carver asked for time to consider his proposal.

"What did he say, daddy?" Willa asked after the meeting.

"Let's just say that the amount of your dowry was foremost in his mind."

"It's just an Italian custom, daddy."

"He's impecunious."

"He's an artist "

"Whatever he is, he's unsuitable. I think it's time we settled you somewhere that you can study art if that's what you want. Get it out of your system."

Seldom does the answer to an urgent question present itself as though the gods had been listening and immediately dispatched their special envoy, but, in fact, that is exactly what happened. The following week, Lily Handel, the wife of Mr. Carver's law partner, invited the Carvers to meet her cousin, Isabella Farnese. Because she was well connected in artistic circles in Florence, Signora Farnese had been invited to speak on the subject of "Italian Art Yesterday and Today" at the annual Women's League luncheon at the Pavilion, a benefit for needy families. Her accent reflected her American upbringing, but her ochre silk skirt and gauzy blouse with patterns reminiscent of the markings of a tabby cat, her paisley shawl drawn aside to reveal finely wrought gold jewelry, and her exquisite leather shoes were entirely Florentine. Willa imagined the Signora's daily life as one of Byzantine magnificence and frequent changes of clothing.

At the Women's League Luncheon the Carvers sat with the Handels and their guest. "Are there many young artists in Firenze?" Mrs. Carver asked.

Signora Farnese nodded. The gilded combs in her hair flashed in the light. "Some attend the Accademia while others go to university or apprentice themselves, as in the old days. Of course, some do work on their own and are mostly self-taught."

Mr. Carver leaned toward the guest of honor. "Tell me, Signora, what do the young, inexperienced artists do?"

"It's now a matter of some debate as to whether they will be classically trained or left to find their way alone. Apprenticeship is largely a thing of the past, I'm afraid. Either way, there are, shall we say, desirable and undesirable results."

"And what is your opinion?"

Signora Farnese's eyelids fluttered. "The value of classical training cannot be overestimated."

Their conversation continued into the afternoon. At the end, Mr. Carver shook Signora Farnese's hand. "I look forward to discussing the plan you suggest with Willa. I think she will be very interested in studying art in Firenze." Later that evening Mr. Carver summoned Willa to the living room. "Pack," he said. "You're going to Italy."

4

NEW YORK CITY, OCTOBER 1934

"Remember, dear, you can never go wrong by saying something nice," Ruth Carver reminded Willa as they stood next to the gangplank. She wiped her eyes with her handkerchief and hugged her daughter. "Oh, I almost forgot. Here's a package for you. Something from Aunt Leonie for you to read on the ship." Willa opened the gift. Inside were three books—*Daisy Miller, Portrait of a Lady*, and *The House of Mirth*—and a note: *Dear Willa, Learn much and don't let these ladies be you. With love from your Aunt Leonie.*

"We read these at Miss Waltham's," Willa said. "They're about women in the *nineteenth* century. They all came to a bad end." *Does Aunt Leonie think I will, too?* she wondered. "Tell Aunt Leonie please not to worry. I promise I won't end up like they did."

"You'll remember to write a thank you note, won't you?" Ruth Carver hugged Willa again. "And write to us as soon as you get there…and do as Signora Farnese advises."

Willa followed Signora Farnese up the gangplank. Inside her cabin, she dropped her purse and carpetbag on the bed and returned to the deck. Her parents' final instructions to avoid strangers and obey Signora Farnese seemed as distant to Willa as the port of New York soon would be. Away from home and uncommitted to another place, she felt the giddy freedom reserved to those who release the past without regret and anticipate a future that unfolds only in their favor.

During the voyage Willa enjoyed presenting herself as anyone she chose for a few hours or, at most, the number of days it took the ship to complete its crossing. She felt increasingly expansive, engaging in animated conversations with her shipmates at dinner, at shuffleboard, on the observation deck, even with people she might have ignored previously; confiding that she was going to Italy to study art, to become an artist, a painter; embellishing her plans and expectations as the voyage continued; marveling at all that now seemed possible just by claiming it was so.

Indeed, Willa developed a way of entertaining herself that involved imagining what other passengers might be thinking about her, imagining that they found her mysterious or attractive, concocting ideas they might have about who she was or what she was doing. One day, she was a famous actress, the next a wealthy émigrée, another day a courtesan, and still another a fiancée on her way to meet her husband-to-be. These imaginary flights seemed to her pleasant and harmless. Perversely, however, such excursions made Willa less certain of her own identity and thus in greater need of the attention of others to affirm that her existence still retained both its substance and its meaning. As the voyage progressed, her fancied roles also created unanticipated problems.

On their last evening aboard, Signora Farnese complained of a headache and went to bed early. "Go to dinner without me," she told Willa, who had been looking forward to wearing a special dress for the occasion, a long aqua chiffon gown and matching satin pumps that had sparkling buckles over the instep. Willa sat at the captain's table with some ten other passengers, an arrangement she owed to Signora Farnese's ingenuity. She unbuttoned her long, white kid gloves and took them off slowly as her tablemates watched. To her left sat her host, Captain Forth, in his dress uniform, and on her right, a large man who, during the cocktail hour, had announced that he was the owner of a company "engaged in the manufacture and distribution of haberdashery goods and services for the gentleman." He looked at Willa as if he were measuring yardage.

"Nice dress."

Willa felt slightly uncomfortable on the one hand and challenged on the other. "Thank you." She returned his frank gaze intending to shame him. She marveled at how small his eyes were in relation to the expanse of his face. *How much of my dress can he actually see?* she thought. He extended his hand toward her.

"Harry Grable." She looked at his hand, noticing the thick, dark hair on the back of it.

"I'll bet she has lots of beaus," Grable said to the entire table. He turned to Willa quickly. "Do you?" He spoke as if he were accusing her of wrongdoing.

"You're a flatterer, Mr. Grable." She recognized something unpleasant, almost threatening, in him.

"Never more sincere." He gestured to include others at the table. "So, hon', how many boyfriends do you already have?" He spoke too loudly.

Willa knew he was vulgar, yet she indulged the temptation to use her power to resist his attention without humiliating him publicly. "I really can't say, Mr. Grable, but certainly none as charming as you," she replied, recalling that her mother's advice justified her complimenting him. She saw the effect of her words, his surprise and then the direct way that he focused on her, a hound picking up a scent. Ignoring his dinner, he pressed on, clearly pleased with what he took to be a conquest.

"Discerning gal, right, Captain?" Grable said. The Captain and the others looked down at their food and began to eat.

"Yes, Mr. Grable," the Captain replied, "but I would be careful in pressing what seems to be an advantage." He turned and looked at Willa. "I believe she may have other interests."

"Yes, I do," Willa said, seizing recklessly on the Captain's safe lead.

"What might those be?" Grable asked placing his hand on his chest and smiling.

Willa stopped eating the prime rib and set her fork down. "I'm a dancer." The idea had just popped into her head, and she said it before she thought about it. She noticed Grable's surprise. The other diners inclined their heads the better to hear.

"Is that what brings you to Italy?" the Captain said.

"I'm going to *Firenze*," she replied, emphasizing the word.

Grable leaned forward. "So am I."

Had her answer appeared to include him? That wasn't what she had intended. She tried to distance herself "To buy costumes," she added, thinking of Signora Farnese's clothing.

"I like a gal who knows how to shimmy," Grable cut in. "How 'bout we have ourselves a little dance after dinner?"

"I'll have to...check my card," Willa said. She had no card and Grable knew it.

"Forget that card business, young lady. We'll show these folks how to do the Milwaukee Two-Step. That's a promise." He winked at the Captain.

After dessert was served, Willa turned to the Captain and began putting on her gloves. "Do you dance, Captain Forth?"

"Nah, he steers the ship," Grable said. He put his sweaty hand on her arm. She looked down at the two greasy fingerprints on her pale leather glove.

The Captain turned to Willa and smiled. "We have a custom on our last evening at sea," he said evenly, looking at Grable. "I ask a lady at my table to dance, and then others at the table follow our example until everyone is dancing." He pushed back his chair and held out his hand to Willa. She got up, and he led her to the dance floor. "I believe you've found an admirer in Mr. Grable. He seems intent on pursuing you, if that is your wish." Across the dance floor, Willa could see Grable rising from the table. He lumbered toward them. She felt uneasy.

"Please excuse me, Captain Forth. I'm not feeling well." Captain Forth escorted her from the dance floor, and she escaped from the crowded dining room. The next morning they would land at the port of Naples, and she would never see Grable again. She knew she had made a mistake. In the future, she would be more careful.

5

ITALY, OCTOBER 1934

Well before breakfast Willa put on her wool suit that was the color of lilacs and secured the matching flowered hat, adjusting the veil so it fell just below her cheekbones. On the lapel she attached a pin that had belonged to great grandmother Carver, a tiny spray of gold flowers with centers of diamonds and pearls. It had been an engagement gift from great grandfather Hugh. She touched her wrists and behind her ears with rose petal water and counted her money. Then, she put on her dark blue coat and buttoned her matching kid gloves just above the wrist. The porter knocked at the door.

In one hand, Willa carried her purse and a carpetbag in which she had stowed the sketchbook from Maestro Ottaviani, several drawing pencils, an eraser, a stump, an Italian novel, and a map marked with the directions to Signora Farnese's villa in Fiesole in case they should become separated. In the other hand, she carried a hatbox papered with scenes of happy travelers with parasols. Signora Farnese was waiting for her near the gangplank. As soon as they left the ship, they boarded a taxi.

The entrance at the train station teemed with people. *They look so poor,* Willa thought. Not at all like the lavish Renaissance paintings she had studied at home. As she got out of the taxi, she saw an elderly woman bent under a load of rags nearby. A man in a uniform shouted, *"Vai via! Vai via!"* Go away! *"You can't stand here."*

"Why is he telling her that?" Willa asked.

"She's just a *cenciaiola*," Signora Farnese said. A ragpicker.

"But why did he tell her to go away? She wasn't doing anything."

"People like that aren't allowed to stand around in public places. They're supposed to stay in the marketplaces."

"Why?"

"Because it looks bad."

Willa wished she could draw the *cenciaiola* unobserved, but knew that her own and Signora Farnese's comparative wealth made them conspicuous.

Nearby, a chestnut seller sat next to his brazier shaking the chestnuts in the hot pan. Several children, ragged and coatless in the raw morning, formed a ring around him. Dragging a scrawny puppy by a cord around its neck, one boy no more than four years old held out his hand. *"Ho fame."* I'm hungry. The puppy whined and the child kicked it. The animal squealed.

A woman with a baby wrapped in a shawl wound around her shoulders and carrying two heavy bundles shouted in the direction of the children, *"No! Vattene! Troppo costoso!"* Get away from there! Too expensive! The children backed away, their dark eyes devouring the chestnuts. The woman set the bundles down, seated herself on them, and began to nurse the baby. Appalled, Willa went to the chestnut seller and bought little bags of chestnuts for the children and the woman.

"Grazie, signorina," they said with one voice, watching her as they ate, eager for more. *They even smell poor,* Willa thought. The puppy begged for some food. The child holding the cord glanced around to see if anyone was watching, then kicked the dog again. The animal yelped. The officer returned and ordered the children and the mother out of the station. Willa moved to speak to him.

"Let it be," Signora Farnese said.

"But she was feeding her baby."

"After you've been here a while, you'll understand why."

A porter stacked their suitcases and trunks on his cart with the hatbox on top and led them inside. The station smelled old, stale, a mixture of fuel, dust, food, dampness, people, and time. The shriek of metal brakes hurt Willa's ears. *Still, it's quite clean,* she thought, surprised.

"The eight o'clock train is a local, and there are no first class seats left," the clerk told Signora Farnese. "I still have seats available on the ten o'clock."

"We'll wait," Signora Farnese said. They bought food for their trip—bread and cheese, several pieces of fruit, some pastry, a bottle of wine, two bottles of mineral water—and Willa put these supplies in her carpetbag. They sat down on a bench together. Willa took out her drawing materials and began to draw, trying to remember the children, the mother, the *cenciaiola*.

She had been drawing for nearly an hour when the sight of two officers escorting a man in a wrinkled suit, the pockets of his jacket nearly torn off, caught her attention. The man had large bruises on the side of his face and he walked with difficulty. The officers, one on each side, held his arms. One of the officers also carried a battered suitcase that seemed to belong to the prisoner. The three moved toward a waiting train and got on.

"What happened to that man?" Willa said.

"I recognize him," Signora Farnese said. "I saw his picture in the paper when he was arrested. He's a journalist who spoke out publicly against Mussolini and the Fascist party. He's been sentenced to *confino*."

"*Confino?*"

"Exile. People who cause trouble are sometimes sent away to remote places so they can't continue their illegal activities."

"What did he do?"

"He didn't follow the rules that everyone knows to follow."

"Why?"

"Because he was foolish."

Could this be the real Italy? Willa wondered.

"There you are!" Willa looked up. "Hey, young lady, you went off and left me last night when I was lookin' forward to a dance. Or two or three." It was Grable. She had forgotten about him. He extended a meaty hand toward her. His eyes seemed to disappear. Just then the children to whom she had given the chestnuts crowded around them. *They must have followed me*, Willa thought. They held out their hands. "Get outta here!" Grable shouted. Willa put her drawing materials in her bag. "Hey, I thought you was a dancer. Instead, you're a draw-er. My mistake." He chuckled.

"I don't believe we've been introduced," said Signora Farnese in a tone that foreclosed conversation.

"Name's Grable," he said. "G-R-A-B-L-E." He offered his hand. "*Piacere.*" He chuckled. "Sounds like *pee-on-a-cherry,* don't it?"

Signora Farnese signaled to the porter. "Willa, it's time to go."

Willa gathered her belongings, grateful to follow. "He sat at my table last night," she told Signora Farnese as they walked along the platform. She glanced back, relieved to see that Grable hadn't moved. He was still watching her.

"He isn't someone you want to know, dear, wherever he sat," Signora Farnese said. "Here, we don't talk to people unless they've been properly introduced and then only if we want to know them. Nor do we allow them to talk to us." Willa hoped Grable was on a different train.

The porter helped them up the steps and guided them to their compartment. Through the glass door of the compartment, they saw a young army officer sprawled across the seats. He was asleep. When they opened the door, he snorted and stirred.

"*Un compagno di viaggi*o," a traveling companion, the porter said, smiling. He stowed their luggage and Willa's hatboxes on the racks above and then took their trunks to the baggage car. Willa and Signora Farnese sat down opposite the soldier. He had a fresh plaster cast on his right arm, which rested in a sling. He had used his jacket as a pillow, and a black felt cap covered most of his face. Willa thought he would make a good study of a reclining figure. She had just taken out her sketchbook when the soldier awakened and sat up, spoiling the pose. The porter appeared in the doorway with their claim checks.

Willa rummaged in her purse, pulled out several bills, and put them in the porter's hand. The porter looked at the money with an astonished smile.

"*Aspetta!*" said the soldier. Wait! He glared at the porter, took the bills from him, and returned them to Willa. "It's illegal for him to accept money," he told her in Italian. "You should be more careful or you'll attract thieves." Willa laughed.

"*Grazie mille,*" she said. *Could the soldier be someone I want to know?* she wondered.

"*Grazie mille,*" Signora Farnese said with a sigh.

Willa's attention was distracted by the sound of pebbles thrown against the window. She turned and looked out through the dirty glass. Below, the children waved to her shouting, *"Per favore, signorina."* They weren't supposed to be in the station. *A little money might make them leave before they get into trouble,* she thought. Taking the bills out of her pocket, she went the window and opened it.

The soldier reached out and caught her arm. "*Signorina,* you mustn't try to end all the poverty in Naples before our train leaves."

Willa turned back to him. "What's wrong with helping them?" she said, speaking in Italian. He smiled and adjusted his cap, leaving its small, red feather at an angle, and looked at her with a kind of directness that compelled her attention. He had a round face framed by almost black, curly hair that grew to a peak in the middle of his forehead. Despite a beak-like nose, he was handsome. *A good subject for a painting.* Though he was sitting down, she guessed he was of medium height, muscular and stocky, with square-ish hands that suggested an earthy strength. Practical. Like a carpenter or a farmer. His olive skin and dark uniform gave him an almost smoky appearance, but it was his soldier's vitality that attracted her as one is attracted to both the warmth and also the danger of flames. Willa put her money back in her purse. "Do you disapprove of helping people in need?" she said.

He laughed again and leaned toward her. "First, you give *una fortuna* to the porter…now, you want to give another *fortuna* to beggars. What will you do when their brothers and sisters and cousins and in-laws come rushing to you like locusts to a grain field?"

"Non lo so." I don't know.

"Our lives and theirs"—he gestured toward the window—"are different."

"But that's cruel," Willa said. "They're people just like us." He laughed and shook his head. *His face is strong. It has character. Perhaps a three-quarter view would be better.*

He shrugged. "They have their fate. We have ours." He accepted these circumstances as if there were nothing to be done, an acceptance suffused with regret perhaps, but the kind of regret that is not accompanied by any sense of responsibility for or commitment to righting an injustice.

"I don't believe in fate," Willa said. Signora Farnese cleared her throat and glanced at the seat next to her. Willa sat down. *Anyway, it doesn't matter what this soldier thinks because I don't want to know him.* Just then, the train lurched forward.

"It's your charity that's cruel," the soldier continued, "and selfish, too. You feel good because you throw your money out the window, but suppose you cause a riot or a fight? They'll be arrested or fall under the train and be worse off than before."

Willa couldn't let his challenge pass. "I know it's possible to do better. Someone—perhaps your government—has to help the poor." Signora Farnese put her hand on Willa's, but Willa was already too involved to remain cautious.

"Where do you come from that you think that it's possible to end poverty?" the soldier asked.

"Erhart. Ohio. America." Willa wished that the place she came from sounded more interesting. "But I live in Firenze now." Signora Farnese glanced over at her, but said nothing.

"I've never heard of this place, Ohio, Erhart."

"But you've heard of Firenze." *He is quite handsome*, Willa thought. She smiled. He returned her smile.

"In any case, our government supports land reform." He spoke with great seriousness. "Many people, including myself, believe that the poverty of the peasants will be alleviated when they are allowed to grow enough food to eat and to keep some to sell instead of giving everything to the landlord."

So he does favor fair treatment for the less fortunate, after all, Willa thought. "If that's what you believe," Willa said, "why is it wrong for me to help them?"

He laughed. The train picked up speed, leaving Naples behind. He seemed to draw up to attention. Willa looked at the gold watch that hung on a chain around her neck and opened the engraved lid. "Anyway, we're too far away for me to start a riot in Naples now," she said.

"But you still have enough time to tell me why you're going to Firenze."

Willa looked at Signora Farnese, who shook her head. A warning. "I didn't say I was going to Firenze," Willa replied. "I said that I live there." She turned the page in her sketchbook, intending to work on the drawing of the children while she could still remember how they looked. "I'm going to be an artist." She wished there had been more time to study the children before drawing them, though Maestro Ottaviani believed that the feeling of life could be captured in a single line in no time at all. She wanted her work to reflect this aesthetic ideal.

"An artist." The soldier seemed to ponder this possibility. "I think that must be the reason that you're so impractical." He spoke as if he were merely restating an hypothesis that had already been tested and verified.

"I'm not," Willa said. She didn't mind being considered impractical, but she didn't believe he could judge her character on such minimal and, to her, irrelevant evidence. *Is that how Italians really are?* she wondered. "What could be more practical than for an artist to study in Firenze with its history of great art and artists?" She took a deep breath, wanting to say more about her ideas about art and why people considered a concern with aesthetics impractical, how that was a mistaken assumption. There was so much she wanted to talk about. *But where to begin?*

The soldier leaned closer to see the sketchbook that lay open on her lap. "Why don't you draw me? I think you were planning to do it anyway.

There's time and I'll sit very still." He adjusted his cap, crossed his knees and moved the armrest to support his cast.

"I was planning to draw the children," Willa said.

"Wait, I'll even pay you."

Signora Farnese shook her head. "That's improper."

Willa was curious about the soldier's offer. "How much?" *My first Italian commission! I must write to Maestro Ottaviani and tell him,* she thought.

"As much as you gave the porter," the soldier said. "A thousand lire."

"A thousand lire. Very well, but half of the fee has to be paid in advance," Willa said.

"Is that how they do it in America?"

"Yes."

"In Italy, we pay only if we like the result." He stood up and worked his wallet out of his back pocket with his good hand. "Since you are an American, I will make an exception." He counted out a thousand lire.

Signora Farnese put her hand between them. "No. She does not accept money from...." Before she could say more, Willa took the note and put it in her purse.

"See how impractical you are?" the soldier said. "You didn't even look at it. How do you know it's the right amount?"

He seems pleased, as if he won a competition, Willa thought. "I know it's double what we said. What else do I need to know?" In an effort to restore some formality between them, she pointed to a place next to the window. "If you will sit over there, please." He didn't move.

"I would have paid you even more, but you didn't bargain with me. Very impractical!"

Despite Signora Farnese's disapproving look, Willa took his bait. "You're mistaken. I didn't need to bargain with you because you gave me twice what I asked. Besides, you don't know whether I can draw or not, so it's you who's impractical." Signora Farnese shook her head and took refuge in a book on Italian art. "Please, move where the light is better," Willa said again, but the soldier refused.

"Draw!" He waved his hand like a monarch. "I want to watch you work."

"You'll make me self-conscious."

"You say you're an artist. I paid for my portrait, so you must do this portrait the way I want it. Ask your...mother?"

"What do you think?" Willa asked Signora Farnese.

"I think you made a mistake to take the money in the first place, but now that you've accepted it, you'll have to draw whatever pose he requests or return the money." Signora Farnese resumed reading her book.

"Don't talk," Willa told him. She took out a hard pencil first and began to block the key points of his shape, aligning his proportions with the length of her pencil as Maestro Ottaviani had taught her to do. She changed to a softer lead to note the curved lines of his body under the fabric of his uniform, the thrust of the jaw, the slight indentation where the mandible met the ear, then followed the line of the long, smooth nose, the outward bulge of his eyelids, the rounded darkness of the iris itself, erasing in the white highlight. Moving to the mouth, she traced the full upper lip, the slight smile, the thinner lower lip, and then the hair, which curled around his face like smoke. She followed the line of his sturdy torso to the left ankle resting on the right knee, ending in the left foot thrust toward her, his left hand on his knee, solid and firm. She traced the passage of each finger, erasing, changing, and correcting the angles of the knuckles. *Does this drawing have life?* she asked herself. *What would Maestro Ottaviani say?* The soldier looked soft, yet fierce; kindly, but capable of slaying gorgons. She smudged the gentle edges of his mouth and dug her pencil into the paper in the places where she wanted to emphasize his strength.

"Do you always draw like you're trying to kill something?" he asked.

"Shhh."

"I'm Gabriele Marcheschi and I live in Orvieto." He lifted his arm from the sling, leaned toward her. "I'm going home to get well."

She glanced at him. "What happened to your arm?"

"*Un incidente.*" An accident. He made a rolling motion with his good hand. "In Ethiopia, the truck I was driving overturned near Addis Ababa. My arm is broken in three places." He pointed to his upper arm, then to just below his elbow, and to his wrist, his eyes on her.

Willa looked down at her work. "Perhaps you're not such a good driver," she said as she erased an area that troubled her. "You should have been more careful." She heard his quick intake of breath.

"But I was almost killed!" He sounded affronted. *Have I said something wrong?* she wondered. "I am not careless or weak," he continued. "I am ready to die for my country." He put his good hand on his chest. "I was never afraid." He reached into his pocket and took out a medallion attached to a crumpled purple ribbon. "Look." He put it on her sketchbook and leaned closer, pointing to the inscription. "It says *'for bravery and courage in battle'*."

"I'm sorry about your arm. Does it still hurt?" Willa said. She handed the medal to Signora Farnese, who returned it to the soldier.

"I don't know if I'll ever be able to work again." His expression included sadness, remorse, and self-pity. Willa found the contradiction of his rough exterior and sentimentality appealing in a romantic way. *He seems overly dramatic,* she thought. *After all, he's here and alive and evidently quite well.*

"What does your doctor say?" Signora Farnese asked. Gabriele leaned toward her as if confiding a secret.

"Signora, in Orvieto we had three doctors. One was my brother who was killed in the same accident. Crushed under the truck. He died instantly. The other fellow, also a doctor…his foot was nearly cut off. They took him to the same hospital where they took me. Gangrene set in. He became a hunk of rotten meat. He knew he was dying and he cried for his mother the whole time. Death is a terrible thing." He watched Willa, assessing the effect of his words. "Now, there is only one doctor left for all of Orvieto: Dr. Lucarelli who knows only herbs." Willa looked out the window at the parched hills thinking of Chip and Eddie. Just then, they—and Gabriele Marcheschi, too—seemed beautiful to her, the idea of their being in a war tragic. "Mussolini wants to restore our greatness like a Caesar," Gabriele continued, "but this is why there is no doctor for my arm in Orvieto." He shrugged. *Did he regard this, too, as a matter of fate?*

"If I were you, I'd go where they had doctors," Willa said, glad that she would be an artist in a city with real doctors.

"You mean you would go somewhere for just such a small thing as a doctor? Why would I leave my home, my family's *podere*?" Gabriele replied. "I'm the only son left and I must always care for the land of my family. Our vineyards. Our crops. Our tenants."

"I think a good arm is more important than a piece of land," Willa said. "How could I be an artist without my arm? How could you take care of your family's land without yours?"

Gabriele shook his head. "Without my land, how could I be a man? Anyway," he said, "if you saw how beautiful my family's land in Orvieto is, you wouldn't say that."

"I would too say it. I'd say it no matter what," Willa said.

"Is this how you think?" he asked. She nodded, erasing a line. "You must be an American to leave your home for such a foolish reason."

"That's not why I left," she said, carefully redrawing the line. "I left to become a painter."

"They don't have painters in America?"

"Not in Erhart, Ohio."

"So people in this Ohio, Erhart, leave the land of their fathers and grandfathers just to be painters?"

"*Erhart, Ohio.* Yes," she said, "we do."

Gabriele threw up his hands. "So, now you have nothing."

The conductor entered their compartment. Signora Farnese gave him their tickets and excused herself. One of Willa's pencils rolled off the seat and onto the floor. Both she and Gabriele Marcheschi reached for it. He put his hand around hers and pressed his medal into her palm. Willa pulled her hand away. He put the medal on her sketchbook.

"A gift from your new friend, Gabriele Marcheschi."

"You can't give me this." She handed the medal back to him. "I don't know you."

"You know me well enough to take my money for a portrait." He fingered the medal. "So now you must tell me your name." It was true. She would have to tell him her name when she signed the drawing. She looked out through the window of the compartment door. Signora Farnese and was nowhere in sight.

"Willa." She pushed a long strand of hair away from her face. "Willa Carver."

Gabriele stood up, bowed slightly, and removed his cap with his left hand and put it on the seat. His dark curls tumbled over his forehead. He held out his hand, and she shook it. "So now we are friends, Willa Carver." Using his good hand, he slipped his identity card out from the band inside of the cap and handed it to her.

"*Per favore.* Write your name and the address on this card. So I know where to come for my picture." She hadn't considered this possibility, but he was right. Of course, he would have to come for the picture. He had paid for it. Since she couldn't deliver it, she must allow him to come for it. *He probably won't come,* she thought. She found her address book and copied Signora Farnese's address in her careful, vertical cursive onto the back of the identity card. He studied it.

"Fiesole? You said you lived in Firenze." The compartment door slid open and Signora Farnese entered. She had a small, pink-striped paper bag in her hand.

"*Vicino.*" Near. Gabriele put the card inside his cap and sat back in his seat.

"Near what?" Signora Farnese asked.

"Near to done," Willa said, indicating the drawing.

"Near Firenze," Gabriele said. "She says she lives near Firenze, but in Fiesole."

"I hope you've not gotten into any more trouble in my absence." Signora Farnese offered Willa a chocolate.

Willa took the candy and ate it in one bite. "I'm just working on this drawing." Signora Farnese held out the bag of chocolates to Gabriele.

"No thank you. I'm working, too," he said, smiling. Signora Farnese sat down and took out her book. They rode in silence. Willa continued to draw, shading the contours of Gabriele's cheeks with a soft pencil, the curve of the brow already etched with fine lines. She traced the drape of his half-lowered eyelids, drowsy in the warm car, carved out the depth of the septum and the definite chin, then the folds of his uniform revealing a powerful chest and the muscles of his arms under the fabric. She imagined him as a marble sculpture. The train came to a stop, and she looked up at him. In Gabriele's eyes, Willa noticed a deeper liveliness within, an animation she hadn't seen earlier. *Was this the life that Maestro Ottaviani thought so important?* She changed her pencil strokes to match the vividness of this presence.

"How long will you stay in Italy?" he asked.

She shrugged. "Long enough to become good at painting *uomini nudi*, I think." Gabriele started. Signora Farnese looked up.

"*Nudi*," said Signora Farnese. "Nudes—not naked men,"

"Yes, *nudi*, I mean," Willa said. "And long enough to cure Neapolitan poverty, too!"

"A long time, then," Gabriele said. Willa thought he looked pleased.

About noon, the train slowed again and moved onto a siding while another train overtook and passed them. When tea service and sandwiches arrived, Gabriele insisted on buying refreshments for them.

"That's very considerate," Willa said, "but I want to finish this drawing." Signora Farnese nodded at her approvingly and declined as well. The train slowed, and the conductor announced their next stop. "Orvieto."

Gabriele stood up. "I get off here," he said. "Let me see my portrait once more before I go."

"Here, it's done. You can take it with you."

"Keep it to remember your friend, Gabriele Marcheschi." He bent over to look at her drawing. "It's worth more than I thought." He took out his wallet and counted out another thousand lire. "For a picture and a frame. I want you to hang it where you will see me every day." Signora Farnese raised her eyebrows.

Willa tore the drawing out of her sketchbook. "Here, you must keep it and frame it yourself."

"I will see you very soon, and my framed portrait." He put the bill in Willa's hand and closed her fingers around it. "I will come next Sunday."

Signora Farnese looked alarmed. "It's quite premature," she said. The train came to a stop. *I shouldn't have given him the address*, Willa thought. *Another mistake.*

"*Arrivederci,*" Willa and Gabriele Marcheschi said to one another simultaneously. Then, Gabriele bent over her and with his good arm pulled Willa to him, held her tightly, and kissed her on the lips, pressing his tongue into her mouth. Willa gasped and flailed. Gabriele released her with a shout, and she fell back against her seat. He dropped the medal into her lap and went out into the corridor, laughing.

Willa laughed, too. "That soldier is *pazzo*," she said to Signora Farnese, but she liked it that Gabriele Marcheschi had kissed her, had surprised her, had done something she hadn't expected. He had a way about him that was confident and certain.

"It's a complete scandal," Signora Farnese said. "You accept money from a stranger of unknown reputation. He gives you gifts. He says he will call on you without a proper introduction or an invitation. And to make matters worse, he kisses you in public."

To Willa these things weren't scandalous or regrettable. She thought them amusing, but she understood that she had let things go too far. "I'll give everything back right now." She went to the window. Gabriele was standing on the platform, looking up as if he had expected to see her. She opened the window and leaned out with the medal, the drawing, and the money in her extended hands. The conductor's whistle sounded again. The train moved forward, stopped, and moved forward again.

"You smell like roses and *biscotti*," Gabriele called out to her. "Until Sunday!" He continued waving until she could no longer see him.

"I couldn't give them back," she told Signora Farnese when she returned to her seat. "He was too far away." She sat down and wrote across the bottom of Gabriele's portrait: "Italian soldier on the train from Naples" and the date. Later, she planned to fill in the background. She placed the medal and the money with the drawing and closed them inside her sketchbook. *Is this what people mean by an "Italian" experience?* She smiled.

"What did he say his name was?" Signora Farnese asked. "I'll have someone find out about him."

"Gabriele Marcheschi. He said he would call on me on Sunday. I'll give the picture and the medal and the money to him then."

"So you gave him my address, too?"

"Yes."

"I see," said Signora Farnese. "Then there is nothing else to be done except to tell you that this, too, is highly improper. You are my guest, and I am your chaperone. I am the one who should invite guests to my house on your behalf. That is how we do things in Italy. Please remember that for my sake, if not for your own. And *never* give my address to anyone."

"Not even a taxi driver?" Willa said, intending to tease her.

"Not even a taxi driver."

"I'm sorry," Willa said. "I didn't mean to upset you. I won't do it again."

"*Firenze, signora, signorina,*" the conductor told them. He looked outside and then at his watch, surprised. "Three minutes early." The train swayed, braked, and came to a stop with a shriek and an exhalation of steam. Outside, the purple grey twilight filled the corners of the day. Through the window, Willa could see the water-stained buildings hunched down against the impending darkness. A thin rain had left everything wet but unwashed.

They followed a porter. The used air of the station carried the odors of dampened dust and wool. Willa hadn't expected it to be so cold. She was glad she had worn her warm coat.

"Wait here while I find Antonio," Signora Farnese said. On the crowded platform, people huddled together in brown-grey bundles. *They look like sparrows*, Willa thought. She had expected Italy to be more colorful. Drizzle settled around her. It glistened on her luggage and left a damp film on her coat. When she buttoned the top button, her glove came back wet. A cold wind lifted loose papers and swirled them around her feet. She shivered and adjusted her hat. At last, the porter arrived with their trunks and put the rest of their luggage on his cart. Willa followed him inside the station. At least inside it was dry and warm. In the echoing waiting room, the porter set their belongings on the moist floor.

"Please wait," Willa said. She took out the map from her carpetbag. *"Dov'è Fiesole?"* Where is Fiesole?

"So there you are!" The voice came from behind her. She turned around. "You missed our engagement, girlie"—Grable shook his finger at her—"and then you and your chaperone walked off." The porter pointed to Fiesole. "Looks like you can find your way around, though. Lemme see. Where is it you're going?" Grable looked at the map. "Fiesole, is it? Who d'ya know in Fiesole?" Willa didn't answer. "I'll help you find it."

"I don't need any help, thank you," Willa said. Grable turned on her, his thick lips parted and curled. He was taller than she remembered. His small eyes contained an unexpected threat.

"Not so fast. You stood me up last night and you ducked out on me again this morning." She avoided looking at him. He moved closer to her, filling up the space between them.

"Leave me alone," she said loudly. People turned to look.

"Boy, you sure didn't act that way on the ship," he said equally loudly. *What would these people think?* "Bit of a tease, ain'tcha?" She saw his fury and knew he would hurt her if he could. *Where is Signora Farnese?*

Grable offered the porter several bills. "Get us a taxi." The porter hesitated. "Now!"

"Willa!" Signora Farnese called. "Here you are."

"Had a hard time finding her myself," Grable said. He held out his black-gloved hand. "'Scuse my glove, signora, and 'scuse us. This young lady and I have an appointment to keep."

"I don't think so," said Signora Farnese. A middle-aged man in a worn, black suit appeared at Signora Farnese's elbow. "Antonio, we'll go to the car. Bring everything with you." Relieved, Willa followed, leaving Grable behind. "In Italy, if a young woman is seen without a chaperone, people assume she's available to anyone," Signora Farnese told her after they were in the car. "Antonio and I will accompany you while you're here." She smiled. "Never mind. Now that you're here, I want you to meet some people who can be helpful to you." The car rattled through the dark and then wound uphill toward Fiesole. "Pierluigi Flavi is a re-spected art and antiquities dealer, and I think you would like each other." The wet streets sparkled in the headlights. Willa vowed not to make any more mistakes.

6

FIESOLE, ITALY 1934

On Sunday, the day Signora Farnese had planned a luncheon in Willa's honor, Willa strolled in the garden, noting the variety of plants—vegetables, herbs, vines, roses, wildflowers—and the fragrance of jasmine. Flocks of birds in delicate formations flew overhead, calling. The impression of wild abundance and casual disorder belied the careful geometry of the central courtyard and fountain and the symmetrical paths radiating out from them toward varied views. The leaves of the deciduous trees flickered to the ground in a confetti of red, gold and orange. Under a piercing cerulean sky marbled with light clouds, the olive groves and vineyards followed the soft curves of the hillsides as if they were tumbling into the valley below, rolling toward the tiled rooftops and tawny buildings of Firenze. *How does one capture the sensation of tumbling?* The sensations of painting—the feel of the brush, the thickness of the paint, the texture of the canvas—didn't match the sensation of falling.

Signora Farnese's maid, Assuntina, approached her. "Signorina, the guests have arrived." Excited and nervous about this first social occasion, Willa followed Assuntina along one of the paths that led up a rise to a terrace sheltered by a pergola supporting a large and twisted wisteria. They entered a glass-enclosed loggia where potted citrus trees blossomed. Willa dropped her jacket on a nearby chair. With a disapproving glance, Assuntina took the jacket away. Willa shook out her hair and adjusted her ivory silk dress, then licked her finger and bent down to rub a bit of dirt off her pale shoe.

Signora Farnese entered the loggia with the first of the guests. "Willa, may I present Pierluigi Flavi and his parents, Stefano Flavi, who directs

L'Accademia d'Arte, and Paola Flavi, his wife and my late husband's sister." She took Willa's hand. "And it is my great pleasure to present Willa Carver, my American guest, who, I may say, is going to make a very fine artist." Signora Farnese said this with a certainty that surprised Willa.

"*Piacere di conoscerLa,*" Willa said extending her hand to each of the guests. She hoped her Italian was correct. *Was it* conoscerLa *or* conoscerLei? *Italian could be so complicated sometimes.*

"You speak Italian very well," Pierluigi Flavi said to her. "I don't hear any accent." *ConocerLa must be correct then*, Willa thought, relieved to have made a good first impression.

A Mr. Bradshaw arrived, guided by Antonio. Though Willa failed to catch his first name, Signora Farnese said that he was an American who imported and exported important works of art. "He's the best," she added, as if Willa might have a need of his services. Next, there was a professor of art history, his wife and their twin daughters, whose names, Salomè and Delilah, seemed far bolder than the girls' shy presences. Finally, a very elderly white-haired couple with beaked noses and black clothing hobbled in, leaning on their canes. They cocked their heads when anyone spoke. Willa thought they resembled crows. "You're both looking very well today," Signora Farnese told them. She spoke very loudly. The two looked at their hostess blankly.

The guests gathered around a small sculpture and two paintings, still lifes in neutral colors, which Signora Farnese had recently purchased from Pierluigi Flavi. Willa preferred brighter colors and did not immediately see great significance in the paintings, but the others pronounced the artist a "seminal figure in twentieth century art." Willa had never heard of Morandi. The sculpture, called "Mother and Child," depicted two figures so narrow and elongated that Willa thought a more descriptive title might be "Starvation." She was surprised when the guests congratulated Signora Farnese on these "important" and "valuable" acquisitions to her excellent collection and thought them "sound investments." Willa wished she understood more about art. *How long would it take to learn?*

"Isabella has an excellent eye," Pierluigi Flavi said.

"You are much too modest," Signora Farnese told him. "You have the eye, and I benefit from your exceptional taste." *Do Italians always flatter one another?* Willa wondered.

"What brings you to Firenze?" Mr. Bradshaw asked Willa. He was a large, broad-shouldered man, solid like a plank, pale and blond, with a flat, squarish face and eyes so pale that he appeared farther away than he was. He looked prosperous, yet out of place.

"I'm studying art," Willa replied, wondering how he fit with the other guests.

Bradshaw took the prosciutto-and-fig appetizer from a tray that Antonio was holding and bit into it. "That so?" Willa nodded, watching as the prosciutto came apart and hung down over Bradshaw's chin. He grabbed the morsel with his fingers and pushed it back into his mouth. "Maybe you'd be interested in working for us," he said. He looked at the front of her dress. "I'm looking for an assistant to help me with clients."

Willa understood Bradshaw's gaze and his gambit. "I'm planning to be an artist, so I'm here to study," she said.

Bradshaw grunted and chuckled. "Fine by me."

Signora Farnese seated them around a large refectory table. Pierluigi Flavi held Willa's chair for her and then sat down to her right next to Signora Farnese, with Mr. Bradshaw to her left. "Pierluigi has agreed to take us to the Boboli Gardens next week," Signora Farnese told Willa with obvious pleasure.

"Thank you. That's very kind of you," Willa said to him. She unfolded her napkin, noting its elaborate cutwork and embroidery. Antonio filled her wine glass. Willa joined the others, answering their "*chin, chin*" with her own. *This is exactly where I belong and where I want to be.*

"How long will you be staying in Firenze?" Bradshaw asked.

"Several years, I think," she said, noting the antique Italian landscape depicted in muted tones of sepia on her plate. *Possibly forever.*

Pierluigi Flavi held a plate of antipasti for her. She noticed his slim, smooth hands and manicured fingernails and forgot her conversation with Mr. Bradshaw. Pierluigi Flavi was a study in subtle contrasts of color:

dark hair and profoundly blue eyes, light blue shirt and dark blue jacket against khaki slacks, and a single stroke of brilliant violet in the silk handkerchief in his breast pocket. The colors played in her imagination: cobalt blue, khaki, ultramarine, umber—each violated by that line of violet. "My father tells me that you've agreed to submit to the tyranny of L'Accademia," he said. "I'm surprised an American would do that."

Willa felt a movement on her left. Mr. Bradshaw thrust his business card in front of her. "In case you change your mind, here's where you can contact me." He pointed to his name: *Edward C. Bradshaw, Import, Export and Customs.* "Most people call me Ted."

"Thank you, Ted." Willa put the card on the table next to her plate and returned her attention to Pierluigi Flavi. "Yes, I want to improve my work."

Pierluigi Flavi nodded toward his father on the other side of the table. "You know, don't you," he said in voice loud enough for all to hear, "that at my father's academy you'll learn to draw like Michaelangelo, but you'll never again have an original idea of your own?" The heavy gold watch on his wrist seemed to underscore his authority on the certainty of this outcome.

Willa took a sip of wine, "So you think that classical training is a waste of time?"

Pierluigi Flavi laughed. "No. I simply mean that L'Accademia turns promising artists into the circus dogs of the old masters. You'll strut prettily with your bag of used tricks, but you'll forget why you wanted to be an artist in the first place and what it was you wanted to say. Ask my father whether that's not so. He'll tell you the same thing—at least he will if he's honest."

Willa's confidence vanished. *Could it be that Pierluigi Flavi was right?* "How can you be sure that will happen?" she said, trying to hold her voice steady.

"Real creativity threatens my father," he continued. "He will pull your originality out of you like weeds out of a garden and replace it with something that can never be yours because it's everyone's." Uneasy, Willa took several *bruschetta* and some additional prosciutto and fig and put them on her plate, and began to eat. "If you don't believe me, ask my father right now," Pierluigi Flavi said.

"Is that true?" Willa said to Stefano Flavi with a smile that failed to disguise her uncertainty.

"*Mio Dio!* Do you hear how my own son slanders me?" Stefano Flavi said to Signora Farnese. "Why are the young so ungrateful?"

Signora Farnese threw up her hands. "*Mah!* You would think a father and son would do something besides insult each other at my table and in front of my guests, too!"

Pierluigi Flavi laughed. "Signora, I'm merely warning your lovely guest of the risk that her drawings will be charming, but entirely generic, like *putti.*" He held the platter of antipasti. "Will you have some more?" Willa declined. She had lost her appetite.

"If this gal has as much talent as she does looks, she'll be famous the day after tomorrow." Bradshaw's hearty baritone filled the room and was seconded amid general agreement and laughter. Embarrassed, Willa blushed.

Stefano Flavi cleared his throat. "Nonsense. There is nothing wrong with beauty," he said, smiling at Willa. "Don't take seriously what my son says. He can't draw. He refused to learn the skills of the masters." He held out his hands, turning them skyward. "Now, he realizes that I was right. This is why he takes every opportunity to tell everyone who will listen that I am wrong."

"Nevertheless," said Signora Farnese, "he has exquisite taste." She gestured toward the loggia where the new paintings and sculpture were. "You cannot doubt that."

"Yes, that I will admit," said Stefano Flavi, "and in that sense he is original and creative. I admire his extraordinary success."

"Art isn't merely a matter of good taste," Pierluigi Flavi said to Willa. "In fact, good taste can be the enemy of the truly great artist. I don't believe good taste necessarily leads to originality or creativity. Do you?"

"Everyone knows that!" Stefano Flavi interrupted. Willa had never thought about the relationship between taste and originality. In fact, she had never heard the subject discussed. Such questions were obviously important. *What other questions might there be?* Questions she didn't know to ask.

"What is your opinion, *signorina*?" Stefano Flavi said to Willa. "Does good taste destroy originality or enhance it?"

"I want to introduce you to the artists whose work no one collects yet," Pierluigi Flavi said to Willa before she could answer, "artists my father doesn't necessarily approve of or know. You'll see that they think very differently about art than he does. They don't worry about taste. They have new *ideas* about what art can be."

Antonio came in and whispered something to Signora Farnese.

"What do you mean?" Willa asked, excited at the prospect of meeting other artists.

"For them, art isn't merely the mastery of traditional techniques. Art is the act of creation itself," Pierluigi Flavi said. Willa had never considered this distinction before. *Hadn't Maestro Ottaviani said they were the same? Could he have been mistaken? What else had he been mistaken about?* It occurred to her that perhaps she knew nothing at all about art and that Maestro Ottaviani didn't either. Perhaps she didn't even know what art was. Perhaps her ideas had nothing to do with real art. This troubling possibility led her to take another sip of wine.

"...on Thursday afternoon, then?" Pierluigi Flavi was saying to her.

Before she could respond, Signora Farnese appeared at her side. "You have a caller," she whispered.

"But I don't know anyone here."

"Antonio says his name is Gabriele Marcheschi. I believe he's the soldier from the train."

"The one with the medal?"

Signora Farnese nodded. "Antonio says he won't be put off. He says he has come from Orvieto and insists that he must see you."

Startled, Willa excused herself and stood up. "I'll tell him to leave," she said to Signora Farnese just as Gabriele blew into the dining room, like wind ahead of a storm.

"*Eccoti!*" Gabriele said with an exuberance that brought all conversations to a stop. "There you are! I was waiting for you in there"—he pointed toward the *salotto*—"but you were in here."

"You must excuse me. We were just discussing plans to visit some artists," Willa told him. She was embarrassed, of course. *What would Signora Farnese think? Pierluigi Flavi? It was a terrible mistake to tell Gabriele Marcheschi where I live.* Gabriele advanced into the dining room and rested his hand on the high, carved back of Signora Farnese's chair.

"This is most unexpected," said Signora Farnese. "May I present Gabriele Marcheschi who has come from Orvieto, I believe."

Gabriele nodded and gestured toward Willa. "She's a true artist," he said as if he were privy to their earlier conversation. "Did she show you her portrait of me?" He looked at each of the guests. They shook their heads, murmuring "No."

"You must show my portrait to everyone," Gabriele said to Willa.

Signora Farnese clasped her hands as if to pray. "We were just having lunch with our guests. Perhaps you could come back at a more convenient time."

"But I said I would come today and now here I am."

"I wasn't aware of it," said Signora Farnese.

"Now that I am here," he continued, "with your permission, it would please me to stay."

"No," Willa said involuntarily. She wanted Gabriele to leave right away.

"Perhaps another time," Signora Farnese said. "Today, as you can see, we have guests."

"Please, I beg you to allow me to stay."

Signora Farnese threw up her hands. "Let's not have a scene." She gestured toward the far end of the table. "Assuntina will set a place for you. Now, perhaps we can continue with our conversation."

"We were just discussing whether technique promotes or inhibits the artist's creativity," Stefano Flavi said to Gabriele. "Perhaps you will tell us your views." His tone was amiable.

Gabriele gazed at Willa. "Art grows out of the relationship between the artist and the subject," he said.

"Then you reject the importance of both technique and creativity?" Stefano Flavi said.

"My picture is in her sketchbook unless she's already had it framed," Gabriele continued. "My face, my uniform, my broken arm. You can see they're all there. They come from our relationship."

"It seems that you have known each other for some time," Pierluigi Flavi said.

"No," Willa said. She did not want to give the wrong impression about her relationship with Gabriele. "Our paths crossed on the train, and he asked me to do a sketch of him. That's all."

"Yes! That's where we became acquainted," Gabriele said. "She comes from Ohio, Erhart, America. Here in Firenze she will study art at L'Accademia d'Arte. She has parents and a brother in America." He reeled off fact after fact about Willa and her life, and Willa realized that while she had been concentrating on his portrait, she had revealed far more about herself than she had intended.

Stefano Flavi laughed. "Well, I can certainly see what you mean about the importance of the relationship between the artist and the subject."

"So do I," Pierluigi Flavi said, looking around the table. "I believe we must see this portrait." Everyone nodded and turned toward Willa.

"It's not finished," she said, blushing. *What will Pierluigi Flavi and the others think when they see the drawing?* She didn't want her work to be judged under such compromising circumstances.

"Everyone must see it," Gabriele said. "I paid two thousand lire for it." Once more a murmur spread through the group as people repeated the extraordinary sum paid for what the artist herself said was a casual sketch.

"But you gave it to me," Willa said to Gabriele. Several people laughed. Willa blushed again.

"So that you would remember me," Gabriele said. He stood up, excited. "Now, you pretend you don't know me. You let these people think that I'm *pazzo*?" Embarrassed and feeling foolish herself, Willa decided to do whatever she must to persuade this intruder to leave.

"I threw it away," she said. Gabriele bounced on his toes like a prizefighter. Signora Farnese raised her eyes toward the frescoed ceiling.

"What kind of artist throws a commission away?" Gabriele asked. "I want to show my drawing to these people." Willa got up from the table and went inside. Gabriele followed her.

"If Assuntina hasn't taken the waste papers, perhaps I can find it," she told him, "but then you must promise to leave." Gabriele laughed. "Promise me you'll go!" He laughed again. Willa went to her room and found the drawing folded in her sketchbook. She wadded it into a ball and returned to the *salotto* where Gabriele waited. "Here's your drawing!" she said. "And here is your money and your medal. Now, please go! Assuntina will let you out." She walked away from him and returned to the dining room. Instead of leaving, however, Gabriele followed her.

"My portrait!" he said to the other guests. He smoothed the ball of paper and pressed it onto the table. "See how talented she is!" The guests gathered around the portrait, comparing the wrinkled drawing to the actual model.

"An excellent likeness," Bradshaw said.

"It has an unusual animation and a liveliness," said Pierluigi Flavi. "If that is missing, there is no magic. Nothing."

Moving around the table, Stefano Flavi examined the drawing from different angles, and, sighting with his table knife, checked its proportions. He smiled pleasantly. "There is much that we can teach you, *signorina*."

7

"I'm going to Firenze today," Willa told Assuntina on the Wednesday morning after Gabriele's visit. She had decided to go to Pierluigi Flavi's gallery herself. "Where do I take the bus?"

Assuntina's eyes widened. Willa noticed that the maid's hands were trembling. "Someone must go with you, Signorina."

"I can go myself if you tell me where the bus is."

"The Signora is just coming in from the garden. She will explain about the bus."

Willa followed Assuntina into the kitchen. Signora Farnese had just set an immense bouquet of roses in the kitchen sink. A large khaki apron covered her skirt and sweater. "Assuntina, get the vases, please. Oh, there you are," she said to Willa. "Did you sleep well, *cara*? I hope our work in the garden didn't waken you."

"No, I was ready to get up." Willa plunged ahead. "I think I'll go to Firenze today." Assuntina returned to the kitchen with several vases; Antonio waited with a broom and a dustpan.

"Yes, the two blue ones, Assuntina, please. You can take the rest back." Signora Farnese began to cut the stems of the flowers. "I won't have time to go today, Willa. Antonio and I have more work to do outside. Come along with us. The view over Firenze is especially lovely. You can see the dome from here. Have you noticed?"

Willa saw Assuntina listening by the doorway. "I can go by myself."

"I'm delighted that you want to see Firenze," Signora Farnese replied, "but today I must work with Antonio in the garden. Do come see it."

"I can go to Firenze if only someone will just tell me how to get there," Willa said. Assuntina filled the vases with water.

"It's simply not done, my dear. We'll go next week, just as I said."
Signora Farnese continued trimming the roses one by one.

"And when I go to school, will I go out alone then?" Willa asked.
Signora Farnese shook her head.

"Antonio or I will take you and pick you up."

Even my parents allow me more freedom than this, Willa thought.
*Does Signora Farnese intend to confine me to Fiesole? It's even smaller
than Erhart.* "I'll just take a walk then."

"You'll find plenty of fresh air right here in the garden." Signora
Farnese paused in her work. "Perhaps I can persuade you to do a little painting for me. I need something to hang here in the kitchen." She
smiled. "A painting of the garden with the rooftops of Firenze in the
distance would be quite lovely, don't you think?" Willa didn't respond.
"Besides, I have some news that may interest you: Next week Pierluigi
Flavi has promised to take us not only to the Boboli Gardens but also to
the Duomo and the museums…"

"He invited me to meet some artists, too."

"There are certain places women of good character don't go…even
with Pierluigi Flavi."

"But I already said yes."

"No, dear, he invited *us.*"

But Signora Farnese wasn't even part of our conversation, Willa
thought.

"In Italy, it's expected that you consult me about your plans before
you go out and, of course, someone must escort you," Signora Farnese
said. Clearly, having a chaperone involved more restrictions than Willa
had imagined. *Respectable women in Italy live like prisoners.*

Later that afternoon Signora Farnese took Willa for a *passeggiata*
around Fiesole. The day was clear and still. As they hiked along a dirt
path, the only sounds were those of birds and insects and the scrunch of
dirt and stones under their feet. Butterflies fluttered around them, and the
fields smelled sweetly of earth and weeds. Signora Farnese pointed out
what remained of the wall built by the Etruscans more than two thousand

years earlier and the ruins of the Roman bath and theater.

A flock of birds circled above them. "The Romans sent a dozen young men here every year to study divination," Signora Farnese explained. "They learned to forecast the future by observing the flights of birds." During their walk, Signora Farnese also introduced Willa to neighbors and shopkeepers in the *mercato*; the *macellaio*, from whom they purchased *salumi* and pork shoulder; and the *cameriere* at the trattoria who served them coffee and *biscotti*. Everyone had questions for *L'americana*: *Why did you come to Italy? How long will you stay? Which is better: Italy or America?* Signora Farnese left the table.

"Signorina, it is my dream to go to America to live with my cousin," the *cameriere* whispered to Willa. "You can help me, yes?" Signora Farnese returned, and the *cameriere* withdrew.

"How are you enjoying your Italian adventure, now?" Signora Farnese asked.

"Very much," Willa said. "I want to see as much of Firenze as I can. And Pierluigi Flavi again, too."

"Pierluigi may not be certain whether you're available now," said Signora Farnese. "That's why it's so important that you not let just anyone call on you."

Was Gabriele just anyone? Willa wondered. "But Gabriele Marcheschi is a landowner. Educated too."

Signora Farnese stirred her coffee and took a bite of her *biscotto*. "So he says."

"You don't believe him?"

"We don't know enough about him to believe him or not," said Signora Farnese. "If you were to decide you wanted to pursue a relationship with him, then I could make some discreet inquiries."

"Inquiries?"

Signora Farnese nodded. "Yes. Everyone has to do that these days, unfortunately. There are so many pretenders. They smell American money and think they've found a ticket to the States or a way to pay off the mortgage on some land their grandfather once owned. Or they need a bribe so they can get a position. Believe me, they will pursue you until you drop from exhaustion."

Willa thought of the way Gabriele had insisted on staying for lunch. *Does he smell American money? What about the money he gave me for his portrait?* "Do you think Pierluigi Flavi wants to go to America?"

Signora Farnese laughed. "Certainly not."

8

Although Willa had studied drawing and painting privately with Maestro Ottaviani for two years and before that in high school, when she began her classes at L'Accademia d'Arte the following week, she was assigned to a beginning drawing class where students drew cubes, spheres, and pyramids, examined the effects of light and shadow on their surfaces, and learned the principles of one- and two-point perspective. Beginning students were also required to do rigorous drawing exercises for one, perhaps two, years until their skills became automatic. These exercises tried Willa's patience. Color theory proved mysterious. Beyond her comprehension, in fact. With time she hoped its principles would become familiar. Art history and composition were new to her as well. She felt confined and frustrated by these first experiences at L'Accademia. Perhaps Pierluigi Flavi had been right: by the time she finished her courses, she would no longer have any ideas of her own. She wished she could talk to him again.

On Saturday morning, Willa slept late. Signora Farnese left word with Assuntina that she had gone out to market with Antonio and then to visit her sister-in-law. Willa knew that she should not go out alone, especially not to visit Pierluigi Flavi. Instead, after breakfast, she went to the garden and strolled along all of the paths. She decided to draw something original, something from the garden, even though such work was reserved for more advanced students. She was returning to the house for her sketchbook when Assuntina came to tell her that Gabriele was in the foyer.

"Tell him I'm not available," Willa said. She meant that she didn't want to see him, that she wanted nothing to do with him. *Better not to know him.*

An hour later, Assuntina sought her out again. "Signor Marcheschi has returned for the fifth time. What shall I do?'

"I'll speak to him myself."

Gabriele smiled the moment he saw her. "Finally, you have come."

"We can speak on two conditions," Willa said. "First, we'll speak now and for no more than five minutes and only right here in the front doorway." That way, Willa reasoned, there could be no concern about her being unchaperoned.

"Very well."

"And, second, we'll speak only if you promise to leave and never come back."

"I promise," he said, "but I think of you constantly. I may seem a fool to you, but I am your true love if only you could see it."

Willa noted the flock of birds circling above them.

"If you will only come with me right now, I'll prove to you that I am your true love this very afternoon," Gabriele said.

Accepting what she regarded as the sign written in the flight of birds, Willa said, "Very well, prove it!" Then, she went out into the piazza with him, where everyone could see them waiting together for a bus.

"You are going to change your view of me," Gabriele told her. "Do you know Leopardi?"

"Yes," Willa said. "My drawing teacher gave me a book of his poems." Gabriele cleared his throat, and recited *L'Infinito, The Infinite,* from memory:

I've always loved this lonesome hill,
And this hedge that hides
The entire horizon, almost, from sight.
But sitting here in a daydream, I picture...

Willa joined him and they continued reciting together. By day's end, they had recited Dante, Foscolo, D'Annunzio, and even a bit of Virgil.

Meanwhile, Gabriele took Willa to places that he claimed only he knew of—a fountain in a deserted piazza, a stone crypt underneath an ancient church, a niche in a private courtyard—describing what that had occurred in each:

"Here they burned an evil priest on a skewer."

"Here they hid a pregnant girl before she gave birth to a *bastardo*."

"Here they buried a bag of ducats that belonged to a duke."

And then Willa told Gabriele how she would paint the priest, the girl, and the duke.

"No one has ever painted these places before. You are the first. The only one," Gabriele told her. "I'm going to bring you to these places and recite poetry to you while you paint."

When they returned to Signora Farnese's villa, Gabriele took a black velvet bag from his pocket and held it out to her. "Open it." Inside she found an antique ring of red gold set with diamonds.

She held it in her palm. "It's a beautiful old ring, Gabriele. Where did you get it?"

"It belonged to my grandmother and to her mother before her," Gabriele said. The diamonds sparkled in the sunlight. *Was it another sign?* Willa wondered. "Try it on," he said.

Why is it that every time I see Gabriele something happens that draws me in deeper? She was both attracted by the unexpected way he courted her and repelled by the loss of control she felt. *It would be best to get away from him.*

She gave the ring back to him. "No. It's quite improper."

"You can keep it because we're going to be married." He pressed the ring into her palm. "You don't believe me yet, but you will see very soon that I'm right."

"You're right. I don't believe you," Willa said. "Besides, I don't want to keep this ring."

"Wait and see. I'll be back very soon." He walked away leaving the ring in her hand. "If you haven't changed your mind by the time you see me again, I'll let you give it back to me." With that he was gone.

Willa went to her room and shut the door. Alone, where no one could observe her, she tried the ring on, admired it, and then put it away in a drawer underneath her underwear where it would be safe until Gabriele returned. *I will never marry Gabriele Marcheschi,* she told herself. Still, she liked the way they had recited poetry together and his promise that he would come with her while she painted. There was something alive and vital about him. He seemed more attractive than she had originally thought, more interesting, and he had never once mentioned anything about money or going to America.

When Signora Farnese returned that evening, Willa told her that she had gone for a walk with Gabriele Marcheschi and had found him to be some- one she might want to know. Signora Farnese shook her head. "He is *un uomo rozzo"*—a boorish man, unrefined—"to take you out without a chaperone. Gabriele Marcheschi knows that you must have a chaperone and yet he ruins your reputation. I'm afraid he has turned you away from proper behavior. He's unsuitable."

"But we did nothing improper."

"We say such people sometimes possess the power of *incantesimo,* enchantment," Signora Farnese said. "They lead us to do things that are against our best interests. This is what has happened to you. You must be careful or you will squander your real opportunities. I must tell your parents that I cannot be responsible for what happens."

Willa measured this warning against her experience of Gabriele Marcheschi and concluded such caution must be the result of supersti- tion. Gabriele possessed the practical skills of a successful vintner, the business sense of the landowner, and the soul of a poet, all of which he was.

Within a week, Willa received a cable from her father: "As a guest, you must follow Signora Farnese's instructions or come home. Your mother's letter follows." When Mrs. Carver's letter arrived, it contained another admonition to be "a good guest," mentioned the importance of "proper behavior" and "making a good impression," and concluded with, "Chip asked for you the other day" and "I think Eddie might marry your cousin Polly if you don't change your mind soon." There was a postscript: "Signor Ottaviani has eloped with the Whitman girl and they moved to Dayton." Willa threw the letter into the fireplace and watched as the message curled and turned to ash.

9

ORVIETO, ITALY 1934

Two weeks later, Gabriele called on Willa. He asked her to come to Orvieto to meet his parents. This time Willa consulted Signora Farnese first.

"Such visits are considered the sign of a serious relationship," Signora Farnese warned. "Is that what you intend?"

"I don't know yet," Willa replied, "and I've never seen Orvieto, but if it's as picturesque as he says, I might want to paint there."

"If you go, it will mean that you have a serious commitment to Gabriele."

"I can't say yet, but I want to go."

"Very well, then. I have a friend in Orvieto. Signora Santori. We can stay with her and invite the Marcheschis to tea if she considers it advisable."

However, just hours before Gabriele was scheduled to come for them, Signora Farnese suffered a fall and had to go to the hospital. "You must postpone the visit to Orvieto until I'm able to travel," Signora Farnese told Willa. "You may allow Gabriele to call on you. Assuntina will be here, but Antonio must escort you if you go out."

Stymied, Willa wandered about the house, snacking on the newly made tiramisu in the refrigerator. It was raining. She sat by the loggia window with her sketchbook and watercolors. She painted the olive groves as a river coursing down the hillside, then decided the painting looked like spinach soup, and began again. Hungry and bored, she returned to the refrigerator. As she nibbled at the tiramisu again, she heard a knock at the door. She waited for Assuntina or Antonio to answer. The knock became a pounding. *Where was Antonio? Assuntina?* Finally, she went to the door herself. It was Gabriele.

"But my parents are expecting you," he said when Willa explained the situation. "They will be very disappointed."

"Antonio must come with me. Otherwise, I can't go." Willa left Gabriele waiting in the *salotto* while she went to find the driver. When she knocked at the door to Antonio's room, he didn't respond, but from outside in the hallway she could hear the sound of snoring. She knocked on the door again, this time more vigorously.

"Antonio! Wake up." He cursed. "Antonio, I need you." At last, he came to the door. She tried to explain.

"Later," he said swinging his arm in her direction. "I'm busy." His breath reeked of alcohol. He staggered back to bed. Several empty bottles lay on the floor. She returned to the *salotto*.

"He has to accompany me when I go out," Willa told Gabriele. "He's not well, and I can't go without him."

"I'll bring you back by this evening," Gabriele told her. "He probably won't notice that you're gone."

"Let me ask Assuntina." Willa found the maid doing laundry.

Assuntina was first surprised and then frightened by Willa's request. "It would be improper," she said.

What choice do I have? Willa thought. *The appointment is made, Gabriele has come for me, and his parents are waiting. Should I be rude to Gabriele's parents because Antonio is drunk and Assuntina is timid?* Besides, she was curious. She wanted very much to go despite the impropriety. Finding no alternative except to stay home, she put on her coat and hat, put her sketchbook in her carpetbag, and went to Orvieto with Gabriele and without a chaperone. She noticed that several neighbors and shopkeepers observed her departure with interest. *Never mind. I'll be back by this evening.*

The Marcheschi's home was situated on a rise in full view of the road. When Willa and Gabriele arrived in Orvieto, many people saw them riding alone together in a horse-drawn cart along the rutted dirt road all the

way from the station. Though Gabriele surely must have known that people were watching them, he didn't mention this to Willa. "We use this cart
during the harvest to carry grapes," he explained instead, emphasizing
the most picturesque aspects of the *vendemmia*. "While you're here, I'll
show you how we make our wine." Ahead of them the narrow, dusty road
wound around the perimeter of a high hill and led up toward the golden
walls of the town. From this perspective, Orvieto appeared distant, like a
mirage. Willa commented on the uncanny light that glowed from within
its walls and gave the town fable-like quality. "That's the façade of the
Duomo," Gabriele said. "It's made of gold mosaic. The reflection can be
seen for miles."

Willa thought Orvieto a perfect place to paint. Luckily, she had
brought her sketchbook. "It's beautiful here and it smells good, too. Like
sage...and something sweet," she said, gazing at the road ahead.

Gabriele stopped and waited while she made brief sketches and a few
notes before calling her attention to the vineyards on both sides of the
road and to the orchards and woods beyond. "This land has belonged to
my family for generations," he said. "I will inherit all of it, and my children will inherit it from me."

Willa inhaled deeply the earthy fragrance of the countryside. "You're
certain of your destiny," Willa said. "It must be nice to know your fate.
As an artist, I can't be sure what my future will be."

Gabriele stopped the cart at the foot of a low hill covered in golden
grass. "Yes, you can. Your future is with me," he said with a confidence
that Willa found appealing. Ahead of them, at the crown of the hill, stood
a house of stone. "That's our home. The original one was built three hundred years ago, but we have added on and changed it. Now, there's a wine
cellar where the animals used to be kept." Willa looked up and saw that
two people had come out of the house. They waited in front. "Come and
meet my parents."

Willa put her sketchbook away, and Gabriele helped her down from
the cart. He held her arm as they walked up the dirt path. Signor Marcheschi, dignified in a black suit and white shirt, the collar too large, and

Signora Marcheschi, erect and formal in her black dress with a white lace bib and collar, stood next to one another watching as Gabriele and Willa approached.

"May I present signorina Willa Carver," Gabriele said. "She has been looking forward to meeting you."

"*Benvenuta*," Signor Marcheschi said, glancing at his wife, seemingly uncertain about what to do next. Then, the Marcheschis smiled at Willa and shook hands with her. "*Molto piacere*," everyone said. Signora Marcheschi looked at Willa and then toward the cart and then beyond to the road.

"*Sola?*" she asked. Alone?

Willa nodded. "The person who was coming with me had an emergency and the others couldn't come, so I had to come alone." Signor Marcheschi stepped forward and looked closely at Willa's face, as if he were trying to understand what sort of creature she might be.

"*Mi dispiace.*" Sorry. Signor Marcheschi said loudly and pointed to his mouth. He paused and took a deep breath, then shouted, "No English!" He stepped back and stood next to his wife.

Looking directly into his eyes, Willa said, "*Parlo l'italiano.*"

"*Questa ragazza e' un'americana*," a startled Signor Marcheschi said to his wife. This girl is an American. Willa understood that in this case being an "American girl" wasn't a compliment.

"Let's sit down. We'll drink to your visit," Gabriele told her. He waited for his parents and Willa to precede him into a windowless living room where a low fire burned in a blackened stone fireplace. The odors of smoke and wood, livestock and vinegar, wine and earth permeated the dusky atmosphere. Signor and Signora Marcheschi sat down on the heavy, worn chairs arranged next to uneven tables. Willa and Gabriele sat opposite them on a nondescript sofa. A spring from the cushion jabbed her hip, and Willa edged toward a more comfortable spot. In the dim light, Gabriele's parents looked as if they had been carved from tree roots. Willa responded to their polite questions in the Florentine dialect, the only dialect she knew, waiting for Gabriele to translate when she didn't quite understand what his parents were saying. Soon, a woman came into the room carrying a tray of refreshments. She appeared to be slightly older than Gabriele and was also dressed in black. Willa noticed her curious glances.

"This is Grazia, our housekeeper and cook," Gabriele said. "She's been with us since she was sixteen."

Willa smiled and held out her hand. Grazia looked at Willa and nodded gravely, her expression unchanged, and then placed a tray of olives on the table. She studied Willa once more. Willa smiled again, hoping to elicit a more clearly positive response. Grazia pointed to her own front teeth.

"*Lo spazio. La sfortuna.*" Then she returned by the doorway though which she had come.

"Sicilian," Gabriele told Willa. "They don't care for strangers. She said the space between your front teeth means bad luck."

Willa laughed. "Superstitious."

"Yes," Gabriele agreed. "Already, it's *good luck* that you are here." Gabriele's father served the wine.

"*Il nostro vino,*" our wine, Signor Marcheschi said with obvious pride. Gabriele waited until Willa took a sip. The wine was acidic, harsh, unpleasant.

"Our Orvieto is the best in the region," Gabriele said. He stood up. "Come, I'll show you." Willa followed him through the musty kitchen where Grazia was chopping vegetables. A pot simmered on the wood-burning stove. Just outside the door was a steep, wooden stairway and next to it a large woodpile. A few feet away a hand-operated water pump dripped into an enamel basin. "Be careful. The top step is loose," Gabriele said. He held her hand tightly as he went down the stairs ahead of her. Gabriele's parents followed behind them. About a hundred feet beyond the house they entered a barn-like structure filled with wooden vats, casks, and pipes. The equipment reminded Willa of laboratories she had seen in science fiction movies. It occurred to her that she had not seen a movie since she had arrived in Italy; she felt momentarily homesick.

"*Nuovo*," new, Signor Marcheschi said gesturing toward the equipment.

"*Carisissimo*," very expensive, Signora Marcheschi said.

Gabriele gestured for Willa to climb up a small ladder to a platform. "This is where we crush the grapes after the *vendemmia*." She looked down into a wooden vat nearly twenty feet in diameter and inhaled its sweet-sour smell. Despite the size of the vat, the facility itself seemed small and dark, almost primitive. She backed down the ladder and followed Gabriele among the casks and barrels, accepting the tastings he gave her from each, until she admitted that she could no longer tell the difference between a new wine and a wine ready to be decanted.

"It takes time," he said, "but I will teach you." Later that afternoon, Gabriele took Willa to the top of the hill next to where the woods began. She was out of breath by the time they stopped at a clearing. There, a low wall of stone surrounded an area marked with gravestones and monuments, many of which were obscured by dry grass. Above them a hawk glided on air currents. "This is our family cemetery," Gabriele said. "All of my relatives who have ever lived on this land are buried here. Some day my parents will be buried here, and I will be too, and so will my wife and, after us, my children."

Willa looked toward the horizon where the sky was a deep, improbable blue, a color so beautiful, she decided, that it must be a sign that she was on the course she was meant to follow. *Perhaps there really is such a thing as fate, after all*, she thought. "I would like to paint here. I would put the vineyards in the foreground to show the importance of the wine and beyond them the house and the hill and the trees, and the golden glow."

"With me you will do this," said Gabriele.

When they returned to the house, Grazia lit the long, partially burned candles, suffusing the sitting room with a glow that seemed to Willa as prophetic and meaningful as the sky outside. She imagined painting this room, too, and Grazia and Gabriele's parents, with their interesting faces, but because they maintained such a cautious formality, she feared she might embarrass them or intrude in a way that might make them uncomfortable if she drew them just yet. There would be time for that later after they had gotten to know one another.

Grazia served dinner: salami, the preserved vegetables, sausages, *gnocchi, sanguinaccio, cotechino con lenticchie, stracotto*, grilled *lombatina*.

"I love country food," Willa told the Marcheschis. She searched for a word, "*È perfetto*." Signor and Signora Marcheschi looked at one another, perhaps for understanding or reassurance. Willa wasn't sure, but as the afternoon grew late, they seemed to grow more at ease with their guest and at last began to smile. "Do you grow all of your food yourselves?" she asked, her fork poised above her plate.

"*Sì*."

"Have you always lived in Orvieto?"

"*Sì*."

"What was it like when Gabriele was growing up?" The senior Marcheschis spoke of a life so different from her own that Willa ate a second and then a third helping followed by more wine just to keep them talking. The Marcheschi family, they said, lived by the *mezzadria,* a form of sharecropping in which tenant farmers exchange housing and supplies. Although many landowners treated their tenants unfairly, the Marcheschis were proud that their land was profitable and their tenants contented.

"We take such good care of them and their children that they are happy here," said Signora Marcheschi. "That is our job, and we want to do it well." She described for Willa her visits to her tenants, how she helped them through illnesses and childbirth and later paid for their children to go to school. "We take care of them so they can take care of us."

Willa wasn't alone in imagining the life of the *mezzadri* to be picturesque, a "natural" existence lived by "simple" people who tilled the land and ate their harvest under the olive trees, enjoying their own wine accompanied by music and dancing. She imagined painting the children and the families that Signora Marcheschi described, a series of paintings based on scenes from their daily lives. "That's exactly the way I think people should treat each other," Willa said with enthusiasm as she dipped her spoon into a dessert of preserved fruit. *Gabriele is a fine man from a good family,* she thought. *I'm glad I came to meet his parents even without a chaperone.* "Next time I come, I would like stay longer and make some drawings," Willa said. No one replied. *Perhaps they don't understand what I said,* she thought.

Gabriele looked at his watch. "If we don't go now, we'll miss the last train." They went outside to the cart accompanied by Signor and Signora Marcheschi, who gave Willa a basket filled with their wine, olive oil, and *un dolce.*

"*Arrivederci, signorina Willa Carver.*"

"Don't say goodbye to her," Gabriele told his parents, "I'm going to marry her. I've set the date for July."

"Gabriele! You haven't even asked me yet!" Willa said.

"Her parents must set the date," said Signora Marcheschi, clasping her hands and looking skyward.

Signor Marcheschi put his arm around his wife's shoulders. "Our Gabriele always does things his own way." Gabriele and Willa put the gifts in the cart and began their trip back to the station. Even Willa knew that for Gabriele to set the wedding date was quite improper. Still, she liked the fact that he felt free enough, bold enough, to do unexpected things. *In his way Gabriele is very creative and original,* she thought.

When they were out of sight of the house, Gabriele turned to Willa and kissed her fully and publicly. *Fortunately, it's twilight and no one can see us,* Willa thought. "The moment I saw you on the train, I saw in your green eyes the sparkle of the dew on our fields and vineyards," Gabriele said. The evening star appeared. "I knew right away that I would marry you and bring you to Orvieto with me." She inhaled the scents of the crisp, country night. A seagull passed overhead, far inland from its usual habitat. *Yes. Orvieto must be the place where I belong, and Gabriele is the person I should be with,* Willa thought. *It's always what you least expect.* Gabriele put his arm around her and made another confession. "Besides, the idea of your looking at other men, even *nudi,* makes me *pazzo* with jealousy," he told her. "I won't let you do it."

"You are *pazzo*," Willa laughed. She looked at Gabriele. "But I believe I might marry you just the same."

10

"You are *la favola della città*," the talk of the town, Signora Farnese told Willa a few days later. Signora Farnese was still convalescing from her fall, and she could stand and walk only if Assuntina helped her. "My friend in Orvieto, Signora Santori, tells me that your visit and speculation about your purity swept the city even before you boarded the evening train to return to us." There was more. Several people in Orvieto claimed to have met Willa and reported in detail on what they remembered: the harlot was unable to converse in Italian; she spilled her wine on her dress, a dress that was not stylish, only immodest; she was "*maleducata!*" Rude. Reliable sources said that the senior Marcheschis doubted her suitability. *La straniera* didn't know how to speak Italian as it is spoken in Orvieto. How could they talk to her? Indeed, she spoke in the Florentine dialect, showing that "she thinks she is better than we are." Even more damning, she had no chaperone. Some were certain Willa had no wedding chest, no trousseau, and no dowry.

That her behavior had elicited such gossip and speculation surprised Willa. *Do people have nothing else to do? Perhaps they're just envious.* She had enjoyed her visit, liked Signor and Signora Marcheschi, liked Gabriele more the longer she knew him. *Although he has been hasty in trying to arrange for our marriage, his actions were innocent and well intentioned. At worst, he is guilty of an overabundance of enthusiasm. These are hardly reasons to condemn either of us,* she told herself.

Following Willa's visit to Orvieto, Gabriele wrote to Howard Carver asking for Willa's hand in marriage, mentioning the marriage date, declaring his ardent love, and, finally, suggesting that they discuss Willa's dowry.

Officially, of course, Willa could not accept a proposal of marriage from Gabriele until her father had given his approval, but for Willa her own intentions were clear and governing. Despite her impatience with Italian customs, she made an effort to respect Signora Farnese's pleas concerning the importance of appearances. When she grew frustrated with Signora Farnese's frequent reminders that "in Italy, respectable young women do not go out freely with their *fidanzati*, especially if the engagement is not yet official," Willa contained her irritation.

She showed Signora Farnese the ring Gabriele had given her. "An engagement is more than a ring," Signora Farnese said. "In Italy, *engagement* is both a legal and a religious matter." Willa wasn't sure what legal and religious matters Signora Farnese had in mind. Both with and without Signora Farnese, she continued her visits to Orvieto. Wherever she went, she carried her sketchbook and drew the people she saw on the street, in church, in the Piazza del Duomo and in the trattoria nearby. Thus, it became usual for people to hide their faces from Willa's gaze and her constant drawing. As she became increasingly involved in her relationship with Gabriele, she neglected her studies at the Accademia d'Arte. At last, she was asked to withdraw.

"Signora Santori tells me everyone she knows is convinced that you have a questionable reputation," Signora Farnese told Willa, "and you don't even live there yet."

"But I've done nothing wrong," Willa said. "Besides, they don't even know me."

"Signora Santori says that the Marcheschis are a respected family, but lost most of their money during the Great War. If Gabriele doesn't marry someone with a large dowry, they will have to sell off some of their land." According to Signora Santori, Gabriele had forsaken Maria Cristina Orsini to follow the American siren because Cupid's arrows had struck him in the heart the moment he saw her. It was *un colpo di fulmine* and *un amore a prima vista*. A bolt of lightening and love at first sight. If Willa had only refused Gabriele in the first place, there would have been no harm because he would not have foresworn Maria Cristina, a fine Catholic girl with a large wedding chest whom everyone had expected him to marry and who was the sister of Gabriele's good friend, Pietro Orsini. Now Maria Cristina would soon enter the convent, and her beautiful wedding chest would be of no use. It is always a mistake, people said, shaking their heads, to make a hasty marriage in defiance of the wisdom of one's parents and the practices of the community. *Che peccato!* What a pity!

Later, Signora Santori reported that many said that Gabriele's *innamorata* demanded expensive gifts despite the growing shortages, gifts of such scarcities as truffles, chocolates, coffee, and even silk stockings—things she didn't deserve, things that other people needed. Such reports grew in size and complexity. In Napoli, they claimed, Gabriele took Willa to a sold out performance of *The Elixir of Love,* where the two sat in the orchestra section, thereby depriving some very important people of seats. Afterwards, the couple met "the greatest soprano of all time," Olivetta Boccale, also known as "La Voce," an extraordinary honor that *la straniera* was incapable of appreciating. They said that Gabriele had also obtained custom-made leather shoes for his selfish courtesan when there was a shortage of shoe leather in Italy because it had been requisitioned by the military where it was truly needed for soldiers in Ethiopia and elsewhere. As a result many soldiers had gone barefoot. In the winter. In the Alps. In the summer. In Africa. Although none of these claims was true, people remembered them, and their memories became a truth that was more true than truth itself.

Upset finally, Willa repeated these stories to Gabriele. He smiled. "Don't worry," he told her. "They'll forget their crazy ideas when they get to know you."

Willa believed him. *Gabriele had always lived in Orvieto. Who would know better than he?* "Yes, people are so silly," she agreed.

For his part, Gabriele had his own version of their courtship. "I overwhelm her," he would announce triumphantly, and then he would hug Willa enthusiastically and often, even in public.

"Gabriele!" Willa scolded, but then she always laughed, too.

"We're *innamorati pazzi,"* crazy with love, they told everyone who would listen.

When Willa's next monthly check arrived with a letter from her father, the engraved stationery of Mr. Carver's law firm signaled that the contents of the envelope included a serious message. Warily, Willa opened the envelope and unfolded the letter: "I do not approve of the marriage proposal from Mr. Marcheschi. He appears to have an excessive interest in your dowry. Arriving in two weeks. Be packed and ready to leave." It was signed, "Sincerely, Howard Carver."

"My father is coming to take me back to America," Willa told Gabriele as soon as they were together. "He doesn't approve of our plans."

"I understand. Naturally, he wants to know me better and make sure that I can take good care of you before he gives his permission," Gabriele said. "I'll speak to him as one man to another. Once I show him our *podere*, he'll see how bright our future is." The elder Marcheschis, however, had a different view. Willa's father, they said, "*arriccia il naso di fronte a tutto*," he turns his nose in the air, "because he thinks the Marcheschis aren't good enough for his daughter." Willa noticed their chilly demeanor toward her on her next visit.

"Your family is upset," she told Gabriele as the two of them walked along the Corso toward the Piazza del Duomo and stopped for something to drink at an outdoor café. It was a feast day in Orvieto, and everyone had come out to enjoy the entertainment. "I don't think they understand how my father feels," she said in an unusual moment of insight, "and they've taken offense when they shouldn't."

"They are very traditional," Gabriele said, nodding. Several of Gabriele's friends greeted him, but they did not acknowledge Willa. In fact, Pietro Orsini, Maria Cristina's brother, stood between Gabriele and Willa and turned his back to Willa.

"Your friends don't like me," Willa said when they resumed their *passeggiata*.

"It's just that they don't know many Americans," Gabriele replied. Willa had to admit that Americans were unusual in Orvieto, but she doubted that Gabriele was correct about the reason people weren't cordial to her. She understood that she had given the wrong impression. She just wasn't sure what she should do to rectify her errors or whether she could.

Along the Corso, flags of many colors fluttered in the breeze. Willa and Gabriele bought *gelato* and afterwards strolled around the Piazza del Duomo. Under the gazes of the Madonna and the saints carved into the stone around the entrance of the cathedral, a ring of people stood watching a fire-eater. They whooped each time a long flame disappeared into the fire-eater's mouth. Nearby, a juggler tossed sharp swords that glinted against the bright sky. The crowd gasped and cheered when he caught the weapons behind his back and never once got cut.

Across the Piazza another crowd formed in front of a wagon with a bright red proscenium mounted on it and the words *Circo Dei Burratini* painted in gold letters on the side. Willa took Gabriele's hand and pulled him over. The little stage had velvet curtains that opened to reveal a painted backdrop, which concealed the puppeteers. The crowd yelled and clapped for the show to begin. The curtain opened with a squeaking sound. On the little stage, Punchinello, the rich hunchback, sought the favors of Columbine, the maid, who tricked him out of his money, intending to use it to marry Harlequin. The crowd shouted warnings and epithets at the hapless and angry Punchinello, who protested until Harlequin knocked him over the head with a stick. The audience cheered and elbowed one another to get a better view. Then Harlequin mimicked an obscene Punchinello making love to Columbine before leaving her at the altar himself. The crowd screamed with delight. After the curtains closed, the proprietor passed a large black hat mounted on a stick into which the audience dropped coins and bills until the hat sagged under the weight of the money inside it.

"What a mean story," Willa said to Gabriele.

"It's just puppets," he said. "It's not a real story." He pointed toward the street leading out of the Piazza. "Look at the people on stilts." The two of them stood in the shadow of the Duomo watching the slow, stiff movements of the costumed figures, a dance of giants. The stilt walkers, the fire-eater, the sword thrower, the puppets: in these Willa saw a world of heightened imagination and color, a magical place she would share with Gabriele. Nothing else really mattered.

11

Mr. Carver declined Signora Farnese's offer of hospitality and, instead, stayed at the Savoy Hotel on the Piazza della Repubblica. "I don't want to put anyone to any trouble," he said. His real purpose was to speak to Willa privately. He took her to dinner at Trattoria dei Tre Cugini located next to the Arno near the Ponte Vecchio. The candlelit room glowed, and around them frescoed walls depicted scenes of opulent Renaissance banquets. Diners spoke in low tones interrupted only by the sounds of chiming glasses and restrained laughter. The maitre d' seated them in a curved booth upholstered in dark leather.

"Daddy, won't you at least come meet Gabriele?"

Mr. Carver shook his head. "There's no need. We're leaving in three days." She understood that her father had made up his mind about her engagement long before his arrival. The prospect of leaving Orvieto, where she had not yet lived, seemed to Willa a profound loss and a certain end to her work as an artist, work that seemed to her more promising and probable with each new painting of country life. Until then, Willa had not let herself believe that returning to Erhart was a serious possibility. *It was unimaginable!* She believed something would surely work out to keep her from leaving Gabriele and Italy and life as a wife and artist.

"But, daddy, Gabriele and my work and my art are here…in Italy…in Orvieto. I love him and he loves me."

The waiter came to take their orders. Willa inhaled the odors of garlic, herbs and wine from a passing cart. "I'd like whatever that is."

"*Vitello, signorina,*" the waiter said.

Mr. Carver waved the menus away. "The *vitello*, please, and I'll have steak, salad. We'll have the *antipasto misto* now."

"Daddy, did you get Gabriele's second letter?"

"Yes. He wanted to clarify his intentions and his situation. I believe he means well toward you, but your interests aren't what the Marcheschis have in mind. They need money." The waiter returned with a platter. Willa took some prosciutto and melon in her fingers and bit into the sweet-salty morsel. "Signora Farnese's friend says they made some unwise investments and lost a great deal during the Great War."

"But, daddy, they own lots of land. They aren't poor."

Mr. Carver seemed to anticipate this objection. "It costs money to develop and maintain one's land. I don't want to become involved in supporting them."

"Besides, it's called *un podere*," she said as if the name mattered. "Would you like to see the paintings I've already done of Orvieto? I'm thinking of having a show in a few months."

Mr. Carver cleared his throat. "If you marry Gabriele and go to Orvieto, you won't become an artist. You'll become someone who works on a farm...a *podere*, if you wish. The consequences for you will be the same, no matter what name you give it."

"Daddy, that's not fair. At least meet Gabriele. Please!" The waiter served their main course. Willa looked down at her plate. "Wait! *Vitello* is veal!"

The waiter took out a stained paper from his vest pocket and ran his finger down a list. "*Sì, signorina.*"

Willa hesitated. "I forgot. That's a baby animal."

"It's what you ordered," Mr. Carver said. "Besides, veal tastes a lot like chicken, and you don't mind eating that, do you?" Willa knew better than to get involved in two arguments at once with her father. Mr. Carver often said lawyers who did that were "muddleheaded" and "not worth their fees."

"Daddy, please just meet Gabriele." She knew from experience that convincing her father to change his mind required small steps rather than big leaps. If only he could see Orvieto and meet Gabriele and his family, he would feel differently. Of this she was certain.

"As long as you're packed and ready on Thursday morning, I'll meet this Gabriele fellow, if that's what you want."

Willa smiled. "Oh, thank you. I'm sure you'll love him as much as I do." They finished their meal. She ordered *zuppa inglese* for dessert. "We can go to Orvieto tomorrow. I'll call and leave a message for Gabriele." Mr. Carver nodded. Willa went to a public telephone. She waited for the operator to place the call, heard the phone trill at the other end. She counted that at least five people picked up their receivers. Their breathing and whispers punctuated her conversation with the telephone operator in Orvieto. When she said goodbye, she counted five clicks on the line before she hung up.

The elder Marcheschis shook Mr. Carver's hand murmuring "*benvenuto*" and "*piacere*." They repeated these greetings throughout the day, but there was little else they could say as Mr. Carver didn't speak Italian. Gabriele, however, showed Willa's father the Marcheschi lands, their winery, and later the city of Orvieto, discussing every aspect of the family business and his plans for the future. "We sell our wine throughout the area," Gabriele said waving his arm in a wide arc.

"What about beyond the area?" Mr. Carver asked. "This region doesn't have many people. How will you grow your business if you don't grow your customer base?"

"We are a local winery," Gabriele explained, "So our production is limited, but we sell all that we make."

"How will you support my daughter and a family if you don't have plans to expand your production?" Gabriele seemed unconcerned that he lacked an answer to this question. *Perhaps he doesn't understand what daddy is asking,* Willa thought.

"He has no business plan beyond what he's doing now," Mr. Carver said to Willa when they were alone for a moment. "You'd find yourself poor and working for nothing."

Willa stared at her father. "But we love each other, daddy. That's what matters."

Gabriele saw Willa's tears. "What's wrong?"

"She's crying because I've told her that I won't give my approval for your marriage until I see evidence that you can support her properly," Mr. Carver said. Gabriele was offended and so were his parents when they understood Mr. Carver's views.

"The Marcheschis always support their family," Gabriele said.

Mr. Carver remained unconvinced. "It's time to go," he told Willa, "or we'll miss our train."

At the station, Gabriele took Willa aside. "We will marry anyway, and you'll paint in Orvieto. It will be good luck to be married in our Chapel of the Lily. Our happiness is certain."

But once Willa and her father boarded the train and found their seats, Mr. Carver voiced even more serious objections. "Do you understand how much work needs to be done just to make that house livable?" He took out a list he had made in the course of their visit. "The roof needs mending and perhaps the timbers beneath it. They apparently don't have indoor plumbing and very little running water. What water they do have may not be clean. In some places the planks are coming off the floor. Somebody is going to get injured on that loose stairstep outside. The new winemaking equipment doesn't work properly because they don't seem to know how to configure it correctly. I could easily see that much of their work is done by hand, and most of their farm equipment belongs to another century. In their present situation, it would be very difficult to make a living even if you contributed your labor, and you don't intend to do that because you say you're planning to paint."

"But Gabriele said that I can paint there."

Mr. Carver shook his head. "That's a pipe dream, Willa. If you're serious about being an artist, you would be better off going to New York or Chicago to study. At least, then you would paint."

It is an unfortunate truism that we are never more attached to something than at the moment we believe we are bound to lose it. This was the case for Willa, who understood her choice to be not just between Gabriele and her parents, but also between her vision of life and the more predictable and conventional life her parents envisioned for her. Once she saw her future in these terms, she thought only of how her soul would die without Gabriele; die if she couldn't capture the light in the Piazza, the sunset over the vineyards, the faces along the Corso; die if she returned to America with her father on Thursday.

Mr. Carver took note of her silence. "What are you thinking?"

"I still want to be with Gabriele and paint *here*. In Orvieto." Willa said.

Mr. Carver shook his head. "I also understand that you have not made a favorable impression on people. Have you considered how that will affect your future if you were to live there?" Willa was thinking of the people in Orvieto in artistic rather than personal terms. Their manner no longer seemed unfriendly to her but, rather, reserved. They were part of her larger canvas, one that concerned contemporary life in a small, Italian hill town. *Daddy must be mistaken*, she thought. *Besides, artists are often misunderstood.*

"Daddy, they don't even know me yet. How could they think anything?"

Mr. Carver remained firm, and his firmness called up within Willa an intense and stubborn determination. "I'm going to marry him," she said, certain of her love for Gabriele and of her wish to become his wife.

12

Several weeks after Mr. Carver returned to America, Willa and Gabriele sat together on a bench that overlooked the Isolotto in the Boboli Gardens. Gabriele handed Willa an apple from their picnic basket. She took a bite, then another. He watched as she ate and put his arm around her shoulder. "You are as rosy and full as this fruit." She smiled at the beauty of the Gardens and the beauty of that moment. *If I had gone back to Erhart,* she thought, *I would have missed this.* Gabriele took her hand. "Are you Catholic?"

"No. Why?" She set the apple down on the bench next to her, then reached into the picnic basket for two sweets and handed one to Gabriele.

"My parents noticed that you didn't take communion when we went to church with them," he said.

Willa nodded. She bit into the sweet, chewed it, and swallowed. "We're Methodists," she said. "We don't have communion." A bird hopped onto the grass near them. She tossed a piece of bread to it and leaned over to kiss Gabriele, thinking of the time very soon when they would always be together. After they were married, he could kiss her whenever he liked, wherever he liked.

He took her hand in his again. "For us to be married in the Duomo, you must be a Catholic," he said. "Otherwise Father Enrico won't say the wedding mass." He traced his finger around the stones in the ring he had given her.

"Maybe we could get married someplace else, then." She reached for another sweet.

Gabriele let go of her hand. "What would people think?" He seemed genuinely surprised by her suggestion, which she had thought a very simple and practical one.

Willa tore the crust from one of their sandwiches. "Does it matter *where* we get married when the important thing is that we're married? We would love each other just as much if we got married right here in this garden." She stood up and threw the crusts to an audience of pigeons that had assembled around them. "Look, all the birds want some." She reached for another crust and tore it up. "Besides, it's our wedding." She tore the bread and tossed it piece by piece to the birds. "So, it's up to us."

Gabriele looked at her and frowned. "My parents would never understand. They would disown us."

"If we don't get married in the Catholic Church?"

Gabriele nodded. "That's why I made an appointment for us to see Father Enrico."

It was Willa's turn to be surprised. "Without telling me first?" She saw his guilty look. "So now you've decided when and where we will get married, who will marry us, and what religion I must be!" She put her hands on her hips and glared at him. "Is there anything else you haven't told me?" He shook his head. "I'd just like to know what I'm allowed to decide about my own wedding."

"Willa, everyone talks to the priest about their wedding."

"I don't," she said. "Not without being asked first." Willa told Gabriele she wouldn't come to the appointment with him unless Gabriele agreed that if they got married in the Duomo, she would never have to attend mass again.

Father Enrico's office and living space was located in a building adjacent to the Duomo that was originally part of a monastery.

"Don't say anything to Father Enrico about our agreement," Gabriele whispered to her as he knocked on Father Enrico's door. They heard the sound of footsteps on stone and then the door opened.

"*Buongiorno*," Father Enrico boomed. "Come in, come in."

"Father, this is my *fidanzata*, Willa Carver."

Father Enrico took Willa's hands in his. "It is a great pleasure to meet you," he said. "I'm sorry to have missed you the day you came to mass. I was away, but still I've heard a great deal about you from others." He stepped back and gestured for them to enter. *What a small room to spend one's life in*, Willa thought. The priest indicated two straight-backed chairs in front of a scarred wooden desk. "I hope you won't be disappointed by my simple surroundings."

She looked directly at Father Enrico, smiled, and held out her hand to him. "Not at all," she said.

"She's not shy, is she?" Father Enrico said to Gabriele with a chuckle. *What does he mean?* Willa thought. She had intended to be polite.

"She's an American," Gabriele said. *What does that mean?* Willa wondered.

In addition to the desk and chairs, the room contained a bed with a brown blanket neatly drawn up under a white pillow. Above the pillow a large crucifix hung on a sturdy peg that stuck out from the stone wall. Next to the bed was a nightstand and on it a lamp and a breviary. In the corner next to the fireplace was another table with a hotplate, its element glowing red-orange under a steaming teakettle. Against the opposite wall was a small bureau with two candles on top and above them a mirror only large enough for shaving. On the floor next to the bureau Willa noticed a ceramic washbasin. *Is this what priests use for bathing or do they have real bathrooms, too?* The teakettle whistled.

"Please sit down," Father Enrico said. "Tea?"

"Yes, thank you." Willa took the chair nearest the bureau. Her father's desk had always been stacked with papers and notes, but the top of the priest's desk was empty. Gabriele sat down in the chair next to hers.

"I have pastries, too," Father Enrico said in a conspiratorial tone as he put out the tea and plates. He sat down behind his desk facing them, and served the sweets. His wooden chair creaked under his bulk. At last, he fixed Willa with a sober gaze. "You are not a member of the Church." Willa nodded. "Still, you wish to be married here in our Duomo..." he paused, clearing his throat, "...in just a few weeks?"

"Yes, Father," Gabriele said. Father Enrico continued to gaze at Willa.

"I am leaving you out of our conversation for now, Gabriele. I need to explain to your *fidanzata* that it is somewhat more complicated to become a member of the Church than simply showing up for the wedding."

"Oh, that was Gabriele's idea," Willa said. "It's all right with me if we don't get married in the Church if it's too much trouble." Father Enrico sat back and coughed. Gabriele leaned forward.

"What she means to say, Father, is that she is willing to come for instruction and do what is needed so that we can be married in the Church. She wants very much to have the wedding mass here on the date we've planned, just as I do. Her parents are coming, too." He paused. Father Enrico didn't say anything. "We hope you can advise us on what we must do."

"Quite simply," said Father Enrico, looking at Willa, "you must become a member of the Church. That process takes time—more time than you have between now and your wedding date. You must begin your instruction immediately." Willa nodded. Father Enrico offered her a beatific smile. "And, of course, once you have children, you will make sure that they are baptized and raised in the Church. That is understood." They had not discussed children. Willa glanced at Gabriele. He looked away. "If you come for your instruction regularly and sign an agreement that your children will be raised in the Church, I will bend the rules so that you can go forward with your plans," Father Enrico continued. "Such is my great respect for the Marcheschi family that I am prepared to hold the ceremony under these conditions." He paused. "But, of course, it cannot be the full wedding mass, you understand?"

"Yes, Father," Gabriele said. "We both understand."

"You agree, then, *signorina*?" Willa nodded. "Do you have any further questions?"

"No," Willa said.

"Very well, then. I'll make you a promise." He leaned toward her, smiling through uneven teeth. "If you come regularly for your instruction from now until the time of your wedding, I will wear my gold robes for the ceremony." He chuckled and stood up. "All of the brides like that, but I don't do it for just anyone."

"Thank you, Father," Gabriele said. "That's very kind of you. We both appreciate it."

After their meeting with Father Enrico, Gabriele and Willa returned to the Marcheschi family home. Gabriele's mother took Willa aside and asked her to come upstairs, suggesting there was something important she wanted to share. Willa followed her up a little-used, back stairway. At the top of the stairs, Signora Marcheschi opened the door to a dusty room and allowed Willa to precede her. Inside, on a lumpy bed lay a wedding dress of heavy white satin, and next to it a floor-length veil attached to a white satin crown. The ensemble had yellowed with the years and bore various stains, including rings under the armpits.

"*Il mio abito da sposa.*"

"Your wedding dress?" Willa said.

Signora Marcheschi nodded and gestured that she wanted Willa to put the dress on. Willa shook her head no, but Signora Marcheschi didn't seem to notice. At last, Willa began to understand: Signora Marcheschi didn't have a daughter, but if her daughter-in-law wore the wedding dress, it would be almost the same. "*Qualcosa vecchia, qualcosa nuova?*" Signora Marcheschi added. "Something old, something new..."

"I don't want to disappoint you," Willa replied in Italian, "but my mother is bringing my dress with her. From Chicago...in America."

Signora Marcheschi gestured again. Willa wanted to please her future mother-in-law, especially since she wouldn't be wearing her dress for the wedding. She took off her dress and Signora Marcheschi lifted the heavy gown over Willa's head. The dress had long sleeves, a high neck, and a bodice that extended down to the hips like a corset. Signora Marcheschi buttoned the tiny buttons all the way up the back to just below Willa's skull. Then she buttoned the tiny buttons from the forearms to the wrists. The sleeves covered Willa's hands. Willa fanned herself. "I'm too hot," she said. "Please unbutton it now."

Signora Marcheschi did not seem to hear. She smiled as she placed the headpiece on Willa's head, arranged the long veil around her feet. Then she pointed to the cracked mirror on the wall and clasped her hands. "You like?" she said with tears running down her cheeks. "Please, you wear for my Gabriele's wedding?"

13

ORVIETO, ITALY 1935

Willa awakened briefly when Gabriele kissed her goodbye at dawn and dozed until the drone of a mosquito brought her to full consciousness. Heat and insects had made their sleep elusive the night before, and already the intense summer sun had turned their upstairs quarters into something resembling a terra cotta oven. She sat up on the edge of the bed and counted the bites on her arms and legs. Ten, plus two that she was uncertain about. This morning, she decided, she would have her breakfast in the shady place outside the dining room and spend the day under the plane trees studying the villa from various perspectives and doing preparatory drawings for the next painting in her Orvieto series. Later, she would have a salad and an icy drink for lunch and then a long nap during the heat of the afternoon, just as she and Gabriele had done on their honeymoon.

She opened the *armadio* where her wedding dress and Signora Marcheschi's still hung together. She needed something cool and clean to wear, but had not yet had a chance to do laundry since she and Gabriele returned from their honeymoon the day before. Gabriele had told her Grazia would take care of it. She touched the wedding dresses. It had been very hot on their wedding day, but she and Gabriele had laughed and danced for hours anyway. She saw the large, red stain on the chiffon skirt of her dress where Gabriele had spilled his wine during one of the toasts. She touched the tear in Signora Marcheschi's dress and winced. Other things had happened that day, too. Better not to think about them. Better to concentrate now on her new life, her work, and finding a place to show her paintings. She found the sleeveless white linen dress and her sandals and put them on the bed and then poured some water into the washbasin. *It will be an adventure to live without indoor plumbing.*

That Willa and Gabriele's wedding day had been more cursed than blessed was already part of Orvieto lore, a memory that grew with each retelling. Few would forget that the bride's family didn't arrive until minutes before the ceremony. Some said that such tardiness showed there was already a dispute between the Marcheschis and the Carvers. No doubt it was about the paltry amount of Willa's dowry.

"We can't wait any longer," Signora Marcheschi had said. "Everyone is seated and Father Enrico is waiting for you." Indeed, nearly everyone in Orvieto who mattered, except the Orsini family, awaited them in the Duomo that day. Signora Marcheschi had lifted her wedding dress over Willa's head, and told Willa to put her arms into the fitted sleeves. Grazia helped to button the tiny buttons.

"This dress is too hot," Willa said. "I'm going to suffocate."

"It's only a short time," Signora Marcheschi replied with a distant smile. Around Willa's neck she placed a gold chain festooned with crystals and gemstones in the form of bunches of grapes and grape leaves, a family heirloom the Marcheschis had given Willa as a wedding gift. Signora Marcheschi held the veil that had been hers. "Just like me," she said, her eyes full of tears.

"Why do you cry when you think of your wedding day?" Willa asked.

"Because I was so happy."

Grazia handed Willa a bouquet of lavender and wildflowers that she had gathered from around the Temple Belvedere near the Piazza Cahen. Willa sneezed, and the button at the back of her waist popped off. Grazia found it and put it in her pocket. Without a needle and thread, the gap at the back of the dress could not be repaired.

"My veil will cover it," Signora Marcheschi said.

"I know my parents will be here in time," Willa said.

"Go now." Signora Marcheschi lifted her veil over Willa's head.

At that moment, a black car pulled up in front of the Duomo, and Mr. and Mrs. Carver got out. A bureaucratic tangle of uncertain origin had made it impossible for the Carvers to disembark from their ship until bribes were paid, something Mr. Carver had refused to do on principle until Ruth Carver, distraught and in tears, threatened to jump overboard.

"Thank goodness! Get me out of this dress!" Willa said when she saw her mother. She pulled at Signora Marcheschi's wedding dress trying to free herself. Unfortunately, the aging fabric gave way, and a tear opened up near the shoulder. Signora Marcheschi gasped and then sobbed, picked up her wedding dress and held it to her bosom.

"I'm so sorry. Please don't cry," Willa said. "I'm still going to wear your veil." Willa put on the new dress, adjusted her hair. Signora Marcheschi sniffled noisily as Grazia helped adjust the veil over Willa's face. When they had finished, the voluminous tulle hung around Willa's feet, making it difficult to walk. "I'm ready to get married now," Willa said. As she made her way slowly to the altar on her father's arm, her borrowed veil once again collected the dust of centuries past.

"Father Enrico is wearing his gold robes," Gabriele whispered to her as they stood together. "That's *porta fortuna*." It brings good luck.

Later, Signora Santori told Signora Farnese that Willa had looked disheveled on her wedding day. She said that Signora Marcheschi was distraught about her wedding dress, which Willa had ruined. Imagine! Not only that, but the wedding mass was short because Willa had not yet completed her instruction, and the couple had to remain outside of the altar rail for their ceremony. *Santo cielo!* Gabriele's wife isn't even Catholic! Who knew if she would finish her instruction? She hasn't even come to mass. *Che disgrazia!* So many problems.

The Marcheschi's were embarrassed by their daughter-in-law's behavior, of course, especially Signora Marcheschi, who could not explain the many irregularities of the wedding to the satisfaction of her friends. And when people learned that Willa's parents had come to the wedding by taxi all the way from Naples, they shook their heads and told one another that Willa's family was *ricca sfondata* by which they meant that the Carvers were rolling in money. Think of it! They came late and did not host the wedding celebration as was customary. Such insults, especially when Signor and Signora Marcheschi always showed such great *cortesia* and *generosità* and are so well respected. It must be, they said, that the Americans are miserly. And what about the wedding chest? No one had seen it. Was it possible that *la straniera* didn't even have one? Well, an unfortunate beginning always leads to an unfortunate end. *Che peccato!* What a shame.

Still, it was clear to all who were present that no matter what their opinion was concerning the suitability of Gabriele's bride, Willa and Gabriele loved one another. As the couple left the Duomo together, Gabriele's shout of joy echoed in the Piazza. He picked Willa up and whirled her around and around with everyone clapping until they were both so dizzy they had to sit down.

After the wedding, however, there followed Willa's permanent exclusion from the friendships and small courtesies that were part of daily life in Orvieto. Gabriele, it was tacitly agreed, was blameless, the guileless victim of an unscrupulous woman. Though nothing was ever said to Gabriele directly, he, too, by degrees came to see himself in this same light and to behave accordingly. Many years later, some people thought that perhaps Willa's exclusion was a mistake, but what difference would it make to admit it then? It was almost always better to keep things the way they are.

Willa finished washing and got dressed. She picked up the envelope on the dresser. Inside was the check that her parents had given to the couple on their wedding day. The amount of the check, Gabriele had told her with pride, was far more than any dowry seen in Orvieto in perhaps a century. In addition, the Carvers had also left a large sum to pay for the expenses of the wedding celebration, an amount that seemed to surprise and please Gabriele's parents because it far exceeded the costs of the wedding, though they didn't tell anyone lest it seem that they were in need of money.

"Consider me your partner!" Mr. Carver had told Gabriele with a broad smile during the toasts at the wedding meal that followed the wedding mass. "Always have enjoyed a fine glass of *vino*." As soon as the toasts were over, he set his glass down and asked Ruth Carver to pass him the water.

Willa put the check back in the envelope and left it on the dresser. Now that she and Gabriele were married, her obligations to the Church were concluded, at least until children were born, and she had made certain that would not occur anytime soon, no matter what Father Enrico said. Anyway, how would he know? She would be too busy painting to think about having children. And she and Gabriele would have to buy a house first. Her parents' check would surely be enough for a down payment. She would ask Gabriele or perhaps Signora Marcheschi. She pulled the linen shift on over her head and buckled her sandals, then went out into the hallway where she could smell newly baked bread. She went down two flights of stairs and along a musty passage at the back of the house.

"...it's already nine o'clock and she's still asleep," Willa overheard her mother-in-law saying as she neared the kitchen. "Does she think this is a hotel?"

When Willa entered the kitchen, she saw six loaves of bread cooling on the counter. Signora Marcheschi was busy with some papers. She wore black stockings and black shoes and had wound her grey hair on top of her head and pinned it in a roll. Her black dress was fully covered with an apron that buttoned at the back of her neck. Nearby, Grazia, also in black, held a dead chicken by its legs. She dipped it into the kettle of roiling water on the wood-burning stove, pulled it out, laid it on the counter, and began plucking the feathers. *She looks like a vulture*, Willa thought, imagining her as a black shape on a greenish-yellow background with dead prey around her.

"*Buongiorno. Come state*," Willa said using the respectful *voi*. She wanted to impress Signora Marcheschi with her good manners. Gabriele had explained that she must wait until her new mother-in-law invited her to call her *mamma*, thus acknowledging their warm relationship. It was an important Italian custom, he said, especially between older people and younger people.

"*Buongiorno,*" Signora Marcheschi said without looking up from her papers. "*Sto bene. E tu, come stati?*" *Tu*? Signora Marcheschi had ad dressed her in the informal way. *Is that an invitation?* Willa wondered. She wasn't sure. Grazia grunted and continued to pluck the feathers off the bird. Some of the feathers floated through the air toward Willa. Her nose started to itch. *Will Signora Marcheschi or Grazia serve breakfast or should I make it myself?* Her nose ran and she sneezed.

"You will be responsible for making lunch for the workers," Signora Marcheschi said, still looking at her papers.

Willa wasn't sure she had understood her mother-in-law correctly. "I'm planning to paint today."

"*Santo cielo!*" Signora Marcheschi waved her hand as if to swat an annoying bug. "We have work to do." Willa wasn't sure what Signora Marcheschi meant. Grazia shook her head and dipped the chicken in the kettle again. Willa stepped closer and stared at the wet, headless bird. "Today, we'll visit our tenants so you can meet them and their wives," Signora Marcheschi continued. *Perhaps the tenants' wives could be the subjects of another painting of life in Orvieto,* Willa thought. *Does Signora Marcheschi mean that I need to bring my pencils and a sketchbook?*

"May I have some breakfast first, please?" She remembered to say *colazione,* the word for breakfast, correctly. Often, she mixed it up with *collasso,* the word for heart failure, which had made Gabriele laugh. Now, every time they made love, he joked that she gave him *un collasso* when he only wanted a cup of coffee. Willa smiled at the thought of Gabriele's little jokes. *How happy we are!*

Signora Marcheschi pointed to a grey enamel coffee pot with a large spout on the stove. "There's bread on the table." Willa looked around for a cup, but saw only one that someone had already used. It was chipped and had a large crack up its side. As there was neither a place to wash it nor any clean cups, she filled it with coffee and said nothing. No need to embarrass her mother-in-law already by suggesting that her dishes weren't clean. The almost black liquid in the cup looked like thick syrup and tasted bitter.

"Is there any cream and sugar, please?"

"*La straniera!*" Signora Marcheschi muttered without looking up. *What does she mean?* Willa wondered. She wished Gabriele were there to explain, as he had done during the previous six weeks on their honeymoon at Montecatini whenever she hadn't understood what people were saying or what was expected. *So much to learn all at once.*

Grazia picked up the bald chicken by its legs. Blood dripped from the bird's neck onto the old linoleum floor. She wiped the floor with a towel she had nearby; it came up with dark streaks of dirt and chicken blood. She tossed the towel on the counter and passed the bird back and forth directly over the fire on the wooden stove, twisting and turning it constantly. The smell of burning pinfeathers made Willa feel lightheaded. She took her coffee to the table in the middle of the room and sat down. Faded green paint flaked off the tabletop. She brushed the pieces away with one hand. Grazia grunted and came over with the towel to wipe the specks from the floor before putting the towel back on the counter and then resumed butchering.

Willa watched her cut open the chicken and pull out the insides, piling the entrails on the counter next to it. Flies cruised nearby. She looked away and cut a slice of bread from the warm loaf. She wished she could have butter and jam, too, but decided not to ask just in case it might seem impolite. As there were no plates, she nibbled at the bread from her hand and took a sip of coffee. Both tasted burnt. A painted clock on the wall above the stove ticked in the silent room.

"It's very warm today," Willa said.

"We're too busy to notice the weather," Signora Marcheschi replied.

Taking up a large black knife, Grazia made a single, sure cut between the thigh and the breast of the chicken; then she twisted the joint where the thighs joined the body in a smooth motion. Willa heard the cracking of sinews and cartilage as the thighs separated from the breast and the back of the chicken. Grazia dropped pieces into a smoking skillet on the wooden stove and then disappeared into the garden. The chicken sizzled in the pan. Willa carried her cup to the counter and set it down. The chicken's head lay nearby still covered with reddish feathers, its red comb drooping, and its eyelids closed as if a whitened film had grown over them while the chicken slept. She noticed the tiny eyelashes, the yellowish beak slightly parted as if the chicken were merely trying to get its breath or were panting in the heat of the kitchen. She looked into its pinkish mouth, open and vulnerable. A wave of nausea swept over her. She looked away until her stomach calmed, then remembered the visit to the tenants and went to get her sketchbook.

The silver coating of the mirror in their room had crazed and peeled, leaving gaps in her image. She found some fresh water in the pitcher by the bed, brushed her teeth, and applied some lipstick. She pinched her cheeks until they looked pink and healthy. By the time Willa returned to the kitchen with her sketchbook, Grazia was stirring tomatoes and herbs into the boiling pot. She poured boiling water into an empty pot and dropped in the neck from the chicken along with its feet, liver, and finally its heart and another organ Willa couldn't identify.

Signora Marcheschi looked at the clock and then at Willa. "It's 9:45. Make late." She had packed two large, wicker baskets with numerous vials; some used clothing, including shirts, socks and a tiny pink dress; and several bottles of wine. She added the loaves of bread on the counter. "Take," she said to Willa, indicating two large, metal containers with handles, which were still sitting on the table.

"Where shall I put my sketchbook?" Willa asked.

"No draw," Signora Marcheschi said.

"Why?"

Signora Marcheschi didn't answer. Willa lifted the heavy containers, holding one in each hand, and followed her mother-in-law outside. As she stepped onto the top stair, the loose step came up. She stumbled, scraping her shin on the metal can, but managed to regain her balance without dropping the containers or falling. She continued down the stairs and followed Signora Marcheschi along a dirt path that led toward a wooded area. There the path ended. Willa stepped over the fallen branches and around stumps. Dirt, sticks and rocks invaded her sandals. She stopped to remove the debris. Signora Marcheschi shook her head and sighed. "Shoes no good." They continued walking for nearly twenty minutes until ahead of them in a clearing in the woods Willa saw a young woman in a tattered, print dress washing clothes in a wooden bucket. Around her, several small children close in age, dirty and dressed in rags, crawled on the ground outside a small, wooden structure, the only building Willa could see. *Could this be their house?* The young woman stopped her work to greet Signora Marcheschi and accepted the gift of the pink dress and a loaf of bread.

"Grazie mille, Signora Marcheschi."

"You're too thin, Theresa," Signora Marcheschi said. "Tell your husband that I said you are to eat more."

"I will, Signora."

"How can she eat more if they don't have enough food?" Willa whispered to her mother-in-law after they left.

"Why must you insult everyone?" Signora Marcheschi said.

14

Willa turned over and looked at her watch. Eight-thirty. She had intended to get up early, as early as Signora Marcheschi and Grazia. As she hurried downstairs and through the passageway, however, breakfast was her only thought. She heard Signora Marcheschi's voice in the kitchen. "Why isn't that *ragazza* around when I need her?" She heard the sound of a metal spoon against a kettle. Willa paused. *They're talking about me. Should I go in?*

"Perhaps she's outside," Grazia said. Willa listened without breathing.

"Painting pictures, you mean? Nonsense! I don't know what she and Gabriele could be thinking." *So this is what Signora Marcheschi really thinks.*

"We say 'To help a husband, help a wife,' Signora," Grazia replied.

Signora Marcheschi laughed. "She doesn't want to learn our ways, so how can I help her? No wedding chest, either. No linens. No furniture. No clothes. She costs us every day and produces nothing except chatter about painting pictures. Gabriele refuses to speak to her, and he won't let me. What am I to do?"

Lies. She's telling lies, Willa thought. She turned away and bumped a small cabinet. The sound echoed in the passageway.

"What's that?" She heard Signora Marcheschi's footsteps. Pretending she had heard nothing, Willa righted the cabinet.

"*Scusate...Buongiorno. Come stati?*" Willa said giving her mother-in-law her best smile.

Signora Marcheschi seemed to take offense. "*Come state,*" she replied, insisting on the formal form of the greeting.

Willa and Gabriele had already been married for nearly two months, and Signora Marcheschi had not yet suggested that Willa call her *mamma* though Gabriele had said she would. "We begin the *vendemmia* today," Signora Marcheschi continued. "You'll supervise the meal for the family and our workers." There wasn't enough space for all of the workers to eat at once, so they were to be fed in shifts. "First, you'll make the soup. There will be bread, cheese, some fruit, wine, coffee. Grazia will help you." The process of preparing, serving and cleaning up would take most of the day. Once again, there would be no time to paint.

"I don't know how to make soup," Willa said.

Signora Marcheschi frowned. "What do girls in America learn?" She picked up a small knife and began to sharpen it. The sound of the knife against the whetstone grew more rapid and urgent. Signora Marcheschi tested the blade with her finger and then handed the knife to Willa. It was so old that the sharpened side of the blade had worn into a curve, and the steel had corroded to a mottled grey color. The newly sharpened edge gleamed with a silvery threat. Signora Marcheschi pointed to an enamel basin on the counter filled with vegetables that still smelled of the soil in which they were grown. "Peel. Cut. *Pezzi piccoli.*" Little pieces.

"Where?" Willa said. Signora Marcheschi pointed at the counter.

"I mean where do I wash them?" Signora Marcheschi pointed to the door. Willa took the knife and the vegetables and went outside, stepping cautiously on the loose plank. *Don't fall with a knife,* she reminded herself. She put the basin under the water faucet and began to work the pump, which sucked and gurgled, until, finally, the water came out, a thin stream that immediately turned brown in the basin. Willa emptied the water and rinsed the vegetables separately—chard, carrots, potatoes, tomatoes, zucchini, fava beans—before returning them to the basin. She pumped more water over the vegetables, ignoring the muddy plot at her feet. The water was cloudy. Signora Marcheschi came out.

"They're still dirty," Willa said. "I'll wash them again." Signora Marcheschi seized the basin and poured the water out. The mud on the ground thickened and stained the hem of her dress.

"Good for soup," Signora Marcheschi said. *Should I even eat the food here?* Willa wondered. She stepped over the mud and went back into the kitchen.

Signora Marcheschi pointed to the vegetables in the basin and made a cutting motion with her hand. Willa put the chard on the counter. The rumpled green leaves gave the newly sharpened knife no resistance. "No." Signora Marcheschi took the knife from her, cut the stems away from the leaves and chopped the stems into pieces. Then, she tore the leaves into small pieces.

"But there's still dirt," Willa said.

Signora Marcheschi seemed not to hear. She peeled the carrots and the potatoes, too, letting the peelings fall on the floor. "Take," she said pointing at the peelings and in the direction of the compost pile outside. "*Forza! Forza!*" Hurry. Willa put the muddy peels and scrapings into the basin and went outside. The compost pile made a faint frying sound as though it were alive. She dropped the scrapings on top. A small, brownish worm crawled out and then burrowed back into the heap. She rinsed the basin before bringing it inside. With a disapproving look, Signora Marcheschi handed her the knife and pointed to the tomatoes. Willa began slicing. The tomatoes succumbed easily to the blade. As she quartered the last tomato, she heard Gabriele and his father on the stairway. She looked up, relieved. During this moment of inattention the knife completed its passage through the soft flesh of the tomato and sliced into Willa's hand between her left thumb and index finger. She dropped the knife and the tomato. Blood erupted over her hand and dripped onto the tomatoes she had just sliced. She knew it was deep.

"Gabriele!" Blood poured from the wound. She couldn't stop it. Willa cupped her left hand with her right. "Help!" Signora Marcheschi came closer, watched the blood flowing, and shook her head. Grazia looked at Willa's hand and crossed herself, then reached for a towel and covered the bleeding wound.

"No. It's filthy!" Willa pulled away and wrapped the skirt of her dress around her hand. The blood soaked through the thin cloth. "I need a clean towel and a doctor," Willa said to Gabriele.

"Come, sit down," Gabriele said. "Grazia will take care of you."

Grazia wrapped the skirt of her apron around the handle of a metal spoon then went to the wood stove and opened a small door in the chimney. Signor and Signora Marcheschi watched silently, their eyes darting from Willa's hand to Grazia. With the spoon Grazia scraped out soot from the hot chimney and carried it to where Willa sat. Gabriele held Willa's shoulders as Grazia pressed put the soot into the wound. Willa pulled her hand away with a shriek.

"Let her help you. She knows what to do," Gabriele said.

Willa held her hand tightly against her body. "She's putting dirt on it!"

"It's not dirt. It's soot." Gabriele took Willa's hand in his and held it out for Grazia. "Be still and let her help you." Grazia pressed more soot into the wound. The bleeding slowed. At last, it stopped. Then Grazia asked Gabriele's father to remove his shirt, the one he had been wearing to work in the vineyards. It was dirty and damp with sweat. Willa watched as he unbuttoned the shirt and handed it to Grazia, who tore it into pieces of varying widths. With Gabriele's help, she wrapped the largest piece around Willa's hand.

"The shirt of an old man makes faster healing," Grazia said. She tied the wrapping with more pieces of cloth torn from the shirt.

"Done!" Gabriele said, pleased. He held Willa's hand with his. "Don't you want to thank Grazia for taking such good care of you?"

Willa pulled her hand away and fled outside. Gabriele followed her. As she walked along the road between the olive grove and one of the vineyards, he reached out to her. She turned away from him. "Liar," she said. "When you said that I could paint here, I believed you. When you said your friends would get used to me, I believed you. When you said your mother would tell me to call her *mamma*, I believed you. You knew that none of it was true. My father was right. You just wanted money."

"No, Willa, don't say that. You're my wife, and this is our home. You are part of our family and our business now." He tried to put his arm around her shoulders, but she shook him off.

"You're my husband, yes, but this isn't my home or my business. I don't belong here." Tears spilled down her cheeks. "And now I know I never will."

Gabriele put his hands on her shoulders once more. "Don't say that. You're just upset."

"You let her rub dirt into my hand. I could get an infection!"

He took her hand and kissed her bandaged palm. "Grazia always treats our cuts this way."

"I can't live like this. I won't."

"This is how we can love you. Please, Willa, this is the only life I have," he said. "You must let me love you the way I can."

"We must have a house of our own."

"A separate house?" She nodded. "What would my family think if I tell them you don't want to live with them?" Gabriele said. "No one does that."

"When you promised that we would have a life together here, I thought you meant we would have a home of our own."

"Families must stay together. That's how they grow. We make my family stronger,"

"We can help your family's business become stronger and still live and work in town."

"But my work is here," he said.

"Mine is not." She remembered the check on the dresser. "My father gave us enough money to buy a house of our own, and I want our house to be in town with a place for me to paint."

Gabriele shook his head. "That's *pazzesco*," a crazy thing, he said. "No one does that."

That evening, as they sat at the dining room table together, Willa listened while Gabriele and his father discussed the upcoming harvest. Willa picked at the cracked veneer on the edge of the table, piling the broken pieces next to her plate. It would be a bountiful year. She studied her bandaged hand and dirty fingernails. In them she saw the ugliness of her existence. She thought of the women she had seen in *National Geographic* gazing at the camera, smiling through black or missing teeth, exhausted by the need to feed themselves and the infants crowded at their pendulous breasts.

Grazia set bowls of minestrone in front of the two men. Willa imagined painting them hunched over the brown table, the candles reflected in their wineglasses; the vaguely green, perhaps grey, walls behind them, all in shadow save the still life of bright vegetables floating in their soup bowls and the fruit piled at the center of the table on the chipped white platter. Their spoons clicked against their bowls. They didn't see her, couldn't value her separately from their own needs and plans. She understood now what her father meant. Grazia set a bowl of soup in front of her.

"Your check will cover the new tractor," Signor Marcheschi said to Gabriele.

"No!" Willa said. "That check is for our house." Signora Marcheschi frowned, but said nothing. After dinner, Willa went upstairs alone. The envelope was gone. She looked in the drawers. Her stomach roiled. *It's their filthy food,* she thought. She lay down on the lumpy bed and fell asleep. When Gabriele came in later, she awakened, heard him undress. He sat on the side of the bed next to her and put his hand on her hip. She turned toward him. "Where is my father's check?" Gabriele remained silent, examined his fingernails. "Gabriele, where is our check?"

He looked up at her. "It was an emergency. I had to use it for the new tractor."

"And you didn't ask me?"

"A husband makes these decisions."

"It's my check, too."

"A husband makes the decisions."

"I thought *we* made the decisions," she said, angry now. "Gabriele, I refuse to live like this."

"I'm sorry, Willa. I planned to make it up so I wouldn't have to tell you."

She took a deep breath. "No, Gabriele, I'm the one who is truly sorry. Our marriage has been a terrible mistake. It's not your fault. It's mine. I imagined something was true that wasn't." In the quiet room, her voice sounded very loud to her. "Gabriele, I'm going to leave." She saw Gabriele's shoulders slump as if he had received a blow.

"Please stay," he whispered. "I love you. We love each other. That's all that matters."

"I imagined that was true, but if I stay, both of us will lose our dreams. Surely, you can see that as well as I can."

"I'll tell my mother again that you should paint whenever you want."

"She and your father are concerned about my dowry and how much I eat because they need a way to make a living."

Gabriele shook his head. "It's not true."

"You don't hear her. You don't see that we can't do this."

"My mother doesn't mean it that way."

"Yes, she does. She dislikes me so much. Why? Because I didn't wear her wedding dress? Because I don't know how to cook soup? Because I want to paint? Because I came without a chaperone? Because I'm not Catholic? Because her friends talk about me? Or, is it because I'm not Maria Cristina? You tell me. Which is it?"

"Our customs are different from yours. That's all. It just takes some time." Gabriele held out his arms to her. "I'm sorry." Willa went to the window. Under the full moon the landscape appeared silver-plated. Gabriele came to her. "Don't think about leaving, not now when you're so angry and upset." Although they continued to stand at the window, looking out at the moon, Willa knew then that they no longer saw the same moon. Perhaps they never had.

15

The next morning Willa still felt queasy. *That dirty soup! At least I won't have to eat it again.* She intended to pack her bag that very day and go to the station where she would buy her ticket to Firenze and leave Orvieto forever. A wave of nausea forced her to lie down. *I'll go to Signora Farnese. A hotel.* She sat up and counted the money in her purse. There was perhaps enough to stay for a few days at a *pensione* until her parents could wire her the money to come home. She felt better and went to find some paper and an envelope, then remembered that she could send a cable from the telegraph office in town. *A cable would be so much faster.* She washed, dressed and went out.

As she walked toward the lane that passed in front of the Marcheschi home, she rehearsed her plan: First, she would cable her parents to send the money to American Express in Firenze. As soon as the money arrived, she would buy a ticket either to Genoa or Naples. From one of those ports, she would take a ship to New York. It wasn't until she neared the telegraph office that she remembered that the operator was a close friend of Signor Marcheschi. The contents of her message would be known in Orvieto within an hour. No, a letter was the only choice, though it would take much longer than she wished. She returned to the house. In the bright sunlight, it looked unkempt. *Had it always looked that way?*

"I'm not feeling well today," Willa told Gabriel the following morning. She stayed in their room until she felt well enough to sit up and write the letter to her parents: *I must come home right away. Please send money for my ticket to the American Consulate in Firenze right away. Very, very urgent.* She put the letter in her purse and lay down again. Soon, she fell asleep. Gabriele brought her some soup for lunch, but she couldn't eat it. The next day and the day after that, she remained ill and unable to eat. On the afternoon of the fourth day Dr. Lucarelli arrived carrying a black leather bag the size of a cat. He chatted with Signor and Signora Marcheschi, shared a joke with Gabriele, and drank coffee with Grazia before Signora Marcheschi led him to Willa and Gabriele's room.

"He brings his herbs in his bag," Gabriele explained to Willa. Signora Marcheschi told Gabriele to leave and close the door. She put a small, caned chair next to the sagging bed so Dr. Lucarelli could sit down. He studied Willa without saying anything. Finally, he spoke to her.

"*Buongiorno. Come state?*" She waited for her mother-in-law to leave, but Signora Marcheschi remained.

"You understand me?" he said.

"Yes. I'm a little ill," Willa said. "From the dirt in my soup. I'll be fine." Signora Marcheschi grunted, but said nothing. Willa heard Gabriele, Grazia, and Signor Marcheschi outside in the hall. She knew they were listening at the door. *Just as soon as I feel better I'll be going home,* she thought. She stared at the waterstained and yellowed ceiling and imagined that she was in Firenze. New York. Erhart.

Dr. Lucarelli tapped his finger on her lips. She opened her mouth. He leaned forward and smelled her breath. He stuck his tongue out and pointed to it. Willa stuck hers out. He glanced at it, apparently satisfied. He pulled her eyelids down and up. He pressed on her stomach, her belly. Another grunt. He asked, *per favore*, to examine her female parts.

"No," Willa said, but Signora Marcheschi told Dr. Lucarelli to continue. Willa threw up on the floor near Dr. Lucarelli's feet.

"Ayyy!" Signora Marcheschi said. She took Willa's washcloth from the washstand and wiped the floor with it. When Dr. Lucarelli completed his examination, he gave Signora Marcheschi a small envelope filled with a powder that smelled like soil.

"Make a tea and have her drink it three times a day," he told Signora Marcheschi. "You'll feel better very soon," he told Willa. Then he closed his bag, stood up, and bowed slightly. *Good,* Willa thought. *Now, he'll leave and so will Signora Marcheschi.*

"*Arrivederci, Signora*," Dr. Lucarelli said to Willa. Outside in the hallway, Willa overheard him announce his findings: "È *incinta*." Pregnant. "*Felicitazioni!*" many good wishes.

"No! You're wrong! I'm not pregnant," Willa called to them.

"*Di quanto?*" How long? Signora Marcheschi asked.

"About four to six weeks," Dr. Lucarelli said. "Perhaps five to seven." Signora Marcheschi and Grazia smiled and exchanged knowing looks.

"No. You're wrong. I took precautions," Willa said again. "It's just their dirty food." Dr. Lucarelli and the family glanced at one another.

Gabriele came to Willa's side and put his finger to his lips. "What would Father Enrico think if he knew?" he whispered to her.

"I don't care what Father Enrico thinks!" Willa said once again, her voice loud enough for everyone to hear. Signora Marcheschi gasped. Grazia crossed herself.

"Don't you see? It's good to begin our family right away?" Gabriele told Willa later that day. They were alone together. "You are fertile, and we have time for many children." He looked pleased, she thought, proud. *Did he forget that I'm leaving?*

"I'm not going to become your prisoner because of this." She handed Gabriele the letter that she had written to her parents and asked him to take it to the post office.

Gabriele chuckled. "So, my little bird, you've decided to tell your parents our good news right away."

16

The pale blue envelope postmarked *Erhart, Ohio* arrived several weeks later. Willa recognized her mother's stationery. She took the letter to their bedroom where she would be alone and opened it, taking care not to tear it in case a money order or a check was inside. She removed the note and unfolded it. Nothing. She searched the floor. Nothing. *Of course. They would have sent the money to Firenze as she had asked. Or perhaps the ticket.* She read the note:

Dearest Willa,

It sounds as if you have become a little homesick. It's something that often happens to new brides, especially those who have decided to live far from their families. I felt quite lonely as a newlywed. So much changes when a woman gets married, doesn't it? We're sure that you will feel much better after this period of adjustment. Meanwhile, if you and Gabriele would like to visit here, we'll plan a reception for you at The Pavilion.

All our love, Mother.

Willa tore the letter into unreadable pieces and let them fall to the floor. Then she threw herself face down on the unmade bed, too exhausted to cry. *I must leave before Orvieto swallows me up. Tomorrow! I'll go tomorrow.* Her thoughts whirled. *At least in Firenze people understood my ambitions. But would they if I had a baby? Could I hide it? Give it to Gabriele or someone else? People do that, don't they? Isn't there a way to stop a baby? Signora Farnese would know.*

Willa put some clean underwear, a nightgown, robe, and two of her loosest dresses in her suitcase. She put an extra pair of shoes in her carpetbag and some jewelry, but left the wedding necklace on the bureau. *I'll need work.* She recalled the American businessman at Signora Farnese's luncheon who had offered her a job. She scrambled through her drawers and suitcase. At last she found his business card inside her address book. She tore a small opening in the lining of her purse where she concealed what little money she could find, her Italian identity card, her American passport, and the business card. Then, despite the warm day, she put on her coat, picked up her carpetbag with one hand and her suitcase with the other, and made her way down the front stairs, wary in the silent house. Once outside, she closed the front door softly behind her, walked to the lane, and followed the main road in the direction of the station. The sounds of insects and birds played against the otherwise silent country-side. She inhaled the scents of grasses and herbs mixed with earth. *I'll miss the smell of Orvieto,* she thought.

Ahead, a car approached. It was a large black Packard with chrome hubcaps like the one Eddie Ingersoll's father had. She glimpsed the driver and the three passengers. They were laughing. The car passed on, stirring a cloud of dust that settled over her. She watched the car as it moved away from her. She had seen such cars in Orvieto before; they always belonged to day visitors, usually wealthy tourists from Firenze or Roma, occasionally more distant places. In the summer, the women wore dress-es made of white lawn and fashionable shoes despite the difficulty of walking on cobblestoned streets. The men wore searsucker or linen suits, and some carried walking sticks with silver heads. Willa often tried to imagine what it might be like to participate in their glamorous, carefree lives and lively conversations, to be someone who traveled, who enjoyed what people called the finer things. The car came to a sudden halt, backed up, and stopped. A man in a pale suit and straw hat got out.

"I'll be right back, Greta," she overheard him say. He walked back to where Willa was standing.

"Buongiorno, signorina. We've come to see the Duomo and buy wine." She couldn't place his accent. "We need someone to guide us. Please, will you help us? We could pay you." She hesitated, thinking of

the other opportunities she had missed and how much she needed the money.

"Thank you, no. I'm on my way somewhere." He nodded at her suitcase.

"I see you are traveling. We can drive you later." Her stomach roiled. *What if I threw up in their car?* Unlike her, they were free to visit for a day, buy wine, dine out, and then return to lives far from this backward province where all the decisions were already made and where it was picturesque only if you lived someplace else.

"Thank you, but not today. You'll find someone in town who can help you." She continued on to the train station. Squinting in the bright sun, she returned to her thoughts of finding a job. She recalled Signora Farnese's luncheon. *If only I could go back to that day and start my life over again. Anyway, it hasn't been so very long. Just a few months. It shouldn't be too late. Keep a positive outlook and be confident,* she told herself.

Donato, the clerk, looked up at her. He had lost his left eye in the Great War and wore a black eye patch. His hands trembled, though he was still young. "Battle fatigue," people called it. Still, his infirmities did not hinder his knowing exactly who came and left each day, their starting points and their destinations, and the reasons for their trips. "Signora Marcheschi! Let me see. I'll bet you're going to Corfu today." He chuckled.

Willa was thinking about what she might say to Signora Farnese. "I'm sorry for my behavior and I ask your forgiveness and your help," she murmured.

Donato laughed. "Excuse me, Signora Marcheschi, the place for a confession is in the confessional. Here we sell only tickets."

"Firenze," Willa said quickly. "Today." Donato took out the tickets and stamped each one carefully, slowly, in several places as if he were stamping them for the first time and wanted to do it perfectly. Then, he noted the transaction in his ledger in several places with equal care. *I hope he doesn't tell Gabriele where I'm going.* She thought about Signora

Farnese again, rehearsed a plan in her mind. *Apologize. Chat pleasantly. Later, ask for "guidance" or "a suggestion," "a recommendation" or maybe "a referral to someone who handles difficult situations." Yes, that was how to put it.* At that moment, Willa wanted to lie down on one of the worn benches in the dim waiting room. *What would Donato think?*

"Firenze is interesting, but you won't enjoy it as much now that you're going to be a mother," Donato said. *If he knows, then everyone does.*

"No, I suppose not," Willa said.

"Signora Marcheschi, I see that you're going to Firenze today, too."

Willa turned and looked into the round face of Sister Maria Cristina. She forced a smile. "Sister, how nice to see you."

Sister Maria Cristina smiled back through crooked teeth. "We'll sit together. You'll tell me all about your happy news." In that moment Willa understood that even in a city as large as Firenze neither her intentions nor her actions nor her condition could be concealed for long. She would have to go much farther away, to a place she didn't know, couldn't imagine. Her head ached.

"Your train arrives in fifteen minutes, and the trip takes two hours." Donato handed her the tickets. "That will be four hundred lire, signora."

"Is that for a round trip?"

"Yes, of course, unless you're not planning to come back." He shook with laughter at his own joke and winked at her with his good eye. *If only I could say, "No, I'm only going one way and I'm never coming back,"* Willa thought. *What if I said that I'm not sure when I'll be coming back? No. Even that would create questions.*

Willa hesitated at the ticket window until Donato looked at her closely and spoke. "Are you all right, Signora Marcheschi? You don't seem well today." Willa gave Donato the money for the round-trip ticket and put the ticket in her purse.

"It's your condition," Sister Maria Cristina said. "Women who come from Orvieto are never sick during their pregnancies." Willa nodded in agreement, knowing that her status as *la straniera* marked her as an unhealthy exception. "Tell me, how do you like your new life here?" Maria Cristina leaned forward slightly. A silver cross dangled from the thin silver chain around her neck.

"It's very nice," Willa said. She watched the cross swing back and forth.

"And what do you like best about our city of Orvieto?"

"The weather..," Willa said.

Maria Cristina moved, and her cross continuted to swing back and forth. She waited like a cat waits for a bird.

"...and the Duomo is interesting," Willa added, thinking this observation might make a favorable impression on Maria Cristina. The cross moved as if Maria Cristina controlled it by her will alone.

Willa looked away. "And what do you like best about Orvieto, Sister?"

"It's been my family's home for many generations."

"I cannot say the same."

Maria Cristina looked genuinely surprised. "Why not? The Marcheschi's have been in Orvieto even longer than the Orsinis."

"Excuse me," Willa said. She hurried to the bathroom at the end of the platform, leaving her suitcase and coat outside the door. Inside, the smell of the open toilet overwhelmed her. She braced her hands on the wooden seat and vomited into the round opening. Her skin felt cold and hot at the same time. She wanted some water. *Never mind. I'll get some on the train.* She opened the rough, wooden door, saw that her train was about to leave. She stumbled over the rocky path and boarded the second-class coach just as the conductor blew his whistle. He closed the door after her. She entered the first vacant compartment and sank down onto the faded red plush seat, pressing her cheek against the cool window. If no one came, she could lie down and sleep. The train began to move. She glanced out the window and saw her coat and suitcase next to the door to the toilet where she had left them. She clutched her carpetbag and her purse close to her chest. Maria Cristina opened the door and entered the compartment.

"Are you all right?" she said. "You left quite abruptly." At that moment Willa felt grateful even for Maria Cristina's false concern.

"A little ill."

Maria Cristina took out her breviary and placed it in her lap. She glanced around the compartment and then smiled, raptor-like. "I don't see your things," she said.

"What will you enjoy most when you go to Firenze?" Willa said, thinking it a safe change of subject.

"I suppose you have time for enjoyment, but pleasure isn't part of my calling. I'm going to Firenze on behalf of my convent." Maria Cristina folded her hands in a steeple and placed them on the breviary. "And you?"

"I'm visiting a friend." Willa took the blue sketchbook out of the carpetbag. Perhaps she could capture Maria Cristina's ominous bulk. She opened the sketchbook to a blank page.

"Does Gabriele know?"

"What do you mean?" Willa asked.

"The Marcheschis never leave Orvieto. All of their friends and relatives are here." It had only been a social question, Willa thought, relieved.

"I have a friend in Firenze, just the same." Willa tried to smile, but her upper lip felt tight, as if it had been stretched and tacked down. She drew a sweeping curve across the page.

"Another artist-type like you?" Maria Cristina leaned forward to examine the line. The conductor came for their tickets.

"What?" Willa said absently. She handed the conductor her ticket. Sister Maria Cristina pounced.

"Your friend. Is he an artist-type?"

"No. Not really."

"A lover then." Stunned, Willa felt her cheeks redden with embarrassment and anger. Maria Cristina watched her discomfort. The conductor raised his eyebrows. He punched Maria Christina's ticket and returned it to her.

"Why would you say that?" Willa asked so that the conductor would hear. "My friend is a woman."

"My vocation doesn't preclude knowledge of more worldly things." Maria Cristina handed the conductor her ticket.

"But why would you say that to me?"

"It's what everyone says," Sister Maria Cristina replied. Willa recoiled at Maria Cristina's revelation.

"Bless you, sister," the conductor said, returning Maria Cristina's ticket.

"And you think this, too?" Willa said.

Maria Cristina nodded. "Yes. Everyone thinks that you're a woman of ill repute."

The conductor stared at Willa.

"If I were what you said, then why would Gabriele have married me?" she asked Maria Cristina.

"You tricked him. One day, he'll see his mistake."

"And this is what you think, too?"

Maria Cristina nodded.

Willa realized how swiftly and fully she had been judged. It was worse than she had imagined. Worse than she could have imagined. Angry, she put her sketchbook away and stood up. "Then everyone is as ignorant as you are."

"The truth is what it is," Maria Cristina said, smiling. "You can't walk away from it."

In another car, Willa found a seat in an empty compartment. Trembling, she leaned into the corner and turned her face toward the wall, checking the scream that welled up inside her, allowing silent tears to course down her cheeks. *It doesn't matter what they think because I'm never going back. Ever. Still, why would strangers think such a thing? Was Maria Cristina telling the truth? Could that be why people had been so unpleasant? What about Signora Marcheschi? Doesn't she know me as a daughter-in-law, a wife, and soon a mother?*

Outside the window Willa looked at the village where the train had stopped. *Here, too, are people who don't know me. What if I get off and stay? What would these strangers imagine about me? That I'm an artist? A peasant? A loose woman? Una straniera? Am I responsible for what people see in me?* A whistle sounded, and the train churned ahead. She imagined that it left behind a hole in the village into which everyone's ideas about everyone else tumbled together in a stew of truths and falsehoods.

17

FIRENZE, ITALY 1935

Condensation on the windows obscured her view. The train entered the station and stopped. Willa left hastily, stumbled on the steps getting off, regained her balance, and hurried toward the entrance to the station. Just ahead she saw a group of nuns. Was Maria Cristina among them? She turned away and went out by a side door where she found a bus ready to depart for Fiesole. She got on and took a seat near the driver. Her thoughts tumbled. *I'll find work this afternoon. Somewhere to stay. How long does it take to get paid?* She looked out the window at the rain, wishing that she had remembered her coat and suitcase. *Perhaps I can borrow some clothes until I can get mine back.*

The bus rattled up the hillside through low-hanging fog and stopped in Fiesole's cobbled piazza. *Could Maria Cristina have made up the whole story because she was jealous? Maybe it was just a lie.* The driver opened the door for her. Fog blanketed the piazza; the chill and dampness cut through her light sweater. *Which way was Signora Farnese's house?* Hunger and the smell of food drew her to a trattoria where the waiter was preparing tables for lunch. She recognized him. Surely, he would remember her, their friendly conversations. She smiled at him and said hello.

"We don't open until noon," he said, continuing with his work.

She looked at her watch. Five minutes to twelve. "Shall I wait?" The waiter looked puzzled.

"*Signorina*, we're closed."

Willa turned and walked away. *Well, no matter. Signora Farnese will serve lunch.* She remembered the lunches that Assuntina had prepared: *pasta e fagioli*, fresh bread, cold roasted pork. Her stomach growled. As she drew closer, she recognized the pink walls of the villa, its tiled roof, and the orderly garden of herbs and flowers set out in a pattern that dated from the Middle Ages. Roses too. These seemed to her part of something she had done long ago. She followed the path to the front door. *Assuntina could be preparing lunch right now.* She lifted the brass knocker, heard the echo inside when she let it drop. Assuntina opened the door.

"Hello, Assuntina."

"Wait here, please," the maid said, alarmed. "I'll find the Signora." Willa shivered on the doorstep.

Signora Farnese appeared at the door. "Willa, what's happened? Why have you come?" She took Willa's red, chapped hands in hers and looked down at them. Signora Farnese's hands felt warm and smooth. On her right hand, Signora Farnese wore a large ring of pink tourmalines surrounded by pearls and diamonds that sparkled even in the pale light of the foggy day. Willa wished that she had remembered to clean the dirt from under her fingernails. "Good heavens, what's happened to you?" Signora Farnese said.

Willa hid her hands behind her back. "I've been working."

"You look frozen, my dear. Such a nasty day. Assuntina shouldn't have left you standing outside. Do come in." Signora Farnese stepped back to let Willa enter. "Sometimes, I think Assuntina just doesn't know what to do." The warmth of the house surrounded Willa.

"I was just reading…," Signora Farnese took her reading glasses off the top of her head and set them on a nearby table. Willa admired the Signora's smooth skin, her eyes the color of tiger's eye, her stylishness. Her dark brown hair was flecked with white and wound in a chignon, secured with tortoiseshell combs, their edges worked with gold filigree. Willa ran her fingers through her own unkempt hair. She couldn't remember the last time it had been cut.

"I was in Firenze and I stopped by," Willa said quickly. She gazed at Signora Farnese's pale blouse the color of apricots, the heavy silk stitching running up the front, her earrings of coral of varied hues. *The colors of heaven,* Willa thought.

Signora Farnese looked anxious."You're still shivering. Are you all right?" Willa nodded. "I'm so sorry. I didn't receive your letter, so I'm not prepared to welcome you properly."

"I'm sorry I didn't write," Willa said.

"Unfortunately," Signora Farnese looked toward the door, "yes... that is...unfortunately, I must be going out. Quite soon, in fact." Signora Farnese glanced at Willa's wrinkled clothes, her purse, the carpetbag, and then toward the door. "Is your husband with you?" Willa shook her head. Signora Farnese seemed to relax slightly. She studied Willa more carefully. "You look pale. Are you well?" Willa nodded. "Come, then, let's sit down for a moment."

She led Willa into her study. Willa looked down at her own scuffed shoes and at the herringbone-planked floor. *How long had it had taken for the floor to attain its golden patina?* She thought of the raw plank floors in Orvieto. Signora Farnese indicated that Willa should sit in the armchair next to the stone fireplace where a fire already burned. The light of the flames danced in the polished brass of the andirons and reflected off the shiny surfaces around the room. Willa inhaled the fragrance of the roses in a vase on the side table and the smell of burning pinewood. Signora Farnese sat opposite her on a small, greenish brocade couch. Its high curving back of wood had been skillfully carved into garlands of leaves and flowers. Signora Farnese's brocade chairs and couches and the windows hung with damask seemed like a silken cocoon. At that moment, Willa desired nothing more than to be spun into it and held fast within its comforting boundaries. She allowed the warmth of the room and the safety of the armchair to embrace her, delaying the reason for her call.

"It seems you're a long way from home today," Signora Farnese began.

"I've left Orvieto," Willa blurted out. It was not what she had planned to say, but she plunged on. "I mean, I came to apologize...if I embarrassed you...I'm sorry."

"It was your reputation that was compromised, my dear, though not fatally so, apparently. You and that soldier married recently, I believe?" Willa nodded. "I'm sorry that I was away and couldn't attend your wedding."

Willa remembered the antique silver chalice that Signora Farnese had given them as a wedding gift. Had she sent a proper thank-you note? She wasn't sure. Embarrassed, she looked away. Watercolors of Tuscan landscapes hung on the walls. *Were they there before? Did I not notice how beautiful they are?*

Signora Farnese followed Willa's gaze. "They're Corots," she said. "My late husband bought them many years ago from Corot's dealer in Paris." Willa realized that there were other things in the room she hadn't noticed either: the large quartz ball on its stand on the mantel with a lightening-shaped crack at its center point. *Could I still return to L'Accademia d'Arte?* she wondered. Assuntina carried in the tea service on a lacquered tray and set it on the low table. The teapot was formed in the shape of pale, pink petals suggesting sweet peas, its handle a twining stem. The cups repeated the flower-and-vine motif, while the saucers and plates mimicked leaves.

Signora Farnese poured the hot water into the teapot, replaced the lid and let the tea steep. Willa watched her careful fingers, gazed at her heavy gold bracelets studded with stones in colors of dawn that echoed the flecks of color in her tweed skirt. Around Signora Farnese's neck an ancient pendant of rough-hewn gold hung on a heavy chain. In its center was a single, smooth stone of shiny, mottled black that reminded Willa of something underwater, perhaps the eye of a sea creature. Signora Farnese offered her a plate of cookies arranged in concentric circles. Willa remembered them, their fragrances of clove and lemon. She placed only one on her own smaller plate hoping to conceal her insistent hunger and, more urgently, the degree to which her own life defied the aesthetic of Signora Farnese's existence.

"So, now you are married," Signora Farnese said. For a moment, Willa couldn't think of how to tell Signora Farnese that her marriage had failed. *Isn't this when most young brides tell of their indescribable happiness?* "Tea?" Signora Farnese lifted a cup and saucer and poured jasmine tea into the cup. Light passed through the thin porcelain petals it imitated.

Willa balanced the cup and saucer on her palm. They felt nearly weightless. Signora Farnese handed her a small, monogrammed napkin of pink linen edged with green stitching. Willa opened it on her lap with her other hand. "Forgive me," Signora Farnese continued, "but you look...I don't know...as if Cinderella had torn her gown at the ball."

Willa took the handle of the teacup between her fingers and sipped her tea. "Signora Farnese, there's so much that I didn't expect." Tears rolled down her cheeks against her will. "They don't allow me to paint, and people say that I'm a...a loose woman." The tea leaves eddied at the bottom of her cup. She dabbed her eyes and cheeks with her napkin, leaving it streaked with tears.

"But you went out without a chaperone," Signora Farnese said. Willa caught her breath and tried to control her growing fear. *Does Signora Farnese feel as Maria Cristina does?* Willa realized that she had created her reputation herself. She had done as she wished, imagining that what she did had no consequences, affected no one, least of all herself.

"Yes, I did." She took another sip of her tea. "I was very much mistaken." The outlines of the leaves in the bottom of her cup were more visible. She drank them with the rest of her tea, tasted their bitterness. Swallowed. "There's something more. I thought...I was hoping...you could advise me...I need...that is, I wonder if...could you...perhaps you would recommend someone who could help me?"

Signora Farnese refilled her cup. "Help you with what?"

Willa realized that she hadn't yet asked her question. She took a deep breath. "Signora Farnese, I don't want to...to have a baby." Willa bit the inside of her cheek so that she wouldn't cry again. She tasted the saltiness of her own blood and sipped her tea, saw the remaining liquid in the cup stained pink with surging trails of minute red filaments.

"You were thinking of an abortion?" Signora Farnese sounded incredulous. Willa nodded. "Does Gabriele know how you feel?"

Willa put the cup down abruptly. A porcelain chip pinged in her saucer. "Oh, I'm so sorry." Willa picked the chip out of the saucer and held it out to Signora Farnese who put it on the tea tray.

"It can be repaired," Signora Farnese said. "It will be good as new."

"Signora Farnese, I don't know what to do," Willa whispered.

The older woman spoke slowly, choosing her words carefully. "You must understand that abortions are obtainable, but only by those with highly confidential and powerful connections or, if you're willing to risk death, with a midwife-butcher out in the country. I know of no one who could help you with such a thing." She looked at Willa, this time with what Willa interpreted as concern. "No wonder you're so distraught." Signora Farnese held out the plate of cookies.

Willa devoured another. "I can't go back."

"How do you plan to live otherwise?"

Willa opened her purse, took out the American businessman's card, and showed it to Signora Farnese. "Mr. Bradshaw gave me his card and asked me to be his assistant." She took another cookie. Signora Farnese looked at the card and returned it.

"I'm afraid your situation is quite different now. Before, you were an attractive, available young woman. Perhaps he saw you as a possibility for himself—or at least as an attractive accessory to his business. It's a sad fact, my dear, that no man wants another man's used merchandise… or another man's baby."

"But I could still work, whether I have a baby or not." Willa lifted the saucer and took another sip of tea.

"Here, women who are married and pregnant stay at home with their husbands and their babies. That is, unless they're *disgraziate,* foreigners, who scrub floors because they have what we call *un frutto della colpa,* an unwanted pregnancy. I'm afraid this is what will happen to you if you don't return to your husband immediately."

"I won't go back," Willa said with an angry gesture that knocked her teacup from her saucer. The hot tea spilled and the cup shattered into an opalescent corona around her feet. Willa gasped. "Oh, no. Oh, I'm so sorry." She dabbed at the wet stain on the carpet with her napkin.

Signora Farnese picked up the shards and put them on the tea tray. "Never mind." Assuntina collected the tea service and departed with the remaining cookies, Signora Farnese settled herself again on the sofa. "My dear, in Italy men have nearly total control of your children and your property. Even if you make money by working or receive an inheritance—sometimes even a gift of money—it belongs to your husband. You must think very seriously about what you're considering. I don't believe you have the slightest idea how difficult it will be for you to live if you don't go back to your husband immediately."

"Perhaps I could stay with you for a short time…just until I get settled, of course?" *It's presumptuous but what choice do I have?* Willa thought.

Signora Farnese shook her head. "You're young. You don't realize yet that a woman creates her own fate. Then she must accept it. Marriage is never an idyll. It's a business. Its goal is to support you and your children. Just because you have an unhappy marriage doesn't mean you must harm your livelihood. Many people make bad choices just as you have done and have unhappy marriages just as you do right now. Sometimes, they find lovers. If they're discreet, then there is no need for divorce or abandonment. More importantly, there's no loss of support for the children, and fewer economic hardships for the wife, in particular. It's a practical and quite accepted way to manage an unfortunate situation. I can assure you that some of the most respectable people do it."

"But, signora, I don't love my husband."

Signora Farnese laughed. "My dear, we're not talking about love. What you have is a *situation*. In time, you could find that you like—better yet, love—your husband again, and then you'll be glad you didn't make the too-hasty decision you're contemplating, which will only lead you into further trouble."

"But I already told him that I was leaving and…."

Signora Farnese held her finger to her lips, leaned forward, and whispered, "You haven't told anyone else, have you?" Willa shook her head. "Excellent. Then, there is no risk that he will lose face or be embarrassed. He'll forget what you said and welcome your return, especially if you return with money. Right now, it's a matter of saving face. You must help him to do that." Signora Farnese stood up. Willa understood this signaled the end of their visit. She didn't want to leave.

"How will I get money if I can't work?"

"You must think carefully about that. Whatever you do, you must return immediately. Your absence must not be noticed." She looked at her watch. "It's nearly one. If you don't take the afternoon train, you'll have to wait until this evening for another, so we must hurry." She looked at Willa. "Now stand up...." She adjusted Willa's shoulders. "Straight... that's right...and comb your hair." She looked Willa over. "Straighten your dress." Willa adjusted her dress. "That's right. Now, your best smile." Willa's face felt stiff and reluctant. "Here are your things." Signora Farnese handed Willa the carpetbag and her purse. "Good," she said guiding Willa toward the door. "We've had a lovely visit. Now, Antonio will take you to the station and help you find your train. In a few hours you'll be home and no one will be the wiser."

Minutes later, a black car appeared at the end of the walkway. Willa got in and sat down in the back seat. The car smelled like a glovemaker's shop. As soon as she had waved goodbye to Signora Farnese, Willa handed Mr. Bradshaw's business card to Antonio. "I need to see this person before I go to the station."

Antonio looked at the card and shook his head. "The Signora said to take you straight to the station."

"I'll only be a moment...really." *I must convince him,* Willa thought. *It's my only chance to escape.* "I left something there and I need to take it back with me."

Antonio shrugged. "It's in the Oltrarno. You could miss your train."

"I'll only be a moment." They drove through the oldest streets dodging vendors with carts and workmen carrying heavy loads and turned onto the Ponte Santa Trìnita. Once across the Arno, they drove along the Lungarno following Via Sant'Onofrio to Borgo San Frediano. Antonio stopped the car at the Via del Leone and turned off the engine. A human tide engulfed the car, surging to and fro amid the warrens of tradesmen and artisans.

"Where is it?" Willa said.

"It's on the left. *Primo piano*," Antonio told her. "I thought you said you were here earlier."

"I've gotten turned around." Willa got out of the car. The smells of the tanneries and lacquer and the ringing of hammers on stone filled the air and made her nauseated. She followed Antonio's directions to the address on the card and rang the bell. A young woman opened the door. Willa noticed her stylish black dress. She felt out of place. "Signor Bradshaw, please."

"Did you have an appointment?"

"He knows me." She showed the woman the card. "I've just stopped by."

The woman looked surprised. "Will he know what this is about?" Willa shook her head. "Perhaps I could make an appointment for you. That way he could give you more of his time. He's very busy today."

"I'm leaving Firenze this afternoon. I really must talk to him now. He knows me."

"Come in, then. I'll see if he's available." Willa followed her up a narrow stairway to a dingy waiting area. The young woman excused herself and vanished behind a door that was fitted with frosted glass on which black letters edged with gold spelled out, "Bradshaw & Co., Fine Art & Antique Services: Imports and Exports, Customs." Willa edged into to a hard chair trapped between two large wooden filing cabinets. She looked down at the worn floor. Her stomach growled just as Mr. Bradshaw emerged.

"Well, well, look who's here." Willa stood up. He looked at her, confused. "Willa Carver. That's your name?"

"It's nice to see you again," Willa said.

"Well, *piacere*." He held out his hand. She shook it. He looked at her hands and then at her dress. "You say we met before?"

"Yes, a few months ago." He shook his head. "At Signora Farnese's home. A luncheon last summer." He looked at her more carefully.

"Sorry...I always remember a face, but I can't seem to remember yours."

"We sat next to each other."

"Well, how are you, umm…I'm sorry. I don't think we've met. He looked into the distance as people do when they are obliged to remember something that is long past and it returns to them in disordered fragments. "Wait! You're that painter girl?"

Willa plunged on. "You said you needed an assistant. I've come to talk to you about the job."

"You staying with Signora Farnese?" He looked attentive again.

"Not right now."

He noticed her wedding ring. "Hey, didja get married?"

Willa put her hands behind her. *Too late*, she realized. *Why didn't I think to take my ring off?* "I'm looking for a place nearby so I can get to work early."

He made an impatient gesture. His attention wandered, leaving Willa alone with his glazed expression, a ghost of his presence.

Willa knew he no longer saw her. "I could begin right away," she continued. The young woman in black handed him a file. Bradshaw touched the young woman's arm and then her hair. Willa tried to recapture his interest. "Today, I mean…I could begin this afternoon, if you like."

"Thank you, Renata." Bradshaw glanced at Willa. "Now, where was I? Oh, yes, a job. I'm sorry. That job isn't available." He nodded to the young woman in the black dress as though she were a beautiful object that belonged to him. "Renata, will you show this young lady out, please?" He turned away and started back to his office.

"Do you know of anything else?" Willa said. "Another job, I mean?"

"Well, if you're desperate, around here they hire shop girls to help in the back rooms. Usually, though, they're family members from the country. 'Country cousins,' as Americans say." He chuckled and then withdrew into his office. The young woman led Willa downstairs and let her out onto the teeming street.

Surrounded and jostled, Willa pushed through the crowd, searching for Antonio and the car. When at last she found it, Antonio was gone.

She tried the door. Locked. She waited. An hour had passed since they had left Signora Farnese's house. *He'll come back soon,* Willa thought. She looked at her watch. It was almost two-thirty. *I can't miss the three o'clock train.* Nearby, she saw a bar. She walked over. Through the window she saw Antonio. She turned away and hurried to the nearest bridge where she found a taxi. "I need to go to the station. I'm going to miss my train."

"There's an extra charge if I have to cross the bridge," the driver said. Willa got in. The taxi rattled through the narrow streets, around the Piazza della Republica, and stopped in front of the station. She had only a few minutes left before her train departed. They both got out, and she handed him the money. He looked at it. "That's not enough."

"It's all I have."

He returned the money to her. "You need it more than I do." He spat on the ground and got back into his taxi. "Next time walk!"

Willa pushed through the doors of the station and past a young couple entwined in one another's arms. A group of schoolchildren in two long lines behind a priest passed in front of her. Dizzy and hungry, she spent her last few coins on a small bottle of water, a dry sandwich, a *biscotto,* and a bruised apple.

A flower seller handed her a wilted rose. "Last one," he said. Willa took it and ran toward the train. The petals scattered. Just as she reached the platform, the conductor closed the door. "Wait!" The conductor shook his head. There was a loud whistle. Engines turned. Desperate, she climbed onto the steps of the train and held the railing. "Wait!" Alarmed, the conductor opened the door and pulled her inside.

"*Pazza!* You could fall under the train." She glanced around. *Is Maria Cristina on this train, too?* She went into the first empty compartment and burrowed into a corner seat, not caring that the linen cover on the headrest was soiled and wrinkled or that trash flowed from the waste container onto the floor. In the glass of the curtained window she saw her reflection. *Old,* she thought. *I already look old.* As the train moved out of the station, she took out the food, put it on her lap, and bit into the mealy apple. The meat in her sandwich had turned a greyish color. She ate it anyway, thinking of what Signora Farnese had said about money: *What work could I do? It might be a long time before my paintings sell. Are they good enough to attract buyers? If not, what then?* She had intended to do so much more, become so much more. She bit into the *biscotto*. The dry flour tasted like dust. She opened the water bottle and drank. In the waning afternoon, darkening towns and villages passed outside the window and fell away one by one. She closed her eyes and allowed her body to take on the rhythm of the train.

18

ORVIETO, ITALY 1935

When the train stopped, Willa looked out, searching for her suitcase and coat. They were no longer where she had left them outside the bathroom. She got off and hurried away from the station, taking care not to let anyone see her, especially Donato. Ignoring the dirt that sifted into her shoes and irritated her now swollen feet, she walked along the road back to the house. It was nearly five o'clock. If Gabriele were still out with his father and Signora Marcheschi were still visiting their tenants, perhaps they hadn't noticed her absence yet and wouldn't guess the fullness of her defeat. She turned the knob on the terrace door, the one with the cracked pane, lifted and held the handle, then pushed the door inward, slowly so that it didn't squeak. She heard the sound of a metal spoon stirring in a kettle and smelled chicken roasting. It seemed almost welcoming.

"Where do you suppose that *ragazza* is now?" It was Signora Marcheschi's voice.

"Perhaps she's left, Signora," Grazia said.

"To paint her pictures, you mean? Nonsense. What could she be thinking? Having children changes everything. Besides, she won't leave if she wants to keep her child." Willa stopped breathing.

"We say, 'To help a husband, help a wife,' Signora."

"How? She refuses to learn!"

Willa let go of the door handle. The door closed with a slam.

"What's that?" Signora Marcheschi said. Willa took off her shoes and scurried up the tiled stairs to their bedroom. She closed the door. The latch clicked. She turned the lock and dropped her shoes on the wooden floor. Dirt and grit trickled out of them. On the bed, she saw her coat and suitcase. She pushed them under the bed. The doorknob rattled. "Willa?" Signora Marcheschi! Willa stood up, dizzy. "Willa!"

She unlocked the door. Signora Marcheschi looked her up and down, stopping at her grimy feet. "There are dirty footprints on the stairs, and you haven't fed the chickens."

Willa felt something rise up within her, something larger than concern for what happened to her or to her baby, something black and red and wild, born of unbounded disappointment, grief, and now rage. She advanced toward her mother-in-law, her body taut, ready to spring. Her voice, low and even, came from a previously unknown place within her. "Get someone with a bigger dowry to clean your filthy house and go feed the damn chickens yourself." Signora Marcheschi held her position in the doorway. "Gabriele promised that I would be able to paint when we got married. He lied to me."

"He should have told you that we can't afford an artist. We need your help just so we can live as well as we did before we had to feed you."

"Your life has made you old and mean. Why would I give up mine for yours?"

"You already have." Signora Marcheschi closed the door behind her. Willa picked up her shoes and threw them against the door with all of the strength she had left. Long black streaks marked the whitewashed wood. Dust floated in the air.

19

The handful of coins Willa had left amounted to less than a few lire, and Gabriele had already spent the check from her parents on a tractor. *If I had enough money of my own, I could start over—perhaps in Paris or Rome or London. But in Orvieto?* Suddenly, she had an idea. She remembered the tourists from that morning, the ones in the big car who wanted to buy wine. *We could sell it to them.* She turned her purse upside down and shook it. Mr. Bradshaw's card fell out along with a handkerchief, a pen, some aspirin, and a lipstick in a color she disliked. She picked up the business card, turned it over. On the back she wrote, "100 cases, immediate shipment, cash" and put the card in her pocket.

When Gabriele returned from the vineyards, he found Willa waiting for him. Smiling, she kissed him. "I want to talk to you about our plans," she said.

"Plans?"

"For expanding the business…and our family, too." She rubbed her slightly rounded belly. Gabriele smiled."I met a group of tourists on their way to the Duomo today," she continued, "and one stopped to ask me where to buy wine—'a lot of it,' he said. I had to tell him that there was no place in the entire town of Orvieto because all the winemakers are out in the countryside. I said that we would sell him as much wine as he wanted. Look, here's his card." She took Bradshaw's card out of her pocket and handed it to Gabriele.

"We don't have a hundred cases. Anyway, he has an address in Firenze. He can get as many cases as he wants there." Gabriele crumpled the card and dropped it on the table.

"But we *could*," she said. She picked up the card and unfolded it.

"We could have even *more* than a hundred cases and we could *sell* to him and to people like him before they buy their wine from someone else. If we had a shop in town, *we could sell our wine.* Wine from other *poderi,* too. And we could make a profit, which we don't do now."

Her enthusiasm pleased Gabriele. He laughed. "What do you know about selling so much wine, my little bird?"

"I know that you are going to be the most successful winemaker in this region…in all of Italy." Willa touched her belly. "Besides, we must to do everything we can for our family." Gabriele didn't answer, but after dinner when Grazia served the fruit, Gabriele told his father that Vino Marcheschi must open an office and shop on the Piazza del Duomo to reach "the tourist trade." Willa sat nearby, pretending to embroider baby clothes.

"I've never heard of this 'tourist trade,'" said the elder Marcheschi. "What tourist buys a hundred cases of Orvieto? It's not even good wine."

"We could make it good, just like the old Orvieto," Gabriele said. They talked long after dinner.

"How would you manage this shop?" Signor Marcheschi asked. "It's too far away."

"We'd have to live there," Gabriele said.

"*Sono d'accordo,*" Signor Marcheschi said. I agree. "It would be the only way to handle this new business idea of yours," inclining his head in Willa's direction. "Perhaps it would be good for your family, too."

Gabriele nodded. "I think we can improve the vintage."

"You have an excellent mind for business, *figliolo.*"

It was well past 2:00 a.m. when Gabriele came to bed. "As soon as you find a place for us to live, we'll move into town," he told Willa. "My father approves of my idea." After Gabriele fell asleep, Willa slipped out of bed and wrote a letter to her parents:

*…and we hope to have a home of our own in town before our
baby comes, one with a real toilet inside and a sink with running
water, though most people here consider such things luxuries.*

All my love,
Willa

The next morning she took her letter to the post office while Gabriele waited for her outside.

The clerk examined the address. "This letter is going to America." "Yes, to my parents."

"I want to go to America one day," the clerk said. He leaned toward her and whispered, "Signora Marcheschi, do you think your parents could help me?"

Later, Willa and Gabriele called on Alvaro, the accountant, who had inherited a storefront on the Piazza del Duomo. The space had been vacant for twenty-three years since the death of Alvaro's wife. Although people believed Alvaro to be very wealthy, the mottled walls of his tiny office had not been whitewashed for decades and the planking on the floors had shrunk and separated. Spider webs hung in the corners near the ceiling. Dirt obscured the light from the two small windows. A frayed electrical wire snaked up the back wall, slithered across the ceiling, and ended in a bare bulb just above a dusty wooden desk where Alvaro sat on an old, wooden office chair with broken springs. Alvaro acknowledged Willa and Gabriele with a wave of his hand, but remained seated, cleaning his fingernails with a nail. So completely had he merged with his surroundings that, except for his sharp eyes, he appeared to be one with his office.

"I'm expanding my business, I need new space immediately," Gabriele told him.

"Today isn't a lucky day to show property," Alvaro told Gabriele.

"But this is very important," Gabriele said. Alvaro put the nail in a drawer and listened to Gabriele describe "my plan to capitalize on the tourist trade. Along with my wife, of course." Gabriele winked.

Alvaro chuckled and rubbed his hands together. "It's a good idea. I'll make you a good deal." He extracted a key from the top drawer of his desk and a can of oil from underneath. "I think this day will be *fortunato* for you." He glanced at Willa. "And your wife."

The lock on the storefront had frozen from disuse. Alvaro squirted oil into the keyhole and on the hinges. The oil ran down the door and puddled on the ground. Alvaro turned the key and pushed the door open. Inside, cobwebs hung in sheets. Alvaro brushed them aside. Vermin droppings crunched under their feet as they walked through the rooms. Willa coughed. There were three rooms downstairs, one of which could be divided into a storeroom and a bathroom, leaving one for a showroom and one for an office for Gabriele. Upstairs, there was room for a kitchen, a bedroom, a small studio, and a baby's room. *It's large enough, especially by Orvieto's standards, but could it ever be clean enough for a baby?* Willa wondered.

The three went outside to talk. "You can pay by the month," Alvaro said. "I'll make the rent very reasonable." He locked the door and held the key in his hand as if he intended to give it to them that afternoon.

"Buy it," Willa whispered to Gabriele. Once Alvaro understood that Willa and Gabriele wanted to buy his storefront, which until that very afternoon he had considered worthless, it became so valuable to him that he could not bring himself to agree on a price. Weeks passed. Each time Gabriele made a new offer, Alvaro increased his price or changed his terms. Sometimes he agreed to a particular deal, but quickly found something to dislike, something that felt to him *ingiusto*, unfair. Meanwhile, Willa's belly grew, and the baby kicked furiously.

Just days before their baby was due, Willa went to the post office where she found an envelope from her parents. It contained a large money order: *For our grandchild with all of our love,* the note inside said. Without hesitation, Willa walked to Alvaro's office and stepped up to the open door. Even at midday the room was in permanent dusk.

"Buongiorno, Signor Alvaro," Willa said to him. Alvaro's lips moved slightly, but he neither looked up at her nor acknowledged her presence. He got up, apparently to search for something. Willa saw the stack of papers on his desk, most of them yellowed except for the paper on top, the letter with Gabriele's most recent offer. Alvaro opened the rusty file

cabinet under the windows and took out more yellowed papers. "I've come to conclude the sale on the property," she said.

"All in good time, Signora Marcheschi." He returned to his chair with the papers.

"I wish to conclude the sale now before my baby arrives." She needed to sit down, but there was no other chair. Alvaro wrinkled his brow and sniffed like an animal downwind of a hunter.

"Your husband must decide these things, Signora."

"Gabriele has made you several offers, and now I've come to make you a final one." She quoted the amount of her parents' check, an amount much greater than Alvaro and Gabriele had ever discussed. "But only if we write out our agreement now and only if you sign it and make no further changes." Alvaro looked at the papers on his desk and shook his head.

"A wife's place is with *la famiglia*."

"If I leave without an agreement, our offer ends forever." She waited. She felt a change deep in her belly. "Am I to have a place for my baby or not?" Alvaro looked down.

"It is not possible. Only a husband can buy property."

"It's my money and my offer. Will you sell the property to me or not?" She found it difficult to stand and put her hand on his desk to steady herself. Alvaro drew back slightly and looked at her. "Signora, a woman cannot buy property."

"Signor, we have little time, and it's in your interest to sell to us." Willa felt a strong pain in her belly. "Why are you delaying?"

Alvaro shrugged. "Signora, what would people think?"

"They will think that you sold us your building that you aren't using." He shook his head.

"Why not?" she said.

"They would say I sold to *la straniera*. You're not one of us."

Willa looked Alvaro straight in the eye, something she knew people in Orvieto considered too bold in a young woman. "Then why didn't you sell to Gabriele?"

Alvaro held out his arms to her like a beggar. "Signora, my father was born in that place. Myself also. My wife and I, we lived there when we were young. Our children were born there. When my wife was still young, she died there." He paused and drew his shirtsleeve across his face. "A terrible thing, the eyes of my children when they saw her. I'll always remember." He seemed to regain control of himself. "I cannot bear to live there," he said, "but what would I do if I sold you my memories? If I could not say 'the place of all that I have loved is still mine'?"

"I withdraw the offer." As Willa stepped out the doorway, she had to shut her eyes against the blinding sun.

"Signora, watch out!" Alvaro called out.

When Willa opened her eyes, Alvaro was above her, the bright blue sky above him. Two people stood behind him, violet statues. Who were they? She wished they would stop looking at her.

"Signora, you fell," one of the statues said.

"I didn't. I'm fine," She pushed herself up. She was sitting on the street, on the Corso.

Alvaro pointed to her leg. "Signora Marcheschi. You fell. See?" She looked down at a large splinter protruding from her skinned knee. Alvaro pulled it out and showed it to her.

"Call Dr. Lucarelli," said one of the statues.

"No!" she said. "Not Dr. Lucarelli." Willa felt something strong in her belly, something biting her from the inside. Involuntarily, she held her belly, then struggled to her feet, her head swirling. Still another bite in her belly made her gasp.

"What is it, Signora? Are you all right?" Alvaro said.

Willa turned on him. "If anything happens to my baby, it will be your fault." She limped a few steps and then doubled up in pain.

"Signora, let me help you," Alvaro said.

"Help me? You've done everything you could to hurt me and our baby!"

"No, Signora Marcheschi. I would never hurt you or your baby."

"Look at me! I'm covered with blood. I can't walk. I'm in terrible pain. You've refused us a place to live again and again even though we've made you many generous offers. What kind of person are you?" Willa gasped and doubled over.

"Forgive me, Signora Marcheschi. I didn't mean to." Their exchange continued, Willa accusing and Alvaro apologizing, until Alvaro could no longer bear the idea that he was the cause of Willa's suffering, the reason for her moans. "Please, Signora, I will sell my property to you. I will sign the offer now to prove to you and Gabriele that I haven't hurt you or your baby." Despite the intense pain in her belly, Willa took the offer from her purse and handed it to Alvaro. He signed it and gave it back to her. "Thanks be to God, Signora. Now, you will not suffer any more because of Alvaro." He looked heavenward and crossed himself. "May God forgive me, I've sold my property to a woman. To *la straniera.*"

"Take me home," Willa said. Alvaro obeyed.

The next morning, Alvaro congratulated Gabriele on the birth of his first child, a daughter named Silvana, and declared that he still intended to honor his contract even though it was only with a woman.

"I know it was really your offer," he said to Gabriele to avoid any misunderstanding. "Your wife did not seem herself after the fall," he added as if this information explained his unprecedented decision to sell his property to her. "I didn't want to upset her when she was in such pain and not in her right mind."

In any case, people said that after Willa's fall that day outside Alvaro's office, she became a person who did things that no one else would think of doing. Buying Alvaro's property without her husband was just the beginning. In the years that followed, even after she became the mother of two more children, Raffaele and Ettore, it was understood that if you wanted to sell an empty building or a piece of land that produced nothing, Willa would buy it no questions asked. Even the authorities responsible for the transfer of property didn't ask. People simply said, "*La straniera*—that's how she is." They said Gabriele couldn't control his wife and that a man with a crazy wife does many things to keep the peace in his family, things other people didn't have to do. A husband could be excused for his actions under such difficult circumstances.

Of course, no one ever said these things to Gabriele himself or to Willa. Why cause trouble? One might want to sell Willa some property that no one else would buy or one might need Gabriele's help, a favor perhaps. It's better to smile and be polite, pretend nothing is out of place, get along. And this was how within a few years Gabriele and Willa became Orvieto's largest property owners.

20

ORVIETO, APRIL 1944

Willa lifted Ettore, their youngest child, onto her lap. In the background the radio buzzed with static, but she could still make out the cheers of the fascist Milanesi even though Mussolini had been deposed the previous summer. "You see? Mussolini is right," Signor Marcheschi said from behind a newspaper that was five days old. "*Tutto nello Stato, niente al di fuori dello Stato, nulla contro lo Stato*," Signor Marcheschi murmured. Everything in the State, nothing outside the State, nothing against the State. *He never tires of his slogans*, she thought. *What does Mussolini know about our sick baby?*

A week earlier *partigiani* moving north through Orvieto had described bloody German and Fascist defeats in the south. Behind the soldiers, refugees huddled along the roadsides as if all of Italy had gotten to its feet and filed north in a long, undulating line of misery. Orvieto itself had been bombed again only two days before, frightening everyone, especially the children, and entrance to the city could now be achieved only on foot. Fortunately, she and Gabriel and the children had moved out of the city several months earlier when the allied bombing of the nearby Allerona Bridge in late January had killed the allied prisoners of war who were on the train and left her terrified for herself and the children. *At least we still have food and a roof. How long until one army or another takes it?*

Willa drew her hand across Etto's forehead. He felt feverish. His eyes, usually bright, looked glazed and unfocused.

"Mussolini will return to power. We will have a Roman Italy. You'll see," Signora Marecheschi added. *"Viva il Duce."*

"Mussolini lied. Remember what the soldiers told us the other day?" Willa said before she could stop herself. She ignored her in-laws' disapproving looks and tried to interest Ettore in some tepid cereal. The baby took some from the spoon, then more. "Look. Etto ate some cereal. He's getting better." It had been nearly seven days. He was listless and no longer wiggled from her grasp or followed the older children squealing with delight. A few minutes later the child threw up on her skirt and began to cry. He pulled his legs in, his body stiff. Willa frowned. *"Tesoro!* Your tummy hurts, doesn't it? What are we going to do?" There was no one to consult. Dr. Lucarelli had gone into hiding after he had been taken for a *partigiano* by the Fascists and for a Fascist by the *partigiani.* In order to escape, he had had to lie in a ditch filled with sewage where he had pretended to be dead until after soldiers had finished looting his house and departed with his valuables.

"All patriots support Mussolini," said Signor Marcheschi. "Why would you listen to some deserters?" Willa almost welcomed this distraction from her worries about Ettore. Despite her constant efforts to feed him, he threw up everything he ate. *Could it be polio?* The image of a crippled Ettore passed through her consciousness, but she blinked it back and clamped her jaw against her fears. *"Boia chi molla."* Who gives up is a rogue.

She turned to her father-in-law. "What's Mussolini given real patriots, as you call them, besides empty speeches and endless war?"

"I don't have time to tell someone who doesn't want to know." Willa stiffened. It was Signor Marcheschi who didn't want to know. She struggled not to argue.

"The country is in ruins," she replied. "Surely you see that just as well as I can." *Have I gone too far, said too much again?* She had promised Gabriele not to discuss politics with his parents.

"La straniera!" Signora Marcheschi hissed. "It's the Americans and the others who bomb us and destroy our country, not Mussolini."

The baby gave a sharp cry. *Never mind. I must think of what to do for*

Etto, Willa reminded herself.

There had been other disagreements. "He's too young to go outside," Signora Marcheschi had said when Willa allowed him to play outdoors with Silvana and Raffaele. Etto was no longer an infant. He had started to walk. Besides, sunshine is good for children, Willa had said. Signora Marcheschi dismissed these views as "something only *la straniera* would believe." *Had he caught something while he was playing outside with Silvana and Raffaele? The older children loved to carry him around with them. What could be dangerous about that? Besides, they had all worn their sweaters and what was left of their shoes and socks.*

"The *malocchio* is still on the child." Willa overheard Signora Marcheschi talking to Grazia. *Why do they always talk about the evil eye whenever anyone is sick?* The two women watched the fussy infant, but Willa knew Signora Marcheschi's comment was intended for her because she had resisted Grazia's efforts to sprinkle salt on Etto to remove the *malocchio.*

"Fire straightens crooked wood," Grazia replied, hinting darkly at unknown trials. Gabriele's mother nodded. *Was burning one of Grazia's cures, too?*

Willa kissed the baby and kept her fears and doubts inside. Although she had promised Gabriele that she wouldn't argue with his parents no matter what they said, she had decided not to give in to their superstitions or their provincial attitudes. It was an uneasy but serviceable peace formed in the aftermath of the difficult times early in their marriage and made manageable because Gabriele and Willa had moved into town years earlier. Gabriele's mother still had not forgiven Willa for refusing to wear her wedding dress or for bringing *disonore* to the family by coming to Orvieto without a chaperone.

Wounded by the rejection of her in-laws and the community, Willa had still found happiness in her marriage to Gabriele, albeit of a different kind than she had anticipated. In her diary she wrote:

Marriage evolves and changes. One finally learns to love reality...or at least accept it. Gabriele is a devoted husband, and our children are an endless joy. There's so little time to paint or even sketch since they were born...perhaps later... but for now, dear God, it's this endless war.

Willa felt Ettore's arms. They had lost their familiar solidity and round-
edness. The energy of his plump body, which had always delighted her,
now seemed restrained, like water in a faucet that is constricted by lime
deposits. The child tightened his legs against his belly. His thighs looked
thin, too. When she lifted him from her lap, he seemed lighter. She wasn't
sure. Perhaps it was simply that he didn't wiggle and kick the way he usually did. *Sometimes movement can feel like weight.* She wanted so much
to believe he hadn't changed.

The baby settled into her lap, his limbs flaccid, then whimpered and
pulled his legs up again with a sudden cry. She looked into his brown
eyes, searching for their usual sparkle, but found them dulled, as if a
scrim had been drawn over them; their darkened rims made them seem as
if they had receded. She saw in his eyes a new absence, as if Ettore had
wandered away from her, withdrawn to a place that she could see, but
not reach, a place where she couldn't protect him. The two older children
crowded around her.

"Can we play with Etto now?" Silvana asked, hopping on one foot
around Willa's chair. Willa shook her head and held her finger to her lips.
Perhaps, if Silvana and Raffaele were quiet, Etto would go to sleep and
wake up well.

Grazia handed her a cup of tea and a spoon and nodded at the baby.
"*La camomilla* is good for babies."

"Later, Silvana," Willa whispered taking the tea. "Etto needs to sleep.
You and Raffaele can play outside for now, but don't go near the lane in
front. There may be soldiers out there." She rocked the child. Perhaps
they could still find a doctor at the hospital, though the younger doctors,
the ones who had trained in Milano or Bologna, had gone to the front
months before, leaving only two or three elderly nuns from the convent
hospital in Orvieto to tend the sick and wounded. She had heard that there
was a doctor in Arezzo. Ettore whimpered. "We must go to Arezzo and
find that doctor for you," she told Etto as she spooned the tea into his
mouth. He took it quickly as if he were very thirsty, but then jerked away
from her and cried out again. He retched, but brought nothing up.

"Can't you drink, either, *tesoro?*" Willa felt his forehead. "He's very hot." No one seemed to hear. She got up, moistened a cloth, and wiped the baby's face and hands. Raffaele and Silvana cooed to him. Around noon, Gabriele returned from town with a large package and several letters. "*Sfolatti* everywhere!" he said. Refugees. "There isn't enough room for all of them. They're like cattle. They've built campfires in the Piazza. The hotels, the schools, the convent—all full. Even the churches have closed. It's impossible to go anywhere. I only got into the post office because they know me. I couldn't leave until after the German soldiers had passed by. Everyone is frightened. You must keep the children inside."

"We must get to Arezzo and find a doctor for Etto," Willa said. "He's worse and he seems to be in pain."

"Let Grazia take care of him. She knows what to do," Gabriele said. "Babies are always sick. It will pass if you'll stop fussing over him. He just wants the attention," Signora Marcheschi nodded in agreement.

The baby lay still in Willa's arms, his eyes wide and glassy. "Etto needs to go to the hospital. He's very sick. Something is terribly wrong."

Gabriele glanced at the child. "There's no one there to take care of him. No one can get in or out of Orvieto. He'll be better in a few days."

"This is different." Willa put Ettore in the crib that she kept in the living room and gave him a toy, hoping that he would go to sleep. He tried to raise his arms to her, failed, and cried softly. "I heard that the doctor in Arezzo is still there."

"The road is blocked," Gabriele told her. "No one can get through. And they said in town that the Allies have bombed Arezzo, too." Ettore cried out and then lay whimpering softly, a sound that seemed as much an expression of bewilderment as of pain.

"God and Mussolini will take care of the children," Signora Marcheschi said, waving her arm. *"Vincere e vinceremo."* To win, and we shall win.

Willa picked up the child and gave him another toy. He groaned softly. "But we must try."

"If he's not better by morning...," Gabriele said. Willa knew Gabriele wouldn't seek a doctor even then. He believed that time and Grazia's so-called medicine resolved everything, especially a child's illness, as though it were a matter of the turning of the clock or a change of season. "I'll have to take Etto to Arezzo by myself." She handed Ettore to Gabriele and unplugged the radio. "There's no real news, anyway." She hid radio in the back of a low cupboard. German soldiers always demanded radios. They used the parts in their own equipment or bartered them on the black market for a few lire to get cigarettes.

"You just don't want to hear the truth," Signor Marcheschi said. *"Credere, obbedire, combattere."* Believe, obey, fight.

Willa opened her mouth to reply, but Gabriele put his finger to his lips and stopped her with a kiss. She stacked her art supplies in front of the radio, the ones she had scarcely used since Silvana's birth. It seemed to Willa that the pencils and paint, brushes and blocks of paper belonged to someone from another life, a life so unlike hers that she was unable to imagine it or aspire to it. With a fleeting sense of regret, she busied herself opening the package Gabriele had brought. It was from her parents, and she had been expecting it for weeks. It contained a box of fine soap wrapped in pleated tissue the color of a brown paper bag and smelled like carnations. They had remembered her favorite fragrance. There were other much-needed things, too: clothing for the children, shoes, canned soup, plus three small teddy bears and some crayons. Willa checked the stitching on the teddy bears and squeezed them feeling for money inside. She wasn't sure. Tonight, after the children went to sleep, she would cut the bears open, look for money, then sew them up before the children awakened. She gave one of the bears to Ettore. He let it fall on the floor. There had been more in the box, but an inspector had opened it first and crossed out certain items on the customs list in heavy black ink and stamped *"Proibito"*—forbidden—in red next to the marked-out items.

"Probably cigarettes," Willa said. "Customs agents are thieves. We're lucky to get what we did."

"Cigarettes aren't *proibite*," said Signora Marcheschi. "The black market is illegal. The inspectors are just doing their job."

"They take whatever they can to sell on the black market," Willa replied in a tone that betrayed her impatience with her mother-in-law's Fascist sympathies.

Signora Marcheschi took the newspaper from her husband and spread it on the kitchen table. She put some hardened bread unfit to eat in the center of the paper along with the end piece of the very dry salami that she had made the previous spring. Next, she took off her gold earrings and put them on the table, tore a scrap from an old dishtowel, wrapped the earrings in it, and then set it next to the salami and bread. On top of the pile she put a few lire from a ceramic jar she kept on the kitchen shelf along with her marriage and baptism certificates. "*Basta!*" Enough. "I never put too much in one place."

Since the allied march north had begun, Signora Marcheschi had hidden many of her things from passing soldiers by burying them around the Marcheschi property. She made a list of what was in the pile on the counter, folded the paper, and put it inside her dress with her other lists. With a length of string she tied the newspaper around the pile and put the package in a scarred wooden box the exterior of which had once been painted with the images of the three graces. She closed the hinged lid, locked the box with a key, and tied the key onto a black ribbon that already held several other keys. Then, she put the ribbon around her neck and dropped it inside her dress, too.

"If they think you've buried supplies, the Germans will execute all of us and dig until they find them," Willa told her mother-in-law as she removed the pleated paper from the soap. "Give me a knife." Grazia handed her a paring knife. Willa cut into the side of one of the bars. It split open without effort. "There it is," Willa said, pulling out a sheaf of bills. She imagined her father working on the concealment, perhaps with the help of his friend, a dentist, who had special tools suited for such exacting deception. "Let's see what's inside the others."

"Thanks be to God, Mussolini has taken care of us." Signora Marcheschi said. She crossed herself.

"If that were true, then why do you bury your food and valuables?"

"Santo cielo!" Signora Marcheschi waved as if she were swatting a fly. "Now that you have money in your pocket, no one can say anything when you're around." She unlocked the wooden box and added some matches, two pairs of socks, and a small doll that belonged to Silvana. The little girl shrieked and rushed for the box.

"Wait, *cara.* This way it will be here for you when the soldiers leave," Signora Marcheschi said. Silvana wailed, but her grandmother ignored her. "Gabriele, come help me dig." She smiled through brownish teeth. Willa hugged the sobbing child, who pointed to her small shovel and bucket and then renewed her cries when she was not allowed to help with the digging either.

"It's a secret," Signora Marcheschi said to her. "No one must know, *cara.*" Willa stood with Silvana, watching through the window as Gabriele excavated a new hole in the soft soil near the compost pile. When the hole was nearly three feet deep, Signora Marcheschi put the box into it and waited while Gabriele shoveled the dirt on top and tamped the soil down. When they had finished, Gabriele and his mother scattered leaves and other debris over the ground. Around the property, Willa could see the sunken outlines of other burial spots containing Signora Marcheschi's secrets. At night, feral dogs sometimes smelled the buried food and tried to dig it up, necessitating daily reburials. This time would be no different.

"I hate *nonna,*" Silvana said. Willa kissed her.

"Let's find you a teddy bear just like Etto's."

"Does she really think soldiers would want her old salami?" Willa said to Gabriele when he returned.

"If it makes her feel better, what difference does it make what she buries or why? You promised to leave her alone." Ettore woke up and whimpered in the crib, but this time he didn't stand up or call for Willa as he usually did.

"I don't give a damn what she does," Willa said, "as long as the rest of us aren't executed for withholding supplies from the soldiers." She picked the baby up. He felt even warmer than when he had gone to sleep.

She took his temperature. The child lay limply in her arms with his eyes closed. Willa checked the thermometer. "It's just over a hundred and four American. We must find a doctor now."

"It's nearly dark," Gabriele said. "It's too dangerous to go out."

"Soldiers will understand about babies. I'll make them understand."

"No, they won't. They shot a woman who went out after curfew to get milk for her children."

"This is an emergency." She handed the baby to Gabriele and put on her sweater.

"Willa, there's no place to go. The road is gone. The bridge, too. It's cold. Going out will only make him worse. You're a mother. Think of your child."

"Then you must find a doctor who will come here."

"Willa, there are no doctors. We have to do our best." Willa took Ettore from Gabriele and carried him into the kitchen where she laid him on a towel on the kitchen counter and took off his clothes and his diaper.

"He's been dry all day," she said. Ettore's lips looked like wrinkled paper. She washed him with cool water and gave him several teaspoons of fresh water. He swallowed the water and vomited almost immediately. She smiled at him and held his hands in hers, examining them, touching his fingers one by one, as if each were new to her, the fingernails, thin, like the papery layer of rice paper on the *torrone*, the white moons taking up nearly half of each nail. She turned his hands over, running her finger across each of the knuckles, seeking the absent dimples. She touched his forehead. His eyelids fluttered, but remained closed. Then, he opened his eyes and looked into hers.

"Here, Etto here," he said softly. It was a game they played with each other.

"Here, mamma here," Willa said to him. She laughed and ran her fingers through his dark curls, noticed that they were no longer shiny or lively. She remembered a lullaby and sang it to him. The muscles of his abdomen tensed making a small dome, but he didn't cry out. Perhaps, he's in less pain now. He shivered. She saw the goosebumps on his legs and arms and dressed him quickly. When she tried to swaddle him in a blanket, he resisted, opening his eyes and pushing at the blanket with one hand.

"Caldo," he said. Hot. She touched his forehead again. She could feel the heat of his body even when she held her hand just above him. His skin looked dry and yellowed. *It must be the poor light in here.* She gathered him in her arms and sat down. With one hand she touched his chest softly. Through his shirt, she felt the hardness of his stomach and the racing of his heart. She watched the synchronous pulsing at his temples, heard his short, quick breaths. At last, he seemed to relax and go to sleep. She sat with him in the rocking chair, rocking him back and forth.

"Let him sleep in his crib," Gabriele said. "That way both of you can rest."

"I want to hold him." Though Gabriele and the others urged her to sleep while Ettore slept, Willa refused. The hour grew late. Everyone went to bed, leaving her alone with the child. As the hours passed, she continued to rock him, felt the pulsing in his chest. From time to time he writhed in her lap, then lapsed back into her arms. Late in the night, she thought that his pulse felt slower beneath her fingertips. She could not be sure, but he seemed to be resting more comfortably. Just before dawn, she, too, dozed. With a start, she awakened from a dream in which Ettore stood before her, waving goodbye. She looked down. He lay still in her lap. She placed her hand on his chest. She felt nothing. She listened for his breath. *He's just asleep.* In the dawning light, she saw that Ettore's skin had become pale, almost colorless. She touched him. At last, he felt cool. *Finally, his fever has broken. He'll be well soon.* She carried him to the window. He remained still in her arms. She touched his face, his arms. His skin felt stiff, unyielding. She shook him lightly, waiting for him to stir.

"Etto," she whispered, "Here. Mamma here." She touched his face and his lips with hers. He remained still, his skin unnaturally cool. She pinched his toes. Shook him. Again. Harder. "Gabriele," she shrieked. "Gabriele." Her calls aroused the family. One by one they gathered around her. She held Ettore close. "He doesn't move anymore."

They shook their heads, looked at one another. Grazia crossed herself. "Against death no house is strong enough."

"See what you've done to my Etto." Willa held the tiny corpse in her arms and wept uncontrollably. "Now he's dead." She rocked the bundle in her arms.

"Willa, don't," Gabriele said. He knelt down beside her, reached for her hand.

"Why didn't you listen to me?"

"Etto is my son, too," Gabriele said, weeping. "He's my son, too."

"You abandoned us when we needed you." She looked around wild eyed, seeing nothing, and shrieked, long high-pitched cries.

"What could I do?" Gabriele asked her.

"I curse you for all time. I curse all of you and your ignorance." She sobbed. "My innocent Etto. You let him die. I curse your soul and the God who made you." She looked at them as from an abyss, no longer caring what happened.

"Call Father Enrico," said Signora Marcheschi. She wrapped a shawl around Willa's trembling shoulders. Willa threw it off. Then Signora Marcheschi brought Willa some tea.

"Get away from me," Willa said through her tears. "Now do you see? This is how your damn Mussolini takes care of the children!"

21

Father Enrico was away. Some said that he had been captured because of his work with the resistance. Another priest came to say the prayers. Afterwards, Willa held Ettore's body until evening, until Gabriele and his father had finished making a coffin, until Signora Marcheschi and Grazia had lined it with soft, blue fabric cut from ragged blankets. Only then did Willa let go of Ettore and allow Gabriele to put him inside the box. She covered him with his favorite blanket and put the new teddy bear next to him, those things only because she couldn't think of anything else. Afterwards, they lit the candles that would burn all night. Willa sat beside him in the rocking chair, her hand covering Etto's hand.

The following morning Gabriele and his father went to the Marcheschi family graveyard at the top of the hill just beyond their vineyard. There they dug the grave among the weeds that had grown up around the markers. When they returned, Willa went outside long enough to gather the few wildflowers she could find, and then Gabriele and his father carried the coffin to the grave. Behind them the family followed in a single line. It was nearly afternoon before Willa allowed them to put Ettore's coffin into the ground. On top of it she dropped the flowers she had gathered, then lifted the first shovelful of dirt herself and tossed it onto the top of Etto's coffin. After the burial, she placed the rest of the wilted flowers on the freshly turned earth. Everyone returned to the house except Willa, who remained next to Etto's grave until the stars moved across the black sky, until the nighttime cold enveloped her. She wrapped her arms around herself and shivered, observing herself from a distance as if she were someone else, unable to will the movement that would mean walking away from Etto and letting go of the thread that had connected them. What would she do without his small warm being next to her? His fingers caressing hers as he fell asleep? A slight breeze carried the smell of the fresh earth at her feet. The long grasses rustled nearby. A dog barked in the distance. She tested herself, the letting go, whether she could give him up, allow the thread to break, will it, will herself to let go. She reached down and took a handful of fresh dirt from the new grave and let it fall through her fingers.

"Here. Mamma here, Etto," she whispered to him. Then she said it aloud for the first time: "Goodbye, Etto. Goodbye." She let the dirt fall from her fingers. Tears poured from her closed eyes. She gasped at the memory of him, so large that it included all of her, leaving nothing of her separate from him. Beyond the broken thread, beyond the letting go, an abyss of loss closed in around her, cut her off from the person she had been just a few hours earlier. A few hours. So short a time, she thought. Just a day. She could still remember who she had been before, when Etto was alive. Minutes passed, one after the other, faster and faster. They would become hours, days, weeks, carrying Etto farther away from her, her away from him, expanding the time and the distance between them, lengthening the thread that had bound them together until it broke, leaving her only a memory of him, a memory that would inevitably become a story about what never happened, a catalog of what never was, until Etto would be utterly and finally and always lost to her. She reached down and took another handful of dirt. She would keep some to remember this day as it really was. Again, she let the dirt tumble from her fingers.

At last, Willa stood up and brushed her dress off. Dirt and pebbles fell softly onto the ground. Her chest felt crushed, unresponsive to breath. She heard gunfire in the distance, but she neither desired nor sought shelter. The image of Silvana and Raffaele's round eyes as they stood holding hands, looking at Ettore's casket came to her, but they, too, felt as distant to her as her own heart. She heard noises on the road and unfamiliar voices from the direction of the vineyards. Probably soldiers. The sounds grew nearer. The thought of going to Gabriele for solace or to comfort him opened within her a river of grief, a torrent that carried her beyond any act of her own choice and swept away all that they had been to one another. Her eyes blurred. Could she pretend a life with Gabriele that no longer existed?

A dog barked next to her. "What are you doing here?" The soldier stood in front of her with a lantern in one hand. He held it up next to her face. He was young. In the glow she saw that he had a round face and large eyes. Curls tumbled out from under his cap. Would Ettore have become a soldier, too? "Answer me. What are you doing out here?"

"Waiting. Waiting with my son."

"It's after curfew. I have orders to shoot." He unslung his rifle. "Where is he hiding, your son? Tell him to come out."

"There." She pointed at Ettore's fresh grave.

The soldier kicked at the dirt. "You don't belong here," he said. "I have orders to shoot."

"I won't leave him out here alone."

"Go. Before it's too late."

"He was just a little more than a year. A baby. He still had curls like yours." The soldier put his hand on her shoulder.

"Go home or I'll arrest you."

"I don't care."

"Go! Now!"

Willa stumbled over the broken stones toward the road, careless of whether she fell or whether the soldier emptied his gun into her body, a bit of matter in a dark universe caroming off the blank walls of an empty galaxy.

22

How does one measure grief? How to measure something that lacks dimension, shape, consciousness of itself, consumes itself only to propagate itself anew, creating a larger blackness than before, infinite in its absence and its presence, lacking beginning, middle, end, height, or depth. Although Willa continued to attend to the older children, she moved in silent abstraction within the family, scarcely noticing anyone. When the War ended more than a year later, there was no relief, no change. Merely emptiness. *We survived, but for what?*

Willa became a familiar figure at the Duomo. Wrapped in a black shawl, she often sat alone in St. Britius' Chapel, while outside the cathedral, where Allied bombs had once fallen, the Orvietani undertook the task of rebuilding their town and their lives. Many days, she walked from the Duomo beyond the walls of the city by way of the necropolises, past the newly planted vineyards, and beyond to the Marcheschi family cemetery where she sat next to Etto's grave.

"Mamma here," she whispered to Etto each time, letting the dirt and stones sift through her fingers, careless of whether the sun shone or whether it rained, careless of whether it was day or night, careless of whether her family expected her or not. At other times, she sorted through Etto's clothing, his toys, touching them, smelling them. Days became months, and months turned to a year, then two, then another. One day, after she returned from Etto's grave, she spoke to Gabriele for the first time in weeks: "Today, I couldn't remember Etto's smile or the color of his hair."

The end of Willa's ability to recall how Etto looked also marked the end of her connection to Orvieto. "I can't bear it here any longer," she told Gabriele. "I want to take the children and go to America."

"Go, then, but I won't allow you to take my children away from me."
Willa wasn't surprised. She knew Italian law was on his side. Even if she
had wanted him to go with her, he wouldn't have agreed to leave Oriveto,
and Gabriele knew Willa would never leave without her children. Thus,
they continued to live together outwardly, while little by little, Willa recalled herself to herself. Smaller withdrawals accumulated, became mutual, and eventually formed the greater part of their marriage, creating a
distance between them that was insurmountable. They became strangers
to one another. They became *stranieri*.

II. MICHEL LOSINE

1

ORVIETO, NOVEMBER 1947

At noon on a Friday in the beginning of November 1947, Michel Losine stood alone in the Piazza del Duomo holding a black umbrella over his head. Memories of his earlier visits to Orvieto with Greta and their friends flooded over him. In the years before their son Paul was born, they had often gone on amiable excursions into the Italian countryside. Orvieto had been among their favorite places "to drink history," as they had told one another, and to fulfill their intention "to live fully and joyously."

Losine and Greta had come to Orvieto by themselves for the first time in 1934, not long after their wedding. It had rained then, too, Losine recalled. They had paused on the steps outside the Duomo, earnest in their sturdy shoes and khaki hats. He had grown up in Brussels, she in Munich, and had met in Milan as university students, married there, and remained. He worked as a jeweler and a dealer in gems, she as a researcher in archaeology specializing in Etruscan civilizations, including the one that had once flourished in Orvieto. The following year, 1935, they had returned to Orvieto after Greta had become pregnant.

"Stand under the statue of the Virgin," Losine had told her as he prepared to take her photograph. His camera was new, a very expensive Leica, her birthday gift to him. "I want us to remember us together here in our favorite place."

"After lunch, I need to make some notes on the necropolises," she had said.

"You must be careful now, my darling. The paths are not well kept." He had held her hand and kissed it, for she was his treasure. There had been a light wind that he had experienced as a kind of threat, but he had banished the feeling, though he still remembered this one detail, now, years later. Rain always stirred his memories. Sometimes he grew confused, lost track of what had happened first, second, and so on, sometimes even of what had happened to Greta, to Paul, and the others. And then, as always, what happened suddenly returned to him: they were gone, gone forever. Swift, dark clouds coalesced overhead. He felt another twinge in his right leg.

Crossing the Piazza, he went into the bar at the Hotel Maitani. He was the only customer. *Well, it's still early.* He removed his gray topcoat and set it down on a chair next to him. The coat of exceptionally fine alpaca had been a gift for his assistance in reuniting the maker with the latter's missing fiancée. He placed his cane on the coat and sat down heavily, taking care to extend his leg so it it didn't swell or become numb. He declined the waiter's offer to store his bag. *No reason to take a chance on losing one's valuables among strangers.* Inside the bag was a fine Hasselblad camera, which he had recently removed from the account of a German client when the latter failed to pay for Losine's services which had included moving a large amount of cash to a numbered Swiss bank account.

"Coffee and some brandy," Losine said to the waiter. He stubbed out his cigarette in the tin ashtray and rubbed his leg again, an effort to counteract the pain behind and just above the knee. *It always aches, especially when it rains,* he thought. *Nothing to worry about.* He sipped his coffee and watched the water dribble down the windows, watched the puddles accumulate, remembering. As usual, images rose up to meet him, danced in front of him. *Memory endures. Nothing else.*

Munich. 1940. Just outside the window of the cafe, he had noticed right away a man in a sparrow-colored coat, his eyes intense, curious. The man had been leaning against a lamppost in the middle of the morning as if he had nothing else to do. Although Losine had known that a warrant was to be issued for his own arrest that morning, Losine had decided he must nevertheless go through with his next appointment with a local police commander of middling importance. It was possible the latter had information about the fate of Greta and Paul and Greta's parents. He couldn't forego the possibility of learning for certain what had happened to them, no matter what the risks might be. Losine went outside where he could see the address on the building across the street and compared it to the number on a piece of paper he took from his pocket. "That's the place, if you're looking for the neighborhood police," the man said to him. Losine stepped back involuntarily, hesitated, and then continued across the street to the address he had been given and entered. He wondered when—if — he would come out.

Inside, the commander, a corpulent man with a thin, uneven mustache, greeted Losine with a hearty handshake—Losine noted the soft ness of his hand—and ushered him into his sparse, grey office; he looked both ways before closing the door and took care to turn the lock. Standing in front of the commander's desk, Losine wondered again whether he would ever leave the room. This would have to be his last contact for a while, that much was certain.

"So, we are ready for our business," the commander said, handing Losine a brown leather bag. Losine opened the bag, shook the contents out onto the coal-colored blotter on the desk. He set the bag aside, and leaned over the desk, resting his weight on long, delicate fingers as he considered the sparkling pile: diamond earrings with ruby centers the size of currants; gold necklaces, one with emeralds set in a meadow of diamonds; a platinum ring with a marble-sized sapphire; scattered wedding bands; strands of gold and silver; humble turquoises, charm bracelets attesting to a love of grandchildren, horses, music, flowers, unicorns. The commander breathed noisily next to him. Losine could see the hairs of the commander's mustache moving as he exhaled and wondered fleetingly whether the commander might be the sort of man who would wear women's undergarments under his carefully pressed uniform.

Losine returned his attention to the jewels in front of him. "With your permission, I'll make an inventory." He reached for his briefcase, unlocked it, and opened the lid. Inside, papers lay in neat stacks like a display in a stationery store window.

"Make two copies," the commander said. "I want a proper record. My collection is far better than the other officers'." He folded his hands momentarily and then reached out to touch one of the glittering objects that lay in front of them. "Of course, you're the expert," he added, as if placating a too-strict father.

Losine moved some of the jewelry aside and looked more carefully. With a start, he recognized the brooch, its concentric petals of diamonds and pink tourmalines, their minute citrine centers. He had designed it for Greta himself. A wedding gift. Inwardly, he slammed into something large, hard, flat. Was he still alive or had he by mistake moved into what he had imagined to be the transition between life and death, a state in which he saw and heard and was conscious, but not? He sucked in his breath, coughed, and covered his mouth in an effort to disguise the trembling of his pale hands. He realized the commander was watching him.

"Is something wrong?" the commander asked. "You look upset. You don't think my jewels are real and you don't want to tell me. Is that it? My wife says it's all cheap costume jewelry. She says I never bring her anything good."

Losine cleared his throat, covered his mouth, and coughed again. "May I have some water, please?" He thought about the warrant. *How long would it be before the commander received word? Or had he already?* The commander unlocked the door, opened it slightly, but kept his foot against it.

"A carafe for my guest!" he said to an assistant. He turned back to Losine and pointed at the desk. "Cover those up." Losine took off his coat and put it over the jewels. The commander smiled at his assistant, took the carafe, and then closed the door and bolted it once more. He returned to his desk with the carafe, but his attention remained on the jewelry. "I want your honest opinion. You don't need to spare me the truth."

Losine moved his coat to a chair and picked up the brooch, held it in the clammy palm of his right hand. *A miracle to have found it! And the gold buttons with her initials, too. Perhaps Greta was nearby. Paul. Greta's parents.* He wanted to seize the brooch and the buttons, run from the dingy command post into the streets, call his family back to him at last.

"I believe in knowing the truth," he heard the commander saying. "It's one of my principles."

Losine roused himself into the present. "The diamonds appear quite fine." He rationed each word, containing himself, imitating the way one might speak when talking about pleasant weather or describing a brief holiday. "I can tell you that much, even without my glass."

A smile swept across the commander's plump face, filling his cheeks like a squirrel's."They *are* real, then! I knew it!" He gave a small clap of pleasure like a child who has been promised a toy. "I'll tell Hedda as soon as I get home."

"This is a very unusual piece." Losine said turning the brooch in his fingers, aware of the commander's black uniform and shiny boots, of the grey walls, the stale air, the black shade over the window. He felt the officer's warm breath near his neck

The commander touched the brooch with the tips of his fingers. "You're sure I can depend on its authenticity? I must be sure. May I tell Hedda that she was wrong?" he asked.

"There's a maker's mark on the back," Losine said. "May I ask where you obtained this piece?" Losine avoided looking at the commander when he spoke, afraid he would betray himself.

The commander eased closer to Losine as if to impart a confidence. "I call these my 'family pieces.'" He laughed pleasantly. "The 'relatives' who owned them left them to me."

"Left them to you?" Losine gasped. He knew that he must speak casually, calmly, knew he must remember that he was talking about business, not about Greta and Paul. Everything depended on it.

The commander leaned toward him, almost touching Losine's head with his own. "Deported," he whispered next to Losine's ear.

"Deported?" Losine thought he might have shouted.

The officer nodded vigorously. "Their parting gifts to me," he said as if they were sharing a good joke or a fine meal. "For my help. That one, for example," he said plucking the brooch from Losine's frozen hand, "wanted safe passage for her son back to Italy. Milano. I think that's where she said she lived." He turned the brooch over and over with his thick fingers and tossed it back into the pile like a piece of coal.

Losine's heart thrashed. *Grab the brooch and run away. No. I must not. No.* "They offered their jewelry in return for your help?" Losine felt as if he were choking. He reached for the water carafe. The commander settled back in his chair.

"Their jewelry. Their property. Themselves. Anything. But, of course, there was nothing I could do except to perform as my duty demanded." He smoothed his uniform and looked up at Losine. "Understand I'm just as patriotic as the next man. Of that you can be sure. So why shouldn't I enjoy the fruits of my loyalty?" Losine clenched his teeth to prevent them from chattering. "Surely, anyone would agree with that," the commander added. Losine coughed once and then again, avoiding speech, afraid of what he might reveal. "Do you agree with me?"

"Yes, of course," Losine heard himself say. "Clearly." The words caught in his mouth. He wondered if he had mispronounced them, like a drunk. Perhaps the commander knew nothing of the warrant, at least not yet. *I must leave immediately,* Losine thought.

"Take some more water," the commander said. "You're not ill, are you?" He looked closely at Losine from across the desk. "I don't want to catch anything. I'm a very busy man."

Losine clutched the glass. "No." His hands trembled. The water swayed over the rim of the glass and splashed onto the concrete floor. As Losine took out his linen handkerchief, the glass slipped from his fingers and shattered. "Forgive me. So clumsy."

The commander came around to Losine's side of the desk. "What a mess." He laughed and clapped Losine on the back. "I hope you don't handle all of your business this way." He paused. "If there's going to be a problem retrieving my money and my jewels after all this is over, I don't want to do it." Losine felt the commander's eyes on him as he mopped

up the spill. He picked up the shards of glass and put them in the recep-
tacle nearby. The sound of the glass hitting the inside of the dented metal
wastebasket echoed in the barren room. He ignored the drops on the commander's boots and stood up. "You're quite unsteady today. Perhaps Munich disagrees with you?" Losine stood up. "Where do you come from?"
"Brussels originally."

"I thought I detected an accent of some sort. What is your language?"

"In my work, I use English, German, French and Italian."

"Is that so? And are you a Jew, Herr Losine?"

"Are you a Christian, Herr Tugendbold?"

"Yes, you're quite right. What does it matter what we are as long as
we do our jobs?"

There was a knock at the door. Losine covered the jewels with his
coat. The commander opened the door, and his assistant handed him a
paper. He read it and dropped it on his desk. Losine realized that the
commander had forgotten his jewelry and was studying him, taking his
time, moving closer. Losine put his damp handkerchief in his pocket. He
tried see what was written on the paper, but the commander, following
Losine's gaze, turned it over.

"The weather, yes, very difficult," Losine said before he recalled
that the weather in Munich had been unseasonably mild for January, less
severe than the weather in Milan. "But, really, no, just an allergy from the
wind." *Had the wind been blowing?* He couldn't remember. "Nothing,
really, nothing at all." He extracted two sheets of paper and a carbon from
his briefcase. "Shall we finish our transaction?" The paper stuck to his
damp fingers. He reminded himself to smile, to hold the papers steady, to
put the carbon in correctly.

"You seem unwell." The commander's grin formed an uneven window around his teeth. His pink tongue grazed his upper lip and touched
his moustache. "I think you should leave as soon as possible. Before your
condition worsens." He studied Losine's briefcase, touched the lock.
"Tell me, how did you get into the smuggling business?" Losine ignored
the question.

"As a dealer in gems," Losine said, emphasizing the word *dealer*, "I would need to know more about this brooch to value it correctly." He willed his hand to write *Commander Dieter Tugendbold, Munich,* and the date at the top of the page.

"How do I know that you will keep my jewels and money for me in Switzerland?"

"It's a matter of trust."

"Yes, but how do I know I can trust you? After all, you're a smuggler." The commander paused, turned away. "What if you're just a thief? What if you don't know anything about jewelry?"

Careful. Keep it businesslike, Losine reminded himself. "I have already given you your numbered account at the bank in Switzerland that you have chosen. Your jewelry will be held for you in Zurich in a deposit box under your name. This is the service you requested and the one that I've agreed to provide for the fee that you've agreed to pay. This is how my business works. I work only by referral, so you must consider whether you trust the word of those who referred you to me. If you are uncomfortable, you are under no obligation to continue with our contract."

The commander looked startled. "Don't misunderstand me. I am quite comfortable. Still, I'd like to know for sure about the value of the jewelry first." The commander sat down on his battered office chair and took a breath. "Does it cost more for an appraisal, more than your usual fee, I mean?" He was sweating now. His brow glistened. "I don't want to pay extra fees. Hedda would never let me hear the end of it."

Losine willed a smile on his lips. "I could overlook my usual fee if you were to help me with something else."

"And that is?"

"Tell me anything you might know about several people," Losine said.

"They said you would have questions." The commander wiped his brow. His breathing sounded as if he were chewing the air as he inhaled.

"I've been asked to check on several people in Munich on behalf of their families in Italy," Losine said. "Perhaps you know of them." He took out a file from his briefcase and read from the cover sheet. "A certain Herr and Frau Bernstein, their daughter Greta, and their grandchild, Paul, it says here."

The commander stared at him through narrowed eyes. "Just how do you know these people?" His voice sounded loud and angry.

"I don't know them," Losine replied quickly. "I simply make inquiries. People give me the names of those whom they are concerned about and pay me a fee. One of my clients is concerned about the Bernstein family."

The commander stood up. "Who are you?" he shouted. "Do the authorities know what you're doing? That you're a smuggler?"

"I believe you understood the terms of our meeting and that you just agreed to them," Losine said evenly. "I'm not a smuggler. I deal in gems and have a license to do so."

The officer strode across the small office, then turned back to face Losine. "I can arrest you."

"For what?" *He knows about the warrant,* Losine thought.

The officer picked up a pen and tapped on his hand as he listed the reasons. "For making unauthorized inquiries, for spying, for smuggling, for being a Jew. For whatever I want." He took a form from his desk drawer and wrote Losine's name at the top.

"In that case, what shall I tell the authorities about your Swiss bank account and your stolen jewelry?"

The officer fell back in his chair. "What do you mean?"

"We both know it's forbidden to send cash and valuables out of the country. You've taken this jewelry from deportees. Their possessions are by law the property of the German government. You know that and so do I. As a dealer who is known to the authorities, I am allowed to carry such items out of the country. Or do I misunderstand our purpose?"

The commander put his pen down. He tore the form into pieces and dropped it in the wastebasket. "What is your interest in these people and their jewelry?" he said quietly.

"I am simply inquiring as to their whereabouts. You asked me to store this jewelry and you told me it belongs—or belonged—to others. Does it perhaps belong to the Bernsteins?"

"I don't know where they are." The commander turned toward the only window in the room. "The jewelry is mine. It belongs to me."

Losine took a folder out of his briefcase. "Would more information help you identify them?" On the desk he spread out pictures of his wife, son, and parents-in-law; a list of their names and birthdates; the Bernsteins' address in Munich. "Perhaps you could look at these." The commander glanced at the pictures and the list, then busied himself putting the jewelry back in the pouch.

"Do you recognize them?" Losine asked. After a long silence, the commander turned and looked at the pictures. He nodded, sweeping his hand over them.

"Yes."

"Do you know where they are?"

"I said they were deported."

"When?"

"They were taken from this neighborhood. It was several years ago."

"You don't remember when?" The commander didn't answer. "Although taking cash and jewelry out of the country is illegal, I've prepared your accounts according to the instructions you gave your intermediary," Losine continued. "Are you dissatisfied with our agreement or my services?"

The commander's body sagged. He turned back to Losine, his face empty. "Very well. It was 1937, and they're dead."

Losine forced himself to hear the information without understanding its meaning. He would think about the meaning later. For now, he would proceed mechanically, without emotion. "Where and how did they die?"

The commander looked down at his desk and then away. "At Dachau. The child immediately of typhus; his mother shortly after they arrived, also of typhus. Her mother soon after that, her father a bit later." He moved the papers on his desk from one side to the other, one by one.

"You're certain?" Losine thought the commander looked upset by the question, as though his skill or competence were at issue.

"I signed the deportation papers myself. I always conduct a very careful investigation to confirm that the decision to deport is correct. I look for evidence. I assess the written records—bank accounts, investments, background. I was a records clerk before the war. I know my work. Much better than most, if I may say so." He seemed to expand with pride. "Few of our local officers have the persistence to follow up the way I do. I am the only one that I know of who takes pictures and personally follows up on each deportee." He seemed to expect praise, a satisfactory review, perhaps a commendation.

"I would appreciate seeing your records," Losine said, maintaining a tone of calm indifference.

"I'll need permission from the highest level."

Losine gestured toward the files on the desk. "Is that necessary, considering your authority?"

The commander smiled. "You make a good point. Involving others is an unnecessary burden and would take too much time." He left the room and returned a few minutes later with several envelopes. He placed them on his desk next to the jewelry on the blotter. "This matter is to be kept strictly between us. Is that clear?"

"Yes. May I?"

The commander nodded. Losine picked up one of the brown envelopes, each of which was stamped in red ink with the word "CLOSED." One by one, Losine opened them. In the first envelope he found Greta's picture, saw her eyes wide and fearful as she sat naked on a stool in an empty room, her arms covering her breasts, her legs crossed. He knew at once what had happened.

The commander pointed to Greta's picture. "That one resisted me until I told her that her behavior was bad for the child."

Though he didn't want to know, Losine forced himself to ask. "And then?" By that time—1937–he had known better than to let Greta and Paul visit her parents. *Why did I agree?*

"I only wanted to look at her. You understand?" the commander was saying. "She didn't want me to look, but she changed her mind after I told her what would happen to the child if she didn't. Mothers are all alike. They do just what you ask if it's for their child." The commander looked away again.

"I don't understand," Losine said. Had he not known in advance what could happen? Wasn't he then responsible for Greta's death and Paul's? He would know everything, absolutely everything, that had happened to Greta, to Paul, to her parents.

"I always keep the mothers in a separate room. They have to let me look before I let them go back to the children. It doesn't take long," the commander said. He seemed unable to stop himself from talking. "It isn't so bad, really, despite what you may think. They just take off their clothes and I look. Sometimes I touch the pretty ones." He pointed to Greta's picture. "She was a pretty one, that one." He looked at Losine. "It's nothing, really."

Losine allowed himself to understand. The commander's words spread over him like an illness. *Wasn't letting Greta and Paul go the same as wishing this to happen? The same as allowing it to happen? Inviting it?*

Losine opened the second envelope and took out the picture of Paul. The boy's gaze was direct, unknowing. In that moment, Losine felt his culpability to be total, his responsibility as complete as if he had personally arranged Paul's fate. The other envelopes contained photographs of his father- and mother-in-law, both expressionless. He saw their signatures on their arrest papers. He read each paper as further evidence of his own failure. That Greta had insisted on going to Munich, begged to go, did not exonerate him. He had known more than she did, intuited the danger, and then discounted it. Such a small thing, a visit to her parents. She would be able to persuade them to leave if only she could see them, she had told him. It meant so much to her, to all of them.

"Like you, I am very thorough," the commander continued. "Most officers don't take pictures at arrests." Losine tried to compose himself, clasped his hands behind his back so that he would not reach for the commander, grab him, snap his neck like a Sunday chicken's.

"And after you looked and touched and took pictures?" Losine adopted the tone of a doctor who inquires about a malady, seeks its etiology, calculates the extent of its progress, tests its hold over the patient.

"I sent them away, as I'm obliged to do. I am not a cold man, you understand," The commander seemed to plead his case

"Not cold. No."

"I remember them when I look at their pictures. I think of them. I don't just forget them. Sometimes I even dream about them." *Does the memory of an inhuman act absolve one of the act itself?* Losine wondered. *If so, then he and the commander would be blameless. Impossible!*

"And then?"

The commander looked surprised. He leaned toward Losine and spoke with sudden guilelessness. "I've never told anyone this. If I look at the pictures, then when I go home, I am a better man to Hedda, and she cares for me again. Tell me, is that so wrong?"

Losine's mind stalled like a flooded carburetor. "Wrong?"

The commander seemed to hear the question as a rebuke. He held up his hand. "Wait. You don't understand." Losine waited, silent, hearing the confession. "I don't rape them or do bad things to them like the others do. It's against my principles." The commander pointed to Greta's picture. "This one cursed me. But she made up for it. She wanted to see her child so she had to make up for it."

"Make up for it?"

The commander glanced at Losine. "For her bad language, of course. I don't allow bad manners." Losine nodded. "I made her touch me. There." The commander pointed to his crotch with a distant smile. "Afterwards, I was stronger than I have ever been with Hedda."

Losine willed his hands to put the rest of the jewelry back in the pouch. He forced himself to speak as if he had merely inquired about his laundry order or the directions to a nearby town. "You say they're dead. Are there remains?" A proper burial might permit him a final act of contrition and consolation. The commander shrugged and patted the papers on his desk.

"These *are* the remains."

"Just these papers?" There was a knock at the door. The commander nodded and went to answer it.

"Excuse me, sir," the assistant said. She whispered something to the commander. Losine put the bag of jewelry into his briefcase, closed the latch, and locked it with his key. The commander went into the outer office, shutting the door behind him. Losine opened the briefcase again and scooped the papers from the desk into the case. The commander was still talking. Losine heard him say, "Arrest warrant?" He put some blank papers in the envelopes, closed them, and laid them back on the desk. When the commander returned, Losine was ready to leave.

"My clients will be pleased with the information. Thank you for your time." The commander blocked his way.

"Just a moment. We're not finished."

"I don't understand." *Will I leave this post alive?* Losine wondered.

"Give me a receipt for my jewelry or I will arrest you." Certain that the commander would regret his confidences and discover the missing papers, Losine rushed for the door.

"I've left it on your desk," he said. Near the outside door, the man Losine had seen earlier stood smoking a cigarette, seemingly indifferent to his surroundings. Losine went out, hurried toward the train station. Seconds later he noticed that the man had followed him and was maintaining a constant distance between them. Losine detoured and doubled back, stopped at a bar, waited at the counter. The man took a table on the sidewalk outside. Losine waited a few minutes, asked for the *klosett* loudly enough to be overheard, and slipped out the rear door.

He was almost inside the station when the man appeared again behind him. Losine looked at his watch as if he were late for an appointment, then rushed into the station and plunged into the crowd on the platform. A group of officers stood talking next to his train; he hesitated, avoided movement. His pursuer approached the officers and pointed in the direction of the train. Losine watched them, waited for an opportunity.

Fortunately, a disturbance on the platform distracted the group just as the conductor blew his whistle. Losine leaped onto the bottom step of the train, grabbed the handrail, and tossed his briefcase ahead of him into the vestibule.

The last thing he heard was the shriek of a whistle, shouts, and then a loud sound, like an explosion. His left leg buckled under him. Using all of his strength, he pulled himself up the steps and into the train. A burning sensation ran up his leg and into his hip. On the floor, a rivulet of blood formed next to his foot. He felt the back of his pants leg with his left hand, found a wet place near his knee, saw the blood on his hand. He twisted to look at the back of his knee. The black cloth of his pants obscured the bleeding. *I must not be found in this condition.* Taking the briefcase, Losine dragged himself into lavatory and locked the door. His heart fluttered and his vision narrowed. He heard shouts outside. He held onto the basin, lowering his head to stay conscious.

He briefly considered jumping out the window as soon as the train cleared the city limits and then taking his chances. He opened the window. Bars. The train gathered speed. He saw his blood on the floor. He threw his overcoat in the corner and lowered his pants twisting around to see the back of his leg. The wound was in his thigh, just above his knee. *A bandage. I must make a bandage.* Despite the pain, he folded his damp handkerchief over and over into a pad. Then he pulled the cloth towel from the wall holder and tore a strip from it. He applied the pad to the wound and wrapped the strip of towel around his leg, tying it tightly. Using the newspaper in his briefcase, he wiped the blood from his shoes and the floor as best he could and dropped the paper through the toilet, saw it fall onto the tracks beneath the speeding train.

Losine removed the pouch of jewelry from his briefcase and retrieved the brooch. He tore open the lining of his jacket and pinned the brooch to the inside seam. Then, he put the pouch in a secret pocket in the side seam of his overcoat. If the police found the jewels, he would claim they were his. He crossed each item off the inventory list and noted "returned to owner" in the space next to it before putting the list back into his briefcase. He took out the papers on his family, held them over the toilet, and lit a match to them, letting the ashes fall through to the tracks below. The lavatory filled with smoke. With shaking hands he lit a cigarette and smoked it quickly then put the butt on the edge of the sink. His vision swirled. He opened the spigot and threw cold water on his face, put on his overcoat, and opened the door of the lavatory. He looked in both directions before stepping into the vestibule.

The clatter of the train and shriek of metal wheels on metal rails filled his ears. Black spots flickered before his eyes and his vision narrowed. As soon as he could focus his eyes, he looked through the window in the door that led to the compartments. Several uniformed officers at the far end of the car advanced along the aisle speaking to the occupants of each compartment. As he watched them come toward him, his eyes went in and out of focus. He braced himself against the wall sweating and shivering, he bent forward, waited for the vertiginous sensation to pass. His head cleared slightly.

He took the briefcase under his arm and edged to the exit door. He set the briefcase down next to him. With great effort he opened the window. It took all of his remaining strength to lift the briefcase and throw it out the window. He watched it tumble down a hillside, waited until the train rounded a curve, then turned away. He refused to faint, but was unable to prevent himself from vomiting. Avoiding the mess he had made, he drew his collar higher around his neck and looked through the window to the compartments. The officers were already next to the vestibule. The door to the vestibule opened behind him; a man and a woman passed by.

"Drunk!" the man said to his companion.

Losine held on, made his way to the next car, gripped railings, braced himself against the walls. At last, in a compartment at the far end of the car, he saw a priest sitting alone. *Was he really a priest?* It was too late to care. He pressed against the door and nearly fell into the compartment. He collapsed into a seat. His vision spun. "I've been shot, father. They're trying to find me. In the name of God, help me."

The priest stood up. He opened his satchel, removed a flask, and unscrewed the lid. "Drink!" he said. He pulled another cassock from the satchel. "Lift your arms." He lowered the cassock over Losine's head and placed Losine's arms in the sleeves, covering him completely. He returned the flask to the satchel and closed it. "You are asleep, no matter what happens." Losine closed his eyes. The compartment doors slid open abruptly. "Good afternoon, officers," the priest said amiably. Losine remained motionless, his eyes closed.

"There is an injured man on the train. A Jew here illegally. He came this way," one officer said.

"He's wanted for theft and smuggling," said the other. "We have a warrant for his arrest."

"Officers, as you can see, we're not injured, but my fellow priest is quite unwell." The priest lowered his voice to a whisper. "He has an infectious delirium. Perhaps fatal. For your own safety, I beg you to leave."

"Yes, Father." Losine heard the rustle of clothing and movement. The officers moved out of the compartment and summoned the conductor. "Quarantine this compartment." When the officers had gone, the priest shook Losine's shoulder. "I am Father Enrico," Losine heard him say. "Quickly, tell me what happened. Before they discover us." Losine lost consciousness. He awoke much later in a makeshift hospital somewhere in the countryside, a doctor at his bedside.

"You're lucky. You'll keep your leg, but I'm afraid you're going to limp for the rest of your life." The doctor smiled at him. "A small thing, really, in such a despicable time, don't you agree?"

2

The waiter returned with a menu, but Losine let it sit unopened on the table. His immediate preoccupation in Orvieto that afternoon was neither the worsening weather nor his impending visit with Father Enrico, but, rather, the unprecedented risk to his business that he had assumed the previous day in Milano. He had received a special delivery letter regarding his recent negotiations to buy an exceptional number of fine uncut gems at well below market prices. He planned to sell shares in the gemstones and return a profit to the investors after selling the stones, taking a percentage of the profits as well as before- and after-sale commissions for himself. It was a speculative, but legitimate, opportunity to spread his own financial risk and gain a handsome return, the prospect of which, he had to admit now, had caused him to overlook the inherent riskiness of a transaction involving untested and unknown parties.

The rough fabric of his tweed suit, a gift from the owner of Knize in Vienna, irritated his skin. As he considered his situation, he reached down to scratch his bad leg. He was not himself, he decided, or he wouldn't have acted so imprudently. It was quite out of character. He had to admit that he had made several misjudgments recently. He had been under strain, though he couldn't say exactly why. It was as if something *within* could destroy him and required all of his strength to control it, ward it off. Perhaps he needed this holiday. He would simply sell the shares in the cache of raw gems when he got back and thereby mitigate any possible losses to himself. The simplicity and certainty of his plan made him feel calmer. *An unwarranted attack of nerves. Nothing more.*

He was sweating. He took out his handkerchief and wiped his forehead, then put the handkerchief away quickly before the waiter could see his agitation. The liquid smoothness of his Washington Tremlett shirt, one of a dozen he owned, and the comfort of his custom shoes from Lobb reassured him. All of his clothing was bespoke. Gifts—very well, *payments*—for risks he had taken during and after the War to find the lost, the missing, and the dead. Most were Jews and most were gone forever by the time he found any trace of them. It would be more accurate to say that he had searched for and sometimes saved the *damned* by supplying them with false identities, papers, even disguises before moving them across borders to a fragile safety. The superficial tokens of gratitude that he now wore affirmed that he was someone who had done this necessary, albeit illegal, penance for his own sins. The latter he considered numerous and beyond forgiveness. He knew that for others he had often made the difference between life and death. *I must remember this if only for the sake of accuracy,* he reminded himself.

His impending appointment that afternoon with Father Enrico intruded on these already troubled thoughts. That Father Enrico had saved his life was a debt he could never hope to repay, and, in that light, his visit seemed paltry and any thanks he offered miserly. Recollection of his own helplessness at that earlier time invariably terrified Losine. Indeed, neediness, helplessness—his own or that of others—repelled him. Between a lightning bolt and the thunder that followed, he lit the cigarette, inhaled deeply, and gazed with half-closed eyes at the façade of the Duomo.

Religion. A lot of fuss over a lot of folderol, he thought. *We're born. We suffer. We die. That's all there is to it. People want to shield themselves from the simple facts of existence.* He adjusted his tie, recalling the way Heinrich Bauer, shirtmaker to the German high command, had only a few days earlier touched it admiringly and begged for its provenance. Losine had revealed the maker of the tie in exchange for information about the operations of the gem seller to whom he had made the now-regretted payment.

He felt an overwhelming and familiar fatigue that sleep did not relieve. Perhaps, now he could concentrate on the other reason for his trip, the photographs he intended to take of the ancient sites in Orvieto. His photographic practices were always the same: after researching a site and preparing a map in advance of his arrival, he paced out the terrain, checked the light at different times of day, noting the exact moment when the sun—or occasionally the moon—reached the right position. Since completing his photographs of ancient Greek, Roman, and Byzantine sites, he had begun work on major Etruscan sites. The following year, he intended to go to Jerusalem. "I'm a lover of ruins," Losine told those who inquired about his expeditions and their motivation. The statement belied his actual purpose. Traveling under the cover of eccentricity enabled him to ask questions that might otherwise arouse suspicion. In the process of examining, say, a temple or a cathedral, he often met local experts and gained information useful in conducting his business transactions and his searches for the missing.

He had made the acquaintance of various experts. Frequently, they, too, provided useful information that went well beyond the technical aspects of photography or archaeology. In Zurich, he preferred to send his film to a laboratory there that was highly regarded for its meticulous attention to clients' privacy, though it could hardly be said that Losine's photographs contained anything personal, unless the viewer surmised that the very impersonality of the photographs was what was most revealing about them. He filed all of his photographs, which numbered in the tens of thousands, in a locked cabinet in the basement of his apartment building in Milano. He neither showed them to anyone nor looked at them himself.

Losine examined the menu in the same manner that he examined gems and jewelry, noticing the stains on the paper, the fine threads within the paper itself, and the watermark. The painting on the cover of the menu—originally a watercolor, no doubt—captured the same view of the Piazza that he had just observed, though on a brighter day. In the corner he was able to make out the signature of the artist: *W. Marcheschi*. The waiter came over to him.

"Something to drink, Signor?"

"Have you a good Orvieto?"

"In my opinion, the quality of the Orvieto is poor, Signore."

"Why?"

"We assume tourists don't know the difference, Signore. Perhaps the Vino Marcheschi." When the waiter returned with the wine, Losine noticed the picture on the bottle. "Is Vino Marcheschi related to the artist whose work is on the menu?"

The waiter nodded and poured some wine in Losine's glass. "Signora Marcheschi paints. Tourists seem to like her work. Customers ask about it."

Losine tasted the wine and gestured that the waiter should fill his glass. "I didn't say that I liked her work. Apparently, you do not."

"Her work pleases tourists, Signor. That's all. You'll find many more in the Marcheschi's *enoteca* across from the Duomo. Would you care to order something to eat?"

In the silence that followed, each man took the other's measure. Losine decided the waiter's opinion on tourists' taste in art was of no importance. He glanced at the menu. The downpour outside became a torrent. Given the weather, completing the Orvieto photography would likely require a second visit. "I'm not a tourist," Losine said to the waiter, "and I'll have the wild boar."

3

That he had never personally thanked Father Enrico for saving his life that day on the train had left Losine feeling ashamed, as if he had lost control. He had tried to ignore these feelings, but, at last, he had decided that he must find Father Enrico and discharge once and for all the obligation imposed by gratitude. In doing so, he imagined that he would be able to forget or at least diminish the anguish of those terrible days. He reviewed once more what he wanted to say, but no matter how he thought about expressing himself, he felt unaccountably awkward and inarticulate. *I should have gotten this over with long ago,* he thought. *Just written a letter. Still, a letter would demand committing facts to paper, facts that must remain confidential. No, a private meeting now is the only option, no matter how awkward.*

In the aftermath of the storm, Losine could still hear water dripping in the Piazza. The downpour had left large puddles in which the reflections of the surrounding water-stained buildings floated like mirages. The façade of the Duomo itself suggested to him a forsaken bride in ruined finery. He noted the plaque outside: *In 1290 Pope Nicholas IV ordered the building of this cathedral to commemorate the "Miracle of Bolsena," which resolved forever any doubt that the communion cup contains the Savior's blood.*

Actual blood? Sometimes Christians are intolerably literal, he thought. He was still early for his appointment and decided to go inside and look again at the Signorelli fresco. Tiny lights in tarnished chandeliers buzzed on fraying wires, as helpless against the twilight as the candles he bought at the entrance to the chapel. A bolt of lightning illuminated the interior

of the Duomo and its silent relics in a barren flash before the returning gloom overcame the few candles that still winked in the drafts. The
stone floor trembled in the ensuing thunder. The odors of dust and mold
enveloped him. The smell of time made him feel even more fragile and
transient than he already did.

Remembering his visits to Orvieto with Greta, he entered St. Britius
chapel, put more coins in the box and waited. The weak lights illuminated
not only the fresco, but also a woman seated nearby on a hard, wooden
chair, her head bowed and nearly covered with a black shawl. The chapel
was so small and she so near that he felt he himself an intruder.

"Excuse me," he said. She lifted her head. "Forgive me for disturbing
you." Tears welled in her eyes. Adrift in his own grief, he offered her his
handkerchief.

"Thank you," she whispered. She wiped her eyes, blew her nose, then
returned the damp linen. "I've soiled it."

"I have more. Are you all right?"

She nodded. "I come here to be by myself."

"With so many tourists, how could you be alone?"

"They pay no attention to me." She sniffled and adjusted her shawl.

He extended his hand. "Michel Losine...tourist!"

"Unless you're born here, you're always a tourist." She took his
hand. "Willa Marcheschi...*La straniera*, as they say. *Piacere.*"

"The artist! Didn't I see your work on my wine bottle?"

She laughed. "I only paint ordinary things." She inclined her head
toward the fresco. "I once imagined becoming a painter here—like the
masters." He waited for her to continue but she didn't.

"What prevented you?"

She shrugged. "I don't have enough history in my blood—or maybe
not enough religion in my soul—to be one of them."

Losine drew up one of the hard chairs next to hers and sat down. "So,
you're a commercial artist, then...like the masters."

"You're gallant, but you've probably came to Orvieto to see the frescoes, too."

"I'm visiting an acquaintance, Father Enrico," Losine said. "Do you know him?"

"Yes. He's Monsignor Enrico now and he won't be back until tomorrow. Does he know you're coming?"

Losine was relieved by the delay. Tomorrow he would be ready. Willa looked at him. "How do you know Monsignor Enrico?"

Losine feared that it was more than a social question.

"A chance wartime encounter." He stood up and examined the fresco.

She got up, too. "Really, where?" He noticed the vivid blue dress beneath her black shawl and her worn black shoes. *Lovely ankles*, he thought.

"Train." He said it abruptly, intending to discourage further questions.

"People say Father Enrico was captured and that they tortured him after he helped a criminal escape from the Nazis. They say that his faith gave him the courage to resist. "

"Was the criminal on a train, too?" Losine asked uneasily. He hadn't known the real cost of Father Enrico's help.

"Yes, I believe so," she answered. "Was that you?"

He looked away. "Only in a moral sense."

"I shouldn't have asked. Would you like to see the cathedral?"

He nodded and put another coin in the light box. Her auburn hair glinted under the light, bringing back a memory of the sparkling angel that his gentile mother had always set on the mantel at Christmastime near his father's menorah. He recalled that he had stored them in an unused corner of the basement. *Are they still there?* he wondered.

"Most of the artists who worked on this cathedral died before they completed their commissions, so Signorelli had to bring all of their work together," Willa said. "They say his style influenced Michelangelo." Losine nodded and followed her out of the chapel and past the front of the altar into another chapel. "This is our reliquary." He peered through a small window in the container. The faded blue cloth inside looked to him like silk.

"I don't see anything miraculous, except the enamel work," he said.

"Seven hundred years ago, they'd have burned you at the stake for saying that."

"And now?"

"Now, you're just another tourist!" she laughed. He smiled at her.

She had a pleasant way about her. He was curious about her real thoughts. "Do you believe Signorelli saw the blood?"

"I believe he gave his customers what they wanted. He made a good living and got plenty of wine besides," Willa said.

"Do you see the blood?"

"Not really, but I don't usually say so."

"And that plaque outside, the one about the miracle: Do you think it really happened?"

"I think they were very devout," she said. "Would you like to see the altar?"

Losine followed her. "You're not Italian."

"No. I came to Italy to be an artist when I was very young. I met Gabriele. We married, had a family, and started our business. The War came, and here I am."

"Do you still paint?"

"Not seriously." She paused and looked at her watch. "I must be getting back. Gabriele will wonder where I am."

Losine followed her. "Why were you crying just now?" He wanted to catch her off guard.

Willa stopped on the steps of the Duomo. "Regrets." She continued down the steps and into the piazza.

He drew next to her. "What is it you regret so much?"

She looked at him. "I regret that you are the only person who has asked me that question."

"You should paint seriously," he heard himself saying. "Italians love art."

"They love the old masters. Women take care of the children and the house and the husband and the guests." She looked away. "But that's only half of it."

"And the other half?"

"If you must know, I don't have the will or the courage to paint seriously." She turned to him. "I managed to get to Italy, but I couldn't go any further. Didn't dare to do what I wanted to do. Once I got here, I felt as if my journey had ended rather than begun. To be honest, I couldn't bear the solitude of it. I had never thought about it. I imagined art with a capital "A" would be here waiting for me. But people expected me to have connections, letters of introduction, a serious portfolio, something important to express. I had nothing—just a few drawings, some watercolors, and mostly a fantasy about becoming an artist. It wasn't enough."

"Surely, it was a start."

"It's no surprise that my work was rejected as the trite scribbles of *una straniera*. Of course, I never considered any of this before I came. I couldn't have imagined it. At first, I believed people would change their minds—that I *could* change their minds—but they saw my efforts as proof of their original judgment. I could have apprenticed myself or perhaps found other work, I suppose, but I wasn't imaginative enough or brave enough to keep trying. I thought being married and being here would solve my artistic dilemma. It only compounded it."

Naive, Losine thought, but he admired her honesty and her ambition, just the same. Yet, saying so would make him appear condescending, and he wanted their conversation to continue.

"I'd like to buy some wine. Would you show me your paintings, too?" *Do I sound sincere? Am I? At least it's something to do,* he told himself. *I'm not hurting anyone.*

"You've earned a drink just for listening to me." She smiled and waved at a passerby. Evidently, his request hadn't offended her.

"Tomorrow morning, I'm planning to photograph the ruins. I need a guide and an assistant," he said on an impulse. He hoped she would come with him. He was feeling especially alone, untethered.

"Orvieto is a very small town. Everyone talks. It would embarrass my husband," she said, "and anyway people already think I'm…well, they think what they think."

"You mean 'no' then?"

"Yes...no." She smiled again. Her green eyes wrinkled at the outer corners where her fair skin had developed fine lines and crevices. *More than thirty*, he thought, *but perhaps not yet forty.* "Our shop is here," she said. "Come in and meet my husband." The paint on the doorjamb had turned to powder. Losine ducked under the transom and followed her inside. The planked floor creaked under their weight. Papers lay strewn on the counter. On the shelves, bottles of wine covered with thick dust lay in stacks. Dim light filtered through the small windowpanes, but not enough to enable him to see what was in the next room.

"Gabriele, a new customer!" Willa called into the dusky interior of the store. She sounded pleased.

"*Sono occupato.*"

"He's busy. He's doing the books today. It's much easier if I do them, but he likes to do the accounting himself." She took several bottles from different shelves. "Try these. I'll find glasses." Losine brushed the dust from the first bottle, studied the label. Willa's arabesques of leaves and branches, the counterpoint of dark tree trunks, the simplified play of sunlight and shadow reminded him of ancient frescoes. She returned with still-wet wine glasses. "These will do." She took the bottle from him, opened it, poured the pale liquid into a glass and set it in front of him.

He tasted it. "It's young and somewhat vinegar-y," he said. "I like the label, though. Would you like to sell me the original drawing?"

Willa showed him a second bottle that had no label. "This one is better," she said. "I shouldn't let you taste it because we have so little. We think it's one of the very old Orvietos." She poured the honey-colored liquid into a clean glass. "Gabriele is certain it's the same as those the Popes drank centuries ago."

The taste was much more complicated, unlike that of any wine he could recall. "I'm surprised that it's held up."

"People believe that the original Orvietos had magical properties. They say if you make a wish and drink the wine, you'll experience a miracle." She raised her glass.

A miracle? Should I make a wish or let fate take its course? Never mind. What difference does it make what I wish for? he thought. "Did *you* make a wish?" he asked her.

"No, but I think it's a nice story." She set her glass on the counter, gathered the papers and moved them out of the way. *Self-conscious*, Losine thought. "Gabriele wants to produce the old vintages again if we can raise the money to do it. I think the miracle aspect would be popular with tourists and profitable for us."

"You're probably right, but you still haven't answered my question. Would you sell me your drawing?"

She laughed and went on with her work. "Why do you want it?"

"It reminds me of a fresco," he said.

"Why don't you buy a fresco then?" she said.

"Do you have one?"

"Yes, but Gabriele would never sell it."

Just then Gabriele appeared. "Sell what?" he said.

"This gentleman wants to buy some wine and see the fresco."

"It's not for sale," Gabriele said to Losine.

"Yes, your wife made that clear," Losine replied. "I'm interested in ancient artifacts—photographing them—and I would welcome an opportunity to examine it."

Gabriele led him down a stairway to a subterranean storeroom lit by a bare bulb. Moisture beaded on the whitened walls. Losine felt the heaviness of the air in his lungs. Amid a profusion of wine bottles, some empty and others full, he could see shards of pottery, several amphorae, a large piece of fresco depicting an early version of the goddess Flora, and an exquisitely sculpted box the lid of which had been fashioned as a head. Losine recognized all of the pieces as Etruscan. He knew they were priceless. "These belong to my family," Gabriele said.

"And you don't want to sell them."

"But I do," Willa said. Her response made him cautious.

"Why, if they belong to your family?" Losine asked.

"We could use the money to make repairs and improvements, and for capital to expand our business."

"You sound like a good businesswoman."

"Willa has no head for business," Gabriele said.

"Have you set a price on the artifacts?" Losine said, glancing away as if something more important had caught his attention.

"No," Gabriele said. "We don't have a license."

"But here they are," Willa said. "They're ours. How would the authorities know?"

She's clearly willing to sell them. "If you change your mind about these or the old Orvieto, I might be interested," Losine said.

"We're not interested," Gabriele said. "My wife has crazy ideas."

4

At half past two in the morning Losine awoke abruptly. His ears rang. He had a headache. He was thirsty, his leg numb. He stretched out under the cold sheets and then withdrew his leg to a warmer spot in the bed. Outside, the wind moaned in the eaves, and rain tapped on his window. A familiar sense of emptiness, of dread, engulfed him. Against the darkness of the room, his failures stood out in relief. He replayed his decision years before to allow Greta and Paul to go to Munich. He retraced his steps to the train station, to the platform, the train, to the moment he had gotten on with them, helped them settle in their compartment. There had still been time, even then, to save them.

Outside the hotel, a noisy crash brought a momentary halt to his self-critique. He closed his eyes and pulled the duvet close to his chin, hoping for sleep. The din continued. He had been cavalier. And stupid to do business with a mere jewel thief. Profligate. Why had he not thanked Father Enrico years ago? He was rude. Why was he not maintaining his health? He was imprudent. As the night wore on, his shortcomings mounted. He chided himself for the triviality of his work and for his own irrelevance. Another hour passed. He was seized by the image of himself adrift in a dark ocean, a white figure flailing in the moonlight.

At last, he threw off the covers and rolled out of bed. His feet touched the icy floor. Startled, he sat back on the mattress and reached for the oil lamp, but couldn't find his matches or his lighter in the dark. The cold room seemed to him an extension of his own body. He got up and went to the radiator under the window, ran his finger across it. He remembered that it had been silent earlier and surmised that the hotel heating system remained another wartime casualty. He saw himself as he was:

middle-aged, alone in a shabby room, a stranger in a village, his where-abouts and existence unknown to anyone save himself and a hotel clerk, his purpose lost, his life shattered. Before he succumbed beneath the dark waters of his own making, would he catch a piece of wood or debris float-ing on the current and manage to stay afloat long enough to save himself? Beggared and lost, he dared not hope for a life raft or his own man Friday.

Grey twilight entered the room. Losine went to the sink. The faucet ran only cold water, and he hadn't reserved a bath. He washed as quickly as he could, added extra layers of clothing, anticipating the thick, hot coffee and the bread that would surely be waiting in the dining room. Pastries too. He would ask the waiter for some food to take with him. He assembled his camera, light meter, tripod, measuring tape, notebook, film, and a thermos for coffee and put them in a large leather knapsack, which he slung over his shoulder. Today he would search out the Etrus-can Temple of Belvedere and confirm to his own satisfaction whether or not it actually reflected the sacred geometry of the school of Pythagoras, as some art historians had claimed. Afterwards, he would move on to the necropolises. He looked at his watch. Quarter to eight. Late, if he intend-ed to photograph both the Temple and the necropolises and then call on Father—no, *Monsignor*—Enrico afterwards.

When he had finished breakfast, he left the hotel, crossing the Piazza della Repubblica and the Corso Cavour. His headache had abated. *Just hunger*, he thought. Though it was out of his way, he turned right at the Via Duomo and continued past the Marcheschi wine shop, which was still shuttered. The emerging sun drenched him in light and gilded the edges of the few remaining clouds. At such moments, he missed Gre-ta and Paul most deeply. By now, Paul would have been a young man. Losine had often tried to imagine whether the boy would have most re-sembled Greta or himself and thus had two images of his son. The day was warming quickly even though it was almost winter on the calendar. He stopped to remove his scarf, folded it, keeping the corners even, and put it in his knapsack before continuing on his way.

Near the Piazza Marconi, where the Via Soliana becomes the Via

Postieria, the image of his wife and son boarding the train once again
tumbled through his mind. Again and again, it copied itself in his dreams,
waited for him when he awoke, insinuated itself into his day. He dreaded
the wave of despair that invariably accompanied it. He closed his eyes
against the unwanted vision and stumbled over the curb of a small public
water fountain in front of the Chiesa di San Bernardino. He fell to his
knees in a puddle with the contents of his knapsack scattered about him.
The tear in his pants exposed the cut on his left knee. He touched it. *Superficial.* Bracing himself with his cane, he tried to push himself to his
feet. A sharp pain shot through his weaker leg. He dropped back onto the
street and looked up to see two boys observing him from the other side of
the Piazza as they might observe an upended tortoise or an insect whose
carapace had become its prison. When they realized that he had noticed
them, they ran away laughing.

Losine turned over on all fours, pushed himself part way up with
his hands and then used the cane to regain his balance. Once upright, he
leaned on the cane and brushed himself off with his free hand. The sun
disappeared under a cloud. His pants and shoes would dry soon enough,
and who would see the tear? *No need to bother going back to the hotel to
change.* He gathered up his supplies.

"Hello." He turned toward the voice. "I've decided to help you after
all." Willa Marcheschi. *The artist manqué. A pleasant surprise, even in
my present condition.*

"As you can see, you're just in time," Losine said, mustering a laugh.
Together, they continued toward the Piazzale Cahen and from there they
entered the park. Now, the sun reemerged at an angle that caused light to
pass through and around objects, giving them the fluidity of a dream. The
warm rays on the damp ground surrounded them in quiet vapor as they
set up his equipment at the Temple.

"Very little is left of it, as you can see," Willa said. "Just a few broken
columns and some steps."

Surprised by the unexpected warmth of her presence, he felt attracted
to her. Immediately, he adopted a firm, businesslike tone. "Hold this tape,

please." He went about his work treating her as if she were in his employ. He instructed her to stand at each corner while he measured the length of the sides, the placement of the columns. Afterwards, they sat together on the steps, and he made his final calculations.

"I believe this temple follows exactly the ideas described by Pythagoras," he told her. "Though they are eighteen hundred years apart, this temple and the Duomo are based on the same mathematical principles." The sun disappeared again. "This demonstrates that knowledge of mathematical concepts in architecture must have spread both farther and earlier than is commonly believed."

Willa drew her jacket up around her chin. "Is that remarkable?" She blew on her hands, stood up and stamped her feet, shivering. "Right now, I'm more interested in how they kept the temple warm."

Losine pointed at the thermos. "Would you care for some coffee?" Vapor wafted around them. She nodded and blew on her hands again. "As soon as the sun comes out again, I can shoot, and then we'll leave." He opened the thermos, poured the steaming liquid into the dented metal cup and handed it to her. "Not very elegant service, I'm afraid."

Willa drank without comment and returned the empty cup to him, then stood to one side, waiting. He had expected her to want more from him. She had seemed so needy the day before. Now there was something so distant and self contained about her that he was uncertain. Perhaps he had only imagined her need of him, of anyone. Had he mistaken his own need for hers? He took the camera out of his knapsack and mounted it on the tripod in what had been the courtyard at the entrance to the Temple. The sun came out from behind a cloud and immediately disappeared again. "Will you show me the necropolises when I've finished here?"

"I'll show you where it is, but I don't want to go in those places," she said. The sun emerged again, this time for good.

As Losine completed his photographs, he handed the film to Willa. "If you'll put these in the container, please." He smiled at her, anticipating a response. She complied silently. "Caring for the film properly determines whether you get good pictures or bad ones," he continued. "That's why having a careful helper is important." Still, she didn't reply. He set up again and took several more shots at the side of the Temple and some of Willa when she wasn't looking, before announcing that they were finished. It was nearly ten. Willa sat down at the entrance to the Temple and helped herself to more coffee and a bit of bread.

Losine sat down beside her. "A successful shoot," he said lightly. "Thank you for your help."

"What do you think about when you're taking all these pictures?" she said.

"I think about the pictures."

"I don't believe you."

"Very well. What do I think about then?" She had asked for more than he was willing to disclose. He wanted to dislike her, find her ordinary, unlike Greta. A little high strung with an inarticulate desire for something more in her life. Certainly more than he could give her, he thought. Still, she was attractive, though perhaps not beautiful. Average, he decided, surprised that he found average appealing. Greta, her purity of intention, her spirit, represented for him a kind of excellence without which he found life nearly intolerable. Perhaps he was cold-hearted, but it was hardly a fault to have uncommon standards. As he grappled with his conflicting thoughts, the silence between them grew until Willa seemed to him to be floating away from him, never to return. Perhaps he had been wrong. He was relieved when she spoke.

"Tell me, then, what do you do with your photographs?"

"What do you mean?"

"Why do you take them? What purpose do you have in all this measuring and setting up and taking down?" She looked directly at him. Under her gaze, it occurred to him that she understood the emptiness of his photographic expeditions, that they were instrumental and pointless. She had noticed so quickly. *Is it that obvious? Are others just too polite to say so? Perhaps. I appear merely foolish*, he thought.

He felt the heat creep up the back of his neck. He stood up and began to repack his supplies. "I think the work speaks for itself."

"No, it doesn't, at least not to me. What do you do after you finish taking pictures?"

"I develop them." He took a sip of coffee from the cup, considering whether he would continue to take any photographs at all.

"And then?"

"I organize them and file them."

"Why?"

Relentless, he thought. "Let's just say I have my reasons," he replied, aware that he had neither a purpose nor a choice.

"Such as?" He could not tell her that failure to complete an expedition amounted to cowardice, bad faith, a capitulation. Perhaps she guessed something from his expression. "Really, I sincerely want to know why you do this." The sun disappeared again. He felt a chill enter his bones. He feared she might withdraw again.

"Because I refuse to give in."

"To what?"

"To nothingness." She reached for his hand and kissed it as if he were someone she recognized after a long separation.

"Why don't you show me where the necropolises are now?" he said. She got up, and together they walked along the ramparts to the old gate and then along the narrow dirt road that wound below the walls of the city to the base of the outcropping. She led him to an overgrown path that was nearly invisible from the road. He limped behind her, using his cane to maintain his balance amid the roots and rocks, dodging branches that caught on his knapsack, avoiding the tall grass that made his eyes itch and his nose run. He felt his leg weaken, but he was determined to go on.

At last, they came to a narrow path lined on either side by contiguous, small, flat-roofed stone structures suggestive of row houses for child-sized dwellers. The roofs were covered with earth, grasses, and other vegetation that had taken root centuries before. Heavy, flat stones blocked some of the doorways, while others gaped open. In shady places on the walls and inside the entrances of the structures where water percolated, patches of moss and lichen were well established. The angle of the noonday sun permitted Losine to look into the interiors of some of the open necropolises, small rooms decorated with decaying paintings of sacred and profane celebrations. Around the perimeter of one otherwise barren room he saw carved stone sarcophaguses, one propped open with a funeral urn.

"People take the artifacts and sell them," Willa said. "It's illegal, but that's how they make money when there's no work." Losine set his knapsack on the ground and crouched down. Dragging his leg, he crawled through the opening and into the chamber. Willa followed him. Crouched inside, he inhaled the smell of damp earth, tasted mold, coughed. Gradually, his eyes adjusted to the dim light. The doorway seemed to recede. A profound awareness of his own solitude came over him. Instinctively, he reached for Willa's hand. She looked at him for a moment and then put her arms around him. He kissed her with an unfamiliar sense of gratitude and then with an urgency that surprised him as much as her eager response. Like solitary wayfarers who meet on a lonely road, he recognized his unexpected kinship with her, a connection he thought he had lost with any other after Greta. It overwhelmed him, filled him with the kind of thanksgiving that honors gods.

He spread his coat on the ground. She sat on it and began to unbutton her blouse, moving slowly and methodically, as if each button required her to make an individual decision about its fate. She allowed her blouse to slip off onto the ground. He eased himself down beside her. She unbuttoned his shirt first and then his trousers. As she slid each button out of its buttonhole, Losine forgot about himself and his original opinion of her. For once, he wasn't conscious of anything except the moment. He helped her slide her skirt off, her bra, her panties and then buried his face in her hair and held her against him, her rosy, silken skin a miracle. He opened his eyes. In the faded frescoes of banquets held long ago he recognized his own hunger.

"I've needed you for so long," he told her.

"And I you." They yielded to one other not as the strangers they were, but as those who have always been together in a continuous beginning.

He felt the universe open to accept them in their first lovemaking. Afterwards, they lay facing one another, shy now in their nakedness. She touched the scar on his leg, tracing its depth and length.

"What happened to you?" He moved her hand away.

"Not now."

"I want to know."

"It doesn't matter anymore." He kissed her nose, found it cold, and helped her to dress. He got dressed himself. She put her gloves on and buttoned her coat.

"Do we have any more coffee?"

"Outside in my pack." He struggled with his jacket, then braced on one leg and using his cane, he got up, grateful that she didn't move to help him. They crawled out of the opening into the light, she after him. He brought the thermos out of his knapsack and poured out the remaining coffee for her.

"Do you have anything to eat?" Willa said. He found some biscuits to share with her along with the last of the coffee from their single cup.

He was curious about her now. "Why have you stayed in Orvieto?"

"At first, I thought this would be only one of my homes. I thought I would go back to Firenze and later home to America…but, naturally, the children—"

"A blessing in itself," Losine said.

"—and then the war," she continued, "and after my baby boy died, my dreams, whatever it was I thought I wanted, didn't matter any more. We had so many people to feed—our tenants, refugees, friends, soldiers looking for their companies. Those poor young men. So sick. Terribly injured. We tried to help them. We would have wanted their families to do the same for our children. The bombs. The explosions. The shootings and executions. It's hard to say who was the worst—the Germans or the Partisans or the Allies. So many people…so hungry. Toward the end, we had no crops. We went to the black market just like everyone else."

"Would you still leave if you could—now, I mean?"

"Yes."

"And your family, too?"

"It would be difficult to leave my children, but there are days when I think that I am ready to pay even that price." She seemed to misunderstand his question, but her answer revealed more than he expected.

"What prevents you then?"

"The war all but wiped us out. We still have our land, but we have to keep working as hard as we can just to survive. We have to make a living."

They sat together in silence. He wanted to help her. "Perhaps you would be interested in an investment in some gems. There is some risk involved, but given the probable payoff, I believe it's a risk worth taking."

5

Late that afternoon, Losine stood outside Monsignor Enrico's study, gathering himself before he knocked on the heavy wooden door. "Come in." He entered the silent cell with its cracked walls and stone floor. A small fire burned in the corner fireplace, and a teakettle steamed on the hotplate. What remained of the afternoon light entered from two small windows near the beamed ceiling. An overstuffed chair failed to contain Monsignor Enrico's girth; his cassock erupted around him and flowed out in all directions like magma. Losine introduced himself.

Monsignor Enrico struggled to his feet, took Losine's hands in his, then kissed him on both cheeks. "I always wondered what became of you." He gestured for Losine to sit down. "How good of you to come." Avoiding the hard, straight chair the priest had offered, Losine continued to stand. He felt his skin and hands grow warmer. He had not expected such hospitality from someone who had suffered so much on his account. He wondered at the warm welcome, and then became annoyed at his own suspicious nature.

"It took me a long time to discover your name. I wasn't sure you would remember me," he told Monsignor Enrico. "Forgive me."

The priest gestured toward the chair, again. "Please, won't you sit down?" Losine lowered himself into the chair opposite Monsignor Enrico's. "I expected you yesterday."

Losine was surprised. "I was told you were away."

The priest smiled and gestured at his ample belly and chuckled. "I didn't know I had become invisible—not yet, anyway." The turned wooden spindles on the back of the chair dug into Losine's spine, and the hard seat pressed against his thin frame and weak leg. "A misunderstanding, obviously. Tell me about yourself."

"I find it difficult to think about what happened, much less talk about it," Losine said.

"We were both in grave danger. It's something all men try to forget and never do, I'm afraid."

"Without you, they would have found me," Losine said.

"You don't know this, but we saved each other. Had I been alone, I feel sure I would have been questioned and my ties to the Resistance discovered right then."

"I'm told that they tortured you because of me."

"Yes, but by the time they discovered who I was and who you were, the information I had was useless. They beat me up a little, but they didn't get much that was useful." He winked at Losine and laughed. "I gave them only the names of the men I knew were already dead."

"They're still looking for me," Losine said. He had never confessed this to anyone.

"You're so important? To whom?"

"The truth is that alive or dead I know too much about too many. They're afraid to arrest me or kill me for fear their records will come to light and they will be exposed themselves. But if they got the chance...."

"You don't say." Monsignor Enrico leaned forward. "Tell me. What did you do?"

Losine shrugged. "Let's just say I specialized in porous borders. What I'm charged with is abetting war criminals by taking from the Germans what they stole from the Jews and keeping it safe for them. It's true, but I exchanged my services for information about Jews who were missing or dead or in need of transport. It seems I'm wanted everywhere. The Italians, for example. The Partisans think I betrayed them. So do the Fascists. God only knows why. The French find my alleged crimes useful in deflecting attention from their own unsavory collaborations. The Allies? Who knows? Capturing someone for an alleged war crime is always a useful cover."

Monsignor Enrico slapped his knee and chuckled. "You're right about that!"

Losine felt a familiar despair rising within him. He told Monsignor Enrico of Greta and Paul, his solitude, his sense of loss. Everything.

"So much has been taken from so many." Monsignor Enrico held his hands out to Losine. "We who are left must take care of one another." He reached for a bottle of brandy and set it along with two glasses on the small table between them. "Shall we thank God for bringing us together?"

"God wasn't involved and doesn't deserve our thanks," Losine said. "I came to thank *you*."

"You're so certain?" Monsignor Enrico leaned back and looked at Losine. There was a wary curiosity underneath his smile.

"If you look at recent history—our own experience, for that matter—the evidence is clearly on my side." Losine felt uncomfortable saying these things to a priest, even one as worldly as Monsignor Enrico. He tried to cross his bad leg over the good one, but the pain was too intense. He folded his arms instead. *What does it matter? Monsignor Enrico is old enough to have met a nonbeliever before.* He adjusted his position on the hard chair, but he was still uncomfortable.

"If life kept the promises we imagine it has made to us, faith would be unnecessary," Monsignor Enrico said. "My parish is filled with holy sites. One sees the truth of faith everywhere."

"We save ourselves with our own actions—or not. Either way, faith is an imaginary necessity—like truth," Losine replied. Involuntarily, he reached for his cane and stood up. He wanted to leave.

"Why? Do you consider yourself an exception?" Monsignor Enrico leaned forward, his eyes holding Losine's. "Please, sit down. You've only just come."

Losine felt small, like a child in danger of a scolding. He resented his position, but he complied. "I've studied many sacred sites," Losine said. "God wasn't there." He stood up again and paced.

Monsignor Enrico leaned back and put his hands behind his head. "Your view reminds me of a story a dying priest told us when I was a

seminarian. We all marveled at his equanimity about his own mortality."
Father Enrico paused. "The story went like this: two men were assigned
to a desert battalion that was responsible for defeating a cruel enemy, one
they couldn't see. In the featureless landscape the members of the battalion stood out like flags. As the battle progressed, heat overwhelmed many
of the soldiers, so as many died of the heat as of the consequences of
battle. Eventually, only the two soldiers remained, and they were quickly
captured and imprisoned in a cave where barred cells had been construct-
ed. As it happened, one was more docile, and he was left to move about in
his cell. The other was a combative fellow—somewhat like you, I should
imagine—and his angry guards bound his hands behind his back and also
bound his feet.

"Each prisoner had a flat plate for food and a bowl into which the
captors poured water if they remembered to do so. The first man died rel-
atively soon, but the second resisted death just as he resisted his captors.
At last, his captors moved on to the next battle, leaving the troublesome
prisoner behind. Through a hole in the ceiling, rare drops of rain fell into
his empty bowl. With his ebbing strength the prisoner managed to edge
near his bowl so that he might put his face down into it and lick. Just as he
was about to do so, he saw that a large and very poisonous scorpion had
crawled into the bowl seeking the same moisture. The question the priest
posed to us was: 'In what may this man believe?'"

"Nothing when all of his choices result in the same end." The story
offended Losine even more than the fact that Monsignor Enrico made a
point of telling it to him. Such stories made light of real losses as if they
were susceptible to solace.

The teakettle whistled on the hotplate. Monsignor Enrico put some
loose tea into a small brown teapot and then poured the hot water from
the teakettle into it. Losine glanced around to see if there was a strainer.
He disliked leaves in his tea. "Yet, you must agree that he has at least two
choices."

"The parable is pointless because he dies either way."

Monsignor Enrico set the teapot between them and handed Losine a cup. "Still, how he understands his choices is what matters, wouldn't you agree?"

"What is there to understand?"

"That faith can give meaning to his suffering if he chooses."

"In such a situation, neither faith nor suffering have meaning. The outcome is the same either way," Losine said. "These problems may interest some, but they are irrelevant to me. They're like mathematical proofs with their own internal logic and foregone conclusions." *Why are people so inclined to propose faith as an antidote for despair?* Losine thought. *How could it be so? Despair is our fundamental condition*—he thought of Willa— *relieved occasionally by the small, merciful connections we have with one another.*

After a silence, Monsignor Enrico smiled. "I'll tell the Pythagoreans you said so,"

"I'm sorry," Losine said. "I'm a poor guest."

"Not at all. We're merely two men speculating on our condition. Now, you must tell me about your visit to Orvieto." He handed Losine a cup of tea. "I believe you've already met Signora Marcheschi." Losine felt his cheeks warming against his will. He disliked surprises. Monsignor Enrico laughed. "We have few secrets here. Cream and sugar?"

Losine shook his head. "I'm certain you know much more than I do." He kept his voice low and spoke easily, but the priest's implication that his actions with Willa had been observed made him uneasy. He ought to defend her reputation, he decided. "Signora Marcheschi was kind enough to guide me to several sites that I wanted to photograph." He took a sip of tea and tasted the bitterness of the leaves. He swallowed them.

"We have several expert guides. I would be happy to refer you," said Monsignor Enrico. "Signora Marcheschi belongs with her family."

Losine placed his teacup and saucer on Monsignor Enrico's desk. "Are you saying that Signora Marcheschi is not permitted to offer her assistance if she chooses?"

Monsignor Enrico held up his hand. "Only that she sometimes offers her assistance too readily."

Losine felt something being snatched away from him. Involuntarily, he raised his hands in an effort to catch it and then pretended that he merely needed to adjust the position of his leg. "I've already completed all of my work, except for the Duomo," he said. He yawned to conceal this new anxiety. "But another time I would greatly welcome your recommendation." He stood up. "I came to thank you for saving my life, and we've ended up talking about other things." He took out his checkbook and pen and wrote a check for an amount far greater than he had planned. He handed the check to Father Enrico. "Perhaps you could use this to support a project that you otherwise couldn't undertake."

"Very generous," said the priest. "Now it's my turn to thank you." He placed the check in his desk drawer. "Redemption is a most difficult mission," he added with a chuckle. "I appreciate your commitment to our work. And the fact that you came to see me."

Losine looked around for his hat. He was eager to leave. Monsignor Enrico pointed to the hat, which was sitting on his desk. At the door, he held Losine's hands in his. "I sincerely meant what I said: thank you for coming. Please, forgive me for having to tell you about Signora Marcheschi. It is one of the less happy aspects of my work."

Losine left Monsignor Enrico's office feeling agitated and annoyed, especially with himself. Reliving those deeply troubling and frightening days had left him anxious and upset. He had said too much, more than was warranted or discreet. It was dangerous. He knew better. Why had he imagined that he was indebted to Monsignor Enrico? Their need had been mutual. He owed him nothing. People don't save others' lives. They do what they do for their own reasons. The balance sheet is almost always even. Still, the reality of their mutual need neither lessened the burden Losine felt nor mitigated his sense of obligation. He spat, an unaccustomed gesture.

He wanted to be near Willa, to touch her pale, warm skin and lie next to her again, feel the warmth of her body against his. *What Willa and I do is our business,* he told himself. *What right does he have...to what?... monitor our activities? Tell us what we're permitted to do?* Losine walked into the Piazza del Duomo. *Willa! She must be in the shop.* He would go there again, say that he wanted to buy some wine to take back to Milano. He could leave his address and have it shipped. If Gabriele were there, he could discuss the purchase of the old Orvieto or perhaps the fresco. What did it matter as long as he saw her again, maintained their connection? As he walked across the Piazza, he imagined her coming to him in his hotel room that night. He felt the familiar numbness in his leg and concentrated on taking careful steps. When he neared the Marcheschi's shop, he saw the sign immediately: "*Apriamo lunedi.*" Open Monday. Two days away. He would be back in Milano by then. Inside the shop, he noticed a bare light bulb was still burning. *Perhaps Willa is there. Yes, she must be. It isn't too late after all.* He tried the door. It was locked. He knocked. *She'll come as soon as she hears my knock,* he told himself. He knocked once, twice, a third time. His fists became an insistent staccato on the door. There was no response. A passerby stopped.

"Vino Marcheschi is closed, Signore. Do you see that it's dark inside? The Marcheschis aren't there." It felt like drowning.

6

FIRENZE, FALL 1948

From a distance, Losine watched the passengers disembark from the train. Against his better judgment and after putting it off for a time, he had begun a correspondence with Willa, formal and businesslike at first, but increasingly personal as time went on. Meanwhile, in the months since their first meeting, Gabriele had, after protracted negotiation, agreed to sell the fresco to him, but under the table and at top price, without permits, insurance, stamps, bribes, or proof of ownership. Losine would take care of all of those himself, and at last, the fresco would finally be his. That is, as soon as Willa delivered it.

Still, there hung in the air the obvious and troubling complications arising from his having become more deeply involved with a married woman. It was true that he had written first and also true that he had continued the correspondence using a false address in another town. He had done so when he was inexplicably upset. No, lonely. She had responded quickly, before she should have, before he was ready to take responsibility for their relationship. Yes, he had to admit that he had kept up their correspondence as a shipwrecked man hangs onto a life raft in a dark sea. Nevertheless, if she hadn't responded... No, he could not deny his culpability or hers. He had acted consciously. Clearly an affair with her was impossible. When they concluded their business, he would simply tell her, politely of course, kindly, respectfully, that their relationship must not continue. The matter would be finished. Furthermore, he could use this time in Firenze to contact potential clients on the Ponte Vecchio. The gemstones would be delivered soon, and the Florentine goldsmiths were eager to return to their pre-war levels of production. With Willa's share of the gemstones invested and as a supplier to the goldsmiths, he would certainly profit and so would she. The risks had been worth it, and he would leave investors better off than when they started. *No fault, no penalty*, he told himself.

Then, he saw her. She stepped down from the train and sought an open spot on the crowded platform. Her breath left small white clouds in front of her. She set her two valises down next to her with great care. The significance of the valises showed in her constant attention to their whereabouts, her protection of them. *Excellent*, he thought, *she has brought the fresco with her.* He was surprised that he had forgotten how she looked. She was smaller than he remembered, pale and freckled, her auburn hair a penumbra of fire under her dark green hat, which lodged to one side of her head, its iridescent feathers curling around her brow. Would she notice him in the crowd? It had been nearly a year since they had seen one another. He watched her movements, curious to see her reaction when she recognized him. She glanced around, then picked up the bulging bags, and, despite their obvious weight, strode toward the station. Her walk was easy, efficient, and rhythmic. Her bias-cut skirt of dark green gabardine swayed against her full hips, emphasizing her curves. She had a narrow waist, and, when her jacket opened, he could see the creamy silk of her blouse falling liquidly over her breasts. *Voluptuous*, he thought. *Not like Greta.*

Her hair caught the brief appearance of the winter sun. In that moment, he saw that she was, in fact, beautiful, much more beautiful than he had realized. He reminded himself again that he must not become more deeply involved with her. The wind dislodged her hat. She set the suitcases down on the platform and pinned her hat back on, then picked up her suitcases, and continued walking. She caught sight of him, smiled, and came toward him.

"There you are, Michel." *She speaks more loudly than necessary*, he thought. *Did anyone hear her?* He felt visible and uncomfortable. He regretted being seen with her in public, revealing something so private about himself. She put down her luggage and embraced him lavishly, kissed him hungrily. "I was afraid you had forgotten." Her laugh traced a musical scale. "I should have known better, shouldn't I? After all, this was your idea!" She didn't wait for his reply. "I've brought the fresco with me and also the Orvietos and the box."

Her enthusiasm made him feel conspicuous. "Shhhh. You never know who's listening."

"Very well," she said in a stage whisper. "Where can we go to be in private?" She buttoned up her coat and took her brown kid gloves out of her purse and put them on. "It's so cold here."

"You'll be comfortable at my hotel." He took her suitcase in his right hand and held his cane with his left. She held the other suitcase and walked alongside him, holding his arm, matching his broken pace.

"I'm so glad to see you." Her voice was breathy. "Your letters have meant so much to me. I've kept them all. Did you keep mine?" Her candor seemed gauche. *Can't she keep anything to herself? No, I did not miss her.* He wondered if perhaps he really had. He focused his attention on getting a taxi. "Not even one of my letters?" He saw that he had hurt her feelings and felt guilty, confused. He hadn't intended to lead her on.

"Here's our taxi. We'll talk of these things later." They settled into the cab.

"I have a ticket on the four o'clock train," she told him. He attributed the stab in his midsection to his awkward position and perhaps to a bit of indigestion brought on by his hasty breakfast on a swaying train earlier that morning rather than to his disappointment at this unexpected change in their plan.

"I thought we said tomorrow." He felt safe calling this to her attention.

"I'm sorry, darling. Gabriele is doing the books tomorrow. If I'm not there, he will find my 'investment' in your gemstones." Their taxi stopped at the carriage entrance at the Savoy Hotel on the Piazza della Repubblica. Losine helped Willa out and brought her to his suite on the fourth floor. A bellman followed with her suitcases. Losine opened the door, and Willa entered the golden yellow room.

"So this is where you stay. Lovely." She took a red rose from the vase on the table nearby and inhaled its fragrance. "I love roses." Behind her, the bellman let the suitcases drop onto the floor.

"Be careful!" Willa said to him. "That will break."

"It's not important," Losine told the bellman quickly. "There's many more where that came from. Start the fire, please." When the fire had flamed up, Losine gave him several bills, and the bellman withdrew, closing the door behind him. The latch clicked.

Willa dropped the rose on a nearby table. "Why did you tell him it wasn't important and then give him that illegal tip?" she said. "If anything breaks, it will be worthless."

"I don't want him to come looking to see what it is when I'm out of the room," Losine replied.

"He didn't look like that kind of person."

"Even the most benign-looking people can be dangerous," Losine said. "Please, sit down. Will you have a drink and something to eat?"

"Yes. Let's celebrate. Together at last!"

Losine had not expected her to be this forward, so openly certain of her feelings. *So willing. Nothing like Greta.* He should not have suggested that they come to his hotel until—unless—he was certain. She would surely get the wrong idea. He must complete the purchase of the fresco and clarify his feelings, his intentions. Certainly, it was not his intention to get involved in something so messy and unpredictable. What had he been thinking?

"Champagne?" Losine opened a bottle of Moet from the bar, poured two glasses, and handed one to Willa. She laughed her melodic laugh.

"To us and to our…our what? Our business transactions." She laughed again. *Guileless*, he thought. *At least, no one can see or hear her. Us.* He felt more comfortable without witnesses to his guilt, to his betrayal of Greta earlier, and now once more with this woman.

"To our transactions," he said. On the table between them he set out the small plate mounded with caviar and toasts. *I'll maintain a business-like distance*, he told himself.

Willa spread a generous portion of caviar on a piece of toast and bit into it. "I love caviar," she said, her mouth full. She sipped her champagne.

"Shall we look at what you've brought?" Losine said. She set her glass on the table. Languidly, she removed a silver key from her purse, unlocked the battered leather suitcases, and opened them. From the first, she lifted out two bundles, both wrapped in white lingerie, and placed them on the wide bed.

"My laundry," she laughed. Carefully, she unrolled one of the bundles. "These are the last two original Orvietos. Gabriele doesn't know," she said. "He wants to keep everything in the family just like his land, but we must raise money if we're going to get our business going again." She unrolled the other bundle. "There's this box, too. It is beautiful, isn't it?" She turned to the second valise and took out another bundle, this one wrapped in a dress. She laid it on the bed and unrolled the small, Etruscan fresco of a goddess of spring. It was far more beautiful and perfect than he remembered. He was flooded with an unaccustomed feeling of happiness.Concealing his excitement, he took out his wallet and counted out the amount they had agreed upon: thirty thousand lire. "What do you think these others are worth?" *Why suggest more than absolutely necessary? Something could go wrong.* "One can't be sure until they're sold," he said.

"Sold? I thought you wanted these for yourself, too." She started to roll up the bundles.

Though he realized that he had expressed an interest in the antiquities, he was surprised that she was so upset. "Your letter said you needed money, and I said I would try to help you liquidate them quickly."

"What about the money from my share of the stones? I have to replace the entire two hundred thousand immediately. Before Gabriele finds out."

"Very well. How much do you want for these, then?"

"One hundred fifty thousand lire for the box." He knew it was worth a great deal more. Did she? "And twenty thousand for the wine."

He didn't want her to think he would take advantage of her. "It's difficult to predict how much they will bring." At least that much was true.

"I know they're valuable."

She isn't a fool. "Everything can be put up for auction immediately," he said. "I'll contact the auction house tomorrow." *There, it's done. A simple business transaction. All above board.*

"But I must have the money immediately."

He studied the pieces. *Beautiful. Rare. Ancient wines? Their historic significance incalculable.* "It takes time to get such objects to auction," he said. "One wants the right house. Do you have permits?" She shook her head.

"Heavens, no! If I had applied for permits, Gabriele would have found out." She wrapped the pieces up and put the bundles in her suitcases.

"What if I give you hundred and fifty thousand for the box today," he said finally, "and let the buyer worry about the permit?"

"Very well, then. One-hundred-fifty thousand for the box. Write that down. And for the wine?" She took off her jacket and settled back in her chair.

"I could give you twenty thousand against sale," he said. "That may be more than it's worth, but I'm happy to do it for you." A slight loss on the wine, he decided, would make him feel less guilty about ending his relationship with her. Still, it could be awkward if he put all this in writing. There could be trouble about a license. Or their relationship, for that matter. He didn't want his name associated with any legal questions. He had enough legal troubles already.

"That covers the two hundred you need if you include what we agreed on for the fresco."

"Very well," she said. "Now, write down our arrangement, please."

He couldn't avoid it, he decided. He went to the desk and took out a sheet of hotel letterhead. He would keep the descriptions obvious, innocuous. He wrote:

Etruscan box without archeological permit, estimated value: 150,000 lire.

Two bottles of antique Orvieto wine, vintage unknown, without permit, estimated value: 20,000 lire

He stopped. How to describe the fresco? It would not leave his hands. A vague description would make it harder to trace, he concluded.

Small painting of unknown origin, estimated value: 30,000 lire

"Now, if you will sign here," he said. He pointed to the space at the bottom of the receipt and handed her his pen. She signed the paper without reading it and returned the pen to him. He left her receipt on the desk.

"I am so grateful for your help." She picked up the receipt, looked at it. "Here, I think you must sign too. That way it's official." He had not expected this. He signed his name so that it was illegible. "Now, we're partners," she said smiling.

Her guilelessness astonished him. He looked at her with new eyes, warmed to her once again. Yes, he had missed her, truly he had. She was beautiful, but it was her obvious trust in him, her unquestioning belief in his inherent goodness that affirmed for him his membership in all that was human. She put the receipt in her purse. It seemed to him that he had given her a receipt for the return of his soul. *No longer lost.* They sat in silence. An awkward formality arose between them.

"You have been well?" he asked.

She smiled at him, her green eyes sparkling. "Well? Of course, my sweet darling. I have been thinking only of you. Us. What about you?"

"Yes."

"Merely 'yes'?" she asked him.

"Yes, I've been well, too."

She sipped her champagne and took another bite of caviar-laden toast. He heard the growing silence in the room, watched as she wiped her lips with a white napkin. He disliked the sight of the lipstick smears and the dark stain of caviar on the napkin. It seemed unkempt to him, an imperfection. He knew he was wrong. He got up and looked out the window at the wan sky and tried to think of something pleasant so as not to spoil their time together. *Her rosy skin....*

"How often do you come to Firenze?" she asked.

The image of her naked body intruded on his thoughts. Reflexively, he thought of Greta, his disloyalty to her with this woman. "Rarely." He sat down in a nearby chair covered in fraying yellow silk.

Willa folded the napkin in quarters and put it on the plate. "So this is a special trip, then?" Was she angling for a declaration from him? *How could she under the circumstances?* She brushed crumbs from her lap into her napkin.

"I have other business here, too." He wanted to sound indifferent, to step back from the precipice. *A married woman. What would Greta think?*

"More business than ours?" She smiled as if they shared a private joke.

"Yes."

She stood up, walked over to where he was, and leaned down to him. "What's wrong? Aren't you feeling well?" She kissed him lightly on the forehead and stroked his hair.

"I wish it were only that," he said, pretending she wasn't there, yet eager to touch her.

"If you wish that, then I do too," she said. She reached down and rested her hand on his knee. He took her hand and held it so she couldn't distract him by touching him.

"Why don't you sit down?" he said.

"Where would you like me to sit?" Seized by his forbidden desire, he drew her onto his lap. They held each other quietly. He unbuttoned her blouse, slid it off her round, warm shoulders, and let it fall to the floor, overwhelmed with gratitude that in a world that was not his home, he was at this moment no longer alone. He held her against him, his cheek against the white satin and lace of the slip that covered her breasts. Slowly, he lowered her slip and bra and buried his face between her breasts, feeling their warmth against his cheeks. He stood up with her and carefully removed her skirt, folded it, and placed it on the chair where they had been sitting. On top of the skirt, he folded her slip, her stockings, and then her garter belt, bra, and panties, all white. Now she stood naked in front of him. It was the first time he had truly seen her body, and he drank in her voluptuousness and the minute wrinkles and stretch marks on her belly. He stroked her breasts, sucked at each nipple, ran his fingers over her hips, and, with her standing in front of him, kissed her between her legs holding her hips to steady himself. Then he guided her toward the bed and stood before her as she removed his clothes, tossing them on the floor like unwanted toys. He remained before her as she kissed him again and again, beginning with his lips, his ears and neck and moving down and around his body until she arrived at his erection, stroking and kissing it, too, until he trembled. He laid her back on the rose silk bedcover with her beneath him and pressed himself hard between her legs into the warmth of her. Wrapping her legs around his hips, she held him immobile. When, at last, she let him go, their slightest movement threatening the loss they both desired and holding it off until, no longer in control, they ended in a mutual cry.

He opened his eyes and wiped the tears from hers and then from his own. "I love you," he said. "I don't know what to do."

Later that afternoon Losine escorted Willa to the station. While he waited with her on the platform, he took a brown paper envelope from his coat pocket. "Here's fifty thousand more in case you need it." She looked at him, her eyes wide. "We mustn't allow anything to create suspicion." She hid the money in a pocket deep inside the lining of her purse.

"I'll sell everything this afternoon," he said. "How soon will you come back?"

"I'll let you know when I get home." She kissed him and taking the empty suitcases, she boarded the train. He waited on the platform until she waved to him from her compartment. When she had gone, he strode out of the station into the crisp, grey-violet dusk. It was still early. He chose one of the beggars from among those who lined the entrance and gave him a fifty lire note. Instead of taking a taxi as he usually did, he plunged into darkening neighborhoods, amid doorways and courtyards blackened by time, beneath the balconies filled with ragged laundry that would not dry until spring, inhaling the aromas of soups and sauces simmering in nearby kitchens, embracing his own unexpected joy. *As soon as I return to Milano, I'll make a gift for her. Something beautiful. Something with emeralds.*

7

Losine checked his valise on the seat next to him once again. *Would the fresco be safer on the floor?* He moved to the corner seat next to the window and placed the valise next to him so that he would be sitting between it and other passengers. He had consigned the other antiquities to the auction house of Flavi and De Angeli, the most respected dealers in Firenze. He was pleased with the arrangements he had made. In exchange for a larger share of the usual consignment fee, Pierluigi Flavi himself had guaranteed "an immediate sale." The sale would bring enough to cover the higher consignment fee, the two hundred and fifty thousand lire Losine had given Willa, and, in addition, the amount of her remaining share in the gemstones, plus interest. Even under such favorable arrangements, he would only break even, but the two prizes he most desired—Willa and the fresco—were now his.

Relieved by the new clarity of his feelings for Willa, he wanted to do something that would affirm their relationship in a tangible way. He found some paper in his briefcase and began sketching the design for a pair of earrings of antique gold. The pinkish hue of the metal would suit her coloring, and the two emeralds in his office safe, when cut, would complement her eyes. He drew the incised rosettes that would conceal the posts. From these, each pendant would hang suspended on a length of braided gold attached almost invisibly at both ends with a gold ring. The cut emerald pendants would move as she moved, reflecting the light in their facets, suggesting the flutter of leaves in a breeze. Losine imagined the sparkle of her hair and the pendants together as the play of sunlight on deep green water. In the corner of the sketch, he wrote, "two ounces of antique red gold." Though less gold would suffice, he wanted to be sure to have enough should he decide to change the design or make a necklace, too. On the sketch, he noted instructions for cutting the stones. He put the drawing in his briefcase.

In Milano, Losine put the drawing in a folder in the back of the file cabinet in his office next to the unmarked one where where he kept Willa's letters. He closed the file drawer and locked it. There was only one key to the cabinet, which he kept with him at all times. He took his briefcase and went out of the office. He closed and locked the door. Tomorrow, he would meet with the representative from the gemstone syndicate and learn the fate of his investment.

When he returned to his apartment building a few blocks away, he was pleased to see that in his absence the concierge had arranged for the polishing of the brass mailboxes, doorknobs, and other fittings, as he had instructed. The advantage of owning the building meant he didn't have to accept any excuses for sloppiness. The concierge mentioned that a telegram had arrived for him. He opened his mailbox and collected the contents. Usually, he ate a solitary lunch on his balcony overlooking the street. Though he would have preferred the quiet of the terrace in back, he didn't want to look at the garden. It was in poor condition just then, and it upset him to see it. He sifted through his correspondence looking for Willa's telegram. *There! She must have sent it as soon as she got home.* He smiled at the thought. He set the stack of mail down on a nearby windowsill and opened the envelope. Dated that morning, it had been sent from Arezzo. Her discretion pleased him:

Darling - All items plus cash found missing. Authorities involved very soon unless everything replaced immediately. Meet Firenze, usual place, tomorrow. Bring everything. Yours in haste - W

Melodramatic, he thought. *Foolish. What if the telegraph operator re-*

vealed the contents of her message to someone else? You never know.
He put the telegram in the envelope and pushed it deep into his overcoat
pocket. Given his situation, suspicion must be avoided at all costs. He de-
spised the shiver of anxiety that passed through him. *A sign of cowardice,*
he thought. He wanted to see her again. As soon as possible. The antiquities could be sold already, and withdrawing her stake in the gemstones
prematurely could seriously undermine his own financial position and
alienate his partners. It was regrettable that the objects had been missed
so soon. He must do what he could for her to protect his own interests.
He picked up the stack of mail and went to his apartment. *There's no
choice but to return her stake and front all of the money myself. What a
nuisance! Perhaps I could sell her share in the gems to another investor.
But who?* He took the fresco with him and went out, stopping first at the
telegraph office where he sent a message to Flavi and De Angeli: *Unfore-
seen problems indicate consignment must be withdrawn.*

Next, Losine called at the studio of an artist and printer he had known
during the War, a specialist in forgeries of all kinds and able to work
quickly. "I'll need a perfect copy of this piece and supporting documentation." The order would be costly. Never mind. *Damn the cost!* He would
still have the fresco. *People like Willa are charming,* he reflected, *but
they don't take into account that all decisions can have unexpected consequences. They confuse their false hopes and unwarranted trust with
diligence. If things don't work out, they expect to start over.* Against what
he regarded as Willa's impulsive nature, Losine contrasted his own ability to evaluate the available alternatives with cultivated dispassion and
then choose the best course of action according to the circumstances.
While it was true that a temperament like Willa's could lead to this sort
of inconvenience, he certainly was not angry. Just then, a tall, stylishly
dressed woman passed him on the sidewalk. *There are many attractive
and interesting women in Milano,* he thought, *but none as beautiful and
lovely and warm as Willa.* Whatever the problems, he looked forward to
seeing her the next day.

In the late fall sunshine, Losine noticed the declining angle of the light that reflected dully in the numerous puddles, the silence left by departing birds, and the absence of street vendors. Spring seemed unimaginable. He thought of Willa, her body curved against his own, bare and warm, her hair tangled on his pillow, under his cheek, enveloping him in the fragrance of carnation and freshly washed white linen. Despite the oncoming winter, he felt in the rush of his own blood a sense of sap rising, and understood the cry of new life within a self long forgotten, a sense of hope that he had not believed possible. As he stood amid the swirl of midday traffic, he recalled Willa's sumptuous delight in him. *Him!* He felt resurrected, willing to do something unprecedented and likely quite foolish.

Nearby, a policeman blew his whistle and shouted at a man to stop. Losine watched the man huddle in a doorway and then look away, avoiding the eyes of passersby. He pulled Willa's telegram out of his pocket and reread it. *Are the police already looking for me?* He continued walking. *What if they have orders for my arrest?* He walked faster. Would they try to arrest him here in Milano, a place where he was known, safe, respected? It would never happen. Or would it? He fled toward the train station. When he had gone a few blocks, he looked back. No one was behind him except a uniformed nanny pushing a baby in a pram. *I must get the antiquities back before this nonsense goes any further,* he thought.

"One first-class ticket for Firenze. Tomorrow," he told the clerk.

"The morning train arrives about noon."

"The night train, then."

"The sleepers and couchettes are already booked, sir."

"I'll sit." His leg would be stiff by the time he arrived. No matter. He returned to his office and cancelled his appointments for the following day, including the one with the gemstone dealer, and booked his usual room in Firenze.

8

When Losine arrived in Firenze the next morning, he went immediately to the hotel. "I want to order twelve dozen roses in twelve vases. Place them around the room," he told the concierge. It was extravagant, of course, and he savored the fact that he could know and feel pleasure again, if only for something as simple as flowers. For the first time in years he took a full, deep breath without choking on the loss of Greta and Paul.

"One exquisite rose would be a very succinct and elegant statement," the concierge said, "and much less expensive."

"It's not enough," Losine said. One rose could scarcely match his growing feeling about himself, about Willa, and about the rush of delight he felt when he anticipated her reaction.

"It will be very difficult to get so many this time of year and very expensive, Signor. I cannot promise."

"Please, it's very important. A surprise."

"A waste when so many people are still hungry. You should give your money to the war orphans." Losine felt momentarily guilty. *Haven't I contributed to the reconstruction effort already? Aren't I entitled to do as I wish with my own money? Haven't I, too, suffered grievous losses?* He waited for the concierge to complete the order, imagining Willa's response, pleased that he had not given up, even in this small matter. *At last, I, too, am beginning to recover.*

He returned to the station. There he bought several newspapers but he felt too restless to read. He stuffed the papers into his overcoat pocket and paced back and forth on the platform. He checked his watch for the third time in as many minutes. Willa's train was already late. Nearby, he observed two pickpockets steal a traveler's wallet. Instinctively, he reached under his overcoat to check that his own wallet was still there, still thick with cash for Willa. He heard the screech of brakes and a relieved hiss of steam. She had arrived.

He watched the passengers disembark seeking among them Willa's corona of auburn hair. At last he glimpsed her in the crowd, her hair unexpectedly restrained under a cloche the color of wisteria. Her cream-colored scarf printed with wisteria blossoms contradicted the severity of her military-style suit of the same color. He had not appreciated her stylishness. Her open-toed, high-heeled oxfords suggested an invitation that her leather briefcase immediately withdrew. He imagined that only he was privy to the luscious secrets concealed beneath her clothes. She waved at him. A throng of passengers surged between them. She threaded her way through the crowd to where he was standing and threw her arms around his neck.

"Oh, my darling. I'm so happy you're here." She kissed him as if they were alone. When she took off her sunglasses, he saw that her eyelids were puffy and dark around the rims, her eyes bloodshot. *Either she hasn't slept or she's been crying.* He kissed her eyelids, assured her that he would take care of her, keep her safe. Uncertain of the implications for him of such vague desires, he hesitated, then kissed her, full and long, his decision made in an instant, mindless of consequences. She released him as if she had suddenly realized where they were.

"Be careful. Someone may see us." She looked around anxiously. "Gabriele wanted to know why I had to go to Firenze again so soon. I said that I took the wine and the box to be appraised because they were too valuable to leave where they were and that I was going back to get them. I know he's suspicious." She ran out of breath. "I wouldn't put it past him to follow me."

Losine wanted to stroke her silky skin, soothe her. "No need to worry now," he said.

"Not if I return with everything immediately."

Better to tell her now, he decided. "That's not possible. I don't have them." Her eyes opened wide. "Yet," he added.

"You don't have the money? The box and the wine? Where are they?" Her voice, a crescendo of incredulity, dwarfed the competing sounds around them.

"We'll discuss it later," he said.

"No, tell me now. What's happened?" Her distress made him anxious. Her voice seemed very loud. What if someone heard her? Saw that a woman was shrieking at him? That he had not pleased her. That he had failed? A warmth and dampness crept into his armpits and around his mustache. What if he lost her? Lost everything? An old fear seized him. He limped beside her, tasting loss. He feigned an interest in something at a nearby newsstand, affected a calm that he didn't feel.

"Can you get them back?" She pulled at his elbow. "Do you understand what could happen to me—to us?" He stopped. If he said "yes," he would only confirm all of her fears, validate her perception of him as a failure. "This may be just a fling for you," she said, "but a woman in my situation could end up on the street or in jail."

He edged closer to the newsstand. "You're shouting."

She drew back as if he had slapped her and then followed him, coming close in a way that made him uncomfortable, anxious. "No," she said. "I'm not."

He handed the news dealer several coins and took another newspaper identical to one that he already had. He folded the paper with deliberate slowness. "It's not a crime to sell or invest what belongs to you," he said.

"Perhaps not in Milano, but it's different in Orvieto. These things belonged to Gabriele and to his family. They regard them like their land: only their children can own them."

Losine put the paper in his other pocket. "Legally, I believe that you are considered a part of Gabriele's family in both cities." He spoke logically, rationally, without looking at her.

"My marriage will be over."

"Could we at least agree that your marriage has been over for some time?"

"Yes, of course, darling, I wasn't talking about us." She began to cry, silent sobs that made her shoulders tremble. Losine hunched forward, a dog on a leash.

"I feel like you want to get away from me." Her voice felt shrill and accusatory, like the point of a knife.

"Please don't blame me for your situation," he said taking her elbow. He wanted to take her outside, somewhere that no one would notice them. "You brought the antiquities to me and asked me to sell them for you."

"I'm not blaming you," she said.

"You were," he said.

"I'm sorry, darling. I'm frightened. I'll have no way to take care of myself."

He leaned nearer to her. "We'll be together," he whispered. "Will that be enough?" Had he wanted to make such a commitment or merely to quiet her? He wasn't certain. He had felt so full of joy, of love for her, just moments before. It was as if Greta were always standing next to him, watching him, reminding him of his failure to protect her and Paul. Was it wrong to think he could go on? Wrong to think he could love Willa?

"Yes. I only want to be with you. Nothing more," he heard her saying. *Well, we can be together in many different ways, some of them imperfect,* he thought. He had won her, secured her for his own. It surprised him that he was capable of this. She hugged him with enthusiasm. Now, her arms felt like tentacles. He extricated himself from her grasp and restrained both of her hands with his.

"Let's talk about it after we retrieve your heirlooms." Over Willa's shoulder, he saw a nun detach herself from a group of other sisters and approach them. The nun pointed her index finger at Willa. He let go of her hands.

"Willa Marcheschi," the nun said. Willa replaced her dark glasses and adjusted her skirt slightly.

"Sister Maria Cristina! It's been so long since we've seen you," Willa said smiling. Losine thought Willa's face looked like plaster cracking. "Are you visiting Firenze today or do you live here now?"

"A visit to another convent in our order." Maria Cristina turned to Losine and extended her hand. "And whom do I have the pleasure of greeting?"

"Sister, may I present my cousin, Michel Losine," Willa said. Sister Maria Cristina stared at Michel Losine.

"Cousin?"

"*Molto lieto,* Sister," Losine shook her hand warmly. It felt cool and strong against his own weaker one.

"We grew up together," Willa said. "Like brother and sister." Maria Cristina looked squarely at Losine.

"It seems you continue to enjoy one another's company very much. I suppose you and Gabriele Marcheschi are quite well acquainted, then." She smiled at Willa through pointed teeth. "Please, don't let me keep you, and do remember me to Gabriele." Sister Maria Cristina walked toward the train that would return her to Orvieto.

"By tonight," Willa told Losine, "all of Orvieto will know your name and exactly how I kiss my cousin."

9

Located near the Ponte Vecchio, the villa, which had once housed the family of a minor Italian nobleman, dominated the Via Lambertesca, a medieval alley. The stone façade rose up to a tower. Double wooden doors, large enough to accommodate a hay wagon, appeared permanently locked, but the bright, brass plaque next to the bell suggested otherwise: *Flavi e De Angeli, Antiquari e Vendite all'Asta*, antique dealers and auctioneers. Losine rang the bell.

"I met Signor Flavi many years ago," Willa said. "He might remember me. Perhaps he'll help us." The *portiere* opened a small, barred window in one of the doors and peered out, first at Losine and then at Willa.

"Signor Flavi," Losine told him. "An urgent matter."

"He's out."

"Nevertheless, we must come in."

The *portiere* closed the window. After a long delay, he admitted them into the vaulted foyer where light poured down from the windows in the tower overhead. They followed him to a desk in the next room where the receptionist accepted Losine's business card. "I'll get someone to help you." She directed them to a circular banquette upholstered in tufted sepia velvet. They sat down. From this vantage point in the center of the room, they could easily view the tapestries mounted on bars bolted to the high, stone walls. Willa leaned her head against Losine's shoulder. A ringlet of auburn hair crept out from under her cloche.

Losine noticed her smeared lipstick, and he wiped her cheeks and lips with his handkerchief, frowning at the pink traces on the linen. He wiped his own lips. "You didn't tell me I was covered with lipstick," he said. "Was it there when I met Sister?"

"I was too surprised to notice." Willa said.

"Yours is smeared," he said. "Do repair it."

Willa sighed and leaned down. "These cheap wartime shoes are so uncomfortable." She untied her shoelaces, allowed her shoes to fall onto the marble floor, and wiggled her toes against the stone. She settled back with another sigh and closed her eyes.

"Better keep your shoes on," Losine said.

"Why?" Willa said wearily. Just then, a slim man in a carefully tailored, black suit entered the room. He glided toward them, saw Willa's feet, and winced.

"Faustino De Angeli, *piacere*," he said to them. Willa opened her eyes. "*La principessa* awakens to find all of her dreams have come true," De Angeli added with a manufactured laugh. He extended his manicured hand, first to Willa and then to Losine. "I see you're enjoying our tapestries. They're a recent consignment from the German owners. Hidden throughout the war. Extraordinary pieces. Gobelins. Seventeenth century." Willa put on her shoes.

"We have come for our consignment," Losine began.

Signor De Angeli gestured toward a low doorway. "Please, come with me." They followed him through a passage so narrow that the cell-like room at its end seemed spacious. Light flooded in through clerestory windows. At one side of the room, doors opened onto a courtyard where a marble Neptune and dolphins frolicked and spouted in a make-believe ocean.

"Originally, this was the bedroom of the villa," De Angeli said. "The tapestries depict the goddess Artemis and the different aspects of her nature." He looked at Willa and then at Losine. "Extraordinary work and very charming," he added, as if there could be only one opinion on the subject. De Angeli adjusted his wire-rimmed spectacles with the sort of deliberation reserved only for the gravest matters, and sat down at a gilded writing table. He opened their file. Willa sat down on a fragile chair in the corner.

"There is a problem with the consignment," Losine said.

"I recall this group. Exquisite pieces. Remarkable, in fact," De Angeli said.

"Regrettably, we must withdraw them," Losine continued. Orsini held up his index finger for quiet. He examined the papers, placing his finger on the first page and tracing a line across the paper.

"I see your contract with us has not yet expired."

"That's correct. However, we've become aware that title is in dispute."

"We often encounter such problems," De Angeli said, laying the contract in the folder. "I shouldn't worry about title problems if I were you. We're very experienced." He closed the folder.

"A sale could result in prosecution for one or both of us. Were I in your position, I wouldn't want to have an association with items that might concern the police."

De Angeli crossed his arms over his chest. "We prosecute any consignor who defrauds us or our customers."

"There's no basis," Losine said evenly. "You knew there were no permits. I made no claims about authenticity or legality when I consigned them to you. I'm coming to you now in the same good faith."

"The box has been sold."

Willa gasped. "No!" Her eyes filled with tears. Losine handed Willa his handkerchief.

"There is nothing I can do, *Signora*. I'm sorry," De Angeli said to Willa before returning his attention to the file.

"For how much?" Losine asked.

"Here it is: six hundred thousand lire," De Angeli said. "We can prepare your payment while you're here, if that's helpful. With the usual deductions, of course, and a small premium for the extra work."

Losine understood that the sale had been especially profitable, but now that they must deflect Gabriele's suspicions, profit wasn't important. "Has the buyer taken delivery?"

"It seems not."

"I bid seven hundred thousand lire. Cash." Pleased by his own boldness, Losine glanced at Willa to see whether she had noticed that he was not merely a cautious man outside the sweep of life, but a decisive player in the events of their time. She blew her nose into the handkerchief. "Send everything to my hotel by tomorrow morning." He took out his wallet and counted out the notes on De Angeli's desk. "Wrap the pieces for shipment in unmarked packages and include a letter over your signature to Signora Marcheschi stating that their value cannot be appraised without further documentation of their origin." He imagined Willa's pride in him and in the excellent outcome he had effected. He had turned their weakness into strength, had protected the interests of all concerned. He imagined her next to him, naked and ecstatic. De Angeli shook his head.

"Signor, the buyer has already accepted the contract." De Angeli got up and put the folder in a file cabinet.

"Cancel the contract. Tell the buyer you've made a mistake. Do whatever you need to do," Losine said.

"It would be very costly, Signor. Much, much more than you would be willing to pay." De Angeli spoke without inflection, as if he were intent on other matters.

"Yes, I assumed that," Losine said, although he hadn't. "How much more?" De Angeli sat back on his gilded chair and folded his hands.

"It's difficult to say, exactly. At least two-hundred thousand more, possibly three hundred. It's only a guess, of course." Losine knew that the deal was made. It was just a matter of his agreeing to the inflated price.

"Very well, but only if I get these pieces today." Losine put his arm around Willa. "Shall we go, my dear?"

"It's for our buyer to decide," De Angeli said. "But I'll prepare the papers just in case your offer is accepted."

10

"Let's celebrate," Losine said to Willa once they were outside. He took her to the once-fashionable Trattoria Dei Tre Cugini. The sounds of the swift water—unusual for the Arno—and of reconstruction work nearby on the Ponte Santa Trinita roared in their ears. Small rapids had formed around the rubble that would later become the reconstructed bridge, a project that had been financed by wealthy Americans. Waves rose and broke against the usually tranquil riverbank. It was still early in the season for flooding, but the authorities had already issued warnings. Losine held Willa's arm as she stepped over a pile of sandbags.

"The Americans know how to win wars and fix monuments. The only question left is whether they can stop a flood!" He laughed and held open the red door of the restaurant for her. They took a table with a view of the roiling waters. Willa huddled against the wall in the corner of their booth. Losine ordered aperitifs and extended his hand across the table to her. She ignored it. "You don't need to hide. This place probably isn't on Sister Maria Cristina's itinerary." He smiled at her, imagining how they would make love all night. "Stay with me tonight."

"I told Gabriele I'd be back," she whispered. "He's already suspicious. What would I tell him?" The waiter served their drinks. She drained her glass immediately.

"Tell him the pieces will be delivered tomorrow morning, and you'll return with them then. That's probably the truth." Losine ordered another aperitif for her. "We'll get them back. It's just a question of how much it's going to cost."

"But if Signor De Angeli doesn't return them by tomorrow morning, then what?" she said. *Then we could make love the entire day, too.*

"Yes, perhaps you should tell Gabriele 'afternoon' instead," Losine said. "That way you can be certain." He looked at the menu. "Shall we try the rabbit?" She remained silent. He placed their order and requested pasta with truffles. "Prosecco or champagne?"

"What about the money?" she said. "I still need the rest of the money." He imagined their spending all of Saturday in one another's arms.

"Money sometimes takes a little longer, but I think we can manage that, too."

She withdrew further into the corner, to a place where he couldn't reach her. "Please don't joke about this," she said. He wanted to bring her back. The memories of Greta, of Paul, of Monsignor Enrico entered his mind unbidden. Without her, he would be left with only his losses. He poured some wine for her.

"I'm not joking. I know you're worried, but successful negotiations do take a little time. I assure you, there is no question that we will get the antiquities back. Leave it to me." She emptied her glass without comment. When their meal arrived, he poured another glass. She drank, but sat unmoving. From time to time she chased the rabbit around her plate with her fork.

"It seems you're not hungry?" he said. "Won't you at least taste the rabbit? I ordered it especially for you. It's really excellent."

She shook her head. "Not just now. Thank you."

"At least you liked the wine." He poured another glass for both of them.

"If I don't bring everything back today, Gabriele will notify the police."

"Why would he do that if you have come here to get the antiquities from the appraiser?" She gave no reply.

"I didn't know everything was going to disappear this way, or that Gabriele would be so angry."

"What do you think I—we—are doing here?" His voice was sharp. "First, you ask me to sell the pieces. You then change your mind. Now, I'm paying whatever premium it takes to get them back for you, yet I'm blamed for losing them."

"I don't mean *lost* lost, just not there when we need them. When I thought they would be."

He held his fork in midair and leaned toward her. "Is there something you haven't told me?"

"Gabriele said he's going to tell the police about you," she said softly. Losine dropped his fork on his plate. The dishes rattled. Willa started. Losine found a cigarette and lit it. "That's why I have to return everything today," she said retreating further into the corner. "I don't think you realize how serious this is." She emptied her glass and tried again to conceal the rabbit under its garnish of parsley before the waiter took her plate away.

"Was your meal satisfactory, *Signora*?" he asked. She nodded affirmatively and looked out the window at the churning river. "Will you have some dessert?" She shook her head no.

"One *zuppa inglese* and two espressos," Losine told the waiter. They sat quietly watching the river.

"Gabriele said he was going to contact the authorities because of something Monsignor Enrico told him about you," Willa said.

The dessert arrived. "Usually, I prefer fruit," Losine said, handing Willa the extra spoon, "but I wanted to make our meal together celebratory." She refused the spoon. He dipped his own into the elaborate trifle. Her silence, he told himself, reflected her own fears. It had nothing to do with him, with them. "What did Monsignor Enrico say about me?"

"I don't know exactly. Gabriele said that he knew all about you." *Betrayed, and by a man of God! How stupid to unburden oneself to a priest. Luckily, I've been warned. I have some time.* Losine understood that she had been trying to protect him. He decided to enjoy his meal, to savor each bite.

"I've been in worse situations than this," he said. "I understand why you were worried. You were right to be concerned. It's good that you've told me." He reached out and took her hand. "I'll take care of everything," he said. "I know what to do." She seemed to relax. He gave her a bite of his dessert and then sipped his espresso slowly.

"What will you do?" she said.

"For now, it's better for you if I don't tell you." He looked at his watch. "It's still early." He ordered cognac.

After dinner, they walked back to the hotel. He unlocked the door to the hotel room and stepped back to let her enter first. The fragrance of roses enveloped them.

"Shall we make up now or later?" he said.

She looked at the flowers and then embraced him. "Now, darling, but only if you're certain that we aren't at our own funeral!"

"We're just starting to live," he said smiling at her. She had come back.

"No one can get a single flower these days, and you got a roomful. How did you...?"

He slipped her jacket off her shoulders. "My secret. Please, stay, Willa."

She walked around the room, gathering roses from each of the vases, and presented him with a bouquet.

"Thank you, but you haven't said that you'll stay."

"I can't." She dropped her scarf on the table and took his face in her hands, kissed his lips, his cheeks, his eyelids. "Let's not argue any more. Arguing makes me lonely and sad." He held his hands against her cheeks, and she kissed each of his fingers, one by one.

"We have everything we need together," he whispered. "There's no need to be afraid."

She looked into his eyes. "Yes, everything," she said.

"I won't let you be lonely, I promise." He held her in his arms and then led her to the bed, where she lay back against the silken pillows. He took a rose from the bouquet she had made, this one the color of burgundy, and handed it to her. She pulled off the petals one by one saying "I love you" as she scattered each petal on the bed. He unbuttoned her blouse. "And I love you," he said.

She dropped the rose stem on the pillow next to her and undid the buttons of his shirt, "And this?" He nodded. She removed his shirt.

"This?" he said. He slid her skirt off and dropped it on the floor.

"Yes, and this?" She undid his belt buckle slowly, as if it were a device she had just discovered.

"Yes, that too." He waited, not moving.

"What about this?" She unbuttoned his trousers slowly, carefully.

"Definitely, yes. Included," he said.

"Everything, then?" She looked into his eyes. Outside he heard the sound of a siren; he held her gaze. "Everything. No buttons at all…if you agree."

"I agree." She traced his body with a rose petal. "Tell me, when shall we begin?"

"Now." He leaned over her.

"And for how long?" She held her finger against his chest.

"As long as we have, God willing." He kissed her.

"No. Wait. The earnest money. Every contract must have an earnest payment first," she said.

"This is your earnest payment," he said showing her his erection. She touched it.

"More than enough, I should say."

"Only if you stay with me." He took her hand and held it in his.

"Gabriele expects me tonight," she said. "I have only an hour more until my train."

"Tell him you're not coming back."

"But my children…."

"Bring them."

"Where would we live? How?"

"We'll have each other. You've agreed that that's all we need."

She frowned. "I don't know what you're expecting," she said.

"I want you to stay with me, to bring your children. Come with me. What more can I do or say?"

"But you hardly know us."

"Forgive me. I had imagined that because we're here together making love—and not for the first time—we were quite well acquainted. You don't share my feelings, then?"

"I do, but you haven't even met my children. It wouldn't be easy for you."

"Why? Am I too old? Too lame? Not the man you imagined yourself with?"

"No, Michel. You are everything I imagined, but there are complications."

"Such as?"

"Gabriele will be vengeful."

"That may be true, but this is our only chance. I've made my decision. Now, you must make yours." She pulled him toward her, held him against her pale and rosy skin. He drew back and kissed her breasts, her body, her private places again and again, then entered her, until, quivering uncontrollably she cried out to him, reached for him, and he for her, until, spent, they lay enfolded in one another's arms.

At last she sat up, looked at the clock. "My train leaves in twenty minutes."

"Do you want me to come for you and the children?"

"Yes. Tomorrow. Come for us tomorrow."

"When do you want to tell Gabriele?"

"As soon as we can."

After Willa had gone, Losine found her scarf on the table where she had dropped it. He picked it up and turned it over in his hands, buried his face in her fragrance. Her sweet scent mingled with that of the roses convinced him that he belonged to a world in which there was, after all, a sort of justice that allowed him to be happy and alive once more. He wept then both for what he had lost and for what he had gained.

11

Losine awoke the next morning exhausted and sweaty. He had dreamed of shielding Willa from a large, grey figure in a long and bloody battle, only to be left to die as the shadow crept away. The mood of the dream hung on, a toxic fog that contaminated his consciousness. In fact, the dream had frightened him. While he didn't believe that dreams literally came true, he did believe in their metaphorical prescience. Had he not dreamed of losing Greta and Paul? *It was a dream about change*, he decided, *about taking Willa from her old life. Nothing more.* In the bathroom, he stood over the porcelain basin and splashed cold water on his face. When he heard the knock, he pulled a towel from the rack and, still dripping, went to the door.

"Yes?"

"A courier brought this letter for you just now, Signor Losine." He saw the auction house name embossed in the upper left corner of the envelope.

"Thank you." He ripped the envelope open, tearing the letter inside. He assembled the torn pieces on the desk with unsteady hands.

...We intend to file charges for fraud unless we can come to a mutually satisfactory agreement before noon today."

A bluff, he said to himself. He noted the time: eleven-ten. He dressed in a dove grey suit and gathered up his homburg, overcoat, umbrella, and cane. He locked the door as he went out. The walk to the auction house involved multiple detours around construction sites and rubble. He checked his watch. Eleven forty-five. An alley became a dead end. He retraced his steps. Eleven-fifty. He increased his pace. At last, the Via Lambertesca appeared on his right. At two minutes before noon he rang the bell. The *portiere* appeared. This time, he was admitted promptly and escorted immediately into Faustino De Angeli's office. Several men unknown to him sat nearby.

Signor De Angeli's mouth formed a grim line. "*Buongiorno,* at last, Signor Losine. I thought perhaps you had lost interest in our transaction." He gestured toward a portly man in a grey suit sitting to Losine's left. "May I present Avvocato Antonio Rossini, our attorney, and *Capitano* Guido Fiorelli of the police department. Of course, you are acquainted with my partner, Pierluigi Flavi,"

"Signor Flavi, I believe you're acquainted with the consignor, Willa Marcheschi," Losine said. "You and she met many years ago. Her name was Carver then," Losine said.

"I don't believe I remember her," Pierluigi Flavi said.

Signor Rossini cleared his throat. He looked mournful, as if a cherished pet had died, and he spoke with funereal solemnity. "Signor Flavi and Signor De Angeli take their obligations to their clients very seriously. Your actions have endangered their reputations," Rossini began. "Fortunately the other buyer has agreed to sell to you." The other men nodded in unison. Rossini handed Losine an itemized statement: double the amount the auction house had received from the buyer of the antiquities listed as "buyer's premium," then the consignment commission, insurance premiums, storage fees, attorney's fees, appraisal fees, shipping charges, "miscellaneous charges"—a police bribe, no doubt—taxes and handling fees, and a permit. Total: one point seven million, five hundred thousand lire. Losine set the bill on the desk.

"This far exceeds my bid. You've added many extraneous charges."

"That, sir, is the price," De Angeli replied. "I warned you."

"If I responded to every blackmailer I met, I wouldn't still be in business. Please correct the figures."

"These are correct," De Angeli said.

Rossini cleared his throat. "The authorities in Orvieto inquired about these items this morning and about the theft of a priceless fresco. We have no record that you consigned a fresco to us. A Signor Marcheschi, who is apparently the real owner, is on his way here to claim these items."

"You can deal with him, then," Losine said. "I have other things to do."

Rossini stood up as if he were taking command. "Unless you want to be arrested for attempting to sell stolen property, I recommend that you deal with Signor Marcheschi yourself. This seems to be a dispute between the two of you. Legally speaking, it's best to keep it that way."

Capitano Fiorelli stood up and turned to Losine. "A very difficult situation, Signor. Unusual, also." He smiled slightly and shrugged. "In all candor, I, too, must recommend that you accept the offer. Otherwise, I am obligated to take action."

"I don't keep extortion funds with me," Losine replied.

"Your check is acceptable," De Angeli said. "When it clears, we'll deliver the pieces to you by courier with your disclaimer. Now, would you like to complete our transaction?" Losine nodded, calculating his immense loss in his head. Still, if the gems paid off...well, then it would matter somewhat less.

"You'll remain in Firenze under Capitano Fiorelli's protection," Rossini added as he departed.

"Am I to be a hostage, too, even though I've paid you enough ransom for a dozen hostages?" Losine said. He tried to appear unconcerned as he wrote out his check and handed it to De Angeli.

"Do you prefer to stay at the jail or hire one of my guards for the hotel?" Fiorelli said. "Naturally, I will respect your wishes,"

"My hotel. Would you care to join me for a drink?" Losine smiled. *Perhaps Fiorelli would be interested in a share of the gems.*

"Very considerate of you," Fiorelli said, "under the circumstances."

12

Fiorelli looked around Losine's hotel room. He picked up Willa's scarf and drew it under his nose. "A lovely fragrance, Signor Losine." He studied the room, smelled the roses. "Obviously, Signora Marcheschi is very important to you." He dropped the scarf where he found it, sat down in one of the armchairs, and put his heavy leather shoulder bag on the floor next to him. There was a knock at the door and Losine answered. A waiter brought in their drinks and set them out on the table nearby. When the waiter left, Losine turned to Fiorelli. "I'm going to Orvieto this afternoon on the two o'clock train. Willa and I intend to return to Milano together with the children." Fiorelli listened. "I would be grateful for your advice...help, I mean. Frankly, I've never been in a situation like this."

Fiorelli took a sip of his drink. "So she's married to this Signor Marcheschi?"

"Yes." Losine took out his cigarette case and offered Fiorelli a cigarette. Fiorelli nodded, took a cigarette, and accepted a light. Losine sat down in the other armchair across from him. "How much would that cost—your help, I mean?"

"It all depends. Legally speaking, Signor Marcheschi has custody of the children, so he can prevent them from going. Most women don't leave unless the husband is willing to let the children go. Is he?"

"It will be a very difficult discussion, but I'm sure he will understand that things cannot go on as they are." Losine lit his own cigarette.

"In that case, I believe a half million should be enough to cover my fees and expenses," Fiorelli said. "I will accompany you solely as a precaution."

"That includes the deliveries of his antiquities, too?" Fiorelli nodded and picked up his leather bag. "And there will be no questions or investigation into the matter of the fresco?"

"That is correct. Absolutely none."

"Nor any investigation involving me. Is that right?"

Fiorelli nodded. "None whatever. You have my word." Losine took out his wallet and counted out the notes. Fiorelli stuffed them into the bottom of his bag and settled back to enjoy his drink and cigarette as if Losine and he were simply old friends. "It is a privilege for me to offer my services," Fiorelli said. He poured himself another drink. Losine began to pack. "In my experience, when two people find each other as you and Signora Marcheschi have, then there is little one can do to stop them, except by using a weapon."

"A policeman deals with extremes," Losine said, "and with criminals. This isn't that sort of situation."

"You would think so, but to tell you the truth, from what I've seen of these situations, nothing surprises me. Mild, law-abiding men become murderers."

"I'm a very moderate man," Losine said. "If I present the matter reasonably and clearly to Signor Marcheschi, I believe we'll come to an understanding."

Fiorelli inhaled and then blew a perfect ring of smoke. "Yes, in your case, I could imagine it. Yet, I have seen cases of seemingly timid men kill their wives and their wives' lovers without warning."

Losine paused in his packing and looked at Fiorelli. "In my business I've learned not to make predictions, but I appreciate your candid opinion."

Fiorelli stubbed his cigarette in a nearby ashtray. Both men turned their attention toward the pounding at the door. "Perhaps you will forgive my offering some unsolicited advice?" Fiorelli said.

"Of course."

"Be careful." Fiorelli walked across the room and opened the door. Outside stood Gabriele Marcheschi, his lips pursed, his expression ferocious. Though he was not particularly tall, he seemed to Losine large and muscular. He held the jacket of his black, wrinkled suit over his arm. His white shirt, unbuttoned at the neck, looked slightly grey. He seemed over-heated, despite the chilly day. He leaned forward on his toes, bouncing as if he were ready to lunge.

"Which one of you is that *bastardo di* Losine?" he said to Fiorelli.

Losine stepped forward between Gabriele Marcheschi and Fiorelli. Gabriele turned on him, his eyes flickering like disturbed embers. "You! They said I would find you here." He strode into the center of the room and faced them, fists clenched. "I am Gabriele Marcheschi." He seemed to Losine to grow larger. Mountainous. Gabriele gazed around the room, at the bouquets of roses, and then at Willa's scarf on the table. He looked at Losine, took his measure.

Losine lowered his eyes momentarily and then returned Gabriele's gaze. *Very well. The moment has come. We will settle things between us now, and then I will go for Willa and the children.* Losine extended his hand. "*Benvenuto.*" Welcome. Gabriele Marcheschi ignored this gesture. *He's rough, unrefined, clearly unsuited to Willa,* Losine thought.

"You will return the antiquities and the money you stole from me now." Gabriele's voice was loud, imperious, uncompromising.

"You're mistaken. I've just paid for the return of the wine and the box that you and your wife decided not to sell," Losine said. "You're indebted to me for getting them back for you."

Gabriele Marcheschi turned to Fiorelli and laughed. "He wants credit for recovering what he stole. What about my fresco?"

"You sold the fresco to me. You have the money."

"That was before I knew who you were. I don't deal with criminals or adulterers. You will give it back," Gabriele said. Losine had the momen-tary impression that Gabriele was full of poison.

"You accepted payment. There is no reason I should return it," Losine replied. "However, if you agree to return my money upon delivery, I will return it to you. That should satisfy your claim." He gestured toward Fiorelli. "May I present Capitano Fiorelli," Losine said. "He will deliver the items to you as soon as they are ready."

"Hummph," Gabriele looked around at the room again and then pointed at Willa's scarf. "What are you doing with my wife's scarf?" He reached for it. Losine grabbed the scarf and held it behind him. "So, you've stolen that too!"

"She left it here," Losine said, unsure of why he felt the need to answer.

Gabriele looked around the room again, glanced at the open closet, the unmade bed, the roses. He glared at Losine, came closer. Losine stepped back. Gabriele moved closer still. Losine felt the warmth of Gabriele's breath, the heat of his body, the smell of smoke and wine.

"What have you been doing with my wife?" Gabriele said.

"I love Willa...." Losine had intended to take more time, to explain, perhaps talk about other things before confronting Gabriele with the truth.

"Hah! Well, you're not the first. Nor the last, either."

Losine was surprised. *I'm handling this badly,* he thought. *Now I've made him say preposterous things about Willa.* He put Willa's scarf in his suitcase, closed it, and shut the latches. He turned back to Gabriele. "Forgive my abruptness. Under the circumstances, I believe it's best if we speak directly. I'm going to Orvieto to bring Willa and the children back to Milano with me."

Gabriele snorted. Losine hesitated, wished that he had sounded more convincing. "First, my antiquities and my money. Now, my wife and children. Do you plan to carry off my vineyards, too?" He turned to Fiorelli. "Have you ever heard of anything so ludicrous?" He looked at Losine again and shouted at him, "They keep people like you at the asylum in Lucca!" He examined his large, rough hands, opened and closed his fists as if to test them. "Let me tell you something, Michel Losine." He made a fist with his right hand and slammed it into the palm of his left hand. "My wife is a delightful woman. She is beautiful. Very desirable." He rubbed the fist on the palm of his left hand. Losine had the impression that Gabriele restrained his fist only with the greatest effort. "Perhaps these qualities in her have led you to believe that she wishes to go to away with you." He pointed his index finger at Losine. "You are mistaken. It is *you* who wish to go away with her. My wife has a husband and a family in Orvieto." He slammed his fist down on the table. Losine started. "That is where she intends to stay and that is where she will stay. And so will our children."

Losine took a deep breath and then spoke slowly, evenly. "I suggest we go to Orvieto and let Willa speak for herself."

"I am her husband. Therefore, I know what her wishes are. She wishes only that you go back to wherever you come from and leave her—us—in peace."

"She didn't say that. She only just left here."

Gabriele went over to Losine's suitcase, opened it and took out Willa's scarf. He shook his head and waved the scarf at Losine. "You stole her scarf because you wanted to keep something of her to remind yourself of what it's like to feel something. Because you are a man who feels nothing, isn't that right?"

"That's mine!" Losine snatched the scarf away.

Gabriele drew a folded paper from his pocket. "I have a letter for you. Willa asked me to give it to you. Read it yourself." He held the note out to Losine. Clutching Willa's scarf, Losine took the wrinkled paper from Gabriele. He turned away so that Gabriele wouldn't see his hands tremble as he unfolded it. The light in the room seemed dimmed to him. He couldn't see clearly. Losine turned on the lamp and held the note under the light.

Dear Signor Losine: I have assured my husband that you intend to return our antiquities and our money immediately. Please tell him how you will do that and confirm the arrangements with him. Thank you.

She had signed it, *"Very truly yours, Willa Marcheschi."* Losine read the note again, saw the blurred ink. The note had gotten wet. Had Willa cried when she wrote it? He crumpled it and tossed it at Gabriele's feet. "This says nothing about us."

Gabriele advanced toward him, fists raised like a prizefighter's. "I tell you she will never go anywhere with you!"

Losine heard the rasping of Gabriele's breath and moved aside, tried to keep his balance. "Your shouting and bullying are unnecessary," he said. "We both have an interest in discussing this rationally. Why don't you sit down? I'll order more drinks."

Gabriele Marcheschi remained standing. "What is there to discuss with you? You imagine you love my wife. That she loves you. You are wrong. If you truly love Willa, you'll leave her alone."

Losine took out a cigarette and lit it. The smoke drifted toward Gabriele. "I do not imagine it. Your marriage to Willa is over."

"Would my wife leave me for a cripple? A tourist? A criminal with warrants out for his arrest?"

Losine coughed. "If you're so certain, then you shouldn't object to our going to ask Willa what she wants to do," he said recovering. He flicked an ash into the glass ashtray on the table.

"Legally, Willa is still my wife. I will never give her a divorce. Legally, the children belong to me. I will never let them be taken from me. Legally, my land belongs to me. I would never let anyone take it away from me. The law is on my side. Surely you know that?"

Losine stubbed out the cigarette. "Do you intend to imprison Willa?"

"I am her husband. Understand: she will never go anywhere with you. As long as I am alive, you can be absolutely certain of that."

"You don't know her wishes," Losine said, "or if you do, you don't care what they are."

"Who would know them better than I? Besides, you are a wanted man. If you go near my wife, I will tell the authorities where you are. You will never escape me." Gabriele waved his hand toward Fiorelli. "Which one of us do you think the authorities would believe?"

Fiorelli glanced at his watch and stepped between the two men. "Signor Marcheschi, it's time to end this unpleasant conversation. Please, won't you join me outside?" Fiorelli linked his arm in Gabriele's and, with a smile, moved with him toward the door. Gabriele looked back at Losine, then at Fiorelli.

"He's paid you off!" Gabriele shouted.

"I understand what you are thinking, Signor Marcheschi," Fiorelli said as he guided Gabriele out into the corridor. "I'm told that your antiquities won't be ready for delivery until tomorrow," Losine heard Fiorelli say. "You can wait in my office, if you like, and perhaps I could assist you in completing this important business. First, I'll need to see your permits." Losine heard Gabriele gasp.

"Permits?"

"The antiquities were sold, and you know, of course, that you must have a permit before you sell antiquities," Fiorelli said.

"But they belong to me."

"That is the point. It's is an unusual situation, I admit—unique in my experience, in fact—but the law is quite clear: you must have a permit merely to *possess* antiquities of this sort. Of course, we normally wouldn't prosecute in a case like yours when it is apparently a matter of inheritance, but, stolen or inherited, you must have permits. Without a permit, the antiquities cannot be returned to you."

"How long would that take?" Gabriele asked.

"Not long," said Fiorelli. "In fact, I could arrange it quite quickly, if you wish."

"Arrange?"

"It won't be too expensive," Losine heard Fiorelli as he closed the door. The latch clicked. He looked down at Willa's scarf still clamped in his damp hand. He spread the silk out on the table, smoothed the wrinkles, and folded it before locking it inside his suitcase. It was time to go. She was waiting for him. He drew a rose from one of the vases and inhaled its fragrance. Petals fell at his feet.

III. FINA

1

ORVIETO, AUGUST 1968

I took my examinations in July of 1968 right after I finished secondary school and did very well. I wanted to go to university and become a history teacher. As soon as I received my test results, I decided to enroll at Università Cattolicà del Sacro Cuore – Cattolicà, as it's called—in Milano, where my teachers had encouraged me to study. Cattolicà had a fine reputation, they said, and it would be a good place for a studious girl like me. *Papà* refused to discuss my plans, but it wasn't until later that I understood his real reasons. At that time—August—*papà* could not have imagined that I would very soon discover all that he and mamma had taken such pains to conceal from me and from each other or that all of our lives would change forever before the end of that same year.

The unraveling of their secrets began on an ordinary day. *Papà* came home early and went into the *salotto*, just as he usually did. He sat down in his faded armchair, which was covered in a prickly, plush material the color of putty. The chair had formed to the contours of his body, become one with his needs. Although the late afternoon sun was still bright, he adjusted his reading lamp to the highest setting, put on his glasses, and opened his newspaper. When he read the newspaper, he demanded absolute silence.

I heard him grunt. "What, *papà*?"

"*Al diavolo!* Strikes in Milano and Torino! *Femministe* rioting in Rome! Workers don't know when they're well off! Women are forgetting their place!"

"What place is that, *papà*?"

He glanced up from his paper and frowned. "I hope you're not planning to join those *puttane.*" The word means "whores," but *papà* meant women who did something to compromise themselves and their reputations, something that wasn't customary or approved, something he didn't like.

"I only want to go to Cattolicà so I can become a history teacher," I said. "That doesn't make me a *puttana.*"

"Girls from good families get married and have babies and take care of their husbands, and their husbands take care of them," he said from behind his newspaper. "That's the way God wants it to be." He put the newspaper down on his lap and looked at me. "You should be thinking about your future, not about history."

"I am, *papà.* That's why I want to go to university."

"Maybe you'll listen to your mother. Where *is* Willa?"

"In bed. She's feeling worse today."

"Hummph!" He shook his head and returned to his paper. Just then, Grazia came in with her broom. "Grazia, has the mail come?"

"I'll check," I said before Grazia could answer.

In the mailbox I found several envelopes addressed to *papà* and a magazine for mamma. Then I saw it, the envelope from Cattolicà with the information about enrollment. I tore it open. *Welcome to Cattolicà...,* the letter said. There was a list of enrollment dates. I would be leaving in two months. At that time, I was excited and anxious about going away from home for the first time, and I couldn't have imagined what the real cost of my intentions would turn out to be. I heard *papà*'s footsteps and slipped the letter inside the magazine and folded the magazine under my arm.

"What's that you're holding, *cara*?"

"It's just mamma's subscription from America." I handed him his mail.

"I want to see *all* of the mail immediately." He tore open one of the envelopes.

"*Papà*, going to university is the only way I can become a history teacher, and I can enroll in October...."

He looked at the address on another envelope and opened it. "There's plenty of work for you here at Vino Marcheschi."

"I just got a letter from Cattolicà. Can I show it to you now?"

He waved his hand as if he were trying to get rid of a fly. *"Basta!*
Come with me."* I followed him into the *salotto.* He handed me his newspaper and pointed to an editorial. "Read this. It's the only history you
need to know." He went out, leaving me to read the article myself:

*We Orvietani believe that mistakes result from hasty or thoughtless ac-
tions. What is correct is already known: the time of the* vendemmia, *the best
families, what is a proper marriage. If an untested action seems needed, we
take time to consult the priest and to wait for agreement among our city's
leaders on what is to be done. We recall that the Orsini and Marcheschi families underwrote the cost of the great bronze doors of our Duomo. Everyone
agreed that their generous gift has bought a sense of solidity to the shimmering façade of our famous cathedral. More importantly, this change occurred
only after several generations had considered the matter, and, thus, it reflects
the collective history and wisdom of our own community.*

*Recently, ridiculous rumors circulated that Orvieto was endangered, per-
haps doomed. Even people who knew better told this story beyond the city
walls with the result that tourists were afraid to visit and our merchants lost
money. Perhaps people told this false story because they found it exciting.
Even though the correct story appeared in this newspaper and others, by the
time it was published, it was already too late. Damage was inevitable. Even
today, some people believe that Orvieto is still in danger.*

*Here is the truth: The porous tufa beneath our city is riddled with ancient
caves and grottoes, some natural, some manmade. From time to time these
structures give way. Such occurrences are so common that they are rarely
publicized. In this instance, after several cars fell into sinkholes and a few
homes sustained damage, our wisest leaders debated whether these were acts
of God or of man and, thus, whether the matter demanded prayer or science.
Once again, two of our distinguished citizens, Pietro Orsini and Gabriele
Marcheschi, urged that we consult with leading experts. The latter advised
inserting a network of piles and pipes into the tufa to prevent further deteri-
oration. When our esteemed Monsignor Enrico also examined the evidence,*

he agreed that our actions were correct and blessed them. Workmen are now placing scaffolding base-to-summit around the perimeter of the outcropping and have begun the difficult work of reinforcement. This exceptional project will keep Orvieto secure for generations to come and once again demonstrates to everyone that by God's grace we are led to success through correct actions.

I dropped the newspaper on *papà*'s chair and took the letter upstairs to my room. Grazia followed me with a basket of laundry. "Grazia, look! It's a letter from the university." I held the letter out to her.

She shook her head and crossed herself. "I can't read letters."

"I'll read it to you." Grazia continued to put the laundry away. "Don't you think *papà* will be proud of me?" I asked her when I had finished.

She shook her head again and made the sign of the cross. "A fruit cannot fall from two trees. *Una grande sfortuna.*" Very unlucky.

"No, Grazia, it will be *good* luck. I'm going to be a history teacher." I lifted the lid of the mahogany wedding chest that had once belonged to Nonna Marcheschi, *papà*'s mother. Leaves and flowers and the goddess Juno had been painted on the front panel. Folded inside was everything I would need when I married: embroidered linens and gowns; tablecloths with cut work, fringe, lace, faggoting; hand-stitched quilts and a heavy, crocheted coverlet begun several generations before that consisted of hundreds of squares sewn together and fringed. There was also a hidden compartment where I put keepsakes: a postcard with a picture of Botticelli's "Primavera," my gold baby ring, the candle I held at my first communion, and an article about James Dean, the American movie actor, that my best friend, Maria Lucarelli, had given me when we were thirteen. I also kept Nonna Marcheschi's pearl necklace and earrings there. I slipped the letter into the same compartment, closed the chest, and locked it.

Just then, I heard the sound of voices beneath my window and went to see who was coming to visit us. It was Dottor and Signora Lucarelli. I knew the box Signora Lucarelli was carrying contained the *confetti,* white sugar-coated almonds that always accompanied wedding announcements. Dottor Lucarelli lifted the latch on our high gate and allowed his wife to precede him. He followed her bulky form as she strode toward our front door. People often told jokes about the Dottore's small stature and the Signora's bulk, the principal one being that he was slight because the Signora was always on top during their lovemaking. Still, the Lucarellis were a very respected family.

As soon as I opened the front door, the fragrances of wisteria and jasmine engulfed me. The vines cascaded over our courtyard walls and obscured the bullet holes made during *la Guerra*, a subject that everyone avoided. Some Orvietani, including *papà* and mamma, had sympathized with the *partigiani* while others, including the Lucarellis, had supported the *fascisti*. There had been many deaths for which each faction still blamed another. The Orsinis, among others, had tried to remain neutral. It was likely only by chance that the retreating Germans spared the Orsini's property and not that of their neighbors. Still, some suspected the Orsinis of collaborating with the Germans. After the War, people found it difficult to forget that these things had happened and to go on with their lives. Often, the smiles with which they greeted one another when they met on the streets and in the shops provided only the thinnest disguise for their bitter memories and suppressed rage.

Signora Lucarelli smiled at me and held out a small box tied with a white ribbon.

"Mamma! Come!" I called. "It's the *confetti* for Maria and Edgardo." When we were little girls, Maria Lucarelli and I had promised that we would attend one another on our marriage days. I already had the blue dress I would wear for Maria's wedding mass. Whenever I had tried to talk to mamma about my marrying Bruno, she always said, "You'll have plenty of time for that later." I knew that girls who waited to get married could miss their chance. Mamma apparently didn't think that was important, but I knew *papà* did. At the time, I thought that mamma was simply preoccupied with her illness.

I untied the ribbon on the box and lifted the cover. Then we all kissed one another on both cheeks and said how happy we were. At that moment, mamma appeared in the foyer. The Lucarellis and I watched in silence as she shuffled toward us like a large shadow, her black leather slippers dragging against the terra cotta floor. By then mamma had been sick for more than a year. Dottore Lucarelli had first diagnosed her problem as "indigestion" and prescribed castor oil and herbs. When she got worse, she went to a doctor in Arezzo, who said she was suffering from a "nervous esophagus." It wasn't until she went to a specialist in Milano that she learned that she had cancer. By then, there was little that could be done to arrest the progress of her disease. Most people regarded this news as fate, but mamma saw it as bad luck. Bad luck that she had the misfortune to live in Orvieto instead of in a place with "real doctors, not quacks." Mamma always had strong opinions. Mine was a less certain temperament than hers, but I had no doubt that I wanted to become a teacher.

"What a surprise!" mamma said looking at the *confetti.* "How long have they known each other?" She didn't appear to be talking to anyone in the room. I saw the Lucarellis exchange glances.

"But our daughters are best friends." Signora Lucarelli looked at me and then at mamma. "You don't remember the banns?" I was embarrassed for mamma. She had become increasingly forgetful and often said odd things. She extended her frail hand toward Signora Lucarelli, who touched it as if it might break. Signora Lucarelli believed that every disease was contagious. She let go of mamma's hand as quickly as possible, and when she thought no one would notice, wiped her hand on her skirt.

Mamma stumbled and nearly lost her balance. She reached out for my arm. "I'm just a little weak today." She continued toward Dottore Lucarelli with her hand extended. He bowed. It seemed to me that their greetings took an especially long time. "What a lovely surprise," Mamma said again. Her voice sounded stronger, and I hoped the Lucarellis felt more welcomed.

"We're disturbing your rest," Signora Lucarelli said.

Mamma waved her hand as if she were removing a cobweb. "It's certainly taken you long enough," she said. She didn't mean it the way it sounded; her Italian wasn't perfect. Holding my arm, she plucked one of the *confetti* from the open box and held it in her yellowed fingers, seeming to forget that it was there.

Signora Lucarelli took one of the *confetti* from the box for herself. When she put it in her mouth and chewed, it sounded like small bones cracking. "We hope that the Marcheschis will honor us with their presence at Maria and Edgardo's wedding," she said to mamma.

"Odd that *confetti* have two tastes," mamma said. "Sweet at first and then bitter afterward." She chewed the candy with difficulty, choked, and then cleared her throat. "Just like marriage."

"But what could be sweeter than my daughter's marriage?" Dottore Lucarelli said.

"Mamma, the Lucarellis think that you've wished Maria and Edgardo an *unhappy* marriage."

"It's my poor Italian," mamma said to the Lucarellis. "Forgive me. On the contrary, I—we—wish Maria and Edgardo great happiness." She brushed a strand of her thin, graying hair from her forehead.

"Yes, great happiness," I said, hoping I sounded more convincing than mamma had.

"I don't suppose Silvana and Raffaele will be able to join us?" Signora Lucarelli spoke very carefully, as if mentioning my older sister and brother were a dangerous and provocative act.

Mamma took another *confetti*. She seemed to swallow it whole. Signora Lucarelli observed her as though she were watching a thief. "I don't think so," mamma said after a long pause. "Silvana and Raffaele have their...." She hesitated, seemingly unable to name exactly what it was that prevented their attending Maria and Edgardo's wedding. "Yes, their work and...other obligations," she concluded in the manner of a child spelling a long and difficult word from memory. She took a deep breath as if she had crossed over an abyss to safety.

Signora Lucarelli smiled and seemed to relax. "Maria and Edgardo will be very sorry that they aren't able to come. Their *nozze* will be the most beautiful anyone has ever seen in Orvieto, I promise you." Signora

Lucarelli's size and her certainty seemed to expand as she spoke. "Edgardo is a very special young man and he's going to be very successful. Very important." Dr. Lucarelli nodded in agreement. When Signora Lucarelli felt her words had achieved the effect she desired, she rubbed her hands together and turned to me. "Now, *carissima,* we're going to the Orsinis and then to see Monsignor Enrico. So much to do when a daughter gets married!" She looked at mamma. "I think you'll find out just how much very soon." She winked at me as if we shared a secret.

Of course, it was no secret that Bruno Orsini had courted me for more than a year, and it was expected that we would soon announce our betrothal and become *fidanzati.* Bruno was considered *buon partito*: excellent reputation, excellent family, excellent prospects. Handsome like an actor. Refined. People regarded him as trustworthy, too, so that even his elders sought his advice. In Orvieto there was nothing more important a young woman could do than to marry a man everyone respected. I was proud to be considered Bruno's intended, though he hadn't yet proposed.

"Bruno is nearly as much *un buon partito* as Edgardo," Signora Lucarelli confided to me. "Don't you agree?" Signora Lucarelli was crafty, and her compliments often meant something else. She intended to convey that Bruno was respected, admired and thought worthy of being emulated, but just not as much as Edgardo was. Despite what Signora Lucarelli said, I knew that everyone admired Bruno more. "Everyone *still* has great respect for the Marcheschis and the Orsinis," she continued. She pressed my cheeks between her hands as if I were a small child and smiled. "Am I right?"

Of course, I recognized Signora Lucarelli's references to Silvana and Raffaele's scandalous reputations and to the recent financial reverses of the Orsini family. She felt free to mention these things because of her powerful position in the community. Few risked conflict with her. Her reputation for vengefulness dated from the time of *la Guerra.* Of course, those stories might have been exaggerated. How does one ever know for sure? But she was right that the Marcheschi and Orsini names commanded great respect. They still do today, despite what happened right after

Maria and Edgardo were married and despite what people say. Just as the Lucarellis were leaving, *papà* returned. *"Benvenuti, carissimi!"* He shook hands with Dottore Lucarelli and kissed Signora Lucarelli's hand. "Has no one invited you to sit down? Come. Come." He saw the box of *confetti*. "And what is this?" He plucked one of the remaining *confetti* from the box and held it between his fingers. "Such wonderful news!" He popped the *confetti* into his mouth and then held his arms wide. "We must celebrate Maria's happiness and Edgardo's good fortune." He led the Lucarellis into the *salotto*. "Grazia," he called, "bring the wine and prepare something to eat! It's not every day that a daughter marries, as well I know." He looked at me and wiggled his little fingers, a gesture to ward off *la sfortuna*. "Imagine! This one talks about going to university and teaching history instead of getting married."

Signora Lucarelli's eyebrows rose and then came together. "Well, this *is* news. I thought you were preparing your wedding chest." She made it sound as if I had violated a law.

"Not *instead* of getting married...," I began.

"Why shouldn't Fina go to university if that's what she wants to do?" mamma said. No one had noticed that she had come into the *salotto* until she spoke. She had always told me that I should leave Orvieto as soon as I could.

"Never mind," *papà* said, turning his attention to the Lucarellis. "Today, we celebrate your daughter's *nozze*." He poured the wine.

At that time, I often wrote my future name, *Signora Orsini*, on slips of paper just to see how it would look, although girls believed that writing down one's married name before the banns was unlucky. "Don't invite *sfortuna* before *fortuna*," we warned one another. Few followed this advice. Just to be safe, I burned each slip of paper in the fireplace until only ashes remained. In fact, I had already planned my own *nozze*: I would wear a crown of flowers tied with long, colored ribbons that would flutter in the breeze during my wedding procession and afterwards during the dancing. I wanted to look like Flora in Botticelli's *Primavera*, a painting I had seen several times when mamma and I had gone to Firenze together. Once, an older man wearing a grey hat was standing next to us in the gallery. He and mamma spoke very quietly, so quietly that I couldn't hear what they said, but as we were leaving, the man gave me a postcard with a likeness of the painting, the one I kept in my wedding chest. He touched my cheek—I still remembered his cool, dry fingertips—and he said, "Someday, you'll look just like Flora."

After the Lucarellis left, *papà* and I watched mamma shuffle back to bed. "She seems weaker," I said.

"She would feel better if she went out more. She spends too much time in her room."

"*Papà*, I got a very important letter today about enrolling at Cattolicà—"

He threw up his hands. "*Santo cielo*! Why won't you give me any peace?"

2

On the morning of Maria and Edgardo's wedding, I unlocked the wedding chest with the key that I kept hidden in my underwear drawer and slid the front panel out. The letter from Cattolicà was still there. I took out the postcard and compared the image on it with my reflection in the mirror. Like Flora, I was fair and lithe. And I loved flowers. I hoped that this would be a good day to talk to *papà* about my plan to go to university because enrollment was only two months away. Celebrations always put *papà* in a good mood. I left the postcard on my bureau and put on the blue dress. Then, I wound pink flowers in my hair the way I knew would please *papà* and Bruno. I wanted them to feel proud of me.

When I was ready, I took out Nonna Marcheschi's pearls. As the eldest granddaughter, Silvana would normally have received them, but after the birth of Silvana's second illegitimate child, *nonna* had given the pearls to me just before she died. I liked keeping things that were part of our family's history, but to avoid hurt feelings, I wore the pearls only when Silvana wasn't present. I didn't want her to feel that she had been left out. She had a volatile temper and a tendency to talk about unpleasant things, especially if she was angry or upset. I held the string of pearls around my neck, but when I tried to fasten the clasp, the old silk thread broke. Pearls scattered on the uneven floor and rolled into the cracks and crevices between the planks. I gathered up as many as I could find and dropped them into a pink porcelain bowl rimmed with silver that had also belonged to *nonna*.

Next to the bowl I kept a photograph of our family that Grandmother Carver had taken twelve years before at The Pavilion during our family's only trip to America. The photograph was mounted in a bronze frame, which had been cast with ribbons and garlands and had once belonged to Nonna Marcheschi's grandmother. In the center of the photograph, *papà* rested his right hand on mamma's shoulder and his left on Raffaele's shoulder. At that time, Raffaele had just turned thirteen, and I was about three. Mamma is holding me on her lap and looks straight into the camera as if she were waiting for the answer to a question. To one side and separate from us, Silvana, nearly fifteen, looks intent on something beyond the picture frame.

"Fina, it's already nine o'clock," *papà* called. "You'll make us late." I opened my door. "*Papà*, after the wedding, I want to talk—"

He shook his head and put his hand up. "*Presto! Presto!* We're going to miss the procession." I went back and put on *nonna*'s earrings, the ones with pearls as big as olive pits. Silvana didn't know about the earrings either. Mamma said it would be best not to tell her about them. I slipped on my new white shoes, then put the postcard away, and locked the chest again. When I came downstairs, mamma emerged from her room. She pushed her grey hair away from her face. I noticed she had a bald spot at the crown of her head. I hoped she wouldn't discover it; she had always taken so much pride in her thick, auburn hair. When I kissed her pale cheek, her skin felt cool against my lips, and she seemed thinner and even less present than when the Lucarellis had brought the *confetti. I must be mistaken,* I thought.

Before mamma had gotten sick, we had always been confidantes, but by this time I could feel her slipping away from me, going to a place where I couldn't follow her. Earlier she would have talked to *papà* about my going to university herself, but by then she no longer seemed to notice what happened in my life. Looking back, I suppose she must have been thinking about dying, understood that her death was nearing. At that time, I didn't have a real understanding of such concerns.

"Please give the Lucarellis my regrets," mamma said. *Papà* moved abruptly, betraying his impatience, but at least he didn't say anything to upset mamma or make her angry. So often he did.

"I hope you feel better by the time we get back," I said. "We'll have so many things to tell you."

"Perhaps Fina will want to discuss *her* wedding plans with you," *papà* said, smiling.

"She's too young to get married," mamma said. A cloud passed over *papà's* face.

"Tomorrow," he said to mamma, his voice unnaturally hearty, "you'll feel like yourself again. We'll make a *passeggiata* together in the new vineyard. The exercise will do you good, and we can talk about it then."

"Gabriele, don't you see that I'm dying?"

"Nonsense," *papà* said, "it's just a question of attitude: you think about yourself and your problems too much." That's how *papà* was: if he couldn't fix something or get his way, he simply dismissed it. Mamma turned and went back to her room.

"What do you want from me?" *papà* shouted. "I've given and forgiven. It's never enough for you." Mamma slammed her door.

"Forgiven what?" I said. *Papà* didn't answer. He never did. Whenever I had asked mamma what *papà* was talking about, she always said, "Some silly idea he has. It's not important." *Papà* and mamma usually treated one another with cautious formality, as though they wanted to preclude any intimacy before it could occur, so their frequent and heated outbursts seemed inexplicable. Underneath, they were engaged in a war that singed their lives and cooked their souls in a venomous stew that I had learned early not to stir. It would be a few months before I would learned the source of their rage.

Papà and I stood together as Maria emerged from the doorway of her family's home on the Piazza della Repubblica. Her white dress and the gold crown that held her veil shimmered in the bright sun. The wedding guests gasped and murmured to one another:

"Che bella!"

"Edgardo has *fortuna* today."

"Together they will make beautiful *bambini*."As we moved along the Corso, more wedding guests joined the procession, everyone clapping and cheering. Bruno and I walked together, holding hands. He kissed me. "You look beautiful," he said.

When a tourist stepped into the road and aimed his camera at us, *papà* reached out and covered the lens with his hand. The man backed away. "Never let *stranieri* take pictures of you!" *papà* said to us. "They're worse than the *Zingari*." Gypsies. "A *zingaro* only steals your belongings. A tourist turns you into an organ grinder's monkey to entertain his friends." According to *papà* there was nothing worse than a *zingaro*. Not even a *femminista* or a tourist.

Our procession wound past the Cinema Etrusco, Orvieto's only movie theater, which was housed in a cave that in earlier times had been a wine cellar. Today, it's used as warehouse. I loved its shadowy interior and the smells of mold, vinegar, and popcorn. On Saturday afternoons, Maria and I sat on the wooden folding chairs in the middle row, each of us with her own bag of popcorn. According to the proprietor, this was what Americans ate when they went to the movies. There were few new films, but we liked seeing the same ones again and again. The year we were thirteen, our favorite film, *East of Eden* starring James Dean, played for six months. Maria gave me an article from a movie magazine that described James Dean's childhood. I had nearly memorized it: despite his fame, Dean wished for "someone special" to care about him. Whenever I saw that film, I wanted to console Cal, the character Dean played. Of course, I knew it was just a story. By then James Dean was already dead, but I imagined that there was someone, perhaps far from Orvieto, who needed me.

"I want to take care of people and make them feel better," I once told Bruno.

"You think you can change what can't be changed."

"No, I think people need to be consoled for what can't be changed," I said.

"Movies have given you a lot of silly ideas. I don't have time for such things."

"I want to go to university and teach history," I said. "That's not a silly idea."

"I could never marry *una femminista*. They just argue and make their husbands wear the horns."

"How does going to university make me *una femminista*?"

"See? You're arguing with me." Most people felt as Bruno did, including *papà*. Nonna Marcheschi had always said that women have to keep their thoughts to themselves.

When we reached the Piazza del Duomo, I looked up above the doors of the Duomo to the carved statues of Mary Magdalene, Rachel, Sarah, and the Virgin Mary. I often felt their presence at the ceremonies inside and also when I prayed for their help. I thought that everyone experienced this sense of spirits being present, but Bruno said, "Spirits are superstitions from when people were less scientific in their thinking." Bruno had attended a viniculture course in Perugia and had become convinced that he and *papà* could apply scientific principles to developing a new vintage. I didn't see any connection between the spirits I felt and winemaking, but I didn't say so because Bruno would have wanted me to "prove it scientifically," and I couldn't. I thought that when I went to university, I would learn how to explain my feelings about spirits in a way that Bruno could understand, but mamma said, "Men and women live in different worlds. Eventually, you get used to it."

Besides, there were many ways that Bruno showed me that he cared about me. He took my arm as we climbed the steps and walked into the Duomo together ahead of Maria and Edgardo. At the altar, Monsignor Enrico waited in the gold robes that he wore only when the bride's family had made a substantial contribution to a special fund to support "parish development." He spoke of the abundance of a happy marriage and read from the sixty-fifth Psalm: *May the meadows cover themselves with flocks and the valleys cloak themselves with grain; let them shout for joy and sing.* I wanted Monsignor Enrico to read this psalm and wear his gold robes at my *nozze*, too. *Papà* had made many contributions to the parish.

After the wedding mass, Bruno stood with me again outside the Duomo. "I have something to tell you," I said. "I received a letter from

Cattolicà..."

"Our walk is going to be long and hot today," he said. He wiped his face with his handkerchief.

"...about when I'm to go to Milano to enroll."

The owner of another vineyard approached us. "Bruno, I'd like you to come next week and give us some advice on our press."

"Yes. Don't save all your wisdom for Gabriele while the rest of us go broke," another laughed.

People believed in Bruno and relied on his judgement, even though he was still young. So did I. *Why is it that some people seem to know what to do and others are often confused or lost?* I wondered. *Was it because Bruno's mother had died when he was young, and he had learned to look after himself? In* East of Eden *Cal lost his mother, too, but he wasn't like Bruno.*

"My teachers said I would be a good teacher," I told Bruno again as soon as we were alone.

"Are you planning to become a nun, too?"

"No. A history teacher. Why?"

"Only nuns become teachers. Otherwise, women with too much education make trouble. Their brains aren't built for knowledge," Bruno said. "It's a scientific fact."

"That's not true."

Bruno laughed. "See? Already, I have to watch you or you'll just argue with me for no reason. You'll be worse if you go to university."

As we neared the funicular, I stumbled. Fortunately, Bruno broke my fall. He helped me up and stood near me while I brushed the grit off my dress. Afterwards, we waited together on the platform for the funicular along with some of the workmen. When *papà* caught up with us, his face was red and he was breathing hard and sweating. He sank down onto a nearby bench that overlooked the entire valley below us and fanned himself with his hat. "This land belongs to our family now," he said moving his arm in an arc. He gestured toward the scaffolding around the perimeter of the outcropping. "I'm responsible for this project," he added loudly.

Everyone turned to listen to him, though most people had already read about it in the newspaper.

"A wise decision," Bruno said, as if the information were new to him despite the fact that his own father, who was mayor at the time, had helped make the decision to reinforce the outcropping. Bruno didn't seem to mind that *papà* often took credit for what other people did, but I wished *papà* could be more generous.

"When our people have a clear explanation, they do what's right," *papà* continued. "We aren't ignorant like tourists." He wheezed and coughed, but when the funicular arrived, he got on by himself and declined the seat Dr. Lucarelli offered him. Everyone was in good spirits as we descended to the station. When we got off, the workmen called out to us. "Save some *spumante* for us!" "Don't forget the *torta!*" "And a dance for me!" I smiled and waved to them.

"Don't do that," Bruno said.

I dropped my hand as if I had touched something hot. "It's a celebration. Everyone wants to be part of it," I said. As we walked away, the sun beat down on us. My dress felt too small, my shoes too tight. I wished that I had brought my straw hat, the one with the wide brim, so that I could hide under it, cool and invisible, like the grapes in our vineyards hanging beneath their canopies of leaves.

"They're workers," Bruno said. "They would never be invited to an important wedding like this one." He was right, of course. In Orvieto it was important to remember where you belonged. Elsewhere, too, I suppose. There were the good families, then the workers, and then the *stranieri*. After them, the tourists and the *Zingari*. Poor mamma was still considered *una straniera* even after she had lived in Orvieto most of her life and was a successful businesswoman. As we neared the train station, *papà* pointed out the ornate wooden sign on which Gianni, the woodcarver, had worked the name *Orvieto*; the sign had been next to the station since before I was born. Just then, the morning train disgorged its cargo of tourists.

"Wouldn't you like to know about the places they come from?" I said to Bruno.

He held his finger to his lips. "Shhh. Gabriele is talking."

"Willa has always loved Orvieto as much I do," *papà* was saying. I thought he must have been talking about the time when he and mamma were courting because mamma always spoke of leaving Orvieto as if she had an urgent appointment someplace else. Sometimes, it seemed that mamma's only interest was leaving Orvieto despite the success of Vino Marcheschi. No one, especially not *papà*, gave her credit for making Vino Marcheschi profitable. I imagined that if I became a history teacher, one day I could manage a school the way mamma managed our business.

"We should have a modern sign now," *papà* continued. "A billboard to announce our new vintage. If we put it here, the tourists will see it." I noticed Bruno looking at the vineyard next to the road, the one we called the south vineyard. It had originally belonged to his father. Mamma had insisted on buying it from the Orsinis when Bruno's family had needed money. The purchase made our family the largest landowners in the region. Afterwards, mamma had persuaded Bruno to come work for us.

"One day my children will inherit this land," *papà* said with obvious pride, "and their children after them, just as I inherited my father's land." I wished he hadn't made such a point of this in Bruno's presence.

"Yes. It surely *is* the right time for a new sign," Bruno said. "We have the perfect combination of soil and climate this year to recreate the original Orvieto." I thought maybe Bruno could help *papà* adopt a more modern way of thinking, one like mamma's.

3

The sounds of the guests merged with the steady hum and buzz of the insects in the surrounding vineyards and fields. Under a wisteria-covered pergola the women had set out the wedding feast on a ring of long tables. The white tablecloths embroidered with their initials reminded the women of cherished memories of their own weddings. I had always loved this evidence of shared experiences. When Bruno and I were married, I, too, would become a member of their circle and would bring the tablecloths in my wedding chest to celebrations like this one. I sat down and slipped off my shoes. Nearby, Maria and Edgardo talked with their guests. Little girls chattered among themselves; they held out their skirts and pirouetted just as Maria and I had once done, while the musicians tuned their instruments and adjusted their music stands.

In the center of the ring of tables, a place had been cleared for dancing. *Papà* stood there so that everyone could see him. He faced the bride and groom and raised his glass. "I am honored to be the first to wish Maria and Edgardo a life of joy and happiness together. Today, I drink to them with a Lucarelli wine, but as you and God are my witnesses, we will drink to the births of your children and grandchildren with our new Marcheschi Orvieto." The guests applauded. *"Bravo! Bravo!"* I thought that *papà* sounded like the ringmaster at the circus in Naples. He kept on. "Soon, I will recreate the original Orvieto beloved by the ancients and by the popes. Vino Marcheschi will return our Orvieto wine to its historic eminence." The guests applauded and whistled again.

"He shouldn't talk about this now," I whispered to Bruno. "It's Maria and Edgardo's day."

"Why not? Everyone is here," Bruno said. I took a square of fried semolina from a platter and bit off one corner. It tasted of rum and vanilla. "He should give *you* credit, too." I brushed the crumbs off of my dress "Why are you always so critical?"

Papà sat down next to Bruno. I hoped they wouldn't talk about business, but another winemaker sat down with them and asked Bruno about a problem he was having with his vineyard. I put my shoes back on and was about to move away from them when Dottor Lucarelli stood up and raised his glass.

"I wish to make a toast to my daughter and son-in-law on their wedding day." He turned to *papà*. "And to your daughter ahead of hers. May our children never drink with *stranieri*." Laughter and more clapping ensued. I looked at Bruno. He lifted his glass to me and motioned for me to remain next to him. Platters heavy with food arrived for us. I served some of the barbecued meats and sausages. The three men took immense portions. Someone passed the fried sage leaves; I put one in my mouth and crushed it with my tongue.

The musicians started to play, and Maria and Edgardo began the first dance. Soon, other couples joined them. I ate slowly, watching. Bruno poured a chilled Orvieto into our glasses and touched his glass to mine. "*Salute.* What are you thinking about now, *cara?*"

I took a big sip, allowing the liquid to remain in my mouth, and then swallowed. "I'm thinking about going to university."

"Why can't you just enjoy yourself?"

"Maybe because you insist that I should." Sometimes Bruno annoyed me.

"You're arguing with me."

"No, I'm not."

Bruno just laughed and led me into the circle with the other couples. I felt stiff, without rhythm. Though I wanted to pay attention to the music and to Bruno, my thoughts remained elsewhere. When the music ended, I went back to the table and sat down. I took long sips of wine, anticipating the moment when my body would become light and free.

Leonardo came over to me. "Will you dance with me?"

Antonio joined us. "After you dance with me?"

Bruno walked over to us, alert and tense. "She's dancing with me."

I laughed. "There's no music, so I can't dance with any of you." Still, I wondered what it would be like to dance with Leonardo and Antonio. Both came from good families, though perhaps not as respected as Bruno's. One of the women placed several slices of veal carpaccio on my plate. I cut a piece and ate it, savoring the bland coolness of the veal against its dressing of olive oil and herbs.

"You're breaking my heart," Leonardo said, refilling my glass.

"Mine, too," Antonio added.

"She doesn't want to dance with you," Bruno said.

"Why not, Fina?" Antonio said.

I laughed again and drank some more wine. "I'm eating. I'm too busy to dance." Antonio and Leonardo moved away from us.

Bruno relaxed. "Don't encourage them," he said. "They only want to cause trouble."

"Trouble?" I liked being wanted, liked having others see that I was desirable.

"People will talk if you dance with anyone else." Bruno was just jealous. He withdrew into silence. Being with Bruno meant giving up something, too. I took another sip of wine before serving both of us some roasted organ meats. Then, a Lucarelli family specialty—ravioli drenched in roasted meat sauce—arrived at the table.

Despite the excitement of the day, I felt as if I were waiting for something to happen. "You expect too much," mamma often said. "A woman's life is mainly waiting. You'll see…especially if you stay here." Soft, slow music began, and Bruno gestured for me to precede him to the dance floor. He held me in his arms as if nothing were wrong. Probably nothing was. Perhaps he just had other, more important things on his mind. I closed my eyes and felt Bruno's body along the length of mine, the warmth of his shoulder, the strength of his callused hand holding mine. My desire to be close to him and yet keep a proper distance, especially in public, created a pleasant tension.

Maria passed by in Edgardo's arms. "You make a beautiful couple," Maria said to us. It seemed like a blessing. The little girls were watching us, too, and their attention made me aware of the significance of my relationship with Bruno to the community. I felt visible, an actor in my own life, and I imagined something important would happen to me soon. I wanted it to be something that would change me and change my life. A transformation.

When the music stopped, Simonetta called for the unmarried women to dance. We began slowly at first, and then faster and faster, competing with the musicians until the frenzied music invaded our bodies, our muscles, and our bones. The sound drove my movements so that I no longer controlled them, so that the movement was formed from the sound that coursed within me. The effortless oneness of sound and motion erased my awareness of the blister on my foot and the heat of the afternoon and I gave myself over entirely to this power, losing my sense even of time and allowing the wild sound and sweet wine to carry me away, as weightless as wind. Even after the music stopped, the rhythmic clapping of the guests continued. In the center of the circle, I danced alone, unwilling to return to the world of the will, aware for the first time of how many possibilities I contained. I imagined gathering my belongings, carrying them to the Piazzale Cahen, descending on the funicular, and boarding an early train to Firenze, Milano, Roma—perhaps beyond.

I felt Bruno's presence next to me before he spoke. "Everyone is looking at you." I opened my eyes and allowed him to lead me away from the circle. The movement drained from my body. "What's wrong with you today?"

I smiled at him. "Nothing. Nothing at all."

4

Right after Maria and Edgardo's wedding, mamma's condition worsened very quickly. Dottor Lucarelli came. "A few more days at most," he said. *Papà* sent for Silvana and Raffaele. I remember that the weather turned unseasonably chilly and rainy. In her bed, mamma was shivering. Grazia made a fire in the fireplace in mamma's room. I sat in the straight, caned chair by mamma's bed and held her hand. Her fingers fluttered against my palm. Her translucent skin clung to the bones and cartilage underneath like thin, wet paper. Her teeth chattered. I pulled the white matelasse coverlet up under her chin, but her trembling continued. She opened her eyes and looked at me.

"I've lived far from my origins," she said in English, the language she spoke only with me. "When I came to Orvieto, I intended to become someone else. I saw the green hills and valleys and I thought I could grow as an artist here." Tears spilled down her cheeks. I wiped them away with her lace handkerchief. "I was so young. I believed everything was possible. So many mistakes." She looked up at me. "It was my fault." She paused, as if she wanted my encouragement to speak further, and then looked away, still trembling. "I couldn't put down roots in such old soil." I adjusted her coverlet.

"It's all right, mamma." I felt how much she grieved for her life, for losses I didn't fully comprehend. There was so little I could do or say to console her.

"The Marcheschis had their memories. I was a tourist. They've always called me *la straniera*. Everyone did." She sighed. "You children have been my consolation." She sought a more comfortable position and exhaled slowly, as if the movement of each molecule of air brought her

new distress. "It's hard work coming into this life and it's hard work going out." I stroked her hand, observed the paths of the veins and delicate
maps of the capillaries over her knuckles. I was about to say, "Don't go
yet, stay with us, wait," when Grazia limped in with a pitcher of water
and a glass. She put them on the table next to the bed.

"Mamma, I have something important to tell you. I'm planning to
go enroll at Cattolicà in a few weeks...." She coughed and then thrashed,
trying to get her breath. "Here, let me help you sit up."

"Don't let anyone look at me after I'm dead," mamma said to me in
Italian so that Grazia would hear, too. "They didn't care to call on me in
this life. Don't let them satisfy their curiosity about how I look when I'm
in the next one. Put me in my coffin and slam the lid. Do you hear?"

"*Santo cielo.*" Grazia crossed herself and went out. Mamma looked
up at me.

"If it hadn't been for me, *nonno* and *nonna* wouldn't have lived so
long," mamma said.

I poured some water and held the glass for her. "You've taken good
care of all of us. We love you, mamma."

"Gabriele has never thanked me for taking care of his parents despite
the way they treated me. He's never noticed when I was there, but he
didn't want me to leave either."

Grazia returned with a bowl of broth and set it down next to the water
glass. I dipped the spoon into the warm liquid and held it to mamma's
lips. "Here, try some." Mamma took it, swallowed, took some more, and
retched. The broth dribbled down her chin and onto the white coverlet
leaving a yellowish trail and the smell of vomit. She leaned back on her
pillow and disappeared into an unseen world. I wiped her chin with a
white napkin. She opened her eyes.

"The past can't accept the present. Not easily." She gasped, looked up
at the ceiling, and twisted. "I wanted to live in the present." She was silent for a moment. "Try to understand: I wasn't a loose woman. The first
time I visited Gabriele's family I came without a chaperone. That's all."

"Of course, mamma. Don't try to talk."

"I was so lonely. Angry. Bitter." Her voice grew stronger. "They refused to accept me, so I didn't acknowledge them. And then Etto. So little and innocent. After Etto, I couldn't bear them...this place...any longer. After Etto I didn't care. I betrayed...." She paused and looked into my eyes. "Do you want to know?" I hesitated, afraid of what she might tell me. She sank back onto her pillow. "I don't expect you children to understand." She looked up at me. "Maybe Gabriele was lonely, too. But he always had his family. His ancestors. His familiars." She closed her eyes, and whispered, "His witnesses. His place. His memories." She reached out from under the coverlet, her hand in a fist. "Whatever you think about me, about what I've done, please try to remember that I had no one! Not even memories." She brought her fist down on the bed with surprising strength, her eyes full of tears. "Gabriele has never had to drink with strangers." I thought her frail body might break with her sobs. "He suffocated me with his rootedness. He couldn't do anything else." Her cold hand clutched mine. "Don't let him suffocate *you*." Just then, *papà* entered the room.

"Suffocate who?" He turned away from us when he spoke as if to avoid a blow.

"I'm suffocating."

"Ah, so you feel better today."

Mamma closed her eyes again. I adjusted the coverlet.

"I'll let you rest then." *Papà* seemed relieved to have found a reason to leave. "Is there anything you want?"

"Yes, Gabriele. I want to be buried next to Etto." Mamma's voice was clear and strong.

"You ask this of me, too?" He meant, of course, that instead of lying next to his wife, as was proper, he would be buried at a distance from her in an eternity of shame for all to see.

"It's the only thing I ask of you, Gabriele." *Papà* backed out of the door.

As soon as the latch clicked behind him, mamma turned to me with a soundless laugh.

"I'm a stranger to him. He only sees the Willa he's invented. I don't exist." She gasped. "Remember, he has invented you, too." I didn't know what she meant because *papà* and I had always been very close. I held a glass of water for her, not trusting myself to say anything. "In the end, we're all *stranieri*. We have to make peace with that."

"Mamma. I've decided to go to university. In Milano."

"Does Gabriele know?"

"Yes. He doesn't want to discuss it."

"I'll talk to him myself. Where did he go?" Her eyes closed and her jaw slackened. I watched the labored rise and fall of her chest and stroked her hand. She opened her eyes again and reached out, her hand claw-like, for her rosary. "Take this," she said. "I'm past prayers."

I turned her rosary in my fingers, examining the beads of jet and pink quartz separated by incised platinum spheres. "I've always loved this rosary," I said. "It seems magical." For the first time, I noticed the thin, platinum tag attached to it and on it an inscription: *Together in heaven.*

"Don't let anyone else have it. Not even Silvana. I'm leaving other things for her and Raffaele, but I want you to keep this." Mamma struggled to sit up. I put another pillow behind her. "And remember, Bruno isn't your only chance, no matter what they tell you." I nodded. "I want you to promise to do something for me." She gestured toward the closet. "In my *armadio,* behind everything, there's a box hidden in the wall." She coughed and gasped. "Bring it to me."

I opened the doors of the painted wood cupboard, which was secured with bolts sunk into the *tufa* so that the latter formed the wall behind it. Pushing aside mamma's clothes, I found a hatbox papered with faded pictures of travelers. I brushed away the dust on it with my skirt, carried it over to the bed, and set it down next to mamma. She raised herself up, seeming to revive.

"I brought this hatbox with me when I came to Italy. I was only twenty." She closed her eyes and smiled. "So full of dreams." I removed the lid from the box and lifted out a green velvet hat with a drooping, iridescent feather on one side. Mamma traced her finger along the length of the feather. "I wore this one in Firenze."

"I don't remember it. Was I there?"

"Let me see the others." Her interest surprised me. I held up a pale, purple cloche streaked with faded blue. A smile spread over her face. "Firenze, too." I held up another hat, this one of red felt with a black veil of dotted tulle. Mamma inhaled deeply, and tears came to her eyes. "Milano. His favorite."

"They're beautiful, but they seem out of style, now."

"I kept them to remember my dreams."

I put the hats away and returned the hatbox to mamma's *armadio*. "You have so many books in here, mamma." I wiped the dust off of my hands with my skirt. "They're in English."

"I was afraid I would forget my own language. I read and kept a diary...like a survivor of a shipwreck. "

"Here are some paints and a notebook." When I picked it up, the edges of the faded blue leather cover crumbled in my hands. A medal slid out onto the floor. I showed it to her. "What's this?"

"Just a war relic of Gabriele's. Did you find the box?"

I returned to the *armadio* again. In the wall at the back I could see the box. I lifted it out. Behind it the crumbling *tufa* had been scraped away to form a niche the way a prisoner might carve out a secret space or prepare for an escape. I saw a chisel and a spoon, the tools mamma must have used. I backed out of the *armadio* and brushed away the powdery residue on the box. "Is this what you wanted?"

"Yes. Tell him that I'll answer his letter as soon as I can go to Arezzo. I've had so much to do these last few days. I still need to get my tickets." She seemed to be dreaming, but her eyes were open. "The letters...where are they?"

"What letters?" I thought mamma must be delirious.

"You've left my letters out where someone could see them." She looked toward the door.

"You asked me to get this box for you, mamma."

"Always lock the door first," she whispered. I went to secure the lock.

"In the top drawer of my bureau there's a brass key." I found the key hanging on a length of frayed grosgrain ribbon; its original red color had faded to shades of lavender and orange. I gave it to mamma. "I took that ribbon from a cap of Etto's." She held it to her nose. "For a time it smelled like his hair." She handed it back to me. "Open the box now." She watched me as I put the key in the lock and turned until there was a dull click. Inside was a bundle wrapped in purple velvet. "Unwrap it," she whispered. "Remember, no one but you must see these." I took the bundle out of the box. Inside were the letters. I looked at one envelope, then another. I didn't recognize the handwriting. They all seemed to be addressed to someone I didn't know...Signora Isabella Farnese...someone in Arezzo.

"Whose are these?"

"Mine. They're from someone I've loved for many years. Michel Losine." *Was that what papà had to forgive?* I had always believed that we children were the fulfillment of all of *papà*'s and mamma's wishes. I had never imagined that they could have had other lives. Especially not mamma. *Weren't she and papà always together except when she went on sales trips for Vino Marcheschi?*

"Promise me you'll take these letters to him," mamma said, "and that you won't let anyone know that they exist." The fire sputtered. I didn't want to meet mamma's *amante*, who had kept an important part of her from us.

"Let me burn them right now, mamma. Then, you won't have to be concerned about them." I didn't want to keep her secrets from *papà*. Like an emissary on a futile errand, I had often felt caught in an unnamed and unresolved struggle between them. I didn't want to continue their battle.

"His address is on the envelope." Mamma's voice trailed off. I picked up one of the letters and saw the address. The letter was postmarked "Milano." Mamma breathed slowly. I tied the letters and wrapped them in the cloth, returned the bundle to the box, and put the box back in its niche. Now I was complicit. *Would it be a betrayal if I decided not to do what mamma had asked? Could I just burn the letters before anyone found out?* Mamma awakened with a start. "He's expecting you." Her eyelids fluttered. "Do you have your money?"

"What money?"

She opened her eyes, anxious. "In the bottom drawer of my bureau, in the back, under the paper liner there's an envelope with your name. Grandpa and Grandma Carver left this money when they died. Gabriele doesn't know about it or he would insist on keeping it himself. Take it! Make a life for yourself away from Orvieto."

Even though mamma had always talked about leaving Orvieto, the possibility of my doing so had always seemed remote to me, something I might read about in a novel or a story in one of mamma's magazines. After I went to university, I planned to come back. "I want you to have more choices than I had," she said. I wasn't as ambitious as mamma was. I only wanted to become a history teacher and marry Bruno. "Have you found a place to live?"

"No, but I have a list of places where Cattolicà students board."

Mamma closed her eyes, breathed softly; then she stirred, a smile rising at the corners of her mouth. "Did I tell you? I'm leaving Orvieto very soon, too?" she whispered. She opened her eyes and looked toward the door. "Why has Grazia let all those people come in here? Tell them to wait for me outside." She waved toward the foot of the bed. "I must be late!"

"There's no one else here."

"Tell Grazia to go now. I don't need her."

"She's not here."

Mamma fell asleep, her breathing slow and quiet. "I love you, mamma. We all do."

There were many more questions I wanted to ask her, but Mamma died that night. I was surprised that she could be alive and then not, surprised by the way that life leaves. Even though her body was still there, her room felt empty. Surprising, too, was my feeling that at last darkness had turned to light, that I could exhale fully without the ominous unease that until then I had thought was mine alone. It is difficult to describe this sense of relief I felt at the lifting of an unidentifiable but familiar oppression. I felt new to myself and also ashamed that these uncanny yet pleasurable feelings arose because mamma had died. I decided to read Michel Losine's letters.

5

Out of respect for *papà* and our family's position in Orvieto, many people felt it their duty to attend mamma's funeral mass at the Duomo and afterwards to call on us at home and express their condolences. I'm sure that some had never had a conversation with mamma during the entire time she had lived in Orvieto, and for most, it was the first time that they had been invited inside our house on *via* Cavallotti. They moved about the *salotto* and the garden in their best clothes, studied our possessions discreetly, and remarked on our taste as they enjoyed the refreshments that Grazia had prepared.

Though nearly a generation had passed since *la Guerra*, many of the guests had lived through that time and carried with them terrible memories. Some had been brought to our house for questioning themselves, and all knew someone who had been executed after these interrogations. Others remembered seeing that the occupying German soldiers had carved their initials or the Nazi symbol on the mantel in the *salotto*, on the cupboard in the kitchen, and on a newel of the stairway. Subsequent sanding and refinishing had failed to erase the marks entirely, and these too rekindled their memories of so many things that remained unspeakable and terrifying.

"A great loss to all of you," Pietro Orsini, Bruno's father, said to us as he entered the *salotto,* where *papà*, Raffaele, Silvana and I received our guests. He bowed slightly toward me and kissed *papà* on both cheeks. "I can well understand. Bruno was only a baby when I lost my wife."

Sister Maria Cristina, Pietro Orsini's sister, followed him into the *salotto* and stood next to him. The wide-winged wimple of her habit made her appear much larger than she actually was and suggested a fierce bird.

"God be with you," she murmured to *papà* and then turned away without acknowledging Silvana, Raffaele or me. Taking her brother's arm, she led him through the open doors and out into the garden. Bruno stood quietly near the fireplace, the black fabric of his suit jacket tense against his muscular arms.

Just then I overheard Signora Lucarelli ask *papà* about the fresco above the mantel. "It's as ancient as Oriveto," *papà* said. "I had it appraised by the leading antiquities dealer in Firenze. It's priceless. I have the certificates to prove it."

While Signora Lucarelli was thus occupied, Dottor Lucarelli seized my hand and looked into my eyes. "Our deepest sympathy," he said.

"Thank you."

He continued to hold my hand in both of his, trembling. *What does he want?* I wondered. "Your mother received proper care, I trust?" He ran his fingers over mine, held my eyes with his. I tried to extricate my hand, but he resisted. *Did Dottor Lucarelli realize that his misdiagnosis had contributed to mamma's death?* "If Willa had been under my care, I could have saved her. It takes time. She was impatient." Perhaps he wanted me to agree with him or to say that we understood that the delay in mamma's care wasn't his fault. I understood how he could have made a mistake. After all, he wasn't a real doctor. Everyone knew that. Besides, he was old. It was a mistake for mamma to consult him in the first place, but *papà* had insisted. "You've always been a hypochondriac," he said when she went to the doctor in Arezzo and later to a specialist in Milano. They argued about it. I don't know why mamma finally gave in and decided not to seek further treatment. I think she just decided to accept her fate.

"Wouldn't you like to taste some of Grazia's wonderful pastries?" I said to Dottor Lucarelli. At this, he let go of my hand.

Signora Lucarelli moved toward me as she dabbed her eyes with a lace-edged handkerchief of thin, black linen. "A closed casket. Very unusual." I nodded. "I understand the burial will be private, too." I nodded again. "Why private?" she said as though this were a decision that should have been discussed with her. "Whose idea was that?" I offered her some chocolates, hoping to distract her. She took the largest one and bit into it. "Was it your mother or your father who decided on a private burial?"

"I'm not sure." It was best not to tell Signora Lucarelli anything definite. She carried tales that she invented to fit her prejudices and could make it seem that you had said something you didn't say or mean.

Signora Lucarelli looked aggrieved. She reached for another chocolate and took a bite, exposing its soft center. "Willa and I were very close," she said, examining the morsel, "but she kept to herself." Signora Lucarelli shrugged and took the last bite. "I never knew why." She inclined her head toward Silvana, whose status as *ragazza madre*, a woman who had given birth to illegitimate children, had scandalized all of Orvieto. More than that, she took them out in public. "Silvana didn't put any of her children up for adoption, did she? I wonder why." I didn't respond. "Willa should have done something about it." She gave me a knowing look. "After all, your marriage prospects are involved." She took another chocolate. "You are Gabriele's true daughter, his best child, aren't you?"

Signora Carmina Santori, Signora Lucarelli's sister and the wife of a successful merchant, nodded in agreement. *"Assolutamente.* His only true daughter." She relished the spotlight and repeated *assolutamente* several times.

Silvana overheard their conversation and approached the two women. "Fina is an imposter," she said with a cackle and sailed off to refill her wine glass. Silvana would say anything if she felt she had been slighted. It was better not to provoke her.

"Gabriele needs you even more now," Signora Lucarelli continued. She glanced at Bruno. "How long has Bruno been working for your father?" Any response would have led Signora Lucarelli to new questions. "Edgardo owns his own business, of course, but I believe Bruno can still be a good husband and a good provider, don't you?" Signora Lucarelli pressed her hands against my cheeks. "You deserve a nice husband, and it will be good if he is involved in your family's business." She lowered her voice to a whisper. "I think he'll marry you, and he'll be a much better husband than someone in your circumstances could realistically expect."

I knew Signora Lucarelli was just voicing what everyone else thought. I offered her the tray with Grazia's tiny, cream-filled *cannoli*. She selected one, regarded its vulnerability, and then bit into it. "When you marry," she added, her mouth full, "you and Bruno will live in this house and take care of your father." Signora Lucarelli leaned closer and whispered. "I hope you're not still thinking about going to university. You must be careful about asserting your own interests before your wedding. Bruno has other choices."

She extended her index finger toward the antique cameo at my throat and ran her finger over its carved surfaces. "What a charming *little* cameo."

"It was mamma's," I said.

"I suppose it's something Willa got on one of those trips of hers. She was always traveling. Always wearing her hats."

6

At dawn the next morning, the morning of mamma's burial, the sun had already cut golden gashes in the pink clouds, formed stark shadows next to bright planes, and turned the edges of buildings and roofs into thin flames. I slipped mamma's rosary into my pocket. Outside, I had to shield my eyes despite my black veil. Already, my dark clothes felt too warm. Silvana put on her sunglasses and pulled at her dress, distorting the diagonal black and white stripes that encircled her torso like a boa constrictor. Despite the early hour, she smelled of vermouth and cigarettes. In the car, *papà* wedged himself between Bruno, who drove, and Monsignor Enrico. Raffaele, Silvana, and I pressed into the back seat. The cart, driven by one of the gravediggers, followed behind us, carrying mamma's casket, Silvana's children, and Grazia.

"I brought Willa home in that cart the first time she came to Orvieto," *papà* told Monsignor Enrico, his voice raspy with emotion. "She never accepted our life here." He shook his head and fanned himself with his straw hat. "Never accepted losing Etto. She was always a mother first and a wife second." He shrugged. "Well, she's with her Etto now."

"*Che stupidaggini!*" Silvana muttered. What stupid stuff!

At the cemetery, Monsignor Enrico waited while Raffaele, Bruno, *papà,* and the three gravediggers carried mamma's coffin along the dirt path to the open grave. Silvana and I walked behind them, then Grazia and the children. Silvana's daughters, aged four and five, and her son, just seven, skipped along, stopping to throw rocks or to reach into snake holes. The children resembled their respective fathers, indeed, so much so that together they left the impression that Silvana wasn't their mother at all, an impression furthered by her evident lack of interest in them and her insistence that they call her "Silvana." Holding onto her large, black hat, Silvana swayed along the uneven path. Suddenly, the heel of one of her stilettos broke; she stumbled and fell to the ground. Laughing and shouting, the children formed a circle around her. "Look! Silvana fell down again!"

"Zitti!" she hissed. Be quiet! The children froze. Raffaele picked up Silvana's hat and helped her to her feet. She reached for her shoe, then tried but failed to put the heel back. *"Accidenti!"* Damn! She put the heel in her purse. Holding Raffaele's arm, she limped toward mamma's grave. Despite the heat, the freshly turned earth smelled heavy and damp. The gravediggers retreated a short distance to the thin shade of an olive tree, where they squatted and smoked. Silvana's children formed a knot around their mother, pulling her arms and vying for her attention. Silvana brushed them away. Undiscouraged, they returned.

"Mamma, we want to look inside the box," Lucio, the eldest child, whispered. "Please, can we see if Nonna Willa is smiling because she's in heaven?" Silvana ignored their pleas. I fingered mamma's rosary and tried not to think about being buried alive. *Is it possible that I could have lived my whole life with mamma and have nothing more of her than this rosary?* I thought about my promise to return the letters. *If mamma was someone I didn't really know, what else about my life might be false?* I felt chilled and provisional, as if a shrieking wind whirled around me, spinning me out of my own existence.

"Let us pray," Monsignor Enrico said. Grazia clasped her gnarled hands together. Once I asked Grazia why mamma always seemed sad.

"Fortuna," Grazia said. Fate. I tried to keep my mind on Monsignor Enrico's words. I wanted to remember everything about that day, remember it as it truly was.

"We know that as Christ gave his spirit to his disciples, so we, too, can be filled with His spirit and manifest it in everything that we do. Guide us, Lord, as we lay our beloved Willa to rest. Return us to our lives to do as You would have us do. Amen." Everyone except Silvana made the sign of the cross.

Raffaele signaled to the gravediggers, who helped to lower mamma's plain wooden coffin into the ground. Just as they finished, *papà* lurched toward the grave with a sob. "Willa! No!" he cried out. His hat fell onto the coffin. Monsignor Enrico and Bruno held him so that he wouldn't fall into the pit. *Did he tell mamma how much he cared for her when she was alive?*

"Silvana! See? Nonno Gabriele is going to look inside the box now," Beatrice said to her mother. "Let us look, too! Please!" Bruno climbed into the pit, retrieved *papà*'s hat, and held it up. I leaned down to take it, and mamma's rosary slipped out of my hand and fell on the ground.

Silvana saw it before I could pick it up. "You took mamma's rosary!"

"Mamma gave it to me." It was a thoughtless answer, and I knew it would only make Silvana feel more neglected than she already did.

"It's time to go," *papà* said. He put on his hat. The children shrieked and ran in circles around the adults. Raffaele offered his arm to Silvana.

"I prefer to walk alone," Silvana said so everyone could hear her. "That way I'll be with someone I can trust." She put on her dark glasses and turned away from us.

"Please, Silvana, not today," *papà* said. The bright sun burned our skins and bleached the hillsides. *Papà* took off his jacket, handed it to me; he rolled up his shirtsleeves and unbuttoned his collar. I looked back. The gravediggers were whistling as they pushed their shovels into the pile of fresh earth and threw it on mamma's grave.

"Silvana, are they done yet? Lucio asked. "You promised we could get gelato when everyone is done with their crocodile tears."

"Basta!" Silvana waved them off. The children retreated, and Raffaele lifted them into the cart next to Grazia.

As Bruno opened the doors of the car, his curly hair caught the light like a kind of halo. He moved easily and rhythmically, unimpeded by the secrets and questions that so often troubled me. We all got back in the car, including Silvana, and Bruno drove back toward town. Near the station, a group of tourists with a guide waited to cross the roadway. Bruno stopped for them.

"Let the *stranieri* wait!" *papà* said.

"Mark my words, these *stranieri* will be very good for Vino Marcheschi and for Orvieto," Monsignor Enrico said. He folded his hands over his belly. Despite his Irish origins, Monsignor Enrico's knowledge of Italy, Umbria in particular, had brought him a measure of fame even among the members of surrounding parishes. Despite his spiritual calling, it was for his business acumen that merchants sought his counsel, and when they did, Monsignor Enrico offered more than prayers for their success.

Papà sighed. "For an ordinary winemaker like me, Orvieto—this town and these valleys—are life itself. A reason to go on." He wiped his face with his handkerchief.

"Che stupidaggini," Silvana muttered. Nonsense.

Monsignor Enrico put a sympathetic hand on *papà*'s arm. "One's family is also a reason to go on."

"And your friends," Bruno added, "and, of course, the new vintage."

"Tanti stupidaggini," Silvana said. Such nonsense!

The car labored upward along the steep, dirt road toward the town, its black hood shimmering in the heat. A workman stepped onto the road in front of us and waved two red flags. Bruno stopped and set the brake. Silvana removed her hat and fanned herself, filling the car with the scent of spices. Bruno sneezed. *Papà* and Raffaele coughed. I turned my face toward the open window and inhaled the hot, still air. The children wiggled out of the cart and came to the window.

"Silvana, now can we have *gelato*?"

"Where do you see *gelato* here?" Silvana said, waving her arm in their direction. The children shook their heads and returned to the shade of the cart where they traced pictures in the dusty road with sticks.

Papà turned to Monsignor Enrico. "Some of the women here were very jealous when I married Willa, you know." He glanced at Bruno then looked down at this lap and covered his face with his thick, tanned hands. "I miss her so much," he sobbed.

"Sometimes God's will exceeds our understanding," Monsignor Enrico replied.

"*Che stupidaggini!*" Silvana muttered.

"Willa thought that Orvieto would be like America," *papà* continued. His steely hair curled over the back of his wilted shirt collar like smoke. "Americans believe they can control their fate. We Italians know better." Monsignor Enrico nodded.

"Even now I feel torn between your Italian state of mind and mamma's American one," Raffaele said. "Sometimes I don't know who I am." I thought that Raffaele's observation applied equally to me. The workman signaled for us to continue. *By the time these workmen are done with their work I'll be finished with university, and Bruno and I will be married with children of our own,* I thought. Bruno started the car.

"Have I told you that I'm retiring?" Monsignor Enrico asked.

"When will you be going?" Bruno asked.

"Very soon," I said, thinking of Cattolicà and of my promise to return Michel Losine's letters to him. Bruno glanced at me in the rearview mirror.

"Yes, several months," Monsignor Enrico said.

"Well, I must leave as soon as we get back," Raffaele said.

"The children are restless," Silvana said, but I knew she was talking about herself.

Papà wiped his brow with his handkerchief again. "Willa would have wanted us to be together today."

"We're all still here with you," I said, hoping to forestall a brewing argument about our filial duty, "but we aren't children any more."

Papà wiped his eyes with his damp handkerchief. "You don't want to be my children now that Willa is gone. I know that."

"*Che boiate,*" Silvana said. Bullshit. "Papà, don't you remember when we all came home for the Feast of Corpus Domini, and *you* told us to leave and never come back?" *Even on the day of mamma's burial, Silvana reminds papà of their ugly disagreement. If only they could forgive one another.*

Papà lowered his head like a bull. "This isn't the day to talk about such things." Once, I had overheard him tell mamma that he would disown Silvana for dishonoring him and our family. Mamma said that she would leave him forever if he cut Silvana or Raffaele off. I thought mamma was right to stand up for Silvana and Raffaele. Making a mistake isn't a reason to abandon someone, especially your own child.

"We're nearby if you need us," Raffaele told *papà*, "and Fina is still here with you."

Silvana peeled a bit of red lacquer from a fingernail. "If we leave now, *papà*, you won't have to talk about what mamma left *me*,"

Raffaele glanced at *papà* and laughed nervously. "Are you sure you want us to stay?"

"Mamma left things for you, too, Silvana," I said.

"Well, *you* certainly wasted no time," Silvana hissed. "What else did you get besides her rosary?"

"*Basta!* "*Papà* nodded toward Silvana. "The devil's work," he said to Monsignor Enrico.

"Now, you call me names," Silvana said.

"Out of respect for your mother, I won't call you by your real name today," *papà* answered. He meant *puttana*. With mamma gone, we all knew he would no longer restrain himself. Bruno swerved to avoid a large pothole.

"Out of concern for yourself, you mean." *Papà*'s words had hurt her, and I knew Silvana meant to hurt him. We were all silent.

"Each of us feels loss in a different way," Monsignor Enrico said. "Our faith helps us bear the unbearable."

"This heat is unbearable," Bruno said.

"I've decided to go on living in town," *papà* told Monsignor Enrico. "It will be easier for Dottor Lucarelli to come to me if I need him." I knew that wasn't his real reason. He simply couldn't bear to be alone and wanted to be near the piazza where he and his friends gathered every afternoon to talk and play *bocce*.

When we came to a stop in front of our home, *papà* got out of the car, opened the courtyard gate, and then unlocked the front door. In comparison to the car, the interior of our house seemed chilly. *Papà* noted, as he often did, that the painting next to the door had originally been a wedding gift to his grandparents. It depicted a young man, *papà*'s grandfather, calling on a young woman, *papà*'s grandmother, who stood on a balcony. Behind his back, the young man held a bouquet of flowers and beside him his mule waited with an air of indifference. "I thought of this painting when I proposed to Willa," he reminded us.

Silvana lit a cigarette. "At least *her* unhappiness is over."

"Is that a way to talk about your mother?" *papà* said.

"You don't care how anyone talks about mamma as long as you look good, " Silvana said. I wanted *papà* to say something conciliatory.

"Silvana, *papà* does care," I said. I may not have really known mamma, but I believed that in his way *papà* cared about all of us.

"Did they give you *nonna*'s pearls, too?" Silvana said to me. I didn't know what to say.

Raffaele put his arms around us. "Come, we'll all feel better if we have something to eat." He guided us toward the dining room where Grazia had set the table with our best linens, silver, and glassware.

At our family meals, each of us had an assigned place that never varied without *papà*'s express direction. *Papà* always sat at the head of the table in a tall, wooden armchair upholstered in tapestry; open-mouthed lion faces were carved into the wood of each arm. Our guest of honor, Monsignor Enrico, sat to *papà*'s immediate right, and Bruno, Raffaele, and I to his left. Mamma always sat opposite him at the other end of the table. More than once a guest had observed that mamma planned the meals and supervised the cooking, but ate only leftovers. *Papà* always laughed. "Willa prefers it this way," he would say. Mamma always said, "Gabriele lives in a world of his own creation."

But on this day, instead of sitting at her customary place to *papà*'s left, Silvana took mamma's seat. There was a sudden hush. Everyone, including Silvana, knew that *papà* would never countenance this change in our dining arrangements, not on the day of mamma's burial. Silvana removed her dinner plate and set it aside in order to examine the pewter charger underneath. She turned it over and then looked up at *papà*.

292 REBECCA J. NOVELLI

"What about these?" she said. "Whose are these?" She put the charger back and planted her elbows on the table as if she were staking out her territory. "Mamma won't be using them anymore." *Papà* ignored her question.

"If you sit in mamma's seat, you have to do what mamma did," Raffaele said.

"You mean weep when she thought no one was looking?" Silvana said, her eyes on *papà*. Grazia carried a platter into the room and set it on the sideboard.

"Willa never did that," *papà* said to Monsignor Enrico. "She was very happy. She had everything she wanted here with me."

Silvana picked up a knife and pointed it at *papà*. "So you say." I had seen mamma weeping, too, but I never thought it was because *we* made her unhappy. She had always been like that. I thought that it was just the way mamma was. Unlike Silvana, I had never considered whether mamma was happy or unhappy. Silvana set her dinner plate back on the charger and began to build a sculpture on it with her silverware. We watched her, anxious. I thought of what mamma said about the letters, that they were from someone she loved very much. *Was she happier with her* amante *than she was with us?* The silverware fell with a crash. We all jumped even though we had been watching Silvana's sculpture the whole time.

"Monsignor Enrico will ask the blessing now," *papà* said. Grazia crossed herself.

The priest cleared his throat. "Our Father, in the name of your Son, Jesus Christ, we ask that you extend the protection of the Blessed Virgin Mary to our dear departed Willa and that you bring the peace of our faith and your devotion to us, your children, especially your children here today, now and forevermore. Amen."

7

Papà held the platter while Monsignor Enrico lifted a large serving of pasta onto his plate.

"Happiness is an elusive thing," the priest said. He inhaled the aromas of garlic, olive oil, and basil with obvious pleasure

Bruno poured chilled white wine into the priest's glass. "This is our new Marcheschi Orvieto. The *originale.*"

Monsignor Enrico lifted his glass and looked around the table, nodding at each of us. "To your happiness," he said. He took a noisy sip and signed his approval. We lifted our glasses and drank, too. I was thankful that Monsignor Enrico was with us because I knew *papà* wouldn't quarrel with Silvana in his presence. "Some, I believe, are born with the gift of happiness, while others seem to have no knack for it," Monsignor Enrico continued. He drank more wine and then began to eat. "I once thought happiness was a matter of faith: If we keep our faith with God, God keeps His faith with us. We are content." He made an exclamation point with his fork and nodded in agreement with what he had just said. "Truthfully," he added, looking around the table, "I have seen many people of deep faith who were profoundly *un*happy." As he ate the pasta, his entire body appeared to relax in pleasure. "Happiness is a great mystery."

"True happiness comes from doing what we should," *papà* said. "I believe duty is as essential to happiness as faith." I took the platter from *papà*. *What is a daughter's duty? A wife's? Is there a duty to myself? Did fulfilling one duty lead to happiness, but fulfilling others not? And what about mamma? Had fulfilling her duty led to happiness?*

Next, *papà* served Monsignor Enrico the *bolliti misti.* The priest heaped his plate with the boiled meats. The sauce dripped onto the embroidered tablecloth. Then, Monsignor Enrico took several slices of warm bread, piling them next to his plate. From another platter, he took a large, marinated artichoke and slices of fresh tomato and *mozzarella di bufala*.

"There is happiness in work well done, too," Bruno said. He poured some wine into his glass and lifted it to *papà*. "For example, your brilliant plan for the new vintage."

Papà smiled and returned Bruno's toast. *Papà should make a toast to mamma because it was her ideas and her work that had made Vino Marcheschi so successful,* I thought.

"Being happy isn't all that matters," I said, "Happiness is the result when we do what is right for us." It was a self-serving idea, of course. I was thinking about university. *Had mamma done what was right for her?* I passed the platter of marinated vegetables to Bruno. *It's easy to make a mistake.*

"That's true," said Raffaele, "but some people don't experience happiness as a result of action, faith or duty. Some find happiness in accepting who they really are." He poured more wine into his glass. I knew Raffaele was referring to the fact that he was unmarried and that *papà* had refused to receive his good friend and business associate Paolo in our home. Mamma had just wanted all of us to be happy. She had told *papà* that Raffaele was especially sensitive and took his disapproval too much to heart. Still, *papà* and Raffaele repeated their same argument whenever they were together. Our funeral meal was no exception.

"We have choices about who we are," *papà* said with a meaningful look at Raffaele. "You aren't interested in the natural choice like I was."

"That's right. I don't want to carry on Vino Marcheschi," Raffaele said. "I don't want to live in Orvieto."

"This so-called happiness of yours is unnatural," *papà* said. "You have no wife, no family. Not even a *fidanzata*. You don't continue our family business. When do you intend to become a man?"

Raffaele answered carefully. "When you state your wishes so forcefully, *papà,* we don't have the opportunity to accept the fact that you and I are different."

"My wishes make no difference to you."

Raffaele tapped his fingers on the table and laughed uneasily. "Your wishes are an added burden." He passed the platter to Silvana. "When will you accept that my life makes me happy the way it is?"

Silvana glared at *papà*. "Just do what *you* want, and we'll all be happy. Right, *papà*?" She set the platter down on the table with such force that I thought it might crack. "Anyway, Fina is right: happiness isn't the point. Not in our family."

Papà turned to Monsignor Enrico. "I don't try to choose my children's happiness for them, whatever they say." He held the arms of his chair and looked around the table at each of us. "Fulfilling one's duty, as I have, has brought me great happiness. It still does, even though I can't do as much as I wish anymore." He stabbed a piece of meat, put it on his plate.

"You do a great deal, sir," said Bruno, "and the introduction of the new wine is a very happy moment for all of us at this sad time."

"*Che boiate!*" Silvana said.

Bruno refilled Monsignor Enrico's glass. "This vintage is only our first attempt."

"An excellent beginning!" the priest said.

Bruno smiled. "If you like our new wine, then it will be a great success."

Silvana drained her glass and held it out to Bruno for more. I hoped she wouldn't get drunk again.

"Each kind of happiness has its own season," Monsignor Enrico said. "Fortunately, in my own case, action, duty and faith have coincided in a single happiness." He wiped his full lips with the white napkin.

Silvana pointed her fork at Monsignor Enrico. "Why is it that God has answered your questions, but not my mother's or mine?" I knew her remark would make *papà* furious. Their inevitable quarrels had always paralyzed us. Only Mamma could divert them.

Monsignor Enrico helped himself to another portion of *bolliti misti*. "Where there is faith, my child, we need not question the answers God gives us."

"God gives us no answers. He accepts the answers we give Him," Silvana said.

Monsignor Enrico looked at Silvana and frowned. "Your view is inconsistent with our faith, my dear." He took up his glass and held it in his plump hand.

"She doesn't really mean that," *papà* said. "She means to say, 'May God forgive me for my willful disobedience.'" A hush fell over the table. We all knew that *papà* had always disapproved of Silvana, even when she was a child.

"I can speak to God myself," Silvana said, "without your help."

"Ask God to forgive you then," *papà* said, "because I do not."

Mamma had once told me that she had to love Silvana twice as much to make up for *papà's* coldness toward her.

Raffaele rose from his seat and raised his glass, his eyes moist. We all stood up.

"To mamma, who loved us all in the only way she could…and has left each of us to find our happiness alone." He took a sip of the wine mixed with his tears.

"As we choose," Silvana added. She wiped her eyes with the back of her hand, leaving a streak of mascara on her cheek.

8

Grazia stopped sweeping and watched as I took out the bundle of letters from the *armadio*. When I removed the purple cloth, she made the sign of the cross. "Be careful. The things of the dead bring *la sfortuna* "

I examined the return address printed on the envelope: *Via Violetta 10, Milano, Italia*. Then, the address on the front: *Signora Isabella Farnese* in care of the post office in Arezzo. The address was the same on all of the letters. "These letters aren't even addressed to mamma." I studied the postmarks: the letters were in chronological order. The first was written before I was born, the most recent one the previous year. Almost twenty years.

"Only Death should keep our secrets." Grazia resumed her sweeping.

I gathered the letters and wrapped them up again. "Is *papà* still out?" Grazia nodded. "If you hide these for me, *papà* won't find them." Eyeing the bundle, Grazia crossed herself again and shook her head. "The dead trick the living into keeping their secrets." She lit a candle and put it above the fireplace. "Never put those letters near your bed. They will get into your dreams and make *la sfortuna* while you sleep."

I put the bundle down on mamma's bed. "I'll hide them myself, then, but first I want to find something of mamma's to give Silvana." I opened mamma's jewelry box and picked out several pieces. "Which of these do you think Silvana would like?" Grazia paused in her sweeping to look at the fan-shaped brooch: reddish gold and enamel made in the form of a peacock with a tail of opals, lapis lazuli, and tiger's eye. "I've never seen this one before." I held the brooch in the shaft of light from the window. Fire danced in the stones. "Look! Such pretty colors."

Grazia crossed herself again. "Opals. *Molto sfortunati.*" I turned the brooch over. The back was engraved.

Just then, the door opened. "*Papà*, I thought you and Bruno were working in the new vineyard."

"Bruno is coming this evening. He has something he wants to discuss with me." *Papà* winked at me. "Can you guess what it is?"

"*Santo cielo*, a guest for dinner!" Grazia said. "I have to get ready." She gathered up a pile of laundry and with it the bundle of letters and went out, closing the door behind her.

"What was that Grazia took with her?" *papà* asked.

"Just some old papers. I'm looking for something for Silvana. Would you like to help me?"

"I don't want her to have any of Willa's...."

I held the brooch out to him. "What about this for Silvana?"

He waved his hand. "We have more important things to discuss. I want to talk to you about your future. Bruno...." His voice trailed off. He took the brooch from me. "I don't remember this." He turned it over in his hand.

"It looks old," I said. "Did it belong to Nonna Marcheschi or Grandma Carver?" I put the wooden box beside the door.

"What's that?"

"An old box. I'm going to throw it away. Do you think Silvana would want any of mamma's clothes?" *Papà* put the brooch down and went to get the box. He touched its dusty surfaces, studied the residue on his fingertips, lifted the hinged lid and felt inside, knocked on the sides, shook it. Unsatisfied, he turned it over and tried to remove the bottom. "*Papà*, it's just an old box."

"Willa hid things from me. Tell Grazia to bring me that bundle. I want to see everything you find."

I pretended I hadn't heard him. "We need to decide what to do with mamma's jewelry."

He picked up a pair of gold earrings, flat like buttons with an elaborate incised design, and turned them over in his palm. "I've never seen these before, either." He seemed to forget about the letters. He took up the brooch again, turned it over and over, moved it until the light caught the mark on the back. "There!"

I leaned closer. "An M and a W intertwined. Mamma's initials."

Papà gasped, his jaw tightened. He clenched the brooch in his fist and then threw it as hard as he could against the wall. "Damn them! God damn them!"

"*Papà* no! Don't!" I knelt down to gather the fragments. The metal was bent and some of the stones had scattered. "Why?" I gathered up the pieces.

"Who does he think he is?" *papà* shouted. His face dissolved. "Willa was *my* wife." He covered his face with his hands.

I put my arms around him. "*Papà*. What is it? What's happened?"

At last, he took a deep breath and looked up at me. "Your mother made a mistake, Fina. A long time ago. Before you were born. Some people, people like Willa, become involved in things they don't understand. Sometimes they do things or say things they don't intend. They agree to do something because they aren't sure how to refuse or because they want to show courtesy. Your mother made that kind of mistake. Americans are like that. Always too friendly. This person thought that she meant something else, something more, and so he gave her things that she didn't want."

"What things?"

"Things people should only give each other when they are very close." I looked down at the stones and the bent gold in my hand. "Willa made a mistake, Fina." He scanned the room. "Did you find anything else?" I shook my head. "Tell me if you find any letters. *Capisci?*" Do you understand? I nodded. "Where's Grazia? I want to see what was in that bundle."

"I put those letters in the potato bin," Grazia told me later that afternoon when *papà* had gone out again.

"If *papà* asks you, tell him you burned some moldy papers."

Grazia crossed herself. "*Porterà sfortuna.*" It will be bad luck.

I took the bundle to my room, set it on the bed, and opened the first letter. *"Carissima,"* it began. It didn't even say *Willa. If papà sees them, he'll see that he's mistaken about mamma's letters,* I thought. I looked at the signature. *"Con tutto il mio amore, ora e per sempre, il tuo M."* All my love now and always. I picked up another letter, read it, read another, and then another. One spoke of a painting of a fish, another of "our garden." There were meetings, trips, then later, mamma's illness. I opened the most recent one.

My darling,

I cannot bear that you are ill and knowing that you will be unable to write to me or receive my words of comfort and love. It is an unjust world that keeps us apart when we most need one another. I will not come to you now only because you say you don't want me to see you as you are. Know how much I love you and long to be with you. Until we are together in heaven.

Grazia always said that secrets have their own lives and that their fate is to betray themselves, like footprints in soft soil, seeds in fruit, acorns of truth from a winter of need. I looked at the signature on the letter: *Your M now and forever.* I didn't want to know this secret about mamma and her *amante* and their letters. *Had mamma always had another life with someone she loved very much? An* amante *named Michel Losine in Milano who wanted these letters?* I decided to burn them and put an end to mamma's double life before any misfortune occured. Just then, *papà* called to me, and I heard his footsteps on the stairway. I looked at the clock. Five-thirty. I had lost track of the time while I was reading. Worse, I had neglected to lock the door. I scooped up the letters. Where to put them? I stuffed them into an open bureau drawer and closed it. *Papà* looked in.

"Did you and Bruno finish?"

"Yes, *cara." Papà* saw the purple cloth on the bed. He stopped like a bird frozen in midflight. "Where are they?"

"There was just a bunch of moldy letters, *papà.* Grazia has already burned them. I saved the cloth for you." His jaw bulged.

"Before, you said *papers*. Now, you say *letters*." He looked around. "Where are they?" He sniffed the air like an animal. "Give them to me." I held out the cloth to him. He snatched it. "They must be here." *Did he know about mamma's* amante, *too?*

I took his arm. "We're not finished with mamma's room yet. If there are any papers, letters…anything…we'll find them for you." He pulled his arm away from me and walked out. I knew he didn't believe me. The letters were more important than I had thought. I decided not to burn them. Instead, I wrapped them inside an embroidered pillowcase and put them in the bottom of my wedding chest under my quilts.

9

Shortly after I read mamma's letters, I dreamed of an unknown man. We feasted together on enormous red strawberries that were from the planet Jupiter. The voluptuous sweetness of the berries lingered on my tongue as I awoke. I kept my eyes closed and tried to summon the man back. He retreated as I drew near him and then disappeared. With a sense of regret I opened my eyes to the ringing of the bells at the Duomo. It was my birthday. I smelled bread baking in the oven and I knew Grazia was preparing her sweet almond *torta* for me. I soon forgot about the dream.

My room was already warm. The shutters cast shadowy ladders at odd angles on the wall opposite my bed where a crucifix hung. I counted the shadow steps up to it, blinked, lost my place, started over. Fourteen. Though the crucifix had hung there for as long as I could remember, the profound suffering it depicted always made me wonder at the cost of redemption. I believed that living a Christian life meant thinking of others before oneself. Although I still had mamma's letters, I didn't want to hurt *papà* by keeping my promise to her. *What would a true Christian do? If I must choose between the living and the dead, I would choose papà.*

When I came down to breakfast, *papà* came over and kissed me on both cheeks.

"Buongiorno, tesoro. Tanti auguri. Nineteen years today! I wish your mother could see how beautiful you are on your birthday." He sat down and smiled. "I've invited Bruno to celebrate with us this evening."

"That's nice, *papà*."

"Nice? I thought you were in love."

"I'm thinking about...."

"What could be more important to think about than your *fidanzato*?

Papà chuckled. "Unless it's your old father." He returned to his breakfast and his paperwork. He was in a good mood.

"I'm thinking about going to university." I waited for his response.

"*Papà*, I'm supposed to enroll at Cattolicà next month."

"Hmmm. What did you say, *tesoro*?"

"I've decided to go to university, and I enroll—"

"Nonsense. Your mother would never have approved. She and I agreed on that." He leaned toward me. "Willa didn't have much of a mind for business, but she would have told me you were planning to ruin your life and our livelihood." He stood up. "Bruno is meeting with those Americans this morning, the ones who don't know how to make wine." I knew them. *Papà* smiled. "Bruno thinks we can do business with them. He needs you to translate." The Americans came into our shop frequently. Although they had told me that they planned to export local wines, among themselves they talked mostly about "tax shelters."

When I arrived at our shop a few hours later, the Americans were already sitting on wooden stools around the table and arguing among themselves. Bruno was there, too, nodding and smiling. I could tell that he didn't understand what they were saying. No one noticed that I was listening.

"You're just too cheap to pay a real expert from the States," the fat one said to the quiet one who wore glasses. "You're making a big mistake. You gotta pay for expertise." I wondered what he meant. Everyone knew that you had to touch the grapes to know when they were ready to become wine. *Papà* and Bruno knew because they cared for the vines themselves. They could feel when the grapes were ready.

"Business is business," said the second. "Let's not waste money on so-called experts." He bit off the end of a fingernail and spit it out on the wooden floor. "It was your so called *tax expert* who got us into this mess in the first place."

"You two don't know grapes from Shinola," the man with the glasses said. "Without grapes, we got nuthin'."

"The question is, how do we ship the stuff?" the second man said.

"Barrels? Tanks? Bottles?" I had seen him before. He always jiggled his feet or his keys and talked constantly of moving from one place to another. I liked to listen to him because he sometimes revealed useful information, such as that American women owned cars and drove themselves wherever they wanted to go on roads that were much wider than the ones we have in Italy. I was sure I could learn to drive a car. I tried to learn as much as I could about cars and about driving by asking questions of Dante, the mechanic. Once I asked Bruno about carburetors.

"So, now you think you can fix cars, too?" he said.

The fat man looked noticed me. "How's tricks, hon'? Got anything we haven't tasted yet?" I went in the back of the shop and found a bottle of the new vintage. I poured out three small glasses and set them on the table while Bruno watched.

The fat man took one of the glasses. He smelled the wine, swirled it in the glass, and drank it all at once like a dose of medicine, then coughed and shook his head. "Geez! It's got a real wallop, sis." Bruno smiled. The fat man looked at Bruno more closely and then extended his hand. "Howdy, son."

"*Piacere,*" Bruno said. He pointed at the wine. "*E'l'Orvieto originale. L'ho fatto io.*"

"It's the original Orvieto. He made it himself," I said.

"*He* made this? Hey fellas. He made this stuff." I translated for Bruno, who smiled and nodded vigorously. "You don't say? Listen," the fat man said to his associates, "this guy knows something about growing grapes around here even if his wine tastes like *benzina.*"

"More than we do, but if this is what he makes…." The man wearing glasses returned his wine to the tray unfinished. He turned to Bruno. "No offense."

"*Nessun' offesa,*" I said. Bruno nodded enthusiastically.

"Listen," the fat man said, "our production problems could be over. Suppose we take their wine, mix it with whatever we can get, and package it under our label?" He looked from one associate to the other. "We'll say it's *indigenous*. Jack up the price." He waved his hand. "Marketing."

"Excuse me," the man with the glasses said, "I didn't hear them say they wanted to sell their wine to us unlabelled."

"If we buy from them and put it in our bottle with our label, it's ours, isn't it?" He turned to Bruno and handed him his card. "Maybe you'd be interested in doing some business with us?"

"È un uomo d'*affari*," I told Bruno. A businessman. Bruno looked at the card and smiled broadly. He shook hands with each of the Americans.

"I think he's interested," the fat man said. He turned to me. "Set up a meeting, hon'. Tomorrow, noon, the trattoria on the other side of the piazza." He waved a coin in front of me and winked. "Make it worth your while, sis."

"Domani a mezzogiorno," I told Bruno, *"abbiamo una riunione."* I felt needed, but I also remembered what mamma had said about her own, very similar role in business meetings: "They think I'm a houseplant. It doesn't matter that I know more than they do."

"Our new vintage is already a great success," Bruno said when the Americans left.

"They only want to mix our wine with someone else's," I said. "They don't care about the new vintage. They don't even like it."

Bruno frowned. "You're always so negative. You don't understand. We're going to be rich."

10

The oblique afternoon sun streamed through the open doors of the *salotto*, washing *papà* and Bruno in golden light. I sat down on the sofa near Bruno.

"We'll need to make an investment if we're to start with new vines in the south vineyard," Bruno was saying.

Papà shook his head. "I'd have to take a large loan or find investors. Either way I'd lose control." I saw that Bruno was disappointed.

"Sir, you have a great deal of land, but no capital to develop it. Any new venture requires capital. What other options do you see?"

I knew Bruno was right, but *papà* seldom changed his ideas no matter how persuasive the reasons for doing so. "*Papà*, maybe you should consider what Bruno is saying more carefully."

Papà slammed his fist down. "As long as I have breath in my body, I won't allow anyone else to take control of Vino Marcheschi."

Bruno shrugged and turned to me. "*Tanti auguri, cara.* Would you like to open your birthday presents now?" He went out of the room and returned with two large boxes, both black and tied with wide gold ribbon. I knew they came from a very expensive shop.

"I thought you went to Firenze to sell wine."

"I did!" Bruno laughed. "These are the profits!" Inside the box was a purse with gleaming gold hardware. It smelled of new leather. In one of the finely stitched interior pockets there was a leather-backed mirror. I knew it had cost more than any gift I had ever received.

"It's beautiful." I stood up and put the handle over my arm. "How does it look?"

"*Bellissima*. Like you." Bruno handed me another box. Inside was a pair of matching pumps. "For when we do business in America."

I ran my fingers over the buttery leather. "They're very beautiful, but much too expensive." I meant more than the price.

"Nothing is too good for you," Bruno said. "Try them on." The soft leather shaped itself to my flesh and bones so easily. I wanted to keep them, but I understood the meaning of such gifts, gifts that reflected Bruno's ambitions, his assumptions about my role in fulfilling them, gifts with a message about how I would live and what my future would be. "I want you to have beautiful things to go with our beautiful life together." He raised his glass. "Always."

I knew I should kiss Bruno then, but that doing so would affirm my consent not only to becoming Bruno's wife, but also to accepting a role that had already been defined for me, my consent to more than I could name. I took off the shoes and put the gifts back in their boxes. "They're much too beautiful for a university student."

"We have more important things to discuss tonight," *papà* said quickly. He removed the faceted glass stopper from the decanter, poured the wine, and then raised his glass. "To the two of you and to our future. Both of you make me very happy today." He sipped the wine and then turned to me. "Bruno has asked me for your hand, Fina. I'm pleased to give my permission and my blessing to both of you and to your marriage." I felt my life moving on without my will. In the light that poured into the room, Bruno's stiff white shirt seemed cast from pale bronze. *Papà* took another sip of his wine. "You have always been my devoted and obedient daughter, *cara*, and you bring me the most happiness of all of my children." I recoiled at the word *obedient*. "You'll be rewarded for your devotion." It seemed to me that he was talking about someone else, someone not in that room. "I'm growing older and I need your help here."

My heart raced. "I want to go to university first."

Papà looked surprised. He cleared his throat. "We cannot always do everything we imagine we want to do."

"Not *everything*. Just *university*."

"It's time for you to learn about our business. I've already discussed this with Bruno."

"But not with *me*!"

Papà's hand tightened into a fist, his knuckles whitened. "Bruno has asked me for your hand. That is what is proper." *Papà* inhaled slowly and then went on. "Together you will make a happy marriage like mine. You will be our assistant, Fina. Our future together is assured. What could be better than that?"

Bruno reached out to me. "Fina, I'm so happy and...."

I felt something close in on me, something that prevented me from breathing. "You planned that I will do what mamma did. Is that what you mean?" I said.

Bruno looked surprised. "Isn't that what we've always said?"

"I don't want to do what mamma did. I want to go to university and then teach history."

Bruno and *papà* glanced at one another. Bruno turned to me. "You mean you want to *leave* Orvieto?" I nodded. "Why didn't you tell me this before now? I would have made very different decisions."

"I did." In the silence that followed, a bird sang in the garden. The fragrance of jasmine wafted on a stray breeze. I put my hand in my pocket and squeezed mamma's rosary, fastened my eyes on the stitching on Bruno's shirt, followed it up to his shoulder, then to his collar just under his chin, just below his mouth where his words would come out. *He'll say something soon.*

"*Basta!*" *papà* said. Enough! "Your job is to take care of your family and your husband. This is God's will. I've been patient and so has Bruno." *Patient? How had they been patient?* "If you love me, you'll do as I say." I felt weightless, a leaf in a whirlwind.

"I want to go to university. That's all."

"*Cretina!*" Idiot! *papà* said. "How could you help your husband and me if you aren't here?"

"Later, when I come back." I didn't really know.

"This is all you have to say?" Bruno's voice sounded cold and distant. "Just that you're going away?"

What more could I say? "I received honors on my exams, and—"

"*University.*" Bruno seemed to summon the word from all of the obscure and distant places he had ever heard of. "Why would you go to a place that isn't good for you?" *How does he know this when I don't?* I wondered.

If they understand how important this is to me, they will change their minds. "I'm sure it's good," I said before they could take more away from me. I studied the weave of my napkin, the threads that went in opposite directions. "University is a perfect place for me to...."

"You're unrealistic. Nothing is perfect," Bruno said.

"I mean for me." *Surely, I know more about this one thing than he does.* "I thought you and *papà* would be proud of me."

"Me, me, me. That's all you think about!" Bruno voice was cold and hard. "You knew that we were supposed to become *fidanzati* tonight." I watched his mouth, afraid that the anger and the disappointment in his eyes would weaken my determination. "You have no right to betray me like this. I thought you cared more about us. About me. Instead, you led me on."

It was the first time I felt truly angry at Bruno. "Does *love* mean only that I must marry you when you decide or work in the winery because the two of you have discussed it? Why does *love* mean that only I must give up what I want to do?"

"We had an understanding and you've violated it," Bruno said.

"No! You betrayed *me!*" My voice was so loud that it seemed as if someone else had spoken for me, someone who was certain. "You're just angry because I have plans of my own."

"If you don't accept Bruno's proposal, he'll marry someone who has more sense than you do," *papà* said. *Was this what Signora Lucarelli meant?*

Bruno stood up. "I can still change my plans." He nodded at *papà* and went out. The front door slammed behind him and then the courtyard gate.

"*Idiota*! You've ruined our lives," *papà* said. My heart throbbed. Loose. Fast. Without brakes.

11

I looked out at the empty dawn with eyes that hadn't closed all night. My body felt hollow, my movements automatic, out of my control. *Even if I don't marry Bruno, people will still speak to me. I'll still live in a house. Sleep in a bed. The sun will still shine. I will still be alive.* I dreaded facing *papà* at breakfast. I hoped he had gone out early.

In the dining room, *papà* sat in his chair, his fingers tapping on the carved lion faces, tense and ready to pounce.

"*Buongiorno, papà.*" I sat down at my usual place. Grazia had laid out my breakfast dishes. She took her time serving my toast, pouring my coffee from the ceramic pot that was formed like a rabbit. I kept asking for things—sugar, some fruit, coffee—anything to keep her there, anything to avoid talking about Bruno.

Papà wiped his mouth with his napkin and leaned toward me speaking as if to a simpleton. "Last night you dishonored me and our family, Fina. Bruno made his proposal in good faith and now he intends to leave Vino Marcheschi. This foolish idea of yours has compromised our livelihood."

"I only intend to go to university. You and Bruno have done the rest."

"Bruno is our manager. He's wise and capable and knows our business. I trust him. The life you enjoy now is the result of my work and his. I planned that you and he would take over the business. You would be comfortable for the rest of your lives. So would Raffaele and Silvana, if I chose." *Papà has his dreams, too.*

"I love our *podere* as much as you do, *papà.*" I meant the smell of the winery, the crumbling walls and cool storage rooms filled with oak casks, the sounds in the fields, the color of the sky. "But I don't want to live mamma's life."

Papà jerked as if he had received a blow. He seemed to widen and swell with contempt. "In my day we appreciated our blessings and were willing to sacrifice some of our own selfish desires for the good of our family." He banged his coffee cup on the table. "You're no different than Silvana and Raffaele." A puddle of coffee formed on the tablecloth and expanded in a widening circle. "Silvana is a tramp and Raffaele is a faggot, but at least they're who they say they are. You," he took a deep breath and then spat the words at me, "are a pretender." Grazia crossed herself, grunted, and began to clean up the table. "I thank Jesus and the Blessed Virgin Mary that my mother and father didn't live to see all of my children dishonor me."

"*Papà*, listen...."

"Listen? To what?" He looked at his hands, turned them over as if they might reveal something important.

"Bruno only asked *you* for permission to marry me. He didn't ask *me.*"

"All of us understood what he intended!"

Grazia gathered our dishes and the tablecloth and went out. I could see that *papà* was considering what I had said.

"You weren't dishonored and Bruno wasn't humiliated. I've always said that I intended to go to university. I told you about my exams. About when I'm supposed to enroll. Neither of you listened to me." His body softened. "When I'm finished...." Grazia brought a clean tablecloth and spread it over the table.

"One thing, *cara*: I won't pay for this university scheme of yours." *At least he doesn't intend to stop me from going*, I thought. Grazia replaced our dishes.

"Mamma left me some money from Grandpa and Grandma Carver." Grazia set out our food.

"Willa gave you money without telling me?"

Papà looked at Grazia. "Did you know about this...this *inheritance*

Fina is talking about?" Grazia shook her head.

"*Papà* leaned close to me. "Willa left money to *you?*" I nodded. "So, she hid money from me, too." He slammed his fist on the table. I jumped. "Willa deceived me just like you've deceived Bruno."

"I didn't deceive anyone. Besides, my teachers think I'll be a good teacher."

"A girl who doesn't keep her word? Anyway, you've no place to live."

"Cattolicà can help me."

"These people who help you do things against your best interests, who fill your head with ideas about going to university, are *pazzi*. What did you do to cause this interest in you?"

"I've been a good student and I did well on my exams and I want to be a teacher. That's all."

"Must be something else." *Could there be another reason, one I hadn't guessed?* "You're just an ordinary girl. I think some clever people are trying to take advantage of you. I'm certain Willa has caused this mischief."

"Well, mamma was clever and she wanted me to go to university."

Instantly, *papà's* face contorted with rage. He tried to control himself. "So clever that my children say she was unhappy with me." He pushed his chair away from the table. "No, Fina, the more I think about this plan of yours, the more I'm sure it's not the proper thing to do."

"*Papà,* I know that God approves."

He laughed. "What does an ordinary girl like you know about what God thinks?"

12

Papà was already sitting at the head of the table when I came into the dining room. "Bruno, my guest of honor, here. Fina, next to me." He gestured to his right. Grazia had set out the silver tray with the decanter and glasses. *Papà* poured our wine.

"Gabriele asked me to come," Bruno said to me. His tone was distant, formal. He turned away.

"We have important matters to discuss," *papà* said. "Grazia, the antipasti, please." He acted as if nothing unusual had happened, but I realized our meeting would be a decisive one. "Bruno, what do you think of our *originale*, now?"

"I'm not certain about the quality, but I believe it's an important step forward." Bruno sounded subdued. *He must regret his decision to leave on the brink of such great success.*

Papà raised his glass to Bruno. "A toast to our future," he said, "and to my most capable and esteemed partner." The three of us touched our glasses and drank. *Bruno isn't leaving, then. No wonder papà is so pleased.*

"I'm honored by your confidence," Bruno said.

"And I by yours," *papà* said. "To our new name, Vino Marcheschi & Orsini." We drank another toast to the new name. I didn't yet understand the full significance of this change.

"I want us to consider the possibility of using the south vineyard for the new vines," Bruno began. "If we age the wine properly, it will cost us less, and we can sell it for more. The profits will support our development of other vintages."

Papà nodded. *"Sono d'accordo."* I agree. I was surprised that *papà* had changed his mind so quickly. He smiled broadly and drank again. "Ahhh." He set his glass on the table and turned to me. "*Cara*, you have so many new ideas. What do you think of this one?"

"I'm not sure what idea you mean, but I think it's wise to continue to develop new products." The votives on the table went out, drowned in their own melted wax.

Papà leaned close to my face and spoke with an air of triumph. "Since you say that you are ignorant of this important change in our business, I will tell you what it is: Bruno has honored me by becoming half owner of our new company, Vino Marcheschi & Orsini, and its permanent manager." Bruno had negotiated well. I knew how much it must have cost *papà* to make this decision, how difficult it must have been for him to give up full control of Vino Marcheschi. Mamma would never have done such a thing. Instead, she would have paid Bruno whatever it took to persuade him to stay. "Don't you agree that my idea is wiser than yours?"

"I think you have done a wise thing to make Bruno your partner."

"Thank you," *papà* said in a way that suggested his wisdom did not require my confirmation. "Certainly, none of my children is capable of taking such responsibility." I knew he was goading me. I kept my anger in check. "Understand, I've given Bruno a good reason to remain with us: when we complete our agreement, half of the new firm will be his. Of course, that means that his part of the business will not be yours unless you and Bruno marry. *Capisci?*"

"Yes. I understand." *He had risked everything. It was a shocking decision.* Grazia brought new votives and lit them.

"Good, because there's more you should know: If you marry Bruno, you and he will hold two thirds of Vino Marcheschi & Orsini together. If you don't, you'll inherit one sixth just like Silvana and Raffaele. *Capisci?*" I understood perfectly: he hoped to coerce me into marrying Bruno, indeed, to make it necessary that I marry Bruno in order to keep our business in the family and to assure my own financial security. He pressed his hands over the carved lion heads on the chair arms and waited for my response.

Bruno turned to me. "I'll speak only for myself. I would be honored to marry you, Fina, either before or after you complete these studies that are so important to you, but unless we announce our engagement now, I won't wait for you."

Papà looked at me. "So, *cara,* now you have something to think about besides history, which you say is more important to you than your family's future." He waved his hand. "Grazia, the *strangozzi, per favore.* And the bread. More wine, too." He adjusted the plates in front of him and cleared his throat. "Bruno expects an answer by the end of our dinner, Fina." My appetite vanished. Grazia returned with a platter of pasta with anchovies, garlic, and black truffles, one of my favorites, and set it on the table. *Papà* plunged the silver serving forks into the food and filled Bruno's plate first. "Of course, we must discuss your plans for the south vineyard in more detail, but I believe you are correct that the new production would subsidize our other projects," he said. He filled his own plate and finally mine.

"Unless we upgrade our equipment, the additional production will be lost to our limited capacity," Bruno said.

"It's too risky to make so many large investments all at once. We could easily lose everything."

"Our arrangements with the Americans will be helpful," Bruno replied. *Papà's* eyes widened. *Already, Bruno sounds more certain and confident, as if their new status made them equals.* I knew *papà* was as surprised by Bruno's attitude as I was, but he and Bruno continued to discuss business as partners naturally would. I broke off a piece of the *focaccia,* which Grazia always made especially for me. I couldn't eat it. As soon as *papà* and Bruno finished their pasta, Grazia served us wild pigeon with cardoons, *papà's* favorite. I picked at my meal while Bruno drew up specifications for the new equipment. Afterwards, when Grazia came to clear the table, most of my dinner was still on my plate. It wasn't until she served the rice *budino* and the espresso that *papà* spoke to me. "We are ready for your decision, Fina."

"Decision?"

"I believe Bruno made you a proposal of marriage."

I stood up and faced them. "The two of you have already made all of the decisions. Now, you want to coerce me into accepting them."

"What kind of way is this to talk to your father and your *fidanzato?*" *papà* said.

"This isn't a proposal of marriage. It's a business arrangement."

"*Santo cielo!*" Grazia muttered. "*Che sfortuna!*"

"Marry each other for all I care," I told Bruno. "*I'm not your fidanzata!* " I left the room.

Bruno followed me, held his hand out to me. "Wait, please!"

"Clever of you to take our inheritances whether I marry you or not."

"Fina, I'm sorry. You're right. I haven't asked you to marry me the way a man should ask a woman. It's my fault for being too proud. Say that you'll marry me now or tomorrow or when you come back." He held my hands in his.

I pulled away. "Do you think that money and property are all that matter to me?"

"No. Please, listen to me. Your father needs a manager, and after what's happened to my family's fortunes, I need a secure future. So do you. Don't let a misunderstanding come between us. For both our sakes."

"I could run this winery by myself." I left Bruno and *papà* together in the *salotto.*

Grazia followed me. "*Che tragedia!* " She held her finger to her lips and motioned for me to follow her. "I'll get my cards." She went to the clock, opened it, and took out the battered tin box that she kept hidden inside. Then, she lit a candle and placed it in the center of the green table. Raffaele had carved a channel in the top of it with his new pocketknife when he was thirteen, and the candlelight danced in it like a bolt of lightening. Grazia sat down opposite me. "Don't tell Monsignor Enrico. He says the Tarot is 'blasphemy.' I don't want to upset him." The light from the candle made a hole in the darkness, enclosing us and separating us from the world outside. Grazia took out the cards from the tin box. Their frayed edges had turned black, and their corners were creased and broken. "This table was still in the old villa when your mother bought this palazzo." Grazia shuffled the cards.

"Tell me about mamma and *papà,* Grazia. What really happened?"

She laid out the cards. "This house was meant to be a new beginning for them, I think, because they had been so unhappy together after Etto died. At first, Signor Gabriele refused. It had been a meeting place for *fascisti.* At night the *squadriste* raided their neighbors' shops. After Mussolini fell, it became a Nazi commander's headquarters. You can't see the crater any more, but an Allied bomb landed just outside the *salotto.* Signor Gabriele said people had bad memories of this house. He thought it might be cursed. A place of *la sfortuna.*" Several cards fell on the floor. Grazia leaned over to pick them up. "But Signora Willa said they could change its fate." Grazia studied the cards. "They argued about it for a long time. Then, just before you were born, Signor Gabriele changed his mind. I think he believed buying this house would keep the Signora's heart at home. He didn't allow himself to see that her heart had already flown far away from him long before."

"Did *papà* know mamma had an *amante?*"

Grazia shrugged and pointed to one of the cards. "Here is the Chariot with the other cards around it." She looked into my eyes. "It says you're going on an important journey where you will discover something new… maybe the answer to your question." She pointed to the Hanged Man. "And here the cards say that you must make an important decision about someone. A decision that could change your life."

"I think I just did that. What about when I go to Milano?"

Grazia pointed to the next card. "This one is your future. I see many things…some good, some not so good. She held her hand over one of the cards. "This one is a very bad person." She closed her eyes, the better to view the malign being. "In my mind I can see this person surrounded by teeth. Maybe someone in the place where you're going. Maybe someone you already know." She looked up at me. "I'm uncertain."

I laughed. "Will this person bite me?"

"Maybe bring you harm. Maybe disappointment. Maybe regret.

That's why I see so many teeth. Harm through words, through something someone tells you or says about you. Something false, I think. It looks dangerous. Not all bad, but something, some one thing, very bad. This card I don't like." Grazia tapped the card. "Never mind. I'm going to put a curse on this person. I'll curse this evil one the way my mother cursed them: with suffering, with pains and agonies, with losses of their valuables and loved ones. A curse so strong not even a priest can take it away!" Grazia paused. "Only God." She rubbed her hands together in apparent satisfaction. "Now, whenever you face danger, you are safe from any harm."

"And what about my journey?"

Grazia touched each of the cards with a gnarled finger: "Here is the Empress. This means you'll face many challenges and perhaps gain success, but you must keep your faith and be humble because you are not as powerful as others around you." I pointed to the last card. "Temperance means you're going to make a change in the world somehow and have to balance what is good and what is bad. Perhaps forgive something that is very difficult to forgive." Grazia crossed herself and put her cards away

Later that evening, Bruno spoke to me again. "Fina. I was wrong not to listen to what you were saying. I want you and I'm willing to wait for you. Say *yes*."

I wasn't ready to say *yes* yet.

In the end, *Papà* decided to go with me to Milano himself and make sure I found a place to live. "It's dangerous for a girl like you to travel alone," he said. "*Cattiva gente* everywhere." Bad people. "*Zingari* could rob you. *Femministe and dimostranti* try to recruit inexperienced people like you for their riots. God knows what could happen. You could be arrested and end up in jail!" He said that he wanted us to go to Firenze together first so that he could tell Silvana and Raffaele about his partnership with Bruno. I think he hoped that my presence might prevent an argument with Silvana. However, just a few days before we were to depart, he injured his back when he was working in one of the vineyards and had to stay in bed. He asked Bruno to take me to Milano and help me get settled. Although it wasn't considered proper for a young, unmarried woman to travel overnight with a man, especially one who wasn't even her *fidanzato* yet, *papà* trusted Bruno. "Your honor will be safe," he said, "and while you're in Firenze, Bruno will have a chance to explain our new organization to Silvana and Raffaele."

13

ORVIETO, SEPTEMBER 1968

When the day of my departure arrived at the end of September, I put mamma's rosary inside the black velvet bag with *nonna*'s pearls and her earrings and packed the bag in my suitcase where it would be safe. Next, I took the crucifix down from the wall, wrapped a sweater around it, and put it in the suitcase, too. I ran my fingers over the frame of the photograph of our family. It had always seemed to me that mamma was the most beautiful person in the world, but even at that much earlier time when the picture was taken, she would often look at herself in the mirror and say, "Without my hopes and dreams, I've become old and withered." She didn't look old and withered at all, but in the picture she seemed out of place, uncertain, as if she might have left the photograph had I not been sitting on her lap.

I felt unmoored, too, my suitcases my only tethers. I wrapped the photograph in another sweater and put it in the suitcase. I looked around at my empty room. It seemed too small to contain my own hopes any longer. I imagined that I was on my way to a larger "room," someplace where I would become a different Fina, the real Fina. I took the bundle of letters out of my wedding chest and set them next to my suitcase. I certainly didn't want to meet Michel Losine, much less know him, but keeping the letters made me feel like a voyeur and disloyal to *papà*. On the other hand, destroying them seemed disloyal to mamma. *What would I say to this* amante *who lived on the other side of my false life?*

Looking out my window, I felt as if I were seeing Orvieto for the first time, though its ancient walls and streets held my own history, too. I wanted to hang onto my memories of the sparkling façade of the Duomo with its stone pillars carved like lace; the vineyards and groves, and the green hills extending beyond the horizon. This was where I had always belonged, where I had known myself. I felt the loss of what had once been and was no longer possible there. Although I had sought this change, I did not expect the profound sense of solitude that accompanied it. I was truly glad that Bruno would escort me to my new life. *Would my new history be just as mutable?*

I took the postcard and the magazine clipping from the compartment in my wedding chest and put them in my suitcase in a way that would protect them. I made sure the money mamma gave me was in my purse. I was packing the bundle of letters as *papà* came to the door.

"Remember, be very careful about unscrupulous people, *cara*." I pushed the bundle into my suitcase. "Stay away from *zingari*. They're still around and they're cunning. *Dimostranti* and *femministe*, too." I tried to close the suitcase, but it was too full. *Papà* paused. "Those are Willa's letters, aren't they? You kept them from me, didn't you?"

"I'm sorry, *papà*. I didn't want to upset you."

"You read them?"

"Yes."

"All of them?"

I nodded. I saw his sorrow for what I had done.

"Give them to me," he said. When I handed him the bundle, some of the letters fell on the floor. I helped to pick them up. "I'm glad you're leaving. I don't want you to come back."

"Papà, don't say that." As he left the room, one of the letters fell on the floor. I picked it up and followed him.

He waved me away. "Deceitful. Just like your mother. Go live in the gutter with Silvana and Raffaele, where you belong."

"Papà, don't make us part this way." He didn't answer. I felt inside my pocket, but I had already packed mamma's rosary. I returned to my room and put the remaining letter in my purse. I wanted to write *papà* a note, tell him how sorry I was, but I couldn't find words to bridge the abyss between us. My *carta d'identita* was still on my bed. I dropped it

into my suitcase, too. Grazia came in. "Have you seen *papà?*" I asked her. "Signor Gabriele is burning papers. He said not to let anyone disturb him." She removed a gold chain from around her neck. On it hung a tiny replica of an animal horn, also of gold. She fastened it around my neck. "Gypsies like to kidnap beautiful young girls like you and feed them spiders and mice. Thanks be to God, there aren't as many as there used to be. My *corno* will protect you." Grazia crossed herself. "Never take it off."

14

FIRENZE, SEPTEMBER 1968

Near the Ponte Santa Trìnita where the Via S. Spirito intersects the Via Maggio, stood the Pensione dell'Oltrarno, a spotless rebuke to Firenze's San Frediano neighborhood. The concierge, a graying but still stylish woman, led us along creaky passages wallpapered in tiny blue flowers to the whitest of rooms. After the crowded train, I welcomed the sight of the large bed and its white coverlet, the sink in the corner, and the prospect of a warm bath in the footed tub down the hall. Though we had left only hours before, both Orvieto and *papà's* anger seemed distant to me, left behind with my previous life, left behind like the villages that passed outside the window of the train that carried us to Firenze.

Dressed for dinner and wearing the birthday gifts Bruno had given me, I waited with him downstairs in the *salotto* for Raffaele and Silvana to arrive. Even before we saw Silvana, I felt the change in the room when she entered as though a wave of something foreign and disturbing swept before it all that was ordered and fixed. The low hum of conversation ceased as all eyes turned to watch her. She wore a sheath of bright yellow printed in enormous red peonies, a red hat, and stiletto-heeled pumps, also red. A cartoon goddess bursting from her dress, she swayed before her audience, blooming under the attention she attracted.

"*Fina! Tesoro!*" Silvana exhaled cigarette smoke and kissed the air next to my cheeks. She waved to the concierge, who was serving the other guests. "*Vino, vino in fretta, per favore.* A big glass. Now. "I'm so thirsty." Raffaele, thin and elegant in a pale and wrinkled linen suit, his pink shirt open at the neck, served as pilot boat to Silvana's steamer. He settled her on the sofa. "*Stupide scarpe!*" These damn shoes! Silvana said, holding one of her stilettoes. "How difficult could it be to make them comfortable?" She rubbed her deformed and reddened toes.

The concierge appeared with another tray of drinks. Bruno served Silvana first. "*Bravo* Bruno. So polite," she said, extending her free hand for him to kiss. Bruno held her hand in his, but he didn't kiss it. "Perhaps you aren't even polite," she added. She gripped Bruno's hand and pulled him down toward her, wrapped her arms around his neck and kissed him forcefully on his mouth. Bruno tried to extricate himself from her grasp, but she held him fast. She was drunk.

"Silvana! Let go *now!*" Raffaele said.

Silvana giggled and released her captive. "He likes it. Don't you? You probably don't get much, do you?" I could see that Bruno was disgusted. I was embarrassed and humiliated. *What else will Silvana do before the evening is over?* I thought.

Raffaele put one arm around Bruno and the other around me. "She's not in control," he said quietly. Raffaele always tried to make people feel more comfortable, especially in difficult situations.

Silvana took a long sip of wine. "Maybe I am just a tiny bit drunk, but I won't let you talk about me behind my back." She stared into her wine as if she were looking over a precipice and sniffed. "Did they get this garbage from us?" She raised her glass. "Let's celebrate! We're here and *papà* isn't." She mimed laughter and drank all of the wine in her glass at once.

"Paolo has invited us to his restaurant," Raffaele said.

Silvana sighed. "Do we have to?" Raffaele gave her a warning look. She put her hand over her mouth. "Don't worry. Silvana will be a good girl." She signaled to the concierge to refill her glass. "I'm so thirsty." Beckoning me to come closer, she pointed at the other guests sitting near us. "Everyone wants to know what we're talking about," she confided in a stage whisper. She put her index finger to her lips. "Let's not tell them!" She threw her head back and laughed loudly. Abruptly, she turned to me once more. "What did *papà* say when you told him you were going to university?"

"Probably '*no*,'" Raffaele said.

I tried to smile. "Something like that," I said. Bruno shifted in his seat and tapped his foot on the floor; it sounded like drumbeats. I drank some wine. "But after he made Bruno his partner, *papà* was more willing for me to go."

"*Partner?*" Silvana dropped her glass. It shattered. The room grew silent. "Oh, no! All that lovely wine is on the floor now!" She shook her head and looked at Raffaele with false innocence. "Silvana is a bad girl tonight, isn't she?" A maid appeared with a mop.

"*Papà* needed help with the work," I said, keeping my voice low, "and Bruno has been the manager for several years, so...."

"You're probably concerned about your inheritances," Bruno said. "Let me be as honest as I can with you. I have a commitment to the business and the new vintage. I believe we'll all prosper."

Silvana squinted at Bruno. "So, let me understand. There are two of you," she said holding her index fingers together, "but just one each of Raffaele and me." She separated her fingers. "So your share will be half and ours a fourth each. What do you think, Fina? Is that fair?"

"For God's sake, Silvana," Raffaele said. "Bruno and Fina will be doing all of the work. Besides, our fortunes in Orvieto dimmed long before Bruno came along. They were sealed when mamma died."

Silvana shook her head. "I think Fina has made quite a nice arrangement for herself, don't you?"

"*Papà* made Bruno a *half* owner with him," I said.

The concierge gave Silvana another glass of wine. She took a large gulp. "So, when do you two plan to marry?"

"We have no plans right now," Bruno said. "Are you enjoying the wine?"

"Mmmm. Delicious," Silvana said. She licked her lips and glared at Bruno. "It's also delicious that you get half of our inheritance whether you marry our sister or not. Would you like anything else?" She held out her glass to Bruno. "Wine perhaps?" The wine in her glass spilled on the rug.

"Sometimes we forget our manners," Raffaele said. He blotted the spots with his handkerchief. "Please excuse us." Bruno merely nodded. He didn't look angry or offended. At least, not then. Silvana grunted and emptied her entire glass, then took out a black cigarette from a case, lit it with a plastic lighter the color of an orange, and exhaled, allowing the smoke to pour out slowly, shrouding us in a haze. Raffaele waved the smoke away. Silvana exhaled again.

"Our father can only do what he does," Raffaele said to Bruno. "Silvana has always felt he favored Fina. She was born after Etto died, after our mother's affair, and you could say that Fina helped them recover that time before...before they suffered so much grief."

So, that's why papà wanted the letters: even Raffaele and Silvana don't know that mamma's affair continued until last year. Papà doesn't want any of us to know. Perhaps he isn't sure himself. I knew Bruno was watching me. I looked down at my lap. *What must he think?* I folded and refolded the corners of my napkin. Bruno put his arm across the back of my chair. I recalled my conversation with Signora Lucarelli and Signora Santori after mamma's funeral. *Do they know, too?* I remembered other things people had said to me. Was it only that they remembered that when she was young, she had come to visit *papà* and his family without a chaperone?

"*Papà* has such a colossal ego," Silvana said. "He's always thought mamma would never want anyone else but him." She laughed. I knew that Silvana was wrong, that *papà* had known about mamma's betrayal and couldn't bear it.

"I'm sure you're mistaken," Bruno said. I felt grateful.

"Well, we don't keep any secrets," Silvana said to Bruno. "You know what you're getting into, right?" Bruno didn't respond. "You've always known, haven't you?"

"Gossip, you mean?" Bruno said.

"*Che boiate!*" Silvana exhaled. "More likely, you know an opportunity when you see one."

"Silvana, that's uncalled for," I said. I knew Bruno wasn't trying to use me.

"Despite what Silvana says, Fina kept our parents together," Raffaele told Bruno.

Silvana took another drag on her cigarette and pushed her glass toward Bruno for him to refill. "So, maybe *you* can keep us together now," she said to Bruno, stubbing out her cigarette on the bottom of one of her shoes, "but I doubt it." Ashes fell on the carpet.

"Silvana, none of this is Fina's fault," Bruno said.

"Why does she have to be such a simp, then?"

I was enraged.

Bruno rose from his seat. "I won't allow you to treat Fina this way. Apologize!" Bruno was a gentleman.

"*Sièditi, ragazzo.*" Sit down, boy. Silvana signaled the concierge for more wine and snorted. "Just because you've stolen my inheritance doesn't mean you can tell me what to do."

"I think it's time to go home," Raffaele said. He helped Silvana to her feet. "My apologies."

"Please forgive all of us," I said to Bruno after they left. "I'm so sorry."

"Let's go out and start over together."

In the Piazza del Carmine a large poster advertised the final performance of *Rigoletto* at the opera house nearby. Vespers had just ended, and parishoners streamed out of Santa Maria del Carmine into the violet twilight. As we entered the emptied church, Bruno dropped coins into the candle box. We lit our candles and then entered a pew. On my knees, I prayed that I would have the strength to set aside my anger and shame and forgive Silvana. I prayed that *papà* would be able to forgive me. As we left, Bruno and I paused together in front of the fresco of Adam and Eve fleeing from the Garden of Eden into an uncertain future. I felt a chill.

Outside in the Piazza, Bruno nodded toward the poster. "It's almost curtain time. Do you want to go?"

Firenze's opera house had suffered extensive damage two years before in 1966 when the Arno had flooded much of the historic center of the city, destroying many important sites and art works. During reconstruction the opera company held its performances in a former warehouse. The production had an informal character: plain sets, wooden seats, raw floors. Patrons dressed simply too. As soon as we sat down, a faded curtain rose on the Duke's court as the Duke sang of the pleasures he hoped to enjoy with Gilda, Rigoletto's daughter. The cast wore shabby, ill-fitting costumes, but sang very well, and their acting was so entirely professional that instead of seeing the ragged assembly before me, I saw a palace and a lavishly dressed court.

I knew the story and the melodies well: Rigoletto, the hunchbacked jester, pondered the curse on his life. The feckless Duke may have truly loved Gilda, Rigoletto's beautiful daughter, as much as she loved him. Gilda's *Caro nome* aria swept me up in her love for him so that even his name called up her deepest feelings. *Does Bruno's name sweep me away with love in the same way?* I asked myself. *Perhaps a little. Perhaps when I write "Signora Orsini" on slips of paper. But is that enough?* At the end of Gilda's aria, the audience rose to its feet shouting, "Brava! Bravo!" It was several minutes before the production could continue. *Love has its own way of growing and expressing itself, too. Real love will carry me away with its power and enable me to do extraordinary things, just as Gilda chose to die for the Duke. Surely, a test of real love is whether one is willing to sacrifice life itself for the beloved.*

Perhaps Gilda's tragedy should have caused me to question further my beliefs about love, but even the wrenching scene with the deformed Rigoletto holding his daughter's lifeless body in his arms did not impress me as an emblem of the destructive power of love and betrayal. Instead, I felt my heart opening to all of the new experiences ahead of me. Especially love. By the time we left the theater, I had forgotten about Silvana and her insults. It seemed entirely natural to me to lean into the curve of Bruno's arm as we walked together. I felt safe and protected.

"Shall we have something to eat now?" Bruno said.

"I feel full."

"That's your heart speaking." He took my hand in his. "My heart is full, too."

We stopped for drinks, perhaps because our suppressed physical longing had seized us, perhaps because we were inexperienced and waited for the other to express our implicit wish. I wasn't thinking so much of what would come next, but I felt a change in myself in relation to Bruno, one I couldn't define except to experience the difference as a feeling of a power of which I was both the center and the orbit. I found this feeling pleasurable without as yet fully recognizing its significance or understanding its consequences. It was as if from far at sea a raft pushed by a wave carried us toward an unknown shore.

"*Grappa* for *la signorina* and espresso for me," Bruno said to the waiter. It was my favorite liqueur. This small courtesy and also the great courtesy he had shown earlier that evening affirmed how much he cared about me. In a way of speaking, I knew that I wanted him to take the tiller of our little craft and guide us beyond our hesitations.

"Gilda's coloratura was excellent," Bruno said. He ate most of his *biscotto* in one bite. "But the tenor lacked passion."

"I think he was very passionate and restrained himself."

"That's true, but I wanted him to express more instead of holding back," he said.

"I think he held back purposely. Not because he lacked feeling, but because of his nature."

"You're defending him," Bruno said.

"I feel sympathy for him, even though he was unfaithful."

"Why don't you feel sympathy for me then when I am utterly faithful to you?" Bruno said. "Can't you see that I, too, restrain myself? I love you with all my heart, but I must restrain myself until you say you return my love." I was quiet. "Do you restrain yourself by leaving me?" Uncertain of the consequences of a definite *yes* or *no*, I waited to be carried beyond the moment. "You know that we would be happy together. Always."

"Let's be happy together now." Bruno got up and kissed me. We finished our drinks and strolled hand in hand along the streets. When we returned to our *pensione*, the concierge gave us our keys and a handwritten note from Raffaele:

Dear Fina and Bruno,

Please accept my humble apologies. I deeply regret the ugly behavior you both endured this evening. I'm sorry to tell you that Silvana cannot help herself any more. Forgive her.

I gave the note to Bruno. He read it, crumpled it in his fist, and dropped it on the desk. I didn't want him to act so harshly, especially not right then. "Raffaele is trying to make amends for Silvana and repair our relationship."

Bruno folded his arms across his chest, a gesture that reminded me of *papà*. "How would that be possible? I'm not *un finocchio.*" A fag. Perhaps I should have noticed something unforgiving and unkind in Bruno's nature then, but at that moment I wanted to avoid the complications of real relationships and to be brought willing, but without my own conscious responsibility, into the new life ahead of me. Inexplicably, I chose Bruno to lead me, though he wanted only to return me to my previous life. Perhaps he was available. Perhaps I didn't know what I wanted or needed. Perhaps, like so many important passages, mine was less a matter of choice than of *la fortuna.*

"*Vin santo*, please,' Bruno said to the concierge.

I looked at my watch. "Our train leaves early."

"We have time." He led me into the *salotto,* to the carved sofa with its red brocade upholstery. We sat down together. On the wall opposite us hung a tapestry depicting an Olympian frolic, a prodigious revel involving men, women and beasts. The concierge returned with our wine and a plate of *biscotti.*

"Espresso, too?" Bruno said to me.

"No, thank you."

"One, then." I dipped the *biscotto* into the *vin santo* and bit off the soaked portion, pressed it against the roof of my mouth with my tongue. The sweet wine warmed me. Hoping to recapture our earlier closeness, I edged nearer to Bruno and put my head on his shoulder. He reached into his pocket. "I want you to have this." He handed me a small box covered in black velvet. Inside was a ring set with a circle of mother-of-pearl and a tiny diamond mounted on top surrounded by waves of gold filigree. It reminded me of a miniscule cake. "My father gave it to my mother on their honeymoon."

I hesitated. *Was it an engagement ring?* "Bruno, I don't…."

"I want you to keep it to remind you to come home to me. That's all. You don't have to say that you'll marry me now. I just want you to remember that I'm ready to marry you and because of my partnership in Vino Marcheschi & Orsini, I have the means to do it." I put the ring on. He took my hand. "Are you still so uncertain?'

"It's not that I don't care about you, but if I don't go to university now, I'll never know what I could have done." He played his fingers over mine.

"But what else could you want to be when you're already everything you need to be with me?"

"I wish I wanted only you, only my life in Orvieto, only what I already know," I said.

Bruno seemed reassured. "So, you would marry me then?"

"Yes," I said, believing it was so.

He smiled at me. "I think you'll come back very soon once you see what is not at your university." He put his arms around me and kissed me. "Let's not think about tomorrow. Just tonight." With desire and restraint, we went upstairs to my room. I turned the key in the lock and went in.

Bruno hesitated and then followed me, closing the door behind him. "Do you want to spend our last night together?"

"Yes." We set our wine glasses on the table next to the old bed. Its large frame lent a sense of solidity to our frail desires. Bruno kissed me again. Then, as if we had always known what to do, we pulled the white coverlet back. The mattress had a hollow in the center. With his back to me, Bruno took off his clothes. I undressed, too, and laid my clothes on a nearby chair. I took off the *corno* and put it on the dresser. *Without its protection our evening would have been much worse*, I thought. We got into the bed, he from one side, I from the other, pulled the covers over us, and lay next to one another naked. *This is exactly what the nuns told us not to do.* Bruno turned toward me and took my hand. It was delicious to be next to Bruno, his bare skin touching mine. I thought of Gilda.

"I am as virgin as you are, Fina." Bruno's confession surprised and pleased me. *He isn't a seducer like the Duke. Does Bruno know what kind of sin it is to do what is wrong, to know that one is doing it, and to make no effort to stop?* I wasn't sure myself. *The next time I go to confession I'll ask the priest.* Slowly, we made excursions of discovery of one another's bodies, both of us learning quickly the rhythm and pleasure of the other. At school the nuns never mentioned that making love would be pleasurable, but I had heard other girls talk, and they had said it was. I was surprised that something I had heard so much about in whispered conversations and about which there were so many rules was, in fact, so uncomplicated. That night, neither of us found the awkwardness of too many knees and elbows a distraction when the moment came for Bruno to enter me.

"You're sure it's okay?"

"Yes," I said, uncertain of the right answer. I felt a quick, sharp pain as Bruno moved above me. I had expected that making love would be much more difficult, more dramatic, more about love. Why else would it be forbidden until one had a husband who knew about such things? Bruno knew nothing at all, and we weren't even married. Bruno gasped and then he rolled away from me. *Perhaps the nuns were so mistaken because they had promised never to make love.* I had always assumed that they didn't make love because it was too difficult for them, even more difficult than giving their lives to Jesus. Priests, too. I was puzzled. *Making love is easy. And very nice, too. And it hurt only a little.* Maria had told me it was even easier the second time.

"Are you okay?" Bruno said. "I didn't hurt you, did I?"

"No." The nuns had told us that making love was very dangerous. Yet, here I was, safe with Bruno and still Fina Marcheschi. *Could this be all?* I wondered. *If Bruno were more experienced, would it make a difference?* I was eager to find out how I had changed.

"Do you want me to stay?" Bruno said.

"Yes." I moved closer to him and put my head in the crook of his arm. He kissed me. "I love you very much, Fina."

"I love you, too."

After Bruno fell asleep, I remained awake for a long time thinking about the future, about the stars outside my window in Orvieto, about whether I had changed. *Did Gilda feel the same way I do? Had Silvana?*

15

When I awoke the next morning, Bruno was still asleep. He snored softly next to me. I lay very still, trying to discover whether I had changed. *As soon as Bruno wakes up, he will kiss me and caress me like he did last night.* Maria had told me that she and Edgardo liked to make love in the morning, too. *That would be nice.* Bruno opened his eyes. He seemed not to realize that I was there. I waited for him to kiss me. "Good morning," I said finally. His body seemed to stiffen and avoid mine like a creature withdrawing into its shell.

He rolled over quickly and got out of bed without looking at me. "I have to go." *Is that a reason not to say "good morning"?* He dressed with his back to me.

I felt very naked. I pulled the covers up to my neck. "Let's have breakfast before we go to Milano. There's still time."

He glanced at the door. "I never eat breakfast."

"But you and *papà* have eaten breakfast together every morning since you became partners." Bruno unlocked the door and turned the doorknob. "At least have some coffee with me while I have breakfast, then."

"I have to go." He opened the door and went out. The latch sounded very loud when it closed. *What could have happened to the warmth and excitement we shared only a few hours earlier?* I went to the basin and filled the sink. *Bruno must not be feeling well this morning,* I thought as I dried myself off. I pulled the plug and watched the water whirl down the drain. As I brushed my hair, I heard a soft knock at the door. I put on my robe, held it closed with one hand, and opened the door with the other. Bruno stood outside in the hall with his suitcase.

I opened the door wider. "Come in."

"I have to go."

"Aren't you coming with me to Milano?"

"I can't."

I opened the door completely, forgetting that I wasn't dressed. "Why not?"

"Shhh. People will hear you." He looked around. "Put your clothes on."

My voice rose. "I want to know why you're leaving." I didn't care that I spoke more loudly and insistently than was considered proper for a young woman from a good family.

"Be quiet!" Bruno hunched his shoulders and withdrew even more.

"What are you keeping from me?" My voice filled the hallway. A man in a dark suit emerged from the next room and glanced at me as he passed by with his suitcase.

Bruno squared his shoulders. "You're disturbing other people."

"Tell me the truth."

"If you wish, I'll go to the station with you now and help you get your luggage." He sounded indifferent, as if we were strangers. A well-dressed couple approached us from the far end of the hallway.

"You slept in my bed last night and now you act like you've never met me," I said quite loudly. I saw the woman take the man's arm and look away. I didn't care.

"Are you coming now or not?" Bruno said. I slammed the door in his face as hard as I could. Our empty wine glasses rattled on the nightstand. The floor creaked outside the door, and the sound of Bruno's footsteps faded away. For the first time, I noticed the tattered carpet beneath my bare feet and the frayed curtains at the window. I looked at the clothes I had left on the chair the night before. *Maybe the yellow dress in my suitcase would look better. When he sees me, Bruno will be sorry for the way he's acted. He's probably downstairs right now waiting to apologize.* After I got dressed, I sat down on the unmade bed with the purse Bruno had given me. A few days earlier it had seemed beautiful. I emptied out the contents. I had my ticket and the envelope with the money from mamma. I was very hungry. We hadn't eaten dinner the night before. I put everything back in my purse, closed the suitcase, locked it, and went out into the empty hallway. Just as I was closing the door, I remembered the *corno*. I returned for it and fastened it around my neck. *Perhaps I shouldn't have taken it off.* I tiptoed down the stairs to the front desk. The couple I had seen in the hall turned away when they saw me. *What should I say to Bruno after the way he has acted?* But Bruno wasn't at the desk. Or in the *salotto* either. *He must have gone to the station. I'll ignore him when I see him,* I decided. *Let him apologize.* The concierge took my key. "Are there any messages for me?" I asked.

"The young man with you said his sister would be down shortly," the concierge told me. I understood that this fiction allowed all of us to overlook my actual situation. *At least Bruno had been considerate about protecting my reputation. Or did the concierge make up the story?* The heat climbed up the back of my neck and settled in my face. I pretended that I had dropped something on the floor. When I stood up, she handed me the bill for both rooms. "Your brother said he was late and that you would take care of the bill." She shook her head and smiled at me in a way that seemed sympathetic. I wanted to ask her—someone—what to think, what to do. Fortunately, I had the money mamma had given me, but Bruno had known nothing about it. *How did he expect me to pay the bill?*

"He had to leave early," I said. "A family matter." The concierge smiled pleasantly, as if this information clarified everything.

If there were any advantage to virginity, the advantage had nothing to do with honor. Rather, the advantage was that it gave one the power of having something to give away, something that someone else wanted, a magic wish granted by a fairy tale witch. Once the wish was made, even if it had been the wrong wish or a mistake, it was gone. How silly that so much depended on so little. Nothing at all, really. I hadn't understood before that moment how angry Bruno was at me for leaving. I hadn't understood that making love could also be an act of revenge.

My taxi crossed the Ponte Santa Trinita. "The Americans paid for this new bridge," the driver said. "It's made with pieces of the old bridge. They used the original plans, but this new bridge is much stronger. It looks exactly the same as the old one. No one can tell the difference." He seemed proud.

Could anyone tell that I'm different? I wondered. I checked the time. "Could we hurry, please?"

The streets near the station were choked with *dimostranti and operaii.* Demonstrators and workers. The taxi could go no further, and I had to carry my suitcase the last two blocks. I scanned the crowd still hoping to find Bruno, talk to him, say something to him. *Dimostranti* milled around me waving signs and distributing leaflets. When they tried to talk to me, I ignored them. In front of the station, I set my suitcase down. A gypsy child ran up to me. Nearby, his parents waited, watching us. Quickly, I picked up my suitcase and went inside.

A stiff-limbed porter smiled at me through broken and missing teeth. "May I help you, *signorina?"* His white hair hung over the collar of his dirty jacket. Frayed gold braid trailed off his shoulders. "Where are you going?"

"Milano," I said, "but first I have to find someone." I gave him the claim ticket for the two other suitcases and the trunk I had left at the station. *"Per favore,* take care of my luggage and wait for me here." Then I saw Bruno ahead in the crowd. I called out to him and waved. He paused but then continued on toward the platform. I hurried after him, watched where he got on the train. I walked along the length of the car scanning the windows. I thought I had found him and waved to get his attention. A man looked up at me puzzled, and then waved back. Humiliated, I went back into the station.

The porter looked at me and cocked his head. "Tsk. Tsk. A pretty girl like you shouldn't be traveling alone." He nodded at a group of gypsies. "It's too dangerous." He placed my trunk on his cart with interminable care. "Don't worry. I'll take care of you."

"I'm not alone," I said. "My brother came with me. He took an earlier train back to Orvieto to help with our business." *That doesn't make sense,* I thought. "Our father isn't well," I added.

The porter shook his head as if I had described an unthinkable act. "Your brother should have seen you to your train." Slowly, he picked up a suitcase. *What would the porter say if he knew the truth?* I checked my watch. *Only ten minutes until departure.* "You remind me of my granddaughter. She's a pretty girl, too, but she stays home. Helps her mother and father. Keeps in her place." He looked at the two suitcases that remained on the sidewalk.

"Yes," I said. "No. I mean I'm a student."

He dragged another suitcase onto his cart and paused for breath, shaking his head. "I suppose it's good that some girls learn a little, but not too much." I checked my watch again. "Don't worry. I'll make sure you're on time," he said. He pulled on the cart. The effort required all of his strength. At last, the rusty wheels squealed and turned. "Follow me." During our slow progress to the platform, we stopped again and again for him to catch his breath. "You're a nice girl," he gasped. "Not like those *femministe* and *dimonstranti* outside," he said. "Watch out for the *zingari.* They get on the trains until the *poliziotti* find them and put them off."

When we reached my train, he tried to help me up the steps. I gripped the handrail tightly to keep both of us from falling. On shaky legs he returned for my trunk and each of my bags, pushing them up to me one by one. "You're lucky I was here today," he said as I dragged the last bag into the vestibule. "Nobody bothered you."

"Grazie mille."

"It's my pleasure." He turned his face up to me with a toothless smile. "Who's going to meet you in Milano?"

"My father...yes, my father."

He cocked his head again and looked at me intently. "But you said your brother went home to Orvieto to help your father. Do you have two fathers?"

Was that what I said?

"Buona fortuna, signorina."

16

MILANO, SEPTEMBER 1968

Alone in the compartment I remembered the way Bruno had looked at me and how he had changed, fled from me. "If you refused his offer of marriage, why did you give yourself to him?" *papà* would have said. "Because I couldn't help it," I would have answered. Because I was curious and wanted to find out who I would be after doing this forbidden thing. I touched the *corno* and tried to think about the flowers that grew in Orvieto instead of Bruno, but it was no use. I was sad, frightened, and very hungry.

The conductor came for my ticket. "We'll be delayed for several hours, *signorina*. The *dimonstranti* have called a strike." *Would they be on the train? Gypsies, too?* I touched the *corno*.

"Where can I get something to eat?"

"The *vagone ristorante* is closed. The waiters joined them."

"Could you help me put my luggage on the rack?" I said. "It's too heavy for me."

"The baggage attendants have joined the strike, too, *signorina*."

I sat down to wait. I had changed, certainly, but what had changed was not so much within me. Rather, the real change was in the way Bruno saw me. *A presumption of virginity was enough to establish a woman's goodness, but the real measure of goodness should be love,* I thought. *If you love someone, whatever you do with that person is right. Becoming lovers was right because I loved Bruno just as Gilda loved the Duke. Does Bruno know that I love him?* I decided to write him a letter. Surely, he would understand. My stomach growled.

I leaned back against the seat and closed my eyes. If Gilda had been *papà*'s daughter, he would say, "You sold cheap" just as he had said to Silvana when she came home pregnant and without a husband. *Of course, Silvana hardly knew the fathers her children. I've known Bruno all of my life, and we're nearly engaged.* I didn't regret that Bruno and I were lovers, only that I had lost my temper. Nonna Marcheschi always said that it wasn't becoming for a lady to lose her temper, especially a young lady who doesn't yet know what is correct.

I opened my eyes when the train moved forward. It hesitated, and moved forward again. I checked my watch. Three hours had passed. The compartment door opened. A group of gypsy women entered, all of them gesturing and chattering in a language I didn't understand. I touched the *corno*. The men remained outside in the corridor. Their swarthy presence added to my uneasiness. The gypsy women stacked their bags and baskets on the floor and in the hallway. It was so crowded that I couldn't stand up, much less escape. *At least they can't run away with my luggage.* I tried to move my suitcases aside. One of the young women smiled and lifted my bags onto the rack above me.

They settled noisily into their seats. Three of the men, each one of a different generation, sat opposite me. They nodded at me. I averted my eyes, but I didn't know where to look. A very old woman sat down to my right, a younger one to my left. The youngest squeezed into the seat beside me. I held my purse on my lap, covered it with my arms, and crossed my ankles, drawing myself in to avoid contact. The more I withdrew, the more the gypsy women spread out around me, their warm bodies touching mine. Their rings looked cheap compared to the one Bruno had given me. *Will they try to steal mine?* They wore scarves over their long hair, which looked like it had never been cut. *Are they clean?* Their necklaces and bracelets of brass and glass beads clanked. I could smell their bodies and feel the warmth of them. *Is the white-haired one the older woman's mother or grandmother?* Occasionally, they smiled at me through broken teeth and dark gaps where teeth were missing. Soon, they opened their

baskets. The spicy odors of their voluminous picnic filled the compartment. I was both attracted and repelled. My stomach growled. The woman sitting next to me tapped my arm, pointed to the food and to me.

Although I was very hungry, I shook my head. *What if papà found
out that I ate with gypsies?* The woman smiled and pushed my purse out
of the way. I put it on the floor underneath my legs. *If they try to steal my
purse, I'll kick them and scream,* I decided. The woman covered my lap
with a greasy cloth. I touched the *corno* and then remembered that gypsies steal gold. I buttoned up my dress to hide the necklace. The woman
next to me laughed, put thick, dark slices of bread on top of the cloth, and
piled the slices with spicy meats. She offered me some pickled vegetables
and an oily salad from a common pot. *It doesn't look like spiders or mice.
Does poisonous food smell good?*

The older man sitting opposite me passed me a bottle of red wine
and a glass. The glass looked dirty. *Doesn't wine make the poison work
faster?* He raised his glass in my direction. *"Salute!"* I tried to be polite.
I pretended to take a sip. He smiled and pointed. *Can he tell that I'm not
drinking the wine?* I wondered. The women ate with their fingers, talking
all the while. *Are they talking about me? About how they can steal my
purse and my luggage as soon as their poison takes effect?* I pressed my
legs against my purse. My stomach growled. Someone burped. I was very
hungry. It had been an entire day since I had eaten. *I'm already far from
Orvieto,* I thought. *Perhaps I'll taste just the meat. No one will know. The
gypsies are eating it and they're still alive, still awake.*

I took a bite of the food. Delicious. I drank more wine and took another bite. The bread was delicious, too. I drank more wine and ate some
pickled vegetables. In fact, I ate everything. They gave me more food,
and I ate that, too. The woman refilled my glass several times. Outside in
the corridor, one of the men began to play a guitar, rhythmic passages that
rippled in my bones. I brushed the crumbs from my dress. *Gypsies are
actually very friendly, very hospitable people,* I thought. *If I hadn't left
Orvieto, if Bruno had stayed with me, I wouldn't have known what was
really true. It must be* fortuna *that I'm going to Milano alone.*

17

Behind my heavy eyelids, between waking and sleeping, between fairy-tale and nightmare, the faces of strangers floated before me: men and women, their mouths moving silently, smiling and frowning, disembodied souls fading into existence and out, unable to return to the homes they had left, headed toward places they couldn't name. Then, Bruno came toward me, smiling. Our wedding day. Just as he slid a gold ring onto my finger, a huge centipede stung me, leaving only a red spot where the ring had been.

"Bologna! Next stop!" The voice penetrated the dream. "Tickets, please." I opened my eyes. I hadn't seen this conductor before. The gypsies didn't have tickets or the money to buy them. The conductor called the *poliziotti* who ordered the *zingari* off the train and arrested them as soon as we stopped. When the train left Bologna, the conductor returned to the compartment and demanded to see my ticket again. He pointed to a sack on the floor. A red, oily substance oozed from it and had formed a thick puddle near my feet. "Can't you people pick up your own garbage?" He studied my ticket and returned it with a grunt. Glancing at the sack, he went out and slammed the compartment door behind him. The sack smelled of the food I had eaten earlier. I picked it up, intending to throw it away. The oily substance dripped on my dress, leaving large stains. I needed to change my clothes.

My suitcases were beyond my reach. I pulled the cord to call the conductor. He didn't respond. I signaled again. No response. At last, I stood up on the seat and held onto the luggage rack with one hand. By stretching as far as possible, I could grasp the handle of my largest suitcase, the one at the bottom of the stack. With my free hand I pulled on the handle with all of my strength. It didn't move. I pulled again. Just then, the train lurched, brakes screeched, and the compartment lights went out. My suitcases tumbled off the rack. One struck the side of my head before landing on the floor. I sank down on the seat and touched my throbbing temple. A beam of light appeared outside the compartment, and two men entered with a flashlight. Their badges shone.

"*Polizia!*" Police! One held the flashlight near my face. I blinked at the sudden brightness, momentarily blinded, and then looked away. One kicked my suitcases aside with his foot.

"What's happened?" I said.

The *poliziotto* looked around the compartment. His eyes stopped at my purse. "*Carta d'identità.*" He held out his hand.

"Why are you going to Milano?" the second *poliziotto* said.

"I'm going to university."

They exchanged glances and laughed. One came closer, peered at me, and nodded. "*Zingara!*"

I pulled my purse closer to me. He ran his finger over it. "Expensive purse for a *zingara* or a student. Where did you get it?"

"*Mio ragazzo.*" My boyfriend.

He held the lantern near the stain on my dress, then next to the abrasion on my forehead. "*Sì, certo.*" Oh, sure. "I suppose he's a student, too."

"*Carta d'identita! Forza! Forza!*" the first *poliziotto* said. Hurry up! Where was my identification? I couldn't find it.

The second officer came closer. "We don't like trouble." He flipped open his jackknife and idly tested the blade with his finger. "Or trouble-makers without a *carta d'identita.*"

"I'm not a troublemaker and there's no trouble," I said. "I just can't find my *carta.* I know it's here."

He looked at me like I was merchandise. I could see his pocked skin. Spittle clung to his untrimmed mustache. He licked his lips suggestively. The lights came on. He pointed his knife at the sack. "Even the *look* of trouble."

"She probably doesn't have one," said the other *polizotto*.

"Yes, I do." At last, I remembered that I had put it in my suitcase. I got it out and handed it to the first *poliziotto*.

"Counterfeit," he said without looking at it. "And stored improperly." The second *poliziotto* nodded and closed his knife with a snap."Watch out, *zingara*. If you cause trouble in Milano, we'll arrest you and seize your *documenti*." He took my arm and squeezed it hard. I knew he intended to leave a bruise.

"Let me go! How dare you!" I said. He jerked my arm, pulling me off balance. I fell back onto my luggage. I heard my dress rip.

"*Stammi bene!*" Take care! They left the compartment laughing.

I got up to make sure that I could still open the door, still escape. My temple throbbed. Using the mirror from my purse, I examined the swelling next to my eye. There was a lump and a large bruise. I combed my hair so it would cover my temple and my eye. *The conductor will get me some ice.* I pulled on the cord again. No response. I got a clean dress out of my suitcase and went into the corridor.

The conductor was talking to an elegantly dressed woman in the next compartment. I edged around them. He followed me and stood in front of the door to the lavatory. "*Zingari* use the lavatory at the station."

"I'm not a *zingara*. I just need to change my dress." I pointed to the stains. "And some help with my luggage."

"You sit with *zingari*. You talk to *zingari*. You eat with *zingari*. You smile at *zingari*. You drink with *zingari*. In what way are not a *zingara*?" He glared at me and crossed his arms. "The lavatory is closed to *zingari*. Do I need to call the *polizia* again?" I retreated to the compartment and put my dress back in the suitcase. Fear settled over me like dust, sifted through my skin, and coated my bones. Trembling, I heard the call for Milano Centrale. At last, the train entered the dim and monstrous maw of the station.

I dragged my largest suitcase into the corridor and then into the vestibule. At the stairway door I saw the *polizotti* watching from a distance, waiting. I held the railing with my left hand. With my right hand I eased the suitcase down the steep and narrow steps onto the platform and returned for the second suitcase, and then the third. At the top of the steps I set the third suitcase down and pushed my damp hair away from my face. My temple throbbed. I held my purse under my arm, picked up my suitcase, and took a deep breath. As I negotiated the final step, I slipped and lost my grip on the suitcase. The suitcase landed on the platform and the latches released instantly. My belongings scattered. I scrambled down the steps and caught my foot in the open suitcase. My ankle twisted. I heard it crack. Stunned by the pain, I bit my lip and suppressed a cry so I wouldn't attract the attention of the *poliziotti*. People gathered around me.

The velvet bag containing Nonna Marcheschi's pearls and earrings and mamma's rosary lay on the pavement next to me. Our family photograph was nearby. I reached for the photograph and pricked my finger on a shard of broken glass. A drop of blood landed on the photo. I wiped it off on my skirt and sucked my finger. Just then, a young man in dark glasses approached me. *He's coming to help.* He stooped to pick up my two largest suitcases and disappeared into the crowd with them.

"Thief!" I screamed.

"Which way did he go?" someone said. I pointed toward the station. More people joined the group around me.

The first *poliziotto* pushed his way through shouting, "Clear the area." The bystanders retreated, watching me from a distance. "Well, *zingara*, it didn't take you long to make trouble."

I tried to stand. "That man stole my luggage."

"Another one of your tricks!" The *poliziotto* reached down for the velvet bag and opened it. "Where'd you get these?"

"My grandmother and my mother."

He laughed. *"Sì, certo!"* He put the bag in his pocket. "Evidence!" I saw the other *poliziotto* coming toward us.

The postcard and the clipping of James Dean lay on the pavement next to me. Before I could put them in my purse, the second *poliziotto* yanked the purse away from me. "What else are you hiding?" He reached inside. *"Molti soldi!"* A lot of money. He dropped my purse and held the envelope with the money in his hands. "Where does a *zingara* get so much money?" He put the envelope in his pocket. "Evidence!" I grabbed my purse and put the postcard and the clipping inside. He pushed my clothes into my suitcase and held it shut under his arm. "We know what to do with thieves." I touched the *corno*.

"I'm not a *zingara* and I didn't steal anything." The *poliziotto* reached down and pulled me up by one arm. I heard the sound of fabric ripping. "Be careful. I don't have my clothes."

He pulled me close to him. I felt his hand on my breast and his warm breath near my ear. "I hear *zingare* don't like to wear clothes," he whispered.

I pushed him away. "Don't touch me!" I put my foot down. Pain shot through my ankle. I couldn't walk. The *poliziotto* took my arm again.

My heart surged. *If papà finds out....* "My trunk is still on the train."

The *poliziotto* held onto me until we came to an opaque glass door inside the station. Gold letters outlined in black spelled *Polizia.* He opened the door. Inside, Alpine travel posters hung at odd angles on the walls, their edges moldy where moisture had percolated from the waterstained ceiling. Directly in front of me a man wearing a khaki uniform sat at a battered desk reading a *giallo*, a popular crime story. "Over there, zingara," the *polizotto* said. I hobbled to a wooden bench near the wall and sat down. My ankle throbbed.

"*Capitano…*," my captor began.

"*Aspetta…aspetta,*" the officer said, holding up his hand. We waited until he came to the end of the chapter. Reluctantly, he closed the book and gazed at me, stroking his large mustache. "*Cattiva gente creano un sacco di guai.*" Bad people make a lot of trouble. *Is he talking about the characters in the book or about me?* I wondered. He was bald except for the long, thin hair that extended from above his right ear over his head to just above his left ear, which he had plastered against his scalp so that his head appeared to be wrapped in thread. He might have been a character from a *giallo* himself, but I was too frightened to enjoy the resemblance.

"I am *Capitano* Fiorelli," he said, indicating the sign on his desk with the same title. "I am in charge of this station." His face was round and full, like unbaked bread with eyes. His shirt pulled at the armholes, and his greyish undershirt showed in the opening where a button was missing. He stood up. His stomach hung over his belt, and his pants strained to contain his girth. I thought of the pale sausages tied in the middle that Grazia always prepared for the Feast of Corpus Christi.

The *poliziotto* handed Fiorelli my purse and *carta d'identità*. "She's one of the *zingari* who made all the trouble on the train, *capitano*." Capitano Fiorelli stood up and leaned over the desk. He studied my dress and shoes, nodded.

"I would like to know why I'm here and why you're staring at me," I said. My own boldness surprised me. *Had I already changed so much that I was capable of challenging a policeman?*

"I ask the questions, *signorina.*" Capitano Fiorelli examined my *carta d'identità* with a magnifying glass. "Serafina Luisa Marcheschi. Who is that?"

"Me."

He held the picture next to my face. "Marcheschi." He leaned back and looked at me, stroking his mustache. "Marcheschi." He returned to the *carta d'identità*. "Where did you get this?"

"Orvieto."

"Orvieto…Marcheschi." He thought for a moment. "How do I know that name?" He looked around. "Where is your ticket for Milano?"

"In my purse."

Fiorelli opened my purse, took out my ticket, and held it up to the bare lightbulb that hung above his head. He rummaged in his desk drawer, found his magnifying glass and examined the ticket again with his glass. Then my *carta d'identità*. "These are real," he told the *poliziotti*. He looked in my purse again and found the letter. He studied the envelope with the grave expression of a professional. "This letter is addressed to a Signora Farnese in Arezzo, but you say you live in Orvieto. The name on your *carta d'identità* is Marcheschi. And so is the name on your ticket. This letter is not addressed to you." He removed the letter from the envelope and read it. "Obviously, this letter is from an *amante,* but the writer doesn't sign his name." Capitano Fiorelli smiled. "Perhaps, he has something to hide." He winked as he folded the letter and put it back in the envelope.

"Why have you come to Milano?"

"To go to university. Someone has stolen my luggage."

"Why?"

"I don't know."

"How can you study if you don't know why?"

"I don't know why that *ragazzo* took my luggage." I pointed at the officer. "And I don't know why he took my jewelry and my money."

"Is there someone in Milano who could identify you?"

"Yes. His address is on the back of the envelope. He is expecting me. His name is Michel Losine." I saw their surprise.

Capitano Fiorelli turned the letter over and looked at the address. He showed it to the two *poliziotti.* "You said you had arrested a *zingara* who was making trouble on the trains." The *poliziotti* glanced at one another. "Your *zingara,* as you call her, says Signor Losine knows who she is." The *poliziotti* looked at their feet. "She says Signor Losine will identify her. In fact, she says that he *expects* her." Fiorelli snorted contemptuously. "Now, I am the one who must call Signor Losine and tell him that two *poliziotti* in my department have arrested Signorina Marcheschi because they think she is a *zingara,* although she doesn't look like a *zingara* and she has an *Italian* name and an Italian *carta d'identita.* Not only that, she is injured." I saw their discomfort and their fear. Fiorelli turned to me. "Please, won't you sit here?" He got up and helped me into his chair. Then he pulled out the drawer of his desk so that I could rest my foot on it. The drawer was filled with *gialli.* He pointed to the books. "Something to read? Please help yourself." My ankle throbbed and so did my head. Fiorelli went out, leaving me alone with the two *poliziotti.*

One took the velvet bag from his pocket and set it in front of me. *"Signorina, mi dispiace."* I'm sorry. *"Per favore* don't tell Signor Losine about our little mistake. Signor Losine doesn't like mistakes." He wiped perspiration from his forehead. "He is a great friend of the *capitano*. In fact, you could say that Capitano Fiorelli works for Signor Losine, in a manner of speaking. If there are mistakes, the *capitano* could lose his job. So could we."

When Fiorelli returned, he set an espresso and a plate of fresh *biscotti* in front of me and handed me a cloth napkin. "Signor Losine says it would give him great pleasure to greet you." He turned to the two officers. "Find her luggage immediately. Make sure they don't sell anything. Bring all of it to me. And no payments! *Capite?*"

"*Sì, capitano. Immediatamente.*" The *poliziotti* turned to leave.

"My trunk is still on the train," I said. "And I want my money back."

"Give her whatever you took and bring her trunk!" Fiorelli ordered. One reached into his pocket and brought out the envelope with my money. He put it on the desk. Capitano Fiorelli counted out the money. "Is that the correct amount?"

"Yes." I took the money and put it in my purse.

Just then, a tall young man entered with my suitcases. He set them on the floor, wiped his hands on his jeans, and took a deep breath. "They told me you were in here," he said in English. He cracked his knuckles. "That guy dropped your suitcases as soon as he saw me coming." He smiled. "Lucky I wore my running shoes today." He ran his hands through his red hair. "This a police station?" He came around the desk and held out his hand to me. "Sorry. I always forget to introduce myself. Joey...Joey Dunne." We shook hands. His eyes were grey blue, perhaps light brown. "*Piacere,*" he said. "That's right isn't it? *Piacere.* Pleased to meet you." He looked kind. "I guess you can probably tell I'm not Italian."

"Yes. *Piacere.* Thank you."

"It was my pleasure...*is* my pleasure, I mean." He shook my hand again. "Already said that, right?" He looked at my torn and stained dress, at my swollen ankle, and then at my face. "Geez, you look sorta banged up. You okay?"

"I hope so."

"You want me to stay here with you? I'm not busy...not right now, anyway." He seemed friendly. Not dangerous.

"*Grazie.* Yes."

Joey Dunne found a chair and set it down opposite me. "I'm an American," he said. "A tourist, I guess you could say. Came to Milano about three weeks ago. I was planning to hitchhike around Europe, but I got interested in all the old stuff here. Today, I went to Lake Como. You been there?" I shook my head. "Beautiful. Saw 'The Last Supper,' too. Wouldn't mind seeing it again, though. Leonardo da Vinci's notebooks, too. He looked at people's insides—cadavers, I mean—and drew what he saw. Page after page of hearts, big toes, brains. A baby in a womb. He put it all in his notebooks so he could remember. That's what I want to do: remember everything I see, save it all up so I can think about it whenever I want."

That's what I need, too, I thought: *a notebook where I can write down everything that I know is true: one true thing added to another true thing to another true thing until everything I know about mamma and papà and Michel Losine is the truth.*

"...Da Vinci could have been arrested," Joey was saying, "and put in prison for what he did."

"Anyone can be arrested or put in prison for no reason. It just depends on who people imagine you are," I said.

"And send you off to war, too."

"Are you a soldier?"

"Not yet, but I could be in a few months. Vietnam. And then it'll be all over. Lights out." I wanted to console him. "I applied for conscientious objector status. Draft counselor says I have a good case. I'll soon find out how good."

"Would you like a *biscotto*?"

"Sure."

I held the plate out to him and accidentally knocked my open purse off the desk. The contents scattered on the floor.

Joey went to pick them up. "Hey, this is a picture of James Dean." He handled the fragile paper carefully. "How come you have it?"

"He just seemed like someone without a true friend."

"You know he's dead, right?"

"Yes, but lots of people feel alone...sometimes, anyway." I was thinking of mamma and now *papà*. "Sometimes they need to be consoled."

"But James Dean made a point of living without consolation."

"Yes, but if he...if people...knew they weren't alone...." *Maybe not Bruno or papà, but other people.*

Joey smiled. "So you want to console the people who feel alone?"

"Yes, the people who must bear more than they can."

Joey looked at me, his eyes full of more light than the sky over Orvieto. "That's very kind of you. Very, very kind."

18

Joey Dunne and I had been talking for more than an hour when a man with a cane entered Capitano Fiorelli's office. Everything about him was thin, so thin that he appeared capable of slipping through walls and materializing wherever he pleased. From where I sat it was difficult to guess his height, but he looked taller than *papà*. He had a long, narrow face with a nose to match. His half-closed eyelids gave him a disinterested, almost sleepy look, but his glacier-blue eyes sparkled, intense and jewel-like. His neatly trimmed goatee and mustache, both soft brown and mottled with grey, suggested tweed. He was well dressed. His carefully-pressed tan suit, the luminous sheen of his ecru shirt, the silvery green tie the color of moonlight, and the carved ivory handle of the cane he held in his manicured fingers gave the impression of elegance and control. Despite this refined appearance, his dominant quality was that of pervasive grief.

He limped around the desk to where I sat. "Please, don't get up," he said as if we had already been introduced. He held out his hand. "Michel Losine." Mamma's *amante*. The *M* of the intertwining *MW* engraved on mamma's jewelry. "*Molto piacere.*" His hand was cool and smooth. "I'm sorry to have kept you waiting."

"Fina Marcheschi. *Piacere.*"

"Well, now you've come to Milano." He glanced around the room, then reached into his pocket and brought out a gold case. "Cigarette?"

"*Grazie, no.*"

He selected a cigarette and put it between his lips with nervous fingers, then put the case away and flicked open a gold lighter, lit the cigarette and drew on it lightly, exhaling slowly without leaving any smoke. I thought of Fred Astaire, but without the dancing.

"Capitano Fiorelli tells me that you've had a problem with your luggage." He winked at me.

"Yes," I said.

"Service hasn't been the same since *la Guerra*, don't you agree?" He waved his cane at his leg and chuckled. "Neither have I." His voice, a smooth baritone, seemed pleasant, dispassionate, as if our extraordinary circumstances were unremarkable. "I was expecting you, but not here. How did you come to meet Capitano Fiorelli?"

I began to cry. Losine reached inside his jacket and took out a cream-colored handkerchief of soft, translucent linen. I blew my nose and wiped my eyes. He leaned over to look at my temple.

"Did these thugs beat you up, too?" He smelled like fine soap.

"No, but the one with the mustache did this." I showed him the finger-shaped bruises on my arm.

"Hey! That's a heck of a bruise," Joey said.

"He should pick on someone his own size if he wants to fight," Losine said. "Don't you agree, Capitano?"

"*Assolutamente, signore.*" Fiorelli bowed slightly. From another pocket in his jacket, Losine took out a small, leather-bound notebook and a silver fountain pen. He wrote something in the notebook, tore the page out, and gave it to Fiorelli.

"*Immediatamente, signore,*" Fiorelli said. "Everything will be taken care of. I'll see to it personally."

"This is Joey Dunne," I said to Losine. "Someone stole my luggage, and he brought it back."

"Very kind of you," Losine said to Joey.

"Happy to help."

"Still, I would like to thank you for helping Signorina Marcheschi." Losine took out his wallet and offered Joey several large bills. I wasn't sure how much, but more than I was accustomed to seeing in anyone's wallet.

"That's very generous, but I couldn't take your money, sir. Not for something like that," Joey said.

Losine put the money away. "In that case, perhaps I can be of help to you in some other way." He turned to Fiorelli. "Would you prefer to discuss the shipment now or at another time?" Fiorelli gave no sign of his preference. Losine took a thick envelope out of the pocket of his jacket. "I believe this is the information you requested."

When Fiorelli opened the envelope, I saw that it, too, was full of money. "*Sissignore*. This information will be very helpful with the shipment."

Losine turned to me with a smile and leaned on his cane. "May I look at your ankle?" He bent down. "Show me where it hurts." I pointed to where the swelling obscured my anklebone and had turned black and blue. "Together, I believe that you and I have a total of two good legs," Losine said smiling. "May I take you to my home so we can have a doctor look at your ankle? *His home? They won't know where to look for me because papà burned all the letters.*

"But I don't know you. Just some ice would be fine."

"As a matter of fact, I don't know you either." Losine looked at Joey. "Do you know her, Signor Dunne?"

Joey shook his head. "Might like to get acquainted, though."

Losine removed two cream-colored business cards from his breast pocket and gave one to me and one to Joey. I read the charcoal grey script on the card:

Michel Losine
Via Violetta 10
Milano
Italy

The address on mamma's letters. "Now that we've met officially, shall I ask Signor Dunne to come with us?

"Yes." I touched the *corno.*

"It seems we need your help again, Signor Dunne." Losine gestured toward me. "Could you carry her, please?" Joey lifted me up. As we went out of the office, Losine said to Fiorelli, "Have Signorina Marcheschi's luggage brought to my address immediately."

Outside the station we followed Losine to a large, black sedan parked next to a sign that said parking was prohibited. Two *poliziotti* whom I hadn't seen before stood next to the car, laughing. As soon as they saw Losine, they nodded and moved away. Losine opened the back door. *Papà would never approve of my getting into a car with strange men, especially not mamma's amante. He would say, "They may not seem dangerous, but they could be." But I'm in danger already*, I thought, *especially without any help. Besides, mamma must have trusted Losine or she wouldn't have asked me to take the letters.* Joey set me down gently on the back seat. I sank back onto the soft leather and put my foot up. Joey got in the passenger seat.

"I'm going to university," I said immediately. "Università Cattolica del Sacro Cuore." I meant that I was expected, that my absence would be noticed.

"Excellent," Losine said. "Cattolica is a fine school."

"Congratulations," Joey said. "That's an honor."

"I received highest honors on my exams."

"I'm certain your family is very proud of you," Losine said.

"My fiance's name is Bruno...Bruno Orsini," I continued. "We're going to be married. He's knows that I'm here...where I am, I mean." I meant that just because I had come to Milano by myself, I wasn't a troublemaker, no matter what the *poliziotti* said about me, and someone had already asked permission to marry me.

"My wife's name was Greta," Losine said. "She died some time before you were born. I buy and sell rare gems. I can see that you would look best in emeralds or sapphires." *What an odd thing to say. Is it a trick?* I touched the *corno*. My ankle throbbed. "I think a doctor should see your ankle immediately."

Joey turned around toward me. "I used to work at a hospital. I've seen broken ankles that looked like yours."

"Do you practice in Milano?" Losine asked.

Joey ran his fingers through his cowlicky red hair, which hung down over the back of his shirt collar. "No. I'm a pianist." He laughed. "A pianist without a piano. I can't practice much of anything." He grew sober. "I just graduated. Music school. Not an essential skill. Got my draft notice." He cracked his knuckles, and spread his fingers apart and then together in different combinations as if he were warming up to play. "I thought about going to divinity school, but I'm not sure I believe in God."

"Always a question," Losine said. I looked out. The street sign said Via Violetta. *It's the right street.*

"My mom's best friend is on my draft board," Joey said. "She fixed it so I could take this trip. If I go to Vietnam, I want to have beautiful memories." Losine stopped the car in front of an older building of grey stone. "I can go back to school later, if I live that long," Joey continued. "If I get killed...well, like Bugs Bunny says, 'That's all, folks!' No more worries about anything."

"Oh, I hope not," I said.

Wide steps led up to two large wooden doors with polished brass fittings. Above the doors, a large number ten had been chiseled into the stone façade. *At least the address is right.* Joey opened the door for me. I put my arm around his neck and he carried me up the steps. In the dim light, I could see the freckles sprinkled across the bridge of his nose. His collarbone, which showed at the opening of his shirt, stuck out so his lean flesh formed a valley around it.

"No, it's true. I could die. Lotta guys do," Joey said. "Can't predict. I try to keep that in mind. 'Army's no tea party, son.' That's what my dad says all the time. The other thing he says is 'Army makes a man of you.' He should know. He was in for a long time. Maybe that's why he thinks filing for C. O. means I'm not a man."

"I'm sure he's mistaken," I said.

Losine opened the front door. "If you'll take Signorina Marcheschi inside, I'll call a doctor." I looked at my watch. It was almost ten. *He's able to arrange a lot of things.* We passed through a foyer and then through another set of doors, these of glass etched with flowers, into a hallway. "Apartment number one to the right." Losine let us in. Joey carried me into the *salotto* and put me down on the pale grey sofa. I inhaled the odor of the leather and the sweet fragrance of the roses in the clear glass vase on the table in front of us. The lights from the faceted sconces made scattered reflections on the walls and ceiling. To my left, a door framed in dark wood led into another room. To my right a wide archway opened to a dining room. On the wall beyond the dining table hung a painting of an immense fish with iridescent scales laid out on a black slab, its red and yellow mouth open as though it had just been caught. It looked alive, able to swim away if it were returned to the water. I remembered reading something about the painting of a fish in one of mamma's letters. It was beautiful. On the polished wooden floors, rugs of intricately woven colors appeared to shimmer like the scales of the fish. A piece of a fresco mounted above the fireplace in front of us depicted a procession led by a goddess scattering flowers before her. I recognized it immediately: it was exactly like the one in the *salotto* at home.

"Beautiful, isn't she?" Losine said. "An ancient goddess of spring. She reminds me of a time of great happiness in my life." He coughed, then went to open the doors that led to a terrace. Above, a full moon hovered in the indigo sky.

Joey saw the piano. "Hey, this is a Bösendorfer, isn't it?"

"Yes," Losine said. "My wife's."

"Mind if I try it?"

"It may be out of tune."

"If it is, I'll tune it for you. I used to tune for the symphony at home. Musicians have to do something to make a living." He sat down at the piano and began to play. The notes merged into an enveloping sound that began with a fugue, passed through a turbulent sonata and concluded in a riff on "Santa Lucia." Joey came over and sat down next to me. "I'd love to have a piano like that some day."

A bell sounded, and Losine went to the door. "She's in here, Marcello."

A man in a dark suit entered the room and greeted us perfunctorily. He bent over my leg and gently moved my foot back and forth. When he felt my ankle, I pulled my foot away involuntarily. "That hurts?"

"Yes."

He finished his examination and turned to Losine as if my ankle belonged to him. "It's a bad sprain, but I don't think it's broken. Rest and elevation for seven days."

Joey stood up. "I'll come back tomorrow and see how you are."

Losine's eyes twinkled in the subdued light. "I think you'll be very comfortable here," he said to me as if the matter of my lodgings were settled. He looked silvery, almost supernatural. I blinked to dispel the image. "Consider it a favor to a solitary man who longs for company."

"Tomorrow is the day I enroll at university. I'm afraid I'll be too busy to keep you company."

Propriety belongs to those who can choose what they do; others have to make do with what is available. *Papà* would have been enraged if he had known that I stayed with Losine. I decided that if he asked, I would tell him that I had gone to a small *pensione* where they served meals. *I've scarcely left home and already I've become a liar*, I thought. *It's true that I've changed, but for the worse, my character repeatedly compromised. Is that what leaving home really means?*

19

Sunlight poured through the tall windows onto the carved *armadio* and the vanity table. My dress lay on the small wooden chair where I had left it the night before, next to a vanity set with an array of crystal vials. On the wall there was mirror in an ornate silver frame. *Did mamma use that mirror?* I sat on the edge of the bed and examined my ankle. During the night, the swelling had increased. Using the furniture to balance myself, I hopped to the windows. Outside on the terrace a table had been set for three. Beyond it in a garden surrounded by high, stacked walls a man in a straw hat weeded a bed of herbs. Nearby, a winding path lined with white flowers led to a sheltered bench that faced a black obelisk. *Did mamma sit on that bench?* I reminded myself that the sky above was the same sky as the one outside my window in Orvieto, though the dark, damp weather in Milano that day suggested otherwise.

The door of the *armadio* creaked when I opened it. Inside, women's clothing—mostly dresses—hung in a neat row. *What sort of man keeps dresses? Had mamma ever seen them? Did Losine's guests often lose their luggage and need something to wear?* I hobbled to the chair and put my tattered and stained dress in the wastebasket. Then, I sat down and looked at myself in the mirror. The bruise on the side of my face was quite large. It hurt to brush my hair. I hopped toward the bathroom, balancing with my hand on the wall. Next to the bathroom door were two small oil paintings of the garden outside seen through the windows in my room. Both evoked a similar tension: though the windows appeared open, the viewer felt imprisoned inside the room. The knock on the door startled me.

"Are you awake?" Losine asked. "It's almost eleven." It annoyed *papà* when I slept late.

"I'm just getting dressed," I said quickly. "I'm sorry. I overslept."

"You're welcome to use the clothes in the armoire." It sounded like a wish.

"My foot doesn't fit in my shoe."

"I've sent Signor Dunne for a wheelchair." *Signor Dunne? When did he come back?*

When Joey pushed me outside onto the terrace, Losine put his newspaper on the table next to his plate and looked at me. "You slept well?"

"I'm sorry. I'm not usually so lazy."

"It's good to rest." *Did he and mamma sleep late?*

"I'll be going to university today. My ankle is much better." Losine and Joey glanced at each another.

"Your registration is complete," Losine said pleasantly, "and it seems everything is in order." *How is it that he can arrange so many things? He seems to anticipate everything and control what happens.* I touched the *corno. Did he have some power over mamma, too?* I decided to leave right away. I would need Joey's help.

"Would you like to have some breakfast now?" Losine set out bowls of immense, ripe strawberries, the largest I had ever seen, and a pitcher of thick cream. I was seized by an uncanny memory. *Did he and mamma eat strawberries for breakfast on this terrace, too?* I spooned some of the berries into my bowl and drowned them in cream. Losine filled our cups with coffee from a silver pot and poured tea for himself from a silver teapot.

"We never had strawberries like these in Orvieto," I said.

"Or in America either," Joey said.

"You may find Milanese customs are quite different from those in Orvieto," Losine said casually as if he were remarking on the weather. He sipped his tea. I felt uneasy. "Milano is an international city and quite different from other places in Italy."

"Places like Orvieto?"

"Or America?" Joey said.

Losine nodded. "You shouldn't feel there's something wrong if people here act in ways that seem unfamiliar or strange to you." *The dresses? The money he gave Capitano Fiorelli? The way he arranges everything?* He offered me a plate of toast, sipped his tea, and then took up his newspaper. We ate quietly. After a time Losine spoke from behind his newspaper. "I wonder if I might ask you a favor since you are going to be resting your ankle for a few days." I waited. He put the paper down. "I have a daughter. She's about your size, I believe. She lives in another city. I would like to send her some clothes for...," he hesitated, "her birthday. Perhaps you would try on some things and help me choose what to give her. You must know what young women like these days."

I thought his request peculiar. "Don't the clothes in the *armadio* belong to her?" He didn't answer. I felt uneasy. "I'm sorry. I would like to help you, but I really must leave right after breakfast."

"Naturally," he said, "that's entirely up to you." I touched the *corno.* My life had certainly changed. I still had to give Losine the letter and explain that *papà* had burned the others. *What could be more disloyal than talking to mamma's amante about papà? Perhaps papà had been right when he said that I was the worst of all of his children. As soon as I leave, I'll try to become a better daughter so papà will want me to come home again.*

20

That same afternoon Joey Dunne pushed me in the wheelchair as we followed Losine from shop to shop. At each store, I tried on the clothes Losine selected, balancing on one foot while he examined seams, evaluated designs. He adjusted each garment, commenting on its cut and on the quality of the workmanship. Often, he wanted to see the same garment in several colors before making a decision. He gave detailed directions for the alterations and tailoring, some of which I thought his daughter wouldn't notice, such as an eighth-inch adjustment at the back of an underarm seam of a jacket. I didn't see why these things mattered to him, but they did. *Eccentric maybe, but not dangerous.*

"He likes to shop as much as my mom does," Joey whispered to me while Losine showed a seamstress the kind of stitch he wanted her to use to put in a hem by hand.

"Shopping must be an important Milanese custom," I said to Joey.

"Yes, they dress like every day is Sunday."

"Deliver these to my address by six o'clock," Losine told each clerk. Extra charges for rush orders didn't matter to him. *Lire* denominated in large numbers flowed from his wallet like scarves from a magician's hat. Among the clothes were a dress of blue-green satin that hung like a waterfall; an emerald green suit; several hats, one with feathers; and a dozen pairs of shoes. Though the salespeople could fit only one shoe on my foot, Losine didn't seem to care. "All of them," he said again and again before I could tell him which ones his daughter would like best. At one shop, he purchased more lingerie for his daughter's birthday than Maria's mother, grandmother, and aunts together had embroidered for Maria's entire trousseau.

"If he asks me to try on those gifts, I won't do it, no matter what the Milanese customs are," I whispered to Joey.

"His daughter must not have any clothes at all," Joey said.

"Maybe she's lost everything she had." I was just about to ask Joey to help me leave when Losine announced that we were finished shopping. By then, so many shopping bags hung from my wheelchair that I was embarrassed to meet the gazes of people on the street. When we reached Losine's apartment, Joey helped me inside and then said that he had to leave. I didn't have a chance to ask him if he would help me escape. Losine collected his packages from the concierge and examined their contents to make sure his instructions had been followed.

"So many presents," I said. "When is your daughter's birthday?" There was a silence. He seemed uncertain of the answer. *Wouldn't a real father know when his daughter's birthday is? Perhaps he just forgot, the way papà often forgets how old I am.*

Losine cleared his throat and coughed, as if he had something important to say. "I won't ask you to try all of these clothes on again, but," he said clearing his throat, "tonight would you wear the green dress for dinner? It would please me very much to see how it looks now that it has been altered." I thought this request was as peculiar as those he had already made, but what reason could I give for refusing to try on one dress? It was small thing and it seemed to be so very important to him.

The zipper on the dress was invisible when it was fully closed. Doubts crossed my mind: *What if Michel Losine doesn't really have a daughter? What if he has another reason for buying these clothes?* The dress flowed gently over my body. I felt as if I belonged to it, as if it possessed me. I reached toward my suitcase to touch my own clothes, the clothes from my real life, the life that was slipping away from me.

Losine smiled when he saw me. "Lovely." He wheeled me into the dining room and helped me into a chair. I spread a white linen napkin over my lap, and Losine sat down across from me. "I have something to show you," he said. "Close your eyes and hold out your hand." I complied, but kept my eyelids slightly open so I could watch what he was doing. In my palm he put something soft, slightly textured, with a tender surface. "You may look now." The small, grey suede pouch was tied with a yellow satin ribbon. "Open it." Inside, I found a pair of gold earrings, two small circles of pearls and diamonds surrounding a large emerald. A thin, gold chain hung from the pouch. I pulled out a matching pendant. "Try them on." His hand shook as he took out a cigarette.

"Are these for your daughter's birthday, too?"

Losine raised his hand to still my questions. "I know it's a nuisance, but, please, if you wouldn't mind very much, may I see how the pendant looks without your *corno*?" I thought about Grazia's warning and about Bruno. *I'll put the corno back on as soon as he sees the necklace. It will be right here next to me.* "I assure you this will be my last request," Losine said.

"Just for a few minutes." I put on the earrings and the pendant. Losine looked at me, but he saw someone else.

"You remind me very much of Willa." It was the first time he had mentioned mamma's name. "Would you like to keep them?"

"No!" I was frightened. "No, thank you." *Arrangements. Clothes. Jewelry.* I felt like a fairy tale princess locked in a tower of secrets. *Grazia was right. The secrets of the dead are sfortunati.* I wished that I had burned the letters before *papà* found them. I took off the earrings and held them out to Losine. "I have no place to wear these. Please. Your daughter should have them or someone else who will enjoy them." Losine remained where he was, his hands in his lap. I put the earrings back in the pouch and set the pouch on the table between us, forgetting that I was still wearing the pendant. "They're too much."

He looked at me steadily. "Accepting a gift would make you feel obligated," he said softly, "and you don't want to feel obligated. Is that right?" My fears seemed selfish and hurtful.

"Grazia always says, 'Things betray you into keeping them. Later, they simply betray you.'"

"Your Grazia takes an unnecessarily dark view." Losine took out another cigarette. With trembling hands, he lit it, and inhaled. "Could you not simply enjoy beautiful things for the pleasure they give?"

"Not these." I didn't want to be alone with him any longer. *If only Joey were here.*

"Consider this: You've given me a great deal of help today, and I am the one who is obligated to you. Wouldn't that make us even?" I moved the pouch closer to him. He left it on the table between us.

"I can't stay here," I said. I pushed myself away from the table. "I want to leave."

"Very well, but please do try some scampi first," he replied lightly. He filled my glass with wine. "It's best at the moment it's ready." He seemed to be laughing and serious at once. "Such a simple antipasto wouldn't burden you with too weighty an obligation, would it?" I felt very young and uncertain. Disoriented. He went to the kitchen. When he returned, he put a portion of the scampi on my plate, then sat down and raised his glass. "As my father used to say, 'May your health and convictions outlast your compromises.'" His eyelids fluttered, as if he were casting a spell.

I returned his toast with unsteady hands. When I tried to eat, my fork tapped against the plate, and the sauce dripped on the white tablecloth. I wiped the spot with my napkin.

"Never mind. It's not important," Losine said.

I spread the napkin on my lap once more and leaned over my plate. The scampi was very good. And so was the wine. I began to eat, oblivious to the quantity.

Losine put more scampi on my plate. "At least you like my cooking, even if you can't accept my gift." He refilled his own glass and nibbled at the single scampi on his fork. Turning it slightly, he contemplated the creature that he would soon devour. "Tell me, what made you decide to leave Orvieto?"

"I wanted to do things that I couldn't do in Orvieto." I pressed the white napkin to my lips. "And I want to live in a different place."

"I see." Losine nibbled another bit of scampi and chewed it slowly.

"Mostly, I didn't want my father and Bruno to decide what I can be." I didn't know why I had revealed such private information about *papà* and Bruno. *He makes it easy to say too much.* I took another sip of wine. *I must be more careful.*

"So, you are a person who intends to make her own decisions." Losine said this declaratively. Unambiguously. As though my decision was understandable and reasonable. It seemed to me the first time that anyone had heard me. My decision to leave Orvieto already seemed clearer. Right. I realized that there was something wounded about Losine, but also something kind. I understood why mamma had cared for him so much.

"*Papà* and Bruno said I was selfish for leaving. Do you think it's selfish?" I said with my mouth full. I was hungrier than I had realized.

"Why would I object to your ambitions?" *The Milanese really* are *different,* I thought. Losine poured more wine into my glass. At that moment I was glad that I had eaten with gypsies, that I hadn't changed my dress, and that I had met mamma's *amante.*

"Mamma wanted me to go to university," I said.

"Why was that, do you think?" He poured some water into my glass.

"I think she lost her dreams and didn't want me to lose mine." Losine nodded. I took the last bite of my scampi.

Losine touched the pouch with his fingertips and inhaled the way people do when they are going to talk about something that is important to them. "Tell me," he said leaning closer, almost whispering, as if the subject did not bear his speaking of it aloud. "When did Willa die?"

I wasn't sure that he had even asked the question. *Did I imagine it? He must have asked. Otherwise, why would I consider telling him when mamma died?*

"In August."

"Recently, then." He was quiet. He seemed almost naked, as if he had dropped a disguise. He looked down at his hands and back at me. "Yes, very well. Under the circumstances, it is extremely kind of you to have agreed to try on the earrings." He ran his fingers over the pouch. "Still, I can't help but feel these should be yours. Would you do me the kindness of putting them on again so I could see them once more?" At that moment I wished only to escape from his palpable and overwhelming sorrow, from his boundless grief. I think I would have done anything to get away from it, and I did do something that was cruel and that I'm ashamed of: I changed the subject to something tangential, irrelevant, as if I hadn't understand the real meaning of his request and the need that prompted it.

"After university I'm going to marry my fiancé," I said. "We'll live in Orvieto and run my family's business. We're going to have our own family, so I wouldn't wear them." I reached for my wine glass. "Anyway, you promised you'd make no more requests."

"But didn't you just say you were *not* going back to Orvieto?"

Against my will, my eyes filled with tears. "Why did you say that?"

"I believe it was you who said you wanted to leave Orvieto, and just now you said you intended to go back." I tried not to cry. "Will you do both?" Tears fell onto the dress.

Losine came to my side. "What upsets you so much?"

"Bruno left me." Losine came and put his arms around me and held me gently. "After we were lovers…in Firenze. He wouldn't tell me why, and I don't know."

Losine kissed my bruised temple. "You believe that it was your fault?"

"Yes. It seemed very right at the time, but now I don't know." Losine handed me his handkerchief.

"Sometimes," he said, "a young man is inexperienced and doesn't know how to treat the woman he loves." I looked up at him. "He feels an urgency to make love, but then he doesn't know what to do after that, so he feels weak and uncertain. He becomes frightened and so he runs away. It takes time to learn to be *un'amante.*" He continued to hold my hand.

"Experienced lovers don't do that?"

"It's unkind, but understandable. Love is often very frightening." *Gilda and the Duke? Were they frightened?* Losine leaned back slightly and waited, holding my hand in his. I looked at his hand, trying to center my thoughts: the raised veins running across the tendons toward his fingers; the thin, almost flat, gold watch on his wrist; the minute stitching of the monogrammed French cuff of his shirt; the initials on his gold cufflink: *GBL. GBL? Does he have more than one name?*

"Would you like to have your dinner now? I've made veal chops. Dessert will be a surprise. Do you like surprises?"

"No. I want to know what's happening."

"But you *must* like surprises or you wouldn't have left Orvieto." He was right again. I began to trust him. He went into the kitchen. I looked down at my plate: delicate, blue porcelain bordered in silver. Losine returned with a platter and served me a veal chop. I cut it with my fork and took a bite. To this day I remember its exquisite taste. I took another bite.

"Why aren't the initials on your cufflinks yours?" I said after I had drunk some more wine.

He inhaled deeply. "They're made from gold buttons on a jacket that belonged to my wife, Greta. The initials are hers."

I set my fork down. "You didn't say you had a wife. Where is she?"

"On the contrary, I said that my wife is dead." His pale eyes reminded me of shattered china.

"What happened to her?" I was afraid he would tell me.

"This isn't the right time for a difficult story."

Are those your wife's dresses in the *armadio*?" I reached for the pouch. "And this jewelry—did it belong to your wife, too?" He didn't answer. I took off the pendant and turned it over. On the back I saw the inscription, a *W* and an *M* entwined.

"Yes. They were Willa's," he said.

"Is that why you're trying to give them to me?"

He looked away for a moment and was quiet. He spoke softly. "Fina, those who can't bear their memories must be forgiven if they sometimes try to make new ones just so they can go on."

"I read your letters, if that's what you want to know."

He looked anxious. "Did you bring them?"

I glanced at the fireplace and made my decision: I would betray *papà*. "Only one," I said. "*Papà* burned the rest." There, I had told mamma's *amante* about *papà*, something I had no right to tell him, something he had no right to know. Not from me.

Losine remained silent for a time. "So, that's all that's left."

"Of what?"

He gestured toward the wall where the painting of the fish hung. "Willa gave me this painting for my birthday the last time we were together. We both loved it. She was very ill. She had come here to see a specialist. We found out that she—we—had very little time." He stood up. "I want to show you something." He helped me into the wheelchair, and pushed it into the room where I had slept. He threw open the doors of the *armadio*, touched the clothes, buried his face in the dresses. "These belonged to Willa." He wheeled me over to the paintings of the garden and pointed to the initials in the corners: *WCM, '48.* I hadn't noticed them. "Willa painted these when we planned the garden," Losine said. "They're paintings of what we both wanted. Full of our hopes for the garden and more." He wheeled me outside onto the terrace. "You can see that I had it built exactly as she painted it." He pushed my wheelchair into his bedroom. The door to a large mahogany cupboard had been left open; inside, were stacks of perfectly folded shirts. He stopped next to a bureau. On it were two silver-framed pictures. "My wife, Greta. Our son, Paul. Before the War." He spoke their names as though they were prayers and then answered a question I hadn't asked: "They died in the camps."

He handed me the second photograph. "Willa brought you here several times when you were very young. I doubt you'd remember." He pointed to the picture. "Here you are with your mother outside on the terrace the day we first talked about the garden." It was as if he were begging me to acknowledge them, their relationship, their affair, to say that it mattered, to say that I accepted it. He wanted me to make it real, witness it, share it with him. I looked at the photograph of mamma and me standing together, mamma wearing a suit, I in my best dress, holding her hand, but I only remembered mamma's hat, the red one with the black veil.

"She looks happy," I said. Losine took a faded photograph from his wallet.

"Willa took this picture that same day. I think you were about two

years old. I've always kept it with me." In the photograph, Losine held
me in his arms. We were laughing and waving at the camera. "We were
very happy because that day we were together. A real family," Losine
said. I looked up from the photograph at our reflections in the mirror. The
resemblance was clear, *pentimenti* of truths untold. I recognized a familiar feeling, something that flickered just beyond my consciousness and
left me with an uneasy feeling of not being fully in possession of myself.

"And I am your daughter who lives someplace else." I understood:
*this wasn't a final errand for mamma's sake. Instead, mamma had tried
to send me home.*

"Willa and I agreed that if you brought the letters, I would tell you.
Are you sorry?" I hesitated, already aware of the changes that this knowledge would make in my life and in my memory of what had been real. *If
papà isn't my father, how many other things that I've taken for truth are
false, too?* The truth contained just as many losses as the lies that had
concealed it, made me someone who both existed and did not, a hostage
to other people's secrets. "Tell me, did I do the right thing?"

I felt for the *corno*. "My necklace...."

"You have another." I understood his hope.

"My losses aren't the same as yours. I can't bring mamma back to
you."

"You've brought me even more than I could have wished for."

"Does *papà* know?"

Losine sat down on his bed facing me. "At this point you *are* his
daughter. Legally, you were his daughter when you were born. He was
determined to make you his own so that Willa couldn't leave him. He said
that if Willa left, he would make sure we never saw you again."

"Why didn't you stop him?"

"That was almost twenty years ago, and circumstances were very different then. It was only a few years after the War. If I had tried to take you
and Willa away—even to another country—Gabriele would have pursued us and revealed my whereabouts. I'm well known to the European
authorities, and some...let's just say that they would have welcomed any

opportunity to make a case—any case—against me, and they would have succeeded. Gabriele knew that. Monsignor Enrico was the only person who knew, the only one who could have given him the information. Willa and you and I would have always been exiles, moving from country to country, hiding, living under a constant threat of my arrest and of your being taken from us. You were innocent, yet the one most at risk, the one who would have suffered the most, had I been arrested. We didn't want to subject you to such uncertainty. Secrecy seemed less damaging."

"What about America?"

"It's very difficult for a fugitive to emigrate to America. Gabriele would have exposed us, and Willa would have had no way to see you or Silvana or Raffaele until they were adults."

"What kind of criminal are you?"

"I'm guilty of many things for which I could be prosecuted, but I'm the only one who can prosecute my real crimes. Have I violated the law? Let's just say many of those same authorities have found it advantageous to themselves to have me do what I do for them. And they reward me very well for doing it. But I also know too much, and so they fear exposure. They wait and watch, aware of the danger I represent to them, and yet they are greedy for my help."

I couldn't be sure that what he said was true any more than I could be sure which of my two fathers was the real one: this father who gave us up—mamma and me—and waited to reveal himself to me? Or the father who pretended to be a real father and became what he had pretended? This father who lost his children or the father who stole another man's child? And what of the secrecy that had kept me unknown to myself? What if the truths of our lives beg for consolation?

21

Losine arranged for Joey to go to school with me until my ankle healed. Each day Joey pushed my wheelchair and waited for me until my classes ended. Afterwards, we sat and talked until late in the afternoon. In the evenings, we ate dinner with Losine, and afterwards Joey played the piano while I studied. Our life together continued in this way even after I could walk again. We became a kind of family. A family of *stranieri*.

Of course, at that same time I was thinking about *papà* and how desperate he must have been to keep mamma from leaving him. I believed that *papà* had acted out of anguish and that he had carried on bravely in the face of doomed hopes and the certainty that his effort to keep mamma with him would ultimately fail. How much had it cost him to be reminded every day by my very presence that mamma had betrayed him? Despite the circumstances of my birth, he had been a loving father to me. Whatever his reasons had been and however wrong he was, *papà* had treated me as he would his own child. He had been the best father he could be to me. I believed that he loved me despite my origins. I still loved him and wanted us to be reconciled.

One morning, I was late to my first class, history. The door was always locked promptly against latecomers. I ran from the streetcar stop to the entrance to the campus, and then into the first of two large peristyle courtyards onto which the classrooms opened. Ignoring the carefully laid out walkways, I ran across the grass. I reached the classroom and pulled on the doorknob. Unlocked! Breathless, I scurried to my seat.

"You just made it," said the girl sitting next to me. "You're lucky." At the back of the room, the door shut and the lock turned. The students grew silent. The professor walked with a backward lean that belied his progress toward the podium. His loose, grey-brown coat flapped around his long, angular frame, giving him the appearance of a large bird whose feathers had been ruffled by the wind. He extracted some papers from a briefcase, oblivious to the rest of the papers that spilled at his feet. Behind his thick glasses, his dark eyes appeared abnormally large. He ran his hands through his hair and fussed in his pockets for a pencil. I saw that he wore a wedding ring. *What sort of wife does he have? Is she absentminded, too? Do they have children?* He cleared his throat.

"Today, we shall discuss our ideas about what history is," he said "Whether history is an actual record of what happens, as many people believe, or whether it is an act of imagination as, say, a work of fiction or drama. Some people joke that history is the story told by conquerors, the recounting of the deeds of great men and a victorious people. Others describe the history of any civilization as a journey between birth and death with a limited lifespan just as our human span is limited. And still others say that it's a record of human progress or, conversely, an oscillation between opposites. He waited for the students to stop writing in their notebooks. "Signorina, you in the front row!" I looked up. He leaned over the podium and pointed his thin index finger at me. "Tell us what your view of history is and what evidence you have assembled to defend it."

So many other questions hovered behind the professor's question: *What if we don't know what our real history is? What if it has been kept from us? If our history is false, but we don't know it's false, is it still true? If we are deceived, do we have a history at all? Is history merely what we believe it is? If we don't know our history, how can we know what our experience means?*

"Why couldn't all of these views be true?" I said. "Doesn't what we call *history* depend on circumstances and on who tells it, on their point of view, on what they need or want it to be?"

The professor's eyebrows snapped together, and his coat shook. "You've evaded the assignment by refusing to take a position."

"No," I said. "I am taking a position: If our history is hidden from us or if we don't know what it is, then we don't have a past. *History* is only what we can remember at this moment. If we forget or if we remember something else tomorrow, then our history changes. It's as if history is written in disappearing ink."

"Nonsense. History—*History* with a capital *H*—is documented and available for research and interpretation. It is susceptible to scholarship. To investigation. We *can* discover its truth." He pointed at me again. "The phenomena you describe belong to the realm of personal history. Your experience, meaningful or not, is irrelevant to the great sweep of time and to the study of history. We are very small, *signorina*. What happens to us individually doesn't matter." I thought he was wrong. *If the events of our individual lives aren't affected by the larger events of our time and vice versa, why would we care about history?*

The young woman sitting next to me smiled. "I'm Francesca. *Piacere.* I like what you just said. Personal and societal histories are intertwined. I think we should study both." Small and wiry with curly hair and a wide smile, Francesca's outgoing and decisive nature made her seem bigger and more powerful than she likely was, though I didn't know that then. She was angry: there weren't enough professors at the school, the method of grading was unfair, and tuition increases had just been announced with more to come.

"Students are going to take over this university very soon," she told me after class, "and together with the workers we'll cripple the country until things improve for all of us." She talked excitedly about *resistenza pacifica* and *resistenza passiva*. Nonviolence and passive resistence.

"Isn't it dangerous?"

"Probably. Why don't you come see for yourself?" I felt for the *corno* but it wasn't there.

I listened as Francesca's friends debated the best way to change a society that fails to provide an education for its students.

"We have to take control of the educational system—curriculum, selection of professors, grading—all of it," Marco said. He sounded certain, sophisticated. *He seems even smarter than Bruno,* I thought.

"But *how?*" Lucia asked. I wanted to know, too.

"By joining with the workers and bringing everything to a stop like we just did in Firenze a few weeks ago," Marco said. "The waiters on the train joined us right away. So did the baggage handlers." *Workers? Firenze? Were they planning to bring the country to a halt with only waiters and baggage handlers and students?*

I spoke up. "How did that actually change anything? I think it just made people late and caused them trouble, including me."

"It didn't change anything. *Yet.* It was a test," Marco said. "Now we know that random strikes are a viable tactic." He had a gentle way of speaking. Calm. "We learned that the workers are *ready* to join us and *willing* if we give them the opportunity. If we can bring the railroad to a halt with a small strike, then we can stop the entire country with a general strike. Now we have the will and the means to do it."

"We'll begin in the north—Torino, Milano—where workers have already responded to calls for strikes, Then, we'll move south," Andreas said. "The police won't be able to stop it."

General strike? Torino? Milano? Police? It was both exciting and frightening to listen to them. *So much is happening that I know nothing about. I would have missed so much if I had stayed in Orvieto.*

"Now you're a co-conspirator," Francesca whispered to me, laughing. "Will you help us? We need people who can be runners and messengers. People who won't be noticed." I remembered what *papà* had said about how *dimostranti* recruited people. *Was this what he meant?* I didn't want Francesca, Marco and the others to think I was a *paesanotta.* A bumpkin. I smiled and nodded, pleased to think of myself as a participant in something important, something much larger than who I was or where I came from, something mentioned in the newspapers. "You can't tell anyone," Francesca said, "but it will happen soon."

22

One afternoon—it was in early November—Joey and I went to the Parco Sempione after my classes. The leaves had already fallen, and the wind whirled them around us in a dance of color. Joey pointed to a bare tree. "That linden tree could almost support our whole life," he said, "We could make tea from the leaves and chairs and a table from the wood, so we'd have a place to sit and drink it." We sat down together on a nearby bench that overlooked a pond. "Won't happen, though."

"Why?"

"My C.O. application was denied. Not enough evidence, they said."

"I know you'll be a good soldier." It was difficult to say it, and to think of Joey's leaving. I liked my new "family."

"And you'll be a good history teacher." He seemed proud of me. "I want to do things, too…when I come back…if I come back."

"Maybe Losine can arrange for you to stay here."

"I'm going to see if I can appeal."

"You'll be okay. I know you will."

"Look, those swans are nesting." We moved nearer until the birds objected. "Once I was preparing a piece about a swan for a concert. I wanted my interpretation to be true to what swans are really like, so I used to go and watch them. They're very competent parents. The males sit on the nest and care for the babies if something happens to the mother, and the mothers raise the babies alone if something happens to the father. Did you know that a single swan won't look for another mate until the babies grow up?"

When another tuition increase was announced the following week, Marco said it was time to act. "We need your help," he told me. Of course, I agreed. I wanted to help.

It was at about that same time that I began to feel ill. I tried to ignore my symptoms. I thought they were temporary. At one point, I scarcely ate or drank anything for several days. Losine was away and no one noticed. I was afraid that if Francesca and Marco found out, I might have to give up my duties, so I didn't tell anyone. Then, one morning, just after Losine returned and just as I was leaving for Cattolicà, I fainted.

When I opened my eyes, Losine's face swirled above me. He touched my forehead. "What's wrong?"

"I don't know. I felt a little bit sick." I sat up quickly. The room tipped and then righted itself. I blinked to clear my vision. "It's nothing. I'm fine now."

"Is your period late?"

How could he ask me about such an intimate matter? Papà would never do such a thing. Was that because he wasn't my real father?

"I need to go to Cattolicà. Someone is expecting me."

"The campus has closed. Are you sure you're not late?" he said. *Is this what real fathers do or only Milanese fathers?*

"Not if I hurry."

"That's not what I asked you." *What he's suggesting can't be true.*

"A little, maybe." I had heard women talk about being "late" after an upsetting or stressful time. It was just temporary.

"How little?"

I felt like a criminal. "A week or two."

"Only a week or two? Are you sure?"

"Maybe a month."

"You need to have a test," he said. *He tells me what to do just like papà,* I thought.

"I'm not pregnant like Silvana, if that's what you think. She sleeps with men she's not married to, men she doesn't know. I didn't do that." Losine looked at me closely. "I'm fine now. Even a little hungry."

"I'll get you some tea and toast."

I drank the entire pot of tea and ate six slices of toast. I was still a little dizzy and slightly nauseated, but I was determined not to faint again. "I'm fine. I need to go. I'm late."

"The test is more important." Losine wrote an address on a piece of paper and gave it to me. "Here's where to go. I want you to go *right now*. Tell them you're married because if you're pregnant and unmarried, they may try to send you away." I put the paper in my purse and picked up my notebook. "It's very important that you make certain."

"Just because I fainted?"

"If you don't get a test, I'll worry." I knew he would check when I got home. *I'll get the test and then go to the university. Francesca and Marco will be annoyed that I'm late, but if Losine finds out I'm helping them...well, better to satisfy his questions so he doesn't make some of his arrangements.* "Stay away from Cattolicà," Losine said as I left. "The police are there." *Too many fathers,* I thought. *One is enough.*

Outside, it was foggy, every surface misted. People hurried by me seemingly enclosed within themselves. As I waited for the streetcar, a blind beggar took up a position a few feet away. He leaned against an iron fence in the only protected area and rattled his cup. I dropped some coins into it.

"*Grazie, signorina.*" He got up, put his blind man's cane under his arm, and counted the money as he walked away. I moved into the spot he had vacated and warmed myself with thoughts of how Grazia always made *dolce*, sweets, for us the way her grandmother had taught her. We ate them with hot chocolate or caffè latte. I helped, and often when we were alone together, she told me stories about her life.

"Tell me again about when you ran away with *il tuo ragazzo*, Grazia." It was my favorite story. At this Grazia seemed to return to the place of her childhood, though her descriptions of Palermo, her father, and her family often changed.

"First, we stowed away on a big ferry that was leaving Palermo." She made a well in the flour and broke the eggs into it, then added the sugar and mixed with her fingers. "I was fifteen and Amedeo, *il mio ragazzo,* was seventeen. We wanted to get married, but my father refused us his blessing. We didn't care. In our hearts we were already married. We were so happy." She poured the milk into the well and mixed it in. "We had *fortuna*: No one discovered us. No one asked where we were from or how old we were. When we reach Roma, we found work right away." Grazia always looked away at this point in the story, as if she could only bear to tell it indirectly, as if it might have happened to someone else. Sometimes, she stopped, unable to bear what had happened.

"Tell me the rest, Grazia."

"*Sfortunatamente,* our happiness was short." Grazia would roll out the dough and then cut it in wide strips. Then she put the filling on top. "My Amedeo was murdered just before we could marry with a priest." At other times she said that Amadeo had "died mysteriously" or "disappeared" or "left" or was "executed by the government." She let me wrap the dough up around the sweet filling. I worked slowly so that she had time to finish the story.

Occasionally, Grazia told the version of the story that I thought was true, the one in which her father had pursued the couple and slashed her beloved Amedeo's throat for dishonoring his daughter and their family. "I had to run away again," she said, "before my father could take me back to Sicily. Where I was born, girls who are dishonored…no one wants them. Not even their families. Sometimes girls are killed by their own families." I pinched the dough together. "Worse than *puttane*. A *puttana* makes a living. A dishonored girl begs for mercy."

Grazia always ran her hands through her grey hair and sighed. "When my father fell asleep, I escaped from him. I ran to the station and bought a ticket. I had so little money—only enough to come as far as Orvieto. An hour. When I got off the train, it was cold and raining. I had no coat. Nothing. It was already dark, and I didn't know where I was. An old *mezzadro* brought me in the cart to your grandfather. These men never touched me. Never. They were *buonisignori*. So honorable."

I thought Grazia's story one of great personal courage, but Grazia always concluded by saying, "I had *fortuna*. The Marcheschis have always been good to me. I've always been safe here. Thanks be to God that my father never found me."

"But don't you want to see your family?"

Grazia's answer was always the same. She waved her arm around the kitchen and smiled at me. "Where I am, that is my family. You, *tesoro*, are my family, now."

"But didn't you want to get married?"

"Always, in my heart I am married to my Amedeo. In heaven we'll be together forever. The angels will be our children. We will be completely happy."

At last, the streetcar came clattering along the tracks, stopped, and swallowed me up into its stuffy interior. It smelled of damp clothes. It was very late. I knew Francesa and Marco were waiting. I showed the driver the address.

"Sixth stop," he said. "Many girls go there." Inside the crowded streetcar the warmth of the other bodies, their human smells, made me queasy. I began to perspire. I wiped my forehead and then held onto a pole near to the front while the streetcar followed the circular streets that girded the city center, streets that seemed to end where they had begun, buildings repeating like beads on a necklace in dizzying conformity.

Sometimes, I tried to imagine what Bruno and *papà* were doing. I could still recall the shapes of their bodies, but not all of the details of their faces. *Was this how Grazia forgot her family? Had Bruno and papà forgotten me, too? I had already become* una straniera *in what was once my home.* I felt mocked by my aspirations and my ignorance. The other passengers looked distorted to me, grotesque. Their faces melted together in a delerious swirl, and my own existence seemed mutable and contingent. I took out the directions again and checked the street names outside.

"Two more stops, *signorina*," the driver said. I folded the paper and put it back in my purse. Passengers got off, leaving room for me to sit down. A newspaper on the seat next to me caught my attention. It was

two days old. An article on the front page said soldiers had been needed to quell large and violent antiwar demonstrations in America. These
traditori, traitors, refused to become soldiers. Some had gone to other
countries to escape, including Italy, where they had become troublemak-
ers. Soon there would be a new law: any *traditori* found in Italy would be
sent back to America and to prison. *Not Joey. He isn't a traitor.* Another
article talked about the threat of the protests by Italian students and workers. Marco's name was mentioned and so was Francesca's. They were
described as "organizers of illegal acts against the state." The article said
that they would be arrested. *I must tell them they're in danger before the
police find them.* The streetcar stopped and the driver got up. He laughed
when he saw me. "Do you prefer to walk in the rain, *signorina*?"

Inside the health service office a single radiator covered in a deep layer
of dust gurgled in a listless attempt to warm the room. I found an empty
chair that wasn't broken and sat down. On the table next to me, a worn
women's magazine featured the Roman police attacking female protest-
ers. Someone had drawn mustaches on the women's faces with a pen and
written *lesbiche*, lesbians, underneath. I opened to the article. Some of
the women had been injured while men stood by calling them *puttane*
and shouting obscenities. *Could I do what those women had done?* I said
a prayer to St. Lucy asking for courage.

"*Signora* Marcheschi."

"*Signorina.*" The nurse glanced up at me and then crossed something
out on the chart and wrote something else.

"*Signorina, sì.* Usually, women who want pregnancy tests are married." The room smelled of iodine. She drew my blood. "Come back in
two days." She paused and looked at me. "I'm not supposed to tell you
this, but you should ignore what the Pope says and protect yourself."

"Like those *femministe* in Roma?"

"Like women who have any sense."

23

It was after three o'clock when I left the health service. I hurried to Cattolicà to find Marco and Francesca. Hundreds of students milled in the streets. Sirens shrilled constantly. *Poliziotti* had blocked traffic around Cattolicà and the entrance to the campus, but I found a way in through an unattended side door and emerged in one of the central courtyards where *poliziotti* were forming a human ring around the *dimostranti,* moving toward them, confining them in a narrowing circle like fish in a net. The students continued marching with signs and songs and shouts, but the territory they occupied became increasingly constricted until the *poliziotti* succeeded in confining them to one corner of the courtyard. The *dimonstranti* shouted and made obscene gestures, but they couldn't escape. I searched for Marco and Francesca in the crowd. Someone threw a rock at the *poliziotti.* I saw Andreas. "Where are Marco and Francesca? They're going to be arrested."

"They went to Torino this morning before the police came," Andreas shouted. "Where have you been? We needed you." Near us, another rock struck a *poliziotto.* And then another. An explosion nearby left us surrounded in a kind of fog. Instantly, my throat burned and my eyes filled with scalding tears. The more I coughed and tried to breathe and to see, the more difficult it became. People shouted and cried out. They pushed against me, trying to escape, but they were caught fast in the net of *poliziotti.*

At that moment, someone—I couldn't see who—took my arm and pressed a handkerchief into my hand. "Cover your face, signorina.

This way." He guided me along. "I'm taking her through," I heard him say to someone. I wiped my eyes, coughed. Gradually, it became easier to breathe. We kept walking. We crossed the street and stopped where a police car waited. "Get in, signorina. It's time to go home." I wiped my eyes and looked up. It was Capitano Fiorelli.

That evening Joey came to Losine's apartment as usual. "How about we go out and find some espresso?" He noticed my silence. "If you want to, I mean." He smiled. "Somethin' wrong? You look like you ate a tennis ball."

"No. I'm fine. Nothing."

"Right. My mistake."

Outside, I buttoned my coat against the cold evening. My eyes still burned adn my throat felt raw. At a crowded *pasticceria*, we ordered an espresso and a *dolce*. I hoped it would be like one of Grazia's. It wasn't.

"My mom's friend on my draft board says they won't accept an appeal from me," Joey said. "'Insufficient grounds,' so I'm going back to the States."

"I read about the *traditori* in the newspaper," I said.

"Listen, the truth is I'd rather die in some godforsaken jungle than be a fugitive and maybe end up in prison. Some guys have the kind of courage it takes for that. I don't." We finished our espressos and went outside again. "I want to introduce you to some so-called *traditori*," he said.

We walked for nearly half an hour before we came to a run-down bar in a seedy neighborhood. The sign out front said *The American*. Inside, the bar was full of young men. "Most of the guys here are expats," Joey said. He motioned toward a group standing around a pool table. "The one in the blue shirt...that's Rex. Used to be a competitive runner. He stepped on a land mine his first day in-country." I looked down. Rex had only one foot; where the other foot had been, there was a stump wrapped in a pod made of leather and canvas. "Most of these guys have already served and been discharged. When they got home, nobody wanted them around to remind them of our national disgrace. So they left. They come to *The American* when they get to thinking about the lives they won't be able to live."

They seemed beyond consolation.

24

Naked, I stood sideways in front of the mirror, pressed on my belly, felt its firmness. *Was there a bulge? Maybe a small one.* Losine liked to cook. *My stomach is bound to stick out because I've been eating so much.* Since I had fainted three days earlier, I had been very hungry. I tried on a skirt. Too tight. I put on a loose dress and looked in the mirror again, pressed the fabric against my body, squinted at my reflection. *No, I look the same. The test will be negative. Nothing to worry about.* I got dressed.

When I returned to the Health Service late that afternoon, a different nurse was preparing to close for the day. She locked the door after me and pulled the shades. The patients in the waiting room—a mother with a child on her lap, an old man, and an elderly woman wearing a black dress—took little notice of me. My turn came last. As I went into the examination room, the nurse gave me a knowing look "It's positive."

"There must be a mistake. I go to Cattolica."

The nurse laughed. "University students often become pregnant, especially if they aren't careful."

"But it was the first time."

She laughed again. "God doesn't care about which time it is. He sees an opportunity for new life and blesses it." Suppressing my panic, I waited while she filled out papers and gave me instructions. "It's much better to have your babies while you're young," she said. "That's what I did." She glanced at my left hand. I was still wearing Bruno's ring. "Go home and tell your husband. I'm sure he'll be very happy. You do have a husband, don't you? It says here in your history that you aren't married. I'll correct that."

"Thank you." *Why do I always say "thank you" when someone gives me something I don't want?* She let me out the back door that opened into a dusky corridor. I walked toward the corona of daylight at the end and into an atrium garden where the lush tropical plants seemed larger than normal, possibly carnivorous, ready to enclose me in their nauseating embrace and prevent my escape.

I found Joey at *The America.*

"Hey, what's up?" he said when he saw me. I willed myself not to cry. "What's wrong?" He smiled. "Someone steal your luggage again?"

"No, Joey. I'm pregnant."

"No kidding?" He took my hand. "Maybe you should sit down."

"I'm going to have a baby."

"I love babies. My sister has four. Two of each."

"I don't know what to do."

"So it's that guy Bruno's baby, right?" I nodded. "You two gonna get married?" I shrugged. "You're gonna tell him, right?" I didn't answer. I wasn't sure. The bartender came over and wiped our table with a towel. "Don't you think he'd want to know?" Joey said.

"Know what?" The bartender shook the towel.

"If you were going to be a father, you'd want to know, right?" Joey said.

The bartender laughed. "I sure would, 'cause I'm sterile." He looked at me. "Somebody pregnant?"

"Nah," Joey said.

The bartender nodded toward the bar. "Lotta other guys here. Want me to take a vote on who wants to know?"

"It's just a hypothetical question," Joey said, "but I think every guy would want to know if he was going to have a family."

"We're the *human* family here," the bartender said.

"Even a guy who doesn't want to be a father," Joey said.

"Most of these people here in this bar don't know what they want," the bartender said. "Anyway, *want* doesn't necessarily matter. Take Rex. No matter how much he wants to walk on two feet, he ain't never gonna have another foot. He's gotta accept it. Like I said, I'm sterile. No matter how much I want to, I ain't never gonna be nobody's real father. Gotta accept it." He wiped our table once more. "Anyway, people usually want the opposite of what they tell you."

What if Bruno didn't want to get married even though he said he did?

"Not me. I just want one thing: *love*," Joey said.

The bartender laughed. "What's that mean? Shit, you tell a girl you love her so she'll sleep with you. You mean it—or think you do—but the next day you don't feel it anymore."

Was that what happened to Bruno?

"You're a pessimist," Joey said.

"That won't happen to me," I said. I felt for the *corno*. It wasn't there. I looked in my purse.

"How come?" Joey said.

"I know what I want." The *corno* wasn't there. *Where did I put it?*

"Give it a while and you won't want it any more," the bartender said.

"Just because you want something and then it happens, you can still want it," I said. *I'm going to write to Bruno tonight and tell him. As soon as he gets my letter, he'll come for me. We'll get married. It's just a small misunderstanding.* "Life can turn out happily, too."

Joey smiled and raised his glass. "To happiness...and getting what we want."

25

"I'm sure Bruno will be a good father," I told Joey. The sun dropped below the horizon, leaving the clouds rimmed in gold. "It's been almost two weeks since I wrote to him. As soon as he writes back, I'll know when I'm going home."

"That's great," Joey said. He put his arm around me.

It was easy to lean into the curve of Joey's arm. *It was easy with Bruno, too. Too easy. I have to be careful.* "Bruno and I will get married at the Duomo and live with *papà*. Grazia will help us with the baby."

"Good idea," Joey said. "My sister doesn't have anyone to help her and she never has time to sleep even."

Did I tell Bruno that Grazia would help us? "I'd better write to Bruno about Grazia," I said. "He probably has a lot on his mind."

"Pregnant ladies need someone to take care of them, too," Joey said. I turned away.

"I can take care of myself." I thought of the *femministe*, the women no one respected. "Women today have to take care of themselves."

"Right. I didn't mean that *you* needed any help. Nope. Not at all."

"I want to finish the semester before I go home," I said, "but they won't let me if they know I'm pregnant. Do you think I can manage two more months without being discovered?"

Joey put his arm around me again. "You can do whatever you want. Would you like some dinner?"

"Yes."

It was almost midnight when Joey brought me home. Losine was waiting for me. "Come, sit down. I was just making some tea. You got a letter today." He handed me a pale grey envelope. The return address was printed in dark red ink: Vino Marcheschi & Orsini, Piazza del Duomo, Orvieto, Italia. I looked for Bruno's name on the front of the envelope and then on the back.

"It must be from *papà*. Bruno must have told him about our baby." I sat down at the table. "*Papà* is like a volcano. He explodes and then he grows quiet and still, as if he had never been angry in the first place." I tore open the envelope and slid the letter out. It had been typed on Vino Marcheschi & Orsini stationery like a business letter.

Dear Fina,

I'm sorry for your sake to get your letter. Naturally, I shall say nothing to your father. This information would only add to his disappointments. I am certain, however, that I'm not the father of your baby because it was the first time for both of us—or so you told me—and everyone knows it's impossible to become pregnant the first time. Of course, it was your choice to leave Orvieto. Still, on a matter of such importance, I don't understand why you didn't come to discuss this with me in person.

Bruno

Stunned, I wadded the letter up and threw it on the floor. *Bruno didn't want to know that he could be a father. Was my pregnancy his revenge for leaving him and Orvieto?* "I don't need him."

Losine retrieved the letter, smoothed it out and read it. "Bruno is ignorant and proud, that's all." He put the letter on the table next to me. "You'll have to tell Gabriele. He'll insist that Bruno marry you immediately." He paused. "Your other choices are much less attractive."

"What could be less attractive than marrying someone *papà* has to coerce? Anyway, what kind of husband and father would Bruno be then?" Losine set out a plate of *biscotti* and poured tea for us. "That's what Bruno and *papà* tried to do to me. I won't be like them no matter what happens." I took off the ring that had belonged to Bruno's mother, held it in my palm, felt its infinitesimal weight, and dropped it on the table. *Certainty. So trivial.* "I'll take care of my baby myself. Whatever happens,

I won't let Bruno take away my dreams. It would be *sfortunato* to make Bruno marry me."

"*Le ragazze madri* usually don't keep their babies," Losine said, "because it ruins their lives and their babies' lives, too. You'll be ostracized and so will your child." He lit a cigarette.

I dipped the *biscotto* in my tea and took a bite. "Silvana kept her babies, all three of them, and I would be a better mother than she is."

"Think carefully about Silvana." He exhaled smoke with his words. "Is a life like hers what you want for yourself and your child?" I remembered what Signora Lucarelli had said about Silvana and the ugly faces people made when her name was mentioned. *Why are people so concerned about the difference between women with no husbands and widows? Is having a husband a measure of one's goodness? Why would children, who have no role in creating their circumstances, be accountable for what their parents had done?* But I knew Losine was right: *bastardi* and their mothers had no real place in the world.

I poured some more tea and ate another *biscotto*. "Silvana doesn't complain. I won't either." I tried to sound certain. I picked up the ring and gave it to Losine. "I can sell Bruno's ring and use the money for the baby." I blew on my tea and took another sip.

Losine looked at the ring and handed it back to me. "A tourist's trinket. The only value is sentimental." The tea burned my tongue. I still had the money mamma left me, but even without counting it, I knew it wasn't enough. "Don't be too proud to do what's in your child's best interests," Losine was saying. "Your other choices are to stay here with me or go to a convent until the baby is born and give the baby up for adoption." He paused. "An abortion might still be possible, but it's illegal and it would be quite dangerous for both of us."

"You've only yourself to blame,"papà would say. I felt benumbed, alone, outside the human family. *Is that how Silvana feels, too?*

In my dream, I wrapped my newborn baby in a white blanket and carried it to the Duomo in my arms on the day of my marriage. At the altar, Bruno trembled with fury when he saw us. The veins in his temples swelled and pulsed. "You've betrayed me," he shouted. Monsignor Enrico nodded in agreement. I looked around at the wedding guests. Signora Lucarelli stood up and said, "Just like her mother and her sister." Then, *papà* came toward me, his hand on his chest. "You've broken my heart. You're lost to me forever."

I awoke certain of what I would do. "I'm going to stay with you and keep the baby," I told Losine. He went to his desk, took the *corno* out of a drawer, and fastened it around my neck.

"I believe this is yours," he said.

"I don't need it anymore."

26

It was snowing. As usual, Joey and I stopped at a trattoria near the Galleria Vittorio Emanuele for espressos. "There's something I've been wanting to tell you," he said. He took my hands in his. "I don't know what's going to happen to me." I didn't want to think about what he was saying. "But whatever happens to me, I want you to know that I care about you." He caressed my fingers. "Going to war has made me think about what really matters. This probably seems abrupt, but I want *you*. Us. To be together."

"Us?"

"I want to know that you'll be waiting for me if I make it back."

"I'll be here taking care of my baby."

"That's what I'm talking about. I want us to get married before I go." I didn't think I had heard Joey correctly. *No man in Orvieto would ever marry a woman who was pregnant with another man's baby. Or in Milano either, whatever the differences in their customs.* "See, I'd get a family allowance in the military" Joey was saying. "It would help you support the baby, and you'd get more if anything happened to me. If I live or die, you could still take care of your baby."

"Bruno is the baby's father."

"Yes, but he says he isn't, right?" I nodded. "And you and he aren't going to get married, right?" I nodded. "So you could marry me. I mean if you wanted to. Then, legally, I would be the baby's father."

Papà was right: Americans are *pazzi.* "What about my mother and my sister?"

"You said your mother died."

"My mother and my sister and my brother have dishonored our family. I have a reputation, too. You and your family would be dishonored."

"Listen, I could be *dead!* If you marry me, no one would be dishonored. Isn't that true?" He was right. Honor mattered less than the appearance of honor. If I married Joey, I would either be a married woman or a widow. If I didn't marry him, I would be *una ragazza madre* like Silvana.

"People will laugh at you behind your back," I said. "They'll say your wife made you wear the horns."

"Where I'm going, people will try to shoot me in the back." Joey paused. "Besides, if we get married, I'll be the baby's legal father and Bruno will just be some guy." He waited. "Just like Gabriele is your legal father."

"But I haven't thought about whether I love you."

"You don't really need to think about it because I'm leaving. But since you *are* thinking about it, what do you think?"

It was true that in just a few weeks I had come to care for Joey very much. I looked for him the way one looks for another part of oneself, cherished him and the way I felt when I was with him. In Orvieto no one called this *love* or thought it a reason to marry. *Could love be anything other than what it had always been: a man and a woman pledged to one another to create a family in the ways of the place where they had always lived? I had forsaken that life. Changed. Must I tell Joey that I don't love him because this love isn't what I thought love was?* The waiter brought us a plate of *amaretti* with our espressos. *Couldn't love be several things at once like history?*

"We might never be together," I said. "We wouldn't have any more than what we have right now."

"All I know is that I've loved you since that day when you first told me about James Dean. You cared so much about someone you didn't know. I want someone—you—to care about me that way." Joey needed me just as much as I needed him. I smiled at him. He took my hand. "You don't hate the idea, then?"

"No."

"Fina, we have more now than some people ever have. Worst case, you'll make a soldier happy and you'd get a flag and a pension for you and the baby. I already checked. Besides, I might come back a hero. Do you like parades?" He looked at me expectantly.

"Yes, but I don't want a flag and a pension. Not for that reason. What about my father? If you don't ask for a father's blessing, it's a great offense."

"Do I have to ask both of them?"

"Yes, but Losine won't be back until tomorrow"

"So *yes,* we'll tell them?"

"No. First you *ask* their permission to marry me. If *papà* doesn't give his blessing, I'll probably lose my inheritance if I haven't already. Losine? I don't know."

"Anything else?"

"*Papà* said he didn't want me to come back to Orvieto, so I probably have no dowry at all."

"That makes two of us. Is that all?"

"He might not receive us."

"In that case I wouldn't have to ask him for his blessing, right?" I didn't say anything. "Fina, the baby would be *legitimate.*" My racing thoughts stopped. *A soldier's wife. A widow with a pension.* "Maybe you should think about it a little more." Joey moved his chair closer to mine. He put his arms around me and kissed me lovingly. And then I returned his kiss. "How about this?" he said. "After we have dinner, you can tell me your decision." He looked at his watch. "It's six o'clock now, so figure around eight thirty you can tell me *yes* or *no.*"

"What if I'm not sure?"

He took my hands in his and kissed my fingertips. "We can toss a coin: heads you'll marry me. Tails, I'll marry you."

27

"You haven't changed your mind, have you?" Joey said as soon as I awoke. On the floor beside the mattress the candle had burned out, leaving a waxy puddle on the plate beneath it. I turned toward him.

"I can't. We've been making love all night." I curled into his arms and pulled the ragged quilt up under my chin.

"But do you want to? Change your mind, I mean?"

"No."

"Good. I have a surprise for you." He sat up. "Because you've answered the question-of-the-day correctly, you've won cappuccino and brioche." He applauded. "Last one up doesn't get any." I pushed him down and scurried out of his bed. Before he could catch me, I dashed into the little bathroom and locked the door.

"I want all of the brioche!" I called. "I'm hungry."

He knocked on the door. "Let me in."

"No!" I started the shower.

"Why not?"

"You're not supposed to see me naked before the wedding." I got into the shower and stood under the thin stream of warm water.

"But I already did."

I didn't know what to say. "It was a mistake. I have to go to confession."

"A mistake? No. Let me in." I got out of the shower and opened the door slightly.

Joey peered in at me. "When you said you would share my life, you didn't say you were going to keep the door locked."

I wrapped a towel around myself and opened the door. "Joey, I think this is wrong...I was supposed to...and we've been...."

"We sure have! I think we should get married today."

"We can't. We need to get my fathers' blessings first."

"Okay, if that's what you want, but we have to get married right away. Before I'm inducted. Without those certificates, you and the baby won't get anything. It takes time to get that stuff, especially in Italy."

"Michel Losine will approve, but *papà* might not agree to see you or to give his blessing."

"Not bless his only son-in-law?"

"I think it would be better if I went alone and told him myself."

"Fina, we have to get married right away." I dropped the towel, stepped back into the shower and closed the curtain behind me. "Are you always this modest?"

"Clearly not, but shouldn't we have a longer engagement?" I said.

"Well, a longer engagement could be a lot of fun, but from the looks of things, we're going to have some fun right now." He got into the shower and kissed me all over. "Must be your lucky day. Good thing you're not modest."

In my mind, I resisted this new temptation, but my body paid no attention, and I returned Joey's kisses.

28

ORVIETO, DECEMBER 1968

"...your ticket, Signora Dunne."

"That's you," Joey whispered to me.

I looked at the name on the ticket: *Serafina M. Dunne.* "It sounds foreign. Maybe if I practice writing it while we're on the train, I'll feel that it belongs to me by the time we get to Orvieto."

Joey winked at me. "By then you'll be an American. I sent the papers."

We walked toward the platform. "I think I should tell *papà* myself first."

"Remember, I'm the guy you married this morning at the marriage bureau, not someone you have to hide."

"I remember."

Our ceremony just a few hours earlier had scarcely been a ceremony. "Great day for a wedding," Joey had said, shaking Losine's hand for the third time. Just before we left to make our vows and sign our marriage papers, Losine gave me a small, black velvet box tied with white ribbon. "To wear on your wedding day," he said. Inside the box on a bed of white satin was a pair of earrings: tiny jewels and pearls apparently suspended from a single diamond on nearly invisible strands of gold.

"Like *confetti*," I said.

Losine kissed my forehead. "I've always hoped that you would wear them on the day you married and that I would be there to see you, even if I had to hide in the belfry." I put the earrings on. "Beautiful." Then, we three went to the Marriage Bureau. I thought of the Duomo and of all my wedding plans. Now, I had married outside the church far from home to someone I scarcely knew. How could any bride have been more of a *straniera* on her wedding day?

At the station Losine embraced both of us. "Blessings. Many blessings."

"Up you go, Signora Dunne," Joey said. I climbed onto the train. We edged along the corridor to the last compartment. I settled into the green plush seat and looked out the window to where Losine stood on the platform below. He blew me a kiss and waved. Joey lifted our suitcase onto the rack. "Did you tell Gabriele that we were coming?"

"I only said that I was coming home." I hadn't thought of a way to prepare *papà* for the truth. I tried to imagine his reaction. *What if he refused to see me?* "I'm going to tell *papà* that something unexpected happened."

"That about covers it." Joey unfolded a map of Orvieto. "Show me where we're going." I traced our route from the station to our home in town, pointed out the villa and my family's *podere*. "Both of these houses belong to our family and also the vineyards around them." I made multiple circles with my finger. "Gee, that's a lotta property," Joey said. "Too bad I married someone who's been disinherited." Outside, as the afternoon faded, clouds foretold rain.

"I warned you." I looked away. "Maybe I'll just say that I'm pregnant and here's my husband. That way, *papà* will know everything at once."

"Good idea."

"On the other hand, it might be better if I see him alone first, in case he gets angry. Then, you could come later after he gets over it."

"Definitely another possibility. Telling my father-in-law that we're married and then watching him explode isn't quite the way I pictured my honeymoon. Should we bring a photographer?"

"Maybe it's better to go together."

"Would you like to get married again in Orvieto so Gabriele knows for sure it's real?" Joey said. "Or don't they allow fallen women to get married in the church?" He winked at me. I started to cry. "Never mind. One wedding is enough for *us*, right? And I've got the proof right here."

He patted the certificate in his back pocket and then pulled me close and tried to kiss me.

I pushed him away. "Joey, you have to let me tell *papà* before he meets you." Outside raindrops slid down the window of the train and pooled against the glass.

He looked hurt. "So who do you want me to be? Your husband or just some guy?"

I took his hand. "I'm sorry."

The train stopped. I drew my hand across the misted glass. Orvieto looked unfamiliar, dreamlike, a place I might have seen once long ago. The platform was wet and shiny in the rain. With a start, I saw Bruno standing there. The lights inside the train came on. I raised my hand, then put it down. Too late. Bruno had seen me. He approached the train and stood below the window, smiling and waving. I stood up on uneasy feet. "Bruno is here."

Joey pulled our suitcase off the rack. "Let's go, Signora Dunne. It's face-the-music time now." I followed Joey along the corridor. The linoleum floor had worn through in places, revealing the splintered subflooring. *Was the train this ragged when I left for Milano?* In the vestibule, I waited while Joey carried our suitcase down the steps and set it on the platform.

Bruno came and stood below me with his arms open as if he were waiting to catch me. "Fina, at last, you've come back to me."

I gripped the damp railing, not moving. "I didn't expect you," I said. Bruno dropped his arms. I stepped down to the platform and gestured toward Joey. "Bruno, this is Joey Dunne." Bruno looked at Joey.

Joey extended his hand. "*Piacere.*"

"*Piacere.*" Bruno turned back to me. "Gabriele told me that you've decided to come home...to me...to us. I've met every train. Fina, I'm sorry about everything. I know I was wrong." He took my hands and lifted them to his lips, kissing the back of each one. Then, he saw my wedding ring. He let go of my hands.

"Ci siamo sposati stamattina," I said. We were married this morning. He stepped back, incredulous. "You told me it was my baby." His voice rose. "Your father said you were coming home for *our* wedding." I saw Bruno's hand form a fist.

"Hey, man. Take it easy." Joey placed himself between us. "My wife is pregnant."

"You've tricked me," Bruno shouted at me. The veins stood out on his temples. "Made a fool of me again." People on the platform turned to watch us. Beads of water ran down Bruno's face. Joey pulled his jacket up around his ears.

"Bruno, that's not true." I pushed my wet hair off my face and felt for the *corno.*

"What's he saying?" Joey asked.

Bruno held out his palm to me. "Give my mother's ring back." I opened my purse.

"Does he want money, too?" Joey said.

"Let's get out of the rain." I moved to a vacant bench and emptied the contents of my purse onto my lap: lipsticks, a pencil, a pen, coins, wallet, comb, mirror, a small notebook. I felt inside the pockets and looked in my coin purse. Then I held the purse upside down and shook it. "It was in my purse before we left." I shook the purse again and then my wallet. Coins rattled onto the platform and rolled between the planks.

"That ring belonged to my mother, " Bruno whispered. "It's all I had of her. "

"I'm sorry, Bruno. I'll bring it back to you as soon as I find it. I promise." I pulled on the lining of the purse. There was a hole in it.

"I never should have trusted you with it," Bruno said. I stuck my finger inside the lining. "Only a fool would give his greatest treasure to a false woman."

I looked up at him. "False? You abandoned me."

"What's he saying now?" Joey said.

I felt the ring inside the lining, worked it out, and held it out in my palm. Bruno reached for it with such haste that he knocked it out of my hand. The ring fell onto the platform, rolled over the edge, and disappeared onto the rocky bed next to the tracks. I bent down. I saw something sparkling in the dim light from the station.

"I think we can still find it."

"At least I found out before we got married," Bruno said.

"Found out what?"

"Everyone knows that you always went with your mother to visit her *amante*. Signora Lucarelli even saw the three of you together in Milano. Sister Maria Cristina saw Willa and her *amante* in Firenze. When they told Gabriele, he said that they were wrong. Even Monsignor Enrico told him, but Gabriele said it wasn't so and made excuses for you and your mother." Bruno's voice was loud. Neighbors and friends, people I had always known, moved closer, gathered around us to listen, nodded as if they agreed. Even tourists paused and drew near. Bruno's mouth continued to move, but his voice sounded far away to me.

"It wasn't like that," I said.

"You admit you were there!" Bruno shouted.

"What's he saying?" Joey said.

"Everyone felt sorry for Gabriele," Bruno continued. I watched his mouth recount the truths of my life. "Gabriele is a good man. Even though his own wife made him wear the horns, he took her back. Forgave her. He was a fool. Now, you've betrayed me, too. But you bring your lover home with you and expect me to shake hands with him." He looked at Joey and made an obscene gesture.

Joey came toward Bruno. "Shut up."

"Joey, no. Don't," I said.

Bruno he turned to me and laughed. "I guess your husband doesn't care that he already had the horns when he married you."

"Hypocrite!" I shouted. "You abandoned me and your baby. Explain that to these people." A hush fell around us. I began to cry. Even then, when it no longer mattered, I still cared about what Bruno thought of me, still wanted to change Bruno's mind, still wanted him to understand my intentions, to say that I was still a good person

"Your husband has done you a favor," Bruno said. "I would never touch you."

"Leave my wife alone," Joey said. Bruno pushed Joey away. Joey shoved him back. "I said, leave her alone."

"Joey, no." I reached for Bruno's hand. "We've hurt each other. Let's try to forgive."

"There's nothing to forgive because you're nothing to me. You can't hurt me."

"Bruno, stop. You dishonor both of us."

"Is it dishonorable to speak the truth? I planned my life with you. What do you expect me to do now? Stay here? Run the winery and wait for...what? Nothing? Didn't you ever think about what might happen to me?" Tears streamed down his cheeks. "I'm lost without you."

Joey put his hand on Bruno's shoulder. "Hey, I'm sorry."

Bruno turned and walked away. I pushed my wet hair away from my face. Joey picked up our suitcase and followed me onto the funicular. I sat in a corner, avoiding the curious looks of the other passengers. My head ached. As we ascended, the moon emerged from behind the clouds. The hills and valleys glistened below, a carpet of silver, grey, and umber etched with the stark patterns of rain-soaked vines and trees. On the upper platform, Joey and I let the other passengers get off before we walked together toward the house where *papà* waited for me.

"Signorina Marcheschi!" The taxi driver stopped and opened the door for us. "I'll drive you." Joey and I got in the taxi. "We've missed you."

"I was at university."

The driver laughed. " Be careful! Don't learn too much or no one will want to marry you."

"I'll be careful."

"Is this a friend of yours?"

"A *straniero* who got lost." I put my hand on Joey's. "I'm helping him find his way."

"It's *fortuna* that he found you. The tourist bureau is closed."

"You told him I was a *straniero*?" Joey said after we got out. He set our suitcase down at the door. I nodded and rang the bell. "Are you ashamed that I'm your husband?"

"He would have told everybody who you are before *papà* knew." Grazia opened the door.

"*Tesoro,* you've come home." She embraced me and then looked at Joey. "A guest?"

"This is Joey Dunne, Grazia. He's an American. We met in Milano." She took Joey's hand in both of hers and inspected his palm. *"Allora, il tuo amante?"*

"No."

Her eyes alighted on Joey's ring and then on mine. *"Dio mio! Cosa hai fatto?"* What have you done?

"Ci siamo sposati." We got married.

Grazia looked from me to Joey, touched Joey's cheek, and then embraced him. *"Benvenuto."* Welcome. "I knew. I saw it in the cards." She crossed herself. *"La fortuna."* We followed her into the kitchen. Her feet were swollen. When she walked, her left foot bore most of her weight, causing her to dip deeply to one side as if she were a pendulum that could swing through only half of its arc. She seemed to have grown more stooped during my absence. How had Grazia become so old so quickly?

"Are you well?" I asked.

"Sì, per una vecchia." Yes, for an old woman. In the kitchen the smells of bread and soup embraced us. Joey and I sat down at the scarred wooden table. "Eat before Signor Gabriele wakes up." Grazia set a tureen of minestrone, bowls, and bread on the table. I reached for the bread and put a slice in my bowl. Grazia ladled the soup over it. I took the first spoonful. "Tell me what happened," she said.

"We got married today...and now we're very happy." Grazia patted her stomach.

"Sei incinta?" Are you pregnant?

"Yes. I...we, I mean...came to tell *papà.*"

"He works, this young man?"

"Un pianista." A pianist. "But first he's going to be a soldier."

Grazia's looked surprised. "Where will you live, then?"

"With my other father in Milano."

Grazia crossed herself again and then went to the old clock where she kept her cards. She cocked her head toward Joey. "He's the baby's father, your husband?"

"No."

"He loves you so much?" I nodded. Grazia put her cards away. "Then, the beginning is *molto fortunato.*"

Papà entered the kitchen. "At last my daughter has come home to me. I heard her voice in my dreams like music." I got up and kissed him. He looked at Joey. "Where's Bruno? He said he would meet you."

"*Papà*, this is Joey Dunne. We've come to ask you for—"

He held up his hand. "Before you say anything, I want you and Bruno to plan whatever kind of wedding you want. What is in my pocket is yours."

"—your blessing, *papà.*"

"You have it already. Grazia!" he called, his voice hoarse with sorrow and joy. "Open the new wine. Fina has returned. Prepare a feast."

"Wait until after you hear what we've come to tell you. *Papà*, I fell in love."

"Is that so unusual when one is about to be married? When I married Willa...."

"No, Joey and I have come to ask for your blessing."

"Blessing?"*Papà* waved his arm as if to banish the sight of Joey. "My blessing for you to forsake your father and be married to this...this Joey Dunne? Dunne sounds like an American name!"

"Yes."

"You come home only to destroy me again!"

"*Papà*, I'm going to have a baby."

Papà advanced toward Joey. "You dishonored my daughter? My family? Now you dare to enter my house to ask for my blessing?"

Joey turned to me. "What did he say?"

"Is this false husband of yours such a coward that he doesn't come himself to ask for your hand first?"*Papà* looked at me. "Maybe you're not really married. He may have tricked you. Americans will do that if you aren't careful."

"Show *papà* our marriage certificate." Joey pulled the certificate out of his pocket.

Papà grabbed it from him, held it in his hands, raised it to the light, read it and re-read it, traced his finger over our names.

"See? Joey is my real husband."

Papà rested his hand on the rough table and gasped.

"Come, sit down." I put my hand on his shoulder.

Papà's body sagged. "I thought you would be different," he said. "Willa didn't stay with me, either...didn't love me the way a wife should love a husband. She wanted...I don't know...excitement, maybe. Someone new. Always searching for something else, something just out of her reach. Restless. So restless. Probably, she came with me in the beginning because I was different from her people. Then, after Orvieto became her home, she wanted another place, another life." He looked at me, shook his head. He braced his elbows on his knees and clasped his hands together. "He tried to take her away from me. I refused. I kept her here... with me...after her heart had already left. It didn't matter what I did. She was like a wild bird beating its wings on the sides of its cage until they broke." *Papà* covered his face with his hands. "Now, this Joey takes you from me, too. It's punishment for my sins."

"*Papà*, Joey isn't Michel Losine."

"You know him?"

"Yes."

"That criminal tried to steal Willa from me, but I saved her. I have always protected you from knowledge of this. Even now, Bruno knows nothing of this. Nothing." He raised his finger to his lips. "No one knows. Our family's honor is secure."

"*Papà*, Bruno abandoned me, and Michel Losine and Joey Dunne took care of me."

"Did you tell Michel Losine that Willa lived long after he ruined her life? Destroyed us?"

"No, it was you who took our lives away from all of us." *Papà* looked up at me.

"So you know everything." Then, he surrendered. "I was too proud, Fina. I twisted our lives over it. I knew what I was doing. I couldn't stop myself. I wanted my vengeance." He looked at me. "At the end, I saw that I should have forgiven her, should have mended my own heart, should have let her go and you with her. Instead, I made her stay with me, but never truly let her come back to me, never shared my heart with her again. The truth is, I was too proud to let anyone be happy." His eyes glistened with old tears. "I've loved you, Fina, as my own child, but God help me, I was so bitter. It's too late."

"It's not too late for us to be reconciled, *papà*." I held his hands and kissed his callused knuckles. "Don't keep your blessing from us because of what we can't change."

He opened his fists and looked at my hands pale against his tanned ones. He shrugged. "If the marriage is already made, what does my blessing matter?"

"It matters for happiness."

He pulled his hand away and glared at me. "So *you* can be happy, you mean. So *you* don't feel ashamed for dishonoring *me!*"

"No. So that *we* can be happy, *you and I.* So that we can be consoled for what we've lost and what we must accept. Bless us, *papà,* so that we can love one another again."

"You ask me to bless what I cannot bear."

"Yes."

In the silence, we heard the sound of the rain, the whistle of a train, and in the far distance the rolling of thunder. In the kitchen the clock ticked out the seconds, one by one.

IV. MILANO

1

THE PRESENT

Mamma, *papà*, Grazia, Silvana, Raffaele, Losine, Joey are gone now. All of them. Leaves scattered by the winds. The things in this box are for you. Remnants of our history, shards of our inconsequence, relics of what might once have been true. Here are the earrings Losine made for mamma and these others for my *nozze*. And the brooch still bent from *papà*'s fury. There's my *corno*. I gave it to Joey when he went to war. Mamma's rosary. *Papà*'s war medal. Nonna's pearl necklace and earrings. Losine's cuff links with Greta's initials. Here's my postcard of Botticelli's "Primavera." This wrinkled paper is the drawing mamma made of *papà* the day they met on the train. And here's the picture from our visit to America. These are mamma's paintings of the garden outside. In this envelope you'll find the documents for the fresco on the wall above the mantel. Keep them in a safe place. There's a copy of the fresco in the museum in Orvieto that belonged to *papà*, but ours is the real one. Take good care of it because it's very valuable. This envelope contains Joey's discharge papers and that one our guardianship papers for Silvana's children. Losine's photographs are in the basement; I think the cameras are down there, too. You'll find the deed to this building in the safe with my will so you can transfer the title.

You already know that Vino Marcheschi & Orsini closed after papà died. That's when we sold the palazzo on the Via Cavallotti to the American couple who turned it into a bed and breakfast. Silvana and Raffaele sold their shares of our land to Bruno. I kept mine for you. The deed is in the safe with the other documents. Bruno will probably leave everything to his other children. I'm sorry he has never acknowledged you. He still may. I hope so. He made a mistake, but I believe he's a good person.

I think this is everything you'll need to know. Of course, my memory isn't what it used to be. I warned you at the beginning that what I've told you isn't the truth. No matter. You wouldn't remember it, anyway. No one does.

ACKNOWLEDGMENTS

This novel would not have been written without the love and support of my husband, Bill Broesamle. Jim Krusoe held the light as the book took shape and offered invaluable suggestions. Special thanks to Chuck Rosenberg, Jim Jones, Sharon Cumberland, Charlotte Herscher, Cecilia Strettoi, Alice Acheson, Alisa M. Walker, Deirdre Gainor, Bronwen Sennish, Brenda Anderson, Reynold Dakin, and Jonathan Silverman, for their assistance, and, not least, to Jerry Gold, my fearless publisher.

Rebecca J. Novelli's varied career has included freelance writing and posts as communications director, events manager, publicist, publications manager, textbook writer, magazine editor, advance person, high school English teacher, and language teacher for recent refugees. When she isn't writing, she enjoys painting and is currently at work on a series of paintings about women, among other subjects. In 2016, her painting, "In the Gallery," won first place in the Gage Academy's 24th Annual Best of Gage competition in Seattle. She holds a BA in English from Pomona College, an MA in Education from Claremont Graduate University, and an MFA in Fiction from Antioch University, Los Angeles. A native Californian, she and her family currently live in Seattle.